DIVISIONS OF THE KNIFE

First Published in Great Britain 2012 by Mirador Publishing

First edition: 2012

Any reference to real names and places are purely fictional and are constructs of the author. Any offence the references produce is unintentional and in no way reflects the reality of any locations or people involved.

A copy of this work is available through the British Library.

ISBN : 978-1-908200-88-4

Mirador Publishing
Mirador
Wearne Lane
Langport
Somerset
TA10 9HB

To Don x
Xmas 2012
Love Max

Divisions Of The Knife
The First Part Of The Broken Chamber Trilogy

By

Chris Gallie

Mirador Publishing
www.miradorpublishing.com

For Mum, Dad, Ruth,
Rachel, Shab, Kayleigh,
Joe, Liam, Coco, Lewis, Judith and Natalia.

Come say 'Hello' on Facebook:

In the Chamber.

The room had three doors. Each of the doors had a small silver plaque with a word written on it. In front of these three doors stood a young man, he was holding something. Behind him stood an older man...much, much older.

Venicoos watched silently. His entire life, his unbelievably long life, had all lead up to this one moment. Shabwan looked back at him, the old Sorcerer wanted to say something; anything that might offer a little comfort. That might just give the boy a little bit of courage.

'I cannot tell you what is beyond those doors, only that you must destroy him.'

Shabwan supposed that it was now or never. After all, they'd come far enough to get here. Enough had already been lost, why not lose just a little more? He looked at the dagger he was holding, closed his eyes and plunged it directly into his own heart.

Thousands of years before the god had done exactly the same thing.

Prologue.

1.

Legends are interesting things. They get thrown around a lot, passed on from father to son, from mother to daughter and from drunkard to drunkard. Details are changed, parts of the story are dropped and others become grossly exaggerated.

It's all just part of the natural evolution of stories. After all, it takes time to filter out that which makes the audience feel sleepy and embellish those bits that cause their eyes to grow wide and hungry. It can't be done in mere lifetimes alone, which is why it is so important to pass things on.

As these stories get older, and the process of 'improving' them continues, they become more and more distorted, until the truth becomes of even littler importance than it was at the start. Indeed, people often forget that there was ever meant to be any element of truth involved whatsoever...and if I may apologize and add the cliché of all clichés: what is truth? Once something has been committed to either word or page, then it has already travelled through the prism of interpretation and lost any illusionary aspirations of truth it ever had.

Thinking about it like that would be a good way to suck the fun out of stories which would be a shame because stories are usually better than truth.

But then truth, as much as it is unattainable, is also important. No one will come to be more aware of this than the two people we just left in that odd little room...Actually that’s not strictly true, one of them has already come to realize it but the process was pretty terrible and it wasn't one that he'd ever care to repeat.

For that particular fellow the difference between knowing the truth behind a legend and not was the difference between absolutely everything. Had he know the truth then the world would probably be a different shape...that was the kind of power that they'd almost had.

The world of our story is the same one in which the legend I am about to tell you of took place. This legend, as it is told by the inhabitants of Svin, is old and has become about as distorted as it's possible to get. Indeed in almost any ale house in the country you could be told the entire tale and not one word of it would be correct. It certainly wouldn't sound anything like the version I am about to relay.

There is nothing unusual about this and most people would argue that this inherent lack of truth doesn't take anything away from legendary tales. Indeed the majority of the time it makes them much better. People would be disappointed to learn, for example, that Famulous, the great warrior of the ice planes, was actually a barber who had one massive piece of fortune on a frosty battlefield that he'd had no desire to be on. Or that Viaana the most beautiful woman to have ever lived was actually...well, not the most beautiful woman to have ever lived, she was the third. Still pretty high, but people rarely remember silver and bronze medalists.

While people might be disappointed they wouldn't really *care*. This isn't why people listen. They listen, not for historical fact or education, but to be entertained and both Famulous, Viaana and the countless others who have been immortalized in tale and song have given much greater entertainment in death than they ever did in life. The legend exists to entertain and who cares if any of it is real or not?

Our story is concerned almost entirely with people who *should* have cared.

If these poor fools had known the truth things would have worked out infinitely better for them. Mistakes would not have been made and power would not have been lost (that's not to say that hundreds of thousands of people weren't happy that it was lost but we'll get to that...eventually). None of the characters, who we will later meet, had the luxury of knowing the truth.

Or if not 'the truth' then at least what we might term 'what really happened'.

At least not when it mattered.

Seeing as we *do* have this luxury it would perhaps be a shame to begin our tale without knowing the truth (whatever that is) behind the gargantuan misconception that lead to conception of this particular story.

So at a risk of irking tradition and before we get lost in too much pretentious rambling, here is the legend as it 'actually happened'.

The story of the fall of Krunk and of the knife.

2.

(Ahem! Adopt moody and suspenseful tone designed to draw the ear of the audience. Glance around darkly if possible and begin...)

There was a time, a time after the gods had left, when the world oozed raw magical power. A time of the ancient kingdom of Krunk when the top sorcerers of the day could, without breaking into a sweat, fly their castles through the air with the agility of a buzzard or create swords so powerful that one swipe could cut down half a forest. The world was largely at peace and few lived uncomfortably; although there were still those who had a lot more than others.

Like all great things, however, Krunk had to end.

It began slowly. Rumours began to spread of normal people, *talentless* people, who had suddenly picked up the ability to use magic. It didn't take long for the sorcerers to realize what was happening. It was what they'd always feared.

The flow was increasing.

Soon it would be more difficult to *not* use magic than to use it.

At first the sorcerer's (and hell, even the magicians!) feared that the sudden 'gift' for magic that the increased flow seemed to create in just about everyone, would threaten their positions of authority. The proletariat, who had always carried on happily enough without magic, would no doubt become discontented with their societal status if they felt that there was no longer a valid reason for their inferiority.

The reality was much, much worse.

3.

Before the Earth began to ooze these increased levels of magic, the sorcerers had been the absolute authority of Krunk. They had ruled, for the most part, fairly well. That is to say they had ruled as well as they could be bothered to after ensuring their own comfort and wealth. But unfortunately, this is about as much as can be hoped for. Power does strange things to people, especially prolonged periods of unchallenged power.

Their authority had come from their rarity. It was true that there was more magic back then (even prior to what became known in legend as 'the great ooze') but it still took a great deal of study and natural ability to be able to use it. Few had the *talent* but those who did became great. Such was the nature of 'the ooze', however, that in the space of a few short weeks you no longer needed to train for four years under the order of sorcery to master even the most basic of spells. You just had to wave your arm.

Something would almost certainly happen. There was that much of the stuff kicking around.

It could have been brilliant; magical empowerment to everybody. If handled right, no one would have ever needed to do a days work again and Krunk could have become the richest kingdom ever to have sprawled across the Earth. Unfortunately it was not to be.

It was clear to the people of Krunk, that the magic they were now using so freely and in the crudest of fashions was a gift. A glorious, liberating gift. Perhaps some ancient forgotten god bestowing his power unto them. They didn't know, they couldn't have known, how every casual wave of an untrained arm was drawing them closer to their own destruction. If only someone had told them that the great skill of the sorcerers, the sorcerers who they now regarded more than ever, as their oppressors, was not in the learning of their magical abilities (although this was no mean feat), it was in the controlling of them.

4.

The guild of sorcery met and decided unanimously to take action against the proletariat magical revolution. Unlicensed magic became a highly punishable offense, punishable even by death. Not surprisingly however, people were not at all keen to give up their new found abilities. Why shouldn’t they move towards a glorious new utopian society where all were equal, where no building was stuck to the ground and where no tree was safe?

The war was catastrophic.

In a last ditch effort to regain control of magic, the sorcerers became militant. They attacked communities leaving no one alive in the hope that fear of using magic would spread and maybe, just maybe, disaster would be avoided.

Again, it was not to be.

A crudely organised army rose up to fight the sorcerers. They called themselves 'the liberation of magic for the good of the common person's movement'. Had they spent less time on that name and more time thinking about what was about to happen, some of them may have survived. Some of them... Maybe.

The battle between 'the liberation of magic for the good of the common persons movement' and the sorcerers took place on a field outside the walls of the capital city of Houdala. It was a beautiful green grassy plain between the forests of Elgara and Ravenswood, about two miles across. Houdala rose up above the plain; it's spectacularly tall buildings glinting in the morning light. It was an awesome sight; one that was worth fighting for.

And fighting there was to be. Although not before the head of the sorcerer's army, a man named Veshel, and the self appointed leader of the movement, a young man named Crid, made one last attempt to arrive at a peaceful resolution. Unfortunately diplomacy was neither of their strong points.

'This is foolish beyond belief,' said Veshel in a threatening yet measured tone, his blue eyes blazing. 'The consequences of this conflict will be greater than you can comprehend.'

'Oh I think I can comprehend them just fine.' Crid spat.

He looked impressive and powerful but this was nothing to the way he felt.

Three weeks ago he had been a trader in the fashionable west end of Houdala selling theatre tickets. Since then he had discovered that, as well as possessing what he saw as an unprecedented gift for unlicensed magic, he was also highly adept at uniting people. For Crid, there was only one perceivable future: a world without sorcerers where *everyone* had access to magic.

He often lay in bed at night enjoying this glorious 'utopian'vision. A vision of the world where he, Crid, would be a king amongst men. Remembered in statue as the leader of the resistance after living out the rest of his days in a castle (airborne, naturally) surrounded by bare breasted beauties. Crid's concept of equality and utopia did, perhaps, leave some unanswered questions but for now that really isn't important.

No one was going to live long enough to talk to him about it.

'Disband and you may live.' Veshel said in the same measured tone but this time with more fire in his eyes. Blue fire, the kind that burns rocks.

Crid looked at him and felt, as he had been feeling for some time, the uncontrollable surge of power and self belief that assured him that he was doing the right thing. His vision of the future became crystal in his mind. You could almost hear it ringing over the unnatural calm of the battlefield. He looked levelly at Veshel and then turned his handsome head to look back at his assembled forces; at least five thousand strong. He felt another surge of the irrational, God like strength which had become so much more than a drug to him.

Slowly he turned back to the sorcerer, smiled and, with all the unlikely calm that people apparently show at times like this, said three words:

'Magic is ours.'

Veshel looked at him once more, this time with a hint of sadness in his eye and turned to rejoin his troops.

Crid did not turn.

The power rising within him was at its peak, and with a burst of delirious, fanatical energy (The kind of burst that apprentice sorcerers would spend years learning to control) he pulled out a dagger. This was, however, no normal dagger (although neither was it the one with which our tale is concerned). It was instead, a dagger which Crid himself had crudely enchanted to fly straight into the heart of whom so ever it was thrown at.

With a cry that was (ironically enough) a far cry from his former dignity he flung the dagger at Veshel's back.

Thus the most talented sorcerer on the planet became the first to die that morning. Normally such an attack would have been laughably easy to ward off. Indeed had Veshel been himself, he would have been reading the energy flowing form Crid's mind, preempted the attack and returned the blade to the heart of his owner.

It was his anger which lead to his destruction. He had found it so hard to maintain his cool while talking to that magic filled knuckle head that he had somehow lost his focus. He knew that this one man, this infernal idiot had just made a decision that was not his to make. A decision which could spell the end the world. And yet, battle law being what it was meant he could never, would never even entertain the idea of ending the brute there and then.

He would, as a matter of course, find him later on the battlefield and hopefully have time to terminate his existence in the most creative of ways. Veshel had once killed a young sorcerer who had attempted to steal from him by transforming his legs into huge snakes which had very slowly eaten away at him. It had taken him days to die. But this would be nothing compared to what would happen to young Crid.

Perhaps it was ironic that he never got this opportunity because Crid broke the same sacred battle law which Veshel felt must be observed. Even when he was overflowing with raw hatred and destructive impulses.

But then again, perhaps not.

The death of Veshel quite naturally sparked two very different reactions from the assembled forces. The movement felt a wave of providence. Their leader had killed the leader of the enemy. What greater sign could there be that the day, nay the world was theirs? They started to cheer; the cheers began to take shape and eventually crafted themselves into a chant. The name of their leader rang across the battlefield again and again.

The three hundred assembled sorcerers felt a descending rage of disbelief, one that distorted their rationale and removed their fear of what was fast becoming inevitable. Sorcerers were proud by nature, probably the proudest group of people ever to walk on the green earth of Krunk. This was why they'd all been so surprised when, earlier that day, Veshel had spoken of retreat. As they sat around the vast table in his hall he'd said, quite calmly, that if the front couldn't be talked out of this fight then the shame of abandoning the battlefield could be preferable to what might follow. They argued with him, claiming that they could finish them off before it would happen.

They all spoke of 'it' yet none had dared call it by its proper name. Some things were better left unsaid.

Veshel had eventually and reluctantly, agreed.

Despite their earlier arguments, it is possible that the remaining sorcerers might still have changed their minds. Once faced with the true reality of what was headed their way, retreat may have won over apocalypse after all.

There was something about Veshel's demise, however, which was just too symbolic. A little too much of an embodiment of the changing times which had snatched them from their powerful and luxurious existences and deposited them in this scrappy conduct. The greatest sorcerer in the world had just been slain by a crudely fashioned and wild magical instrument made by a *talentless* trader. A trader who had just broken one of the oldest and most sacred laws of a battlefield which he should never have been allowed anywhere near.

For the assembled population of Krunk's sorcerers the world had changed quite enough. They charged.

The battle was short, possibly the shortest battle in the histories of all worlds. It was over in just under three minutes. By the end of it every man and woman who stood on that field had died. Well... that is to say they were gone.

As the Front followed the sorcerer's lead and began a charge of their own, they fired all kinds of crude magical blasts from weapons which they had enchanted to do just that. The sorcerers created a shield which easily deflected the blasts, but the energy from all this condensed magic began to boil and swirl in the air. The light blue sheen of the shield bounced balls of lethal energy back towards the advancing mass but as it did so these balls began to merge and change colour into fiery reds and oranges. They also began to take shapes. Terrifying shapes.

The use of magic is exceptionally dangerous for one key reason: magic is *alive*.

If used in regulated quantities and with a measure of skill, this life form can be completely manipulated. Allowing the manipulator to enjoy a swift flight in his castle or whatever else he desires. But if enough raw *talentless* energy is unleashed in the same place at the same time it begins to take form. Much worse; it begins to have will.

To use magic safely one must never draw so much of it that it becomes aware of its own existence. Magic is, by and large, a peaceful entity. It means no harm to the earth through which it flows or the creatures who dwell upon it, quite the opposite in fact. However, if it ever becomes aware that it is being used and exploited...Well, like anything it seeks to defend itself.

Perhaps it is best to think of the magic as a great forest, existing harmoniously and completely at peace with itself. But more importantly: sleeping...or at least hibernating. All the elements that make up this great wood exist together in a collective consciousness that has no reason to think because it is safe. Instead it just flows. One can borrow from this great force all they desire, for the forest won't not notice if a few leaves disappear here and there. But if you suddenly start large scale deforestation then you might just find that the seemingly peaceful forest wasn't as asleep or as peaceful as you'd perhaps thought.

The sorcerers knew all about this, the front didn't.

The shapes forming between the Sorcerers and the front became horrible twisted monstrosities; fiery demons which began to swoop at both armies. Wreaking bloody destruction and growing by the second. Before the two forces had reached each other there were hundreds of these monsters, all attacking both the armies and each other in a frenzied and deadly dance.

The forest had woken from its slumber and wasn't the least bit pleased with what it had found.

Viewed from far away it looked spectacular. A mass of swirling fire and darkness plunging into the crowds below, bright flashes of light firing upwards, scything through the demons. The scene was chaos embodied, apocalyptic madness. It was everything Veshel had feared. Although he would now have considered himself the luckiest man on that field. Were he still able to.

A sorcerer named Vix saved the planet from complete destruction.

Every sorcerer present that day knew of only one spell which they though they would never use, not under any circumstances. It was known as the ultimate spell. One which would return all the magic energy on the planet into a single point thus forcing it all to explode outwards again. As it had never been cast no one knew how big the resulting blast would be but the general consensus was that it would be big...really big.

This spell was undesirable. Not only because of its destructive tendencies but also because, it was hypothesised, that it would render all remaining magic useless The flow would be damaged and would retreat into the very centre of the Earth, safe from the volatile surface which had done it such damage. For how long the planet would be dry, they could only guess but it would be safe to say that anyone who survived the blast would not be using magic again in their lifetime, nor would their children, or their grandchildren, or theirs.

As powerful as magic was, the flow was fickle. If the spell was cast and the energy dispersed then the wood would doubtless survive. It was so much bigger than the minions who were now exploiting it. It would settle back into its old sleepy ways; calmly and peacefully flowing. Just not into the world any more.

They knew all this because Veshel had spoken to one of the guardians. She was named Sheeba, she was appointed by the gods and she had spoken to him only once.

Vix would never have believed he would live to see a situation where this spell seemed a feasible option let alone a good one. But as he looked up from the madness of the battlefield, he saw the biggest and most diabolical of the beasts break away from the swirling mass of the battlefield and fly toward the city walls. He knew then, in a moment of horrific clarity, that he had but one option. Even above the infernal racket of the field he could hear the screams of the people who had assembled there to watch. Those damn fools. They were, like all the others, hoping for a front victory on the field, where the 'tyranny' of sorcery would be over and the revolution complete. Now they would die in the most horrific of fashions. These things might be frenzied at the moment, like sharks around a seal pup, but Vix had an idea that they would soon grow calmer and then they would begin to enjoy their kills. Taking their time over the feast of countless bodies.

'The magic is good,' Sheeba had told Veshel. 'But make no mistake. That which it will unleash to defend itself will have no concept of mercy.'

Vix thought of his own wife and daughter, a long way from here, in the nomadic regions of the mountains of Halling. He didn't doubt for a moment that once these beasts were done with Houdala they would eventually reach them too. He had to stop this and there was only one way to do it. He raised his staff to the air and bellowed the unthinkable.

5.

Watching from the city walls, the terrified Houladians screamed. A black and red dragon at least a hundred feet long and seemingly made from flashes of lightning encasing a smoke filled transparent body was separating itself from the chaos. It rose up out of the melee and in a graceful arc turned towards the city walls. They watched in horror as it flapped its massive wings and began its slow measured descent towards them. Now it was out of the mayhem of the birthing ground it had an awful calmness to it which was so much more terrifying than the screeching carnage of the battlefield. Its terrible eyes were locked on its prey. Eyes which spoke only of a vicious hunger, one that would not be sated, even when the earth's last life forms had been reduced to embers. Every person who stood on that wall, from oldest hag to youngest toddler, suddenly became awfully aware of their own mortality.

The dragon shaped horror was only fifty feet from the wall when it happened.

There was a soft popping sound, a bit like when you put your finger inside your cheek and then pull it out, followed by a brief period of blissful calm. All eyes, both demon and human, were focused on the pale watery light at the end of Vix's staff. There seemed to be a beautiful noise coming from it, like singing, but the sweetest singing anyone or anything present had ever heard. Even sweeter than the fabled buxom goddesses of the river kingdom of Otta, thought one of the more whimsical members of the Front. The calm was shattered by an ear-bursting rushing noise that unlike the singing, sounded like it had come straight from hell itself, and a clear expanding sphere blew out of the brave sorcerer's staff, engulfing everything.

Opaque yet clearly visible, like a swirling, misty film, it rushed over the entire planet in a matter of seconds and once it had circled the earth and touched itself, possibly giving itself a little high five, it began to retreat back to the epicenter.

When the spell first left Vix's staff it had harmlessly rushed through everyone and everything it touched, giving one the sensation of being stood in a nice cool breeze for the briefest of moments. It had wanted to be harmless then, now it was sure it had the whole planet within its grasp it had a purpose.

As the spell retreated at breakneck speed, it picked up any magical person or object in it's path, It ripped caldrons out of houses and plucked sorcerers, too old to attend the battle, from their beds .It roared across the world a thousand times faster than any conceivable object could ever have moved, carrying with it the magical legacy of the entire planet. It returned to the field outside of Houdala, and dragged all the magical beasts, sorcerers and front members into a tiny point. It hovered there for a moment, a single glowing ball of concentrated power and possibility, at the end of a now owner-less staff and then it blew.

The blast was over five miles in diameter. It blew the front of the city, facing the field into smithereens. The men women and children who stood watching on the wall were vaporised instantly. The buildings crumbled into dust as the ball of white energy, perhaps with a hint of blue, roared outwards, removing all traces of magic from the planet.

All except one.

6.

As spectacular and devastating as the events of that day were, they are not really the concern of our prologue. Our main concern is in fact a twenty eight year old drunk called Idla.

Some of the stories which are told around the inns of Svin in the time of *our* tale, some three or four thousand years later, actually contain some accuracy with regards to this last part. Some of them claim that there was a battle, some of them claim that it lead to the end of Krunk and some of them even make the link between this and the demise of the magic. But not one of the old codgers, who'll bend your ear until it comes off with this story, will ever mention a young man called Idla.

But they might mention his knife.

7.

Idla, like so many felt like he'd wasted his life.

As a younger man, he'd been quite a hit with the womenfolk of northern Houdala. That was until he'd got far too into the old liquor. It's amazing how even the most accomplished man in this arena can soon become powerless once the jar takes him. During his fifteen long years of hitting the moonskank bitter, Idla had become angry and degenerate, loving fighting almost as much as alcohol and the memories of better times and his 'conquests' were fast becoming distant.

The sad story of his life had been winding its depressing way towards its inevitable conclusion until he'd been given a glimmer of hope. In recent weeks Idla, like so many others, had discovered an unexpected and brilliant new skill. Suddenly he had something to live for…revolution.

Instead of drinking himself to death, Idla began channeling all his anger into the revolutionary cause. He admired Crid as a leader and thought of little else but joining him on the battlefield. Oh what a day it would be! The day they would crush the oppressive reign of the sorcerers and move toward a new future. A future where magic would restore him to his former glory and, as he saw it, God like status among the women folk of Houdala. Idla and Crid would have probably got on like a flying house on fire if they'd only spent more time together.

On the night before the battle Idla, for fear of breaking tradition, got outrageously drunk, so much so that he passed out and woke up when the sun was already a third of the way through its daily arc. Still steaming he was distressed to find himself in his home in the north of the city over six miles away from the field of battle. Amazing, he thought, all the times he'd woken up in bizarre locations and this was the one time he'd actually made it home. He vaguely remembered predicting that he would spend the night somewhere under a bridge near the southern wall. Nice little walk away from his desired location…Perfect plan, but one, for reasons he could not comprehend, he had neglected to follow through. He cursed and rolled out of bed grabbing his dagger as he went. He was about to set off when he remembered, Gods that would have been stupid, he'd almost forgotten to enchant the dagger. No point turning up on a field of battle without a magical weapon.

It was only the night before when he'd eventually decided on what his enchantment would be. He'd been playing with a range of different ideas, united only by their ludicrousness. But there was one which he liked more than any other. One idea that, for Ilda, was perfection. He would enchant his dagger, a rusty heirloom from his poor dead father, so that whosoever plunged it into themselves would instantly become…*Three*.

“That’s right,” he had told the bewildered listeners in the inn the previous evening. “Three!”

He had seen the magic of sub division as a child and, with the same arrogance bestowed into his heart seeking blade by Crid; he imagined it not to be too difficult.

It would be hard to put into words just how much Idla loved this idea. For him it was the perfect combination of martyrdom and strength. He would stand on the battlefield, face to face with his sorcerer foes but before any of them could so much as whisper the first syllable of a spell he would plunge the dagger into his own chest. While his opponents would be lost in confusion he would then divide into three, as many times as was necessary, and surround his poor hapless prey. And should some of him be killed? Well it was no problem. He, the original Idla, the one who bore the knife, would doubtless survive the day. Then he would split himself into three once again to enjoy thrice as much victory coitus with the three (or more) beauties of his choice.

The stupidity and lack of real thought behind the enchantment of the knife made it strikingly ironic that it would be the only magical implement to survive the time of Krunk. If anyone of any magical knowledge had been approached with the idea they would perhaps have pointed out one or two problems. Like, for example, the fact that when Idla came to attack his enemies he would not kill them but divide them into three as well. Or maybe they would have raised the issue of what he would do with all his subdivisions after the battle and resulting coitus had climaxed.

The weapon was not in the least bit exceptional, except perhaps for its stupidity. The reason it becomes important to our story is most certainly not in the quality of the enchantment, neither is it in the skill of the enchanter. Instead it is in the timing: the impossibly unlikely moment of the knife’s birth that would eventually change everything.

Thanks to Idla's drinking habit, he was still two miles from the battle when he finally got round to it. He drunkenly stumbled into a wall and sat for a moment, bloodshot eyes running up and down the blade of his dagger. He could hear some colossal noise coming fom outside the city and he knew he needed to hurry. But he didn't want to run into the fray with just a battered old shank in his hand. Just as he was about to mutter the words which, he believed, would turn this blunt and rusted old blade into a glorious silver saber of destruction, the wall of Vix’s spell rushed outwards through the city.

A few moments later it returned and the mixture of intoxication and excitement in Idla was such that he didn’t even realise that it was bringing back the entire magical property of the earth with it; smashing it's cargo through the buildings above him. It even drilled a cauldron directly through the wall to his left. Had he been standing slightly to that side it would have killed him and there would have been no need for us to continue.

Manic with excitement now Idla enchanted his dagger. Three seconds later the blast smashed through the city, instantly dissolving Idla leaving, just for a millisecond, a faint smell of liquor. His dagger however, his stupid pointless creation, exceptional only for the lucky moment of its creation, was flung high into the expanding magical light. Like a surfer on a huge and terrible wave it spun and danced catching the late morning sun on its now shiny blade. As the light of the explosion seemed to melt away the knife spun onwards, hitting an unfortunate bird, who was more than a little surprised to find he was suddenly three birds. It landed in a clearing in the forest to the north of the remnants of the capital.

The last magical artifact of Krunk; the only one to survive.

8.

You can see why this legend, more than most, got a head start on its journey towards the twisted and distorted version that later lead to so much misconception. So many ill advised actions and eventually the fall of one who people believed could not fall...Nobody who actually saw what happened, no one who could claim to have grasped at that elusive moment of objectivity where they can experience a moment as close to truth as can ever exist, survived.

No one was left.

And so the story of the fall of the worlds greatest magical empire was built almost completely out of speculation and the piecing together of the ruin that was left.

It was a long time before anyone found out about the knife and when they did…well, they got it wrong; massively wrong. But that, as they say, is a story for another day.

Book 1

The Romantic.

Chapter 1.

Vericoos.

1.

Vericoos needed to find someone.

The pretence was simple but the process was proving to be one of the most difficult and challenging episodes of his exceptionally difficult and challenging existence. To say that he was getting annoyed would be like saying that the sun was getting a bit warm.

Let us say for now, that the journey he has been on to reach this point would fill more volumes than this author could hope to produce in one lifetime. He has seen the worst and best things imaginable. He has battled demons so powerful that the very fabric of reality trembled around them. His life has been one of triumph and disaster, one of terror and glory, of loves and losses. A life where empires have both risen and fallen and where he played no small part in either.

A life of magic.

But none of this mattered anymore because he hadn't found the person he was looking for.

The main problem, although not the only one, was that he knew so little about the subject of his search. Male or female? He didn't know. Young or old? Vericoos had no idea. Human? He damn well hoped so but he couldn't be sure…All he knew was that whatever he was looking for had to be *compatible*. A link, so complex and intricate that even he didn't really understand how it would work, needed to exist between their two minds. For once they reached the chamber and the subject eventually came to use the object, everything would rest upon that connection.

His search had taken him to the small agricultural communities which lay along the western arm of Corne (although the Gods knew why) and he'd been travelling for two weeks along the dusty road which linked one depressing coastal hovel to the next. When all you know is that *somewhere* on this miserable dried up husk of a world is *something* you're looking for, the world seems awfully big.

Spectacularly big almost…no, we'll stay with awfully; Vericoos' tale is not one that calls for much exaggeration. And (as we clumsily return to an already strained thread) with no real criteria, other than the vague hope that the subject of his search would be human, Vericoos needed to take everything, everywhere into account.

No small task, although one which was made considerably easier by the fact that Vericoos was the only remaining sorcerer on the planet…probably.

'Probably'.

It was not a word he had used much in the past. In the past he had known things. Doubt was not an emotion which had ever flourished in his brilliant mind. Now there was a lot of it. For all he knew, he *was* the only sorcerer left on the planet, he certainly hadn't seen any evidence to the contrary. But then there could be others, certainly not in this part of the world but through the forest and over the mountains...It was possible, and worrying to boot.

Vericoos' last brush with doubt had occurred some time ago, much longer than you or I could conceive. It had been quite an intensive session. One in which the old man had doubted that he would ever see this world again. Now that he'd defied every divine and magical law and returned, he did not like the weak and impoverished position in which he found himself. Things had changed so much and not in a way that pleased him. Vericoos wasn't really a man you wanted displeased, it tended to bring out his bad side.

In the sea of doubt and frustration he now found himself immersed there was one thing which he did know with absolute certainty and that was that the brainless farmer he was currently being harassed by was getting on his last nerve. If only *he'd* know a tiny fraction of what Vericoos had been through, he probably wouldn't have been behaving as he was. What he would probably have done, when Vericoos entered this God forsaken bar in this God forsaken cesspit of the world, was bow and leave respectfully, never once making eye contact with the tall, skinny stranger..

Again, probably.

In truth the farmer's behavior would have been no easier to predict than the weather which battered and baked their crops year in year out. The world had changed a lot, it was true, but this was a strange part of the world. One which Vericoos had never visited before and he wondered if, even all those years ago when the magic had returned and the new empire of Durpo had arisen, when he had last been free; would this place have been any different?

Being cut off from the rest of Svin, as they were, and so immersed in their crop production Vericoos wondered if the Corneian people would have ever shown the proper respect for a Sorcerer, even back in the old days. And we are talking *old* days, for although Vericoos was still a good couple of thousand years younger than the dagger, so crudely fashioned by Idla in the time when the magic decided it was time to flow just a little harder, he was still old.

Very old.

One would, however, be greatly mistaken in making any link between age and fragility. Physical prowess is laughable to those who have something so much more.

While the old sorcerer was indeed slim and wiry and looked, from a distance, like he could be snapped like a twig; he radiated strength. Not physical strength like the brutes in the pub who spent the years hauling great bails of hay about the place, but a strength that had often been perilously underestimated. Strength you could only truly see once you could see his eyes.

And strange eyes they were too. The steely grey of the iris seemed to blend with the jet black of the pupil and the whites were brilliant. Not at all tarnished with bloodshot reds or subtle tired pinks. Indeed, unlike with most eyes it was the white that you noticed first. There was something deeply unsettling about such flawless colouring in something supposedly natural.

Had the rowdy farmer, who will now make an ever so brief interlude into our tale, seen these eyes a little earlier he might have behaved differently and averted the great tragedy that befell him. A tragedy so small in the mind of Vericoos that it was completely forgotten by the same time the next day. But one that, for the farmer and his unfortunate friends, would be their ultimate tragedy. The one that we never really believe will actually happen until it does.

This little story, while not massively important to our tale as a whole, is a good example of why, in the animal kingdom, strength is shown by great outward displays of size and aggression. It keeps a nice natural order to things and, on the whole, prevents things from getting into confrontations that they don't have a hope in hell of winning. It's a lot less messy that way, as the luckless barmaid whose duties include scrubbing the floor of the Inn, will soon be able to testify.

2.

John Masters had endured a long day and not a great one either. When your wife is openly cheating on you with the town mayor it's hard to have, what one might conventionally term, a great day.

The jealousy, which was now a way of life to John, hung around him like some bitter air borne poison, contaminating and souring everything he touched. Like Midas he was cursed but at least Midas had had the luxury of being left with some pretty valuable produce after he'd laid his hands upon his loved ones. No such luck for old Johnny Masters…

Not that he'd ever been a great man, he thought savagely, but he'd done his best for his children and always put bread on the table. Had he really deserved this? to be laughed at by the entire village while the woman whom he'd loved, dammit who he still loved, sometimes to such a raw extent that it still brought tears to his eyes and pain to his stomach, lay in another man's bed.

Unfortunately this self pitying version of himself was the one that John liked the most these days, he never hung around for long and was always chased out of the yard, like a small wounded dog, by the rabid, drooling and much larger hound who really ruled the roost.

This was the, oh so familiar, shift that John now felt in himself as the warm frothy ale began to do its work; transforming him from impotent self-pittier to the bitter, frustrated and sometimes violent thundercloud that his co workers, who would have once called themselves his friends, were now oh so used to.

You know those moments in the pub where one noise manages to cut through all the rest, those sudden bangs or shouts that create a momentary silence throughout the hubbub? Well, that was what just happened.

The noise was the lovechild of John's fist and a hard oak table. The two of them had never originally planned to perform together but, as any great musician would tell you, sometimes the best work is created with little or no planning. The dull thud that the two unconscious entities produced was by no means a great symphony. People didn't talk about it for much longer. In fact the two would never work together again which was, as I'm sure you've guessed by now, a direct result of the owner of the fist soon becoming just as dead as the table upon which he thumped it.

The unsung hero of the whole fist to table business was, of course John's brain. It was this fellow who had really put the whole thing together, while remaining modestly behind the scenes. However, having now finished this brief act, which inexplicably (especially with how little time John has left) has taken up half a page, it turned its attentions elsewhere…back, of course, to her.

He always pictured them in bed. Him a kind of ghoulish, possessive old beast. Her, a young maiden, which she no longer was, giggling and crooning as if a worry was something that only happened to other people. John could bare this image no longer and there was but one way to banish it…

'Sod this.'

The words were said in a low hissing tone which, to John's three assembled co workers, who knew a lot about this kind of thing, seemed much more dangerous and threatening than an outright bellow. They had long ago stopped thinking of John as a friend but, the Gods knew, they had tried not to. They had spent night after night with him, either in this ale house or in the less cosy Fiddler's Crescent across the street, allowing him to vent his spleen at the evils of the world. But after months of this, they could no longer take the lack of improvement he was showing. If anything he actually seemed to grow worse as time marched along indifferently. And, like the poison that it is, jealousy had begun to extend its ugly tentacles out of John's original dark sphere of anger and wrap them around those closest to him.

His friends had become his co workers, yet old habits die hard, especially in parts of the world like Corne, and still they would find themselves sitting with him in the ale houses, half out of some tired old sense of loyalty and half out of fear.

Actually it was probably more like a seventy thirty split.

The happy John of old was your archetypal gentle giant. A man who was well aware of his physical strength and had never had anything to prove to anyone. While no one would have wanted to challenge him, no one feared him either. But this, like so much else in John's life, had slowly but surely changed. The strength which once seemed reassuring now seemed vicious and dangerous, as if it were its own entity. Its threat existing both within the control of its owner and also completely outside of him. This constant but unspoken menace had robbed the three men sat around the table of the confidence they needed to tell John they'd simply had enough of him.

'Sod this!' He said again, as if annoyed that the first attempt had yielded no reaction.

Bored yet wary glances were exchanged around the table.

'Maybe I'll just kill both of them.'

This ridiculous avenue had been plowed many times and Samyel who was sitting to Johns left sighed, just a little too loudly.

'What? ' John spat. 'Don't believe I'd do it? We're not all cowards you know Sammy boy.'

Sam felt a hot surge of anger rising in his guts; he was close to breaking point with this kind of nonsense but not yet close enough to respond.

'Let me tell you something' John began.

His body language was shifting, subtly but visibly, from inwardly seething to outwardly aggressive. An inevitable but always destructive shift within those who can't deal with their own emotions.

'I've had about enough of all of you. It's bad enough that that bitch is off with his lordship, but when you're so called mates are a bunch of brainless cowards who assume you share their flaws, well' he laughed, a drunken ugly bark. 'It doesn't get any easier put it that way.'

He took a deep swig and finished his pint. As he drank Samyell and John's two other co workers Marti and Splice, all looked at each other in the same way they seemed to each and every night. What the hell were they doing?

The cause of their misery slammed his empty tankard down onto the table, rose wordlessly and lurched off towards the bar.

3.

Vericoos had noticed the four men upon entering the bar, completely unremarkable they were. Indeed they looked almost exactly the same as everyone else in the place. With little difficulty and almost by instinct, Vericoos had got the measure of the group. It was amazing that such things as human emotions and feelings still interested him after all these years.

In the past, his ridiculous abilities to evaluate and understand people, their motives, their drives, what hurt them and what freed them, had come in handy it was true. But even, at times like this, when there was no need to exercise his practically all seeing gaze, Vericoos still found himself doing so. Indeed, he seemed unable to stop himself. Something always drew him back to that one small talent far more strongly than to any of his others. This had always confused him and on occasion troubled him. Now, as he looked though the candlelit gloom of the bar, he saw not four men as anyone else would have seen but one leader and three weaker, still dependent on him despite their obvious disdain. He saw not the people in front of him, but the tapestry of the dynamic that their occupying of the same small space created. He saw not equals and fellow humans but tools or pawns. There is nothing foolish about believing your self to be above others, but believing yourself to be above the need to understand them, that is truly the realm of the idiot. Many a king has spent their last few moments, as the noose is slipped around their neck, wishing that they hadn't presumed so much about those they had up until so recently controlled.

Not Vericoos, his downfall had been unavoidable.

As he looked around the bar he could no longer contain his feelings, the frustration surged through his body and it was a miracle that only one barmaid noticed the little flashes of energy lighting up the ends of his fingertips.

Frustration is an emotion we are all well aware of, the feeling of bubbling up with suppressed rage, the out of control surge which holds its roots in childhood and always drives you back to that immature state. Yet, while we might share an understanding of this emotion, what we can't (and believe me, don't want to) share with Vericoos, is the intensity that this feeling can reach when you've spent many, many human lifetimes searching for something.

The frustration which Vericoos felt prickled in the air, it was frustration that had been to hell and back and still promised no redemption only an ever increasing dosage. The cliché of bubbling over with the stuff took on a very literal meaning with the old man, the raw power from within seemed to stretch outwards warping the air around it, making it crackle and glow.

As dramatic as this sounds, it is worth noting that none of it got through to John Masters who, instead of marveling in the incomprehensibility of multiple lifetime based frustration, tripped and clattered straight into Vericoos as he made his way to the bar for the last time.

4.

John was aware that he'd fallen into someone, but he didn't care? His life was ruined, what did it matter if somebody else had their drink spilt? Soon John would learn, although only for a very short amount of time, just how much his 'ruined' life meant to him.

Vericoos turned slowly, his hooded eyes still hidden from view.

'Perhaps you'd like to apologise.'

He said this quietly yet as soon as he spoke the entire bar fell silent, proving that, no matter how far from Hollywood you are, certain rules must be acknowledged. John was only vaguely aware of the strange and unsettling sensation of suddenly being watched by everyone. It wasn't a feeling he was used to.

'Perhaps you'd like to sod off you old git!' He spat.

John's co-workers, friends, whatever you would call them were a loyal bunch. Despite all that John had put them through for who knows how long, they still didn't want him make a fool of himself or, once he'd sobered up, have to deal with the guilt of having beaten up a helpless old traveler.

They needn't have worried.

'Apologise'

This time the word was swimming with so much more than just anger. All the pain and frustration of Vericoos journey, his epic-beyond-comprehension journey, swilled around in this one word, four syllables of hate, rage, desire, frustration and who could possibly say what else.

Like everyone else in the bar (everyone except John), Samyel, Malti and Splice felt the impending danger. They had originally risen from their uncomfortable seats with the noble intention of dragging John back to his, now they had a different objective.

'John!'

It was Samyell who was yelling his name. John heard it, but it wasn't a tone he recognised. Had he been more himself he may have noticed Samyell's panic stricken yell for what it was. But he suddenly wasn't himself, he was anything but.The stranger in front of him had raised his hood and everything had changed.

All that mattered now were the eyes.

John Masters was completely absorbed in them, in their piercing, terrible beauty. John Masters, a man who less than five minutes ago would have described himself as a very practical man, who didn't believe in any mumbo jumbo, saw a great deal in those eyes. He saw his wife, he saw the mayor and he saw himself. All of his essence and all which destroyed it seemed to swirl around those two grey black zeniths and suddenly he felt absolved. Suddenly he appreciated not only the insignificance of his problems but the insignificance of his very existence and instead of seeming frightening or depressing (as one might suppose such a realisation would be), it was joyful.

He was, he now knew, a mere speck in a vast and beautiful force, a force which governed everything and to which even the highest mountains were like seeds to a field. Just this one flash of a moment was enough; John Masters now saw his place in *everything* and despite all the troubles that had up until so very recently dominated his life, he knew that this momentary glimpse of his connection to...to *it,* had saved him. He needn't worry anymore for he was free.

Or was he? He thought as the colours changed.

As quickly as this wonderful sensation had appeared it was gone. In its place there were questions. Wasn't this stranger just tricking him? What was this? How could a man he'd never met know so much about him and make him feel like this, offer him some kind of fake redemption and happiness? Sod this!

What a strange and irrational reaction, you may be thinking, but then you've never seen Vericoos' eyes.

5.

Everything happened very quickly. John swung his muscular arm up and round aiming to bring the tankard he held down onto Vericoos' head. Vericoos moved very little but all present saw him flick his withered old hand out of his hooded traveling robe and draw a line in the air.

To the complete horror of those who sat in the pub, John's body was instantly cloven in two. The top half, the part with his head, still wearing its last mask, not one of jealousy or rage, the one that had eaten away at the once happy face of its owner, but one of mild surprise, spun around and fell to the floor. His legs didn't even twitch; they just fell over forwards with a dull thwunk!

Samyell, Marti and Splice weren't ready for this. How could they have been? The sight of one's friend, whatever one thinks of him, exploding in a shower of blood in front of one's eyes is something that would surprise most of us. The three men had hated the mess which now lay on the floor in front of them. They'd even, in their darker moments, wished such an event on him. None of them, however, had been blessed in the imagination departments and therefore their visions of John's demise had been much less dramatic than those they now found themselves confronted with.

They stood for a moment, three friends showered in the blood of a fallen comrade. Their former hatred dying along with the subject of it.

Samyell, the youngest of the three, was the first to react. Rage rushed up from his stomach pumping energy into his strong lean frame, whilst simultaneously driving rational thought back from whence it came. He grabbed the most obvious weapon he could see: a stool, and swung it at Vericoos with back breaking force. He moved so quickly that neither Marti nor Splice could have stopped him.

If they could have they most certainly would have.

For both had seen, or perhaps understood, what Samyell had not: the ease with which Vericoos had issued his mortal blow. The young man had assumed, through the haze of panic, anger and adrenaline which had flooded his mind, that to create such a mess as he was now looking at, the old man must have had a sword or some kind of huge scythe or something. Although...he couldn't seem to see one now and....thinking about it.... had he actually seen the old man move...at all?

Now, at this tragically late hour, that he came to think about it, he didn't think he had.

The two older men had realised quickly that this was a man, the likes of which they had never met before. Gods, was he even a man? They couldn't have said, and now they would never get the chance. Earlier the old sorcerer had wondered if people in this part of the world would ever have known how to treat a sorcerer. If Marti and Splice could have had their last few moments again they might just have surprised him.

Vericoos saw the situation perfectly, as he always did. Three men now stood the other side of remains of the unfortunate John (he should clean up before he left, he thought). The two on the outside were quick learners, they had clearly weighed up the situation and had realised how well they were going to have to behave to walk away from this. The middle one was different, younger and stupider. Vericoos sensed his will even before the younger man had begun to act upon it. He watched the chair accelerating towards him with a sort of lazy interest. His left hand was still raised, his finger, which had brought about the climatic scene of John's story, was still extended.

He flicked it back in the other direction.

The stool Samyell was holding froze instantaneously. Then the wood seemed to warp and contort and the air around the stool twisted and melted. All was still for a second and then, soundlessly, the stool's three legs left the place where they had served their purpose for many a long year. They moved too quickly for anyone present to see and when they stopped moving they were sticking into the necks of the three friends. Samyell, Marti and Splice collapsed on top of their former companion.

The bar was still silent once more.

6.

Vericoos looked around at the faces, fearful faces, innocent faces, many faces who doubtless had never seen death before and had now been exposed to murder at its most cold and clinical. As a younger man, and a man who had killed less, he would have felt remorseful; he would have said something to the patrons of this awful public house. Not to excuse himself or to make himself feel better, but for them. For Vericoos, killing was no big deal, sometimes unfortunate, yes, but nothing to lose sleep over. For the onlookers it was different. They would feel less terrified by what they had seen if they felt there was some kind of humanity, some reason, some justice involved and not just the cool termination of that which all hold as their dearest treasure.

If he showed a human side, the story of what happened that night would be one of a lone traveler who acted in self defence. It would be a story that people would feel they could relate to, in the very smallest of ways. If he said nothing, however, he would forever be just an evil breeze which blew into their quiet little bar, a terrible old force who robbed four families of their husbands and fathers for...for who knew what reason? Who knew how the minds of the demons from the darkest corners of the world worked?

Saying nothing would mean that the stories would be different, equally as untrue, all involving near attempts at heroics and bravery and finished with dark glances and mutterings about the fate that would await the nameless stranger if he ever returned to this part of the world.

This false bravery would have a much darker side however, as the little town would always remember the truth of how that which they most feared had been realised in such a terrifyingly incomprehensible way that they would never again feel safe or secure. The memory, the true memory, of the raw evil that took place in the pub that night would haunt every man, woman and child to the grave.

Such was the way of things: give people a little bit of humanity something to cling to and they will heal, they will move on, they will change some things and forget others. All you need to do is give them a few words.

Understanding is the first step towards conquering the ridiculous fear of mortality that these idiots will forever try to unburden themselves from. It wasn't that Vericoos didn't fear mortality himself, he just didn't think these air wasters had any right to.

He walked out of the bar without a sound.

7.

He regretted it later, but only a little. Regret was an emotion with little practical use and Vericoos, as he so often did now (at least with anything vaguely human), surveyed it only from a distance. He'd become a casual and uninterested observer of something which, when he was younger, would have torn at him, forced him into introverted and dark behavior. For while Vericoos had always been good at killing and was now completely removed from it emotionally, that did not mean that it had never affected him.

Sitting trapped in the inescapable prison of his own head, he would once have pondered how he could have done things differently, had he done the right thing? Who even was he? The feeling of regret would have sat in his gut dragging his mind into sadness and despair. The two elements, the gut feeling and the thought, were inseparable; connected by an emotional highway, along which all traveled and along which he had been powerless to place any form of traffic control.

Not so anymore.

Now Vericoos saw his regret as an anonymous and distant carriage, one on a highway to nowhere. The inseparable bond between gut and head had been well and truly severed, just like the body of a certain unfortunate farmer. There was nothing left there. The regret would fall into the void and soon be forgotten, along with so much else.

Vericoos sat on a boulder half way up a fairly steep hill that overlooked the town. The sun, a giant red orb, was just beginning to set. Hanging over the town it had a strangely threatening look to it. The pinky orange light was playing off the buildings as well as the surrounding cornfields casting brilliant shapes and shadows. Vericoos idly wondered if the town had begun to grieve yet or if they were still in that manic state of shock that is the tock to death’s tick.

Grieving? Thought Vericoos, a grieving town? What an odd concept. Funny that one could apply the same word one uses for a collection of wooden houses, streets, churches, shops and pubs to its inhabitants. Together they were just 'the town', individually...he laughed, individually they were nothing, just as they were together; pointless peasants living out a pointless existence.

Vericoos had no time for them or their grief, there was only one person on this dried up husk of a planet who concerned him and he didn't have a clue who it was. The sun was almost half set now, the shapes of the taller buildings wobbled in the last of the light.

Once again it was time for Vericoos to move on.

Chapter 2.

San Hoist.

1.

In the town of San Hoist, about thirteen miles south of where we just left Vericoos, preparations were well underway. Excitement was well and truly in the air. Indeed as this little town prepared for its annual blast of debauchery, music and merriment one would have trouble believing that such a barrel of adventure lay just around the corner for its residents. One a hell of a lot more so than the others. We won't meet him for a little while; he's currently on the toilet. Let us, for now, turn our attentions instead to the center of the town.

'No! Higher, I said higher, what part of 'higher' gives you the biggest problem.'

These words were bellowed through a makeshift megaphone, menacingly wielded by Anika, the formidable yet lovable mother of the town's annual music festival: Laffrunda. Ah Laffrunda! What a week it was, a time of dancing, a time of loving, a time of underage ale consumption, a time of mushrooms and thinly cooked 'aya' bread (both of which shared equally halucanagenic qualities). A time also, of stonk and sronkette; two substances which will later feature heavily in our tale.

Laffrunda was built on the most artistic and noble of foundations, story telling, music, poetry, and art and then made all the more interesting by the fact that everyone, yes everyone, holy men, mothers, grandmothers, took it upon themselves to alter their consciousness in any way possible. And what a wonderful selection of herbs, funguses and potions one could lay their hands on in this part of the world. People think that the best drugs are the ones which you get in the cities, the ones you can buy from people who look like they'll carve you in half after they've sold them to you and then beat your mother to death with your stolen belongings just to pass the time, but they're so mistaken.

No group of people in history have showed the creativity, the flare, the intuition of a bored group of rural youths looking for mind altering fun and amongst these alchemist, these inventors, these pioneers, the young men and women of San Hoist stood like royalty.

There was no local plant or herb, no brew or potion that hadn't been inhaled, ingested or stuck up someone's bottom at one time or another. This put the parents in a great position. While their youngsters would wade their way through all sorts of experiments, battling 'bad trips', crashing anxiety and general overwhelming madness to find their perfect cocktail the parents only had to wait until they had discovered perfection and then rob them of it. Grounding rarely worked but the paternal sector of San Hoist didn't mind, their art was in confiscation not containment.

Anika watched the town's decorations going up around her and smiled. For this week she was queen: every demand would be met, every chore completed with a smile by the young, the old, the rich and poor alike. Everyone, yes *everyone!* loved Laffrunda. The festival was centered in the town's 'Plaine' an amphitheatre of grass about a hundred feet from side to side. A lush green arena that, in just seven days, would play host to all sorts of madness. Anika stood on a crate in the middle of the Plaine surveying. In front of her, the stage, a humble wooden affair, was beginning to take shape, the erection of the green and red lanterns around the perimeter of the plaine, was coming on less well. The lanterns were hanging off their supports in some places and sagging all the way to the floor in others, while a raucous bunch of youngsters attempted to elevate them all to their proper height. Anika smiled to herself, it didn't really matter, they still had a week, a whole week, and the group of giggling lads with their rickety ladder were having a lot of fun. Let them enjoy it, she thought.

Beyond the Plaine the narrow dirt streets of this small agricultural community were also coming to life. Bunting hung out of windows, flags and banners stretched across from house to house. Old feuds between neighbors, the kind which begin as small debates over hedges and end in murders, were forgotten simply for the sake of decoration. Next to the Plaine was the town square, a roughly cobbled together affair, completely surrounded by ale houses. This would be the secondary site of the festival, a haven of drunken debauchery, a gateway to outdoor sexual adventuring in the fields beyond, a den of laughter and quickly extinguished outbreaks of casual, disorientated violence.

On this particular evening however, the square was surprising peaceful. A lot of the townspeople were either in the Plaine helping erect the stage or out working in the fields to ensure that there was enough food to sell to the huge influx of revelers they played host to over the festival weekend. Not Shabwan though. Shabwan, having finished his business with the toilet, was enjoying a quiet moment to himself sitting on the large granite rock which formed the central décor of the square.

Perhaps saying that Shabwan was enjoying his quiet moment would in fact be misleading; he had not really enjoyed anything in quite a long time. Enjoyment was something reserved for those whose hearts were in tact. That said, on this particular evening, there was a faint glimmer of optimism in there with thunderclouds that, like huge moody blankets, continually patrolled the skies above his mind. He was sad, that was for sure, but perhaps not as sad as he had been. Laffrunda was exactly what he needed, the opportunity to get off his head, storm about the place, dance his limbs off and forget all about her.

Easy…although probably a lot easier if she wasn't going to be there as well.

Shabwan rose slowly to his feet, a young man, only twenty two and fairly muscular. Good looking in a kind of dopey uninterested way. He had a broad nose, quite a square chin and dark eyebrows which sat over eyes that were slightly too far apart, something he hadn't realised until his school years when his classmates had been good enough to point it out. He began to walk towards the Plaine, just a couple of weeks ago he wouldn't have even done this. He'd been keeping very much to himself for a while. Well, ever since...it had happened.

But, he told himself for the fiftieth time that day, as if repetition would make the impossible a reality, he was beginning to feel... he wouldn't have said better… but he was most certainly going to get amongst it this Laffrunda and in order to do this, he was going to have to start acting much more like his old self. As he thought this, he acknowledged, somewhat pessimistically, that, even hidden within these supposedly optimistic sentiments, was a cruel reminder of his current condition. For even if he were to start acting like his old self, unfortunately that's exactly what it would be...acting. He could act like the Shabwan of old, the merry, loveable stonk dealer, who carried himself around the streets of San Hoist without a care in the world, but he wouldn't truly be *being* that man. That old bean had been damaged beyond repair and boy did Shabwan miss him.

It was while he walked from the square to the Plaine; the most innocuous of activities, that Vericoos first saw him and every life on the surface of the planet was changed forever.

In the same way that we would never be able to understand the frustration Vericoos felt earlier, we would stand little chance of engaging with his surprise, excitement and relief at this juncture. It seems a strange contradiction that a man (if you want to call him that) who has been described as someone who watches his emotions drift by with little interest or interaction can also feel things more strongly than we can comprehend. You must understand, however, that the search, which had, oh so recently, reached it's unexpected conclusion had robbed Vericoos of so much, but at the same time had made other parts of him so much stronger. He had little capacity left to interact with shallow and meaningless human emotions but the part of him which was concerned with his search well...that was another matter.

As you've probably realized by now, it would be a safe bet to describe him as a complex character.

Anyway, enough of this poor attempt at psycho evaluation (Freud probably wouldn't have liked to have had Vericoos on his couch, that is assuming he defied all odds and actually got him to lie on it). What I'm trying to say, and not doing a very good job of, is that this is a crucial point in our story. The end of one tale (one of which you will here much more later) and the beginning of another; the end of the search and the beginning of the attack.

2.

Vericoos was struggling to organize his thoughts. He'd never given up on his goal but he'd definitely stopped believing he was ever going to achieve it and that was saying a lot. Self belief wasn't something which came unnaturally to Vericoos, modesty he found more difficult, but then, if there isn't a single soul on the face of the earth whose opinion matters to you then modesty is a defunct emotion.

This was what he'd been looking for... that was all he could say, it was all he could think. He didn't know why, and once the relief had worn off he suspected that he definitely wouldn't like it, but he knew it with more certainty than he'd ever known anything. His search was over, and that meant that his quest was really just beginning. The great quest, the ultimate quest, the one he'd been born for, the one which had forced him to live in agony for human lifespan after human lifespan. And for some reason he was going to have to take this simple country lad along with him.

Vericoos was reeling with excitement but the cold clinical part of his nature, the truest part of his nature, told him to wait. Don't act yet, it said, lie low, observe. It had taken him long enough to reach this point, waiting a week or so longer definitely wouldn't hurt (even Vericoos couldn't have known that these words that would be proved catastrophically inaccurate). He needed to know every little thing he could about this individual. He needed to assess him, preferably in a range of different situations. He needed to know his strengths (which he guessed weren't plentiful) and his weaknesses (probably in better supply).

Yes, he needed to know everything he possibly could about the individual who would open the God Chamber.

3.

Three hundred miles to the north the three looked at each other.

'He's in San Hoist' said the tallest.

The other two looked at each other.

'San Hoist? Are you sure?' They said.

But they already knew he was because they were too. Same as they'd been sure of everything for the last year. Sure as sureness itself.

'It's just,' the smallest one started. 'How do you know?'

The other two looked, once again, at each other. They didn't know how they knew, neither did the first. Three sets of glazed eyes took it in turns to meet, all looking where they should but just not...not...they couldn't have said exactly what. They couldn't have said anything much beyond the will of their controller; in fact even as they exchanged these confused words he sensed that something was wrong: they were thinking again. The three figures twitched, the moment of almost coherent thought lost, their bodies became rigid, tense and alert their eyes remained blank and glazed.

'We will travel to San Hoist,' said the smallest. 'And we will kill them both.'

The other two didn't need to respond, they knew this was the right thing to do, they were sure... So very sure.

Their controller sat on a rock, farther away than could possibly be comprehended, separated by dimensions, by enough space and time to bend your mind round until it faced the other way. He grimaced horribly; Vericoos might still be stopped before he'd even started. The controller began to laugh. A manic spluttery laugh which eventually became a cough and then shuddered to a stop.

'Damn you!' he screamed at the top of his lungs.

There was no one to hear him and for this, if he'd had a grain of sanity left, he would have been eternally grateful.

4.

Vericoos was sitting on a hill about a mile to the north of San Hoist. Below him, the surprisingly grassy fields rolled into the north of the town, somehow the land around this placed didn't seem to have been dried out quite as savagely as elsewhere in Corne during the early summer drought.

It was late evening and he was still reeling, his mind was chasing itself around and around. Questions and possibilities were ricocheting around his skull making his whole head ache. He'd found the person he was looking for, this finally sealed shut the question of 'who?' something which Vericoos was immensely pleased about. This question had been the biggest in his life for a very long time; it had all but consumed him. But now it was completely dwarfed by the swelling juggernaut that was 'why?' flanked by the slightly smaller but equally as formidable 'how? How *had* Vericoos known it was this man, this boy who he was meant to take? He wasn't used to not understanding things. There was much to think about, and a lot to do but for the moment he had time, not much but a little. Long enough to stay in this strangely enticing little place for a while and observe. First observe then gradually begin the approach.

Time would also be invaluable in allowing him to gather up one of his most prized possessions: his wits. The same wits that had instantly sized up the group dynamics and troubled relationships of the four late farmers at his last ale house stop. The same wits which had always carried him and had somehow ensured not only his miraculous survival but also his return. These wits of his had been his loyal and trusted companion through many an apparently unwinnable battle. Many a terrible situation had only been saved by those little razor sharp flashes of instinct and ingenuity of which he always seemed capable. Consequently almost every man who had thought he could outthink Vericoos was now dead. Yet, at this moment, his beloved wits weren't needed for conflict, they were needed for recruitment.

Not something he believed would present him with many problems, for the old sorcerer was nothing if not contradictory and despite his inability to relate to people, he was incredible at reading and understanding them. Just because he did not feel something himself did not, for one minute, mean he couldn't see it in action and understand its exact implications upon the tiny mind it was flowing through.

Vericoos would have hated to admit it but, despite his disdain for humans, he was fascinated by them and when he found something fascinating, brilliance was never far away.

This man was clearly coming with Vericoos whether he wanted to or not, but it would be far better to leave together on amicable terms, to leave as friends and co-adventurers, not master and prisoner. Although however the young man ended up perceiving it, this would inevitably be the nature of the relationship

He now set off for his room which he had rented in the nicest looking guesthouse in town with a new spring in his step. He wondered how far away the possessed were. He wasn't worried. Not yet. But if they got here before he'd convinced the young man from the square, then the situation could become extremely complicated. Vericoos scowled, sensing the will of his old adversary.

'Will you continue to try it?' he muttered, his eyes raised to the sky. 'You lost; you lost good and hard and believe me, one day you'll die properly.'

This made him feel better, a lot clearer in the head, as if in answer to his call his wits had begun to prickle and raise their heads, they had taken a momentary blow as their master was subjected to the second biggest surprise of his life but it had been a thing of the moment and already they were dusting themselves off and returning to their long life of servitude.

'For now, just enjoy being completely powerless...you can't stop me.'

He could sense the rage, it moved the sky...he loved it.

5.

Unaware that he was the subject of an inter-dimensional slagging match, Shabwan was sitting in the Plaine talking to Anika.

'So how're you today my lover,' she asked. This was not meant in any kind of traditional way. Anika was thirty years Shabwan's senior and quite homely looking, although something about her face suggested that earlier in life she had been quite beautiful. 'Lover' was just a common phrase used amongst the people of Corne.

'Yeah, you know...I'm doing ok.'

His voice trailed off a little and his eyes slipped to the ground, an area they'd become well accustomed to over the last few months.

Shabwan, like many of the other youngsters in the village, was immensely fond of Anika; she was strict yet maternal, comforting and spiritual. Just being in her presence made you feel younger, there was no need for any proof of manhood or assertion of maturity.

'I just...you know, you go through a good patch but there's always a bad one waiting for you.'

Ah the young! Thought Anika, had she ever been like this? Of course she had, but a lifetime of hard work, stress, raising children and the annual, heart rate accelerating, process of organising Laffrunda had changed her. Heartbreak was for the young, when you got older you just coped, and coping was something the young man in front of her didn't look like he was doing very well at all.

'Listen,' she said. 'I know you've probably heard this from everybody, but you're gonna be alright. It's gonna take time and it’s gonna hurt a lot, but you'll get there. People always get there.'

She was interrupted by a raucous burst of laughter from the group of lads who had, for the seventh time, failed to get the lanterns into position. They now lay coiled like some tired old snake, too lazy to raise its head and strike, upon the inexplicably lush grass carpeting of the Plain.

'Oi!,' yelled Anika. 'We've only got a week you know, don't you think my life is difficult enough without your, (ahem!) 'help", maybe I just should just hang you lot up there and get Morldron to light you all up like a string of stars, how would that suit?'

They fell silent and Shabwan smiled. It was a testament to the respect that Anika commanded that this threat had any effect on the young boys. It had been an exceptionally hollow one, but it seemed to have worked all the same.

'Funny to imagine Morldron doing anything useful at all really,' said Shabwan as the gaggle of would be helpers began attempt number eight.

'Yeah I know, useless old bat, how that man is the only one in this town who can use magic I'll never know.'

'There's been talk you know.' said Shabwan.

'Talk, what kind of talk?' Anika was suddenly interested; no amount of work and stress would ever crush her love of gossip.

'You'd probably be too busy to listen.'

Shabwan's teasing made him seem more like his old self, in spite of his earlier pessimistic rejection of this possibility. He had the old glint back in his eye, the glint that was, in many ways, responsible for his current predicament. She'd always loved his eyes.

'Ar, shut up and tell you young rascal.'

Shabwan flirted with the idea of pointing out the contradiction in Anika's latest instruction but thought better of it.

'Well, the thing with Morldron is, well, you know the way he can use magic but he's kind of...terrible at it'

This was no secret; the town’s only magical engineer was a crazy old fellow to say the least. He lived in the mill just to the north of town and carried himself with the reverence of one of the sorcerers which the old legends spoke of. This was amusing to the residents of San Hoist as they knew that, however thin on the ground legendary material became, there would never be a legend which spoke of Morldron.

Even if the only two people left on the planet were Morldron and a young poet who had, all his life, wanted nothing more than to write an epic ballad which remembered one of the great figures of his time, there would still be nothing written. The young poet would probably cast his eyes to the heavens and ask why he had been left alone in the world with the least legendary character to ever walk upon it. It's probably quite hard being young and poetic anyway. I imagine such things probably all just blend into the general gloominess of being.

Morldron's erratic and all but useless command of magic caused a lot more harm than it ever did good. So much so that people actually preferred the help of Ellarus, the drunk and incompetent town doctor, to Morldron's magical remedies.

'Yeah, that'd be one word for it I suppose.'

'Well, I heard that apparently Georgie Bales was out walking his dog the other day and he was up by the old Mill.'

'The barmy barn?'

The very same, and while he was up there, he swears that he saw old Morldron doing some things.'

'I bet he did, that perverted old devil.'

'Not like that, magical things.'

'Well he is a wizard, supposedly,' said Anika, stressing one word more than the other four.

'Yeah I know, and that's exactly it. According to old Georgie, this magic he was doing actually looked...good.'

'Like the time he set the pub on fire?'

They both laughed and paused for a moment to enjoy the memory of Hull the innkeeper watching in despair as his beloved pub burned, all because Morldron had attempted to turn a shrew into gold to pay for his drink. Hull was an idiot though, and to say that he'd deserved it would have been a huge understatement. The ugly innkeeper had been ripping off the community for years, considering himself to be a man of the people, while fleecing money from those who could barely afford to eat.

They'd managed to put the pub out eventually, something which Morldron still took credit for, attributing the extinguishing of the fire to the fine jets of water he was shooting out of the end of his staff (which instantly evaporated on impact), rather than the ingenious human chain the townspeople formed between the lake and the pub. Hull had attacked Morldron in a blind rage throwing the skinny balding figure across the square and kicking him savagely in the ribs. The San Hoisters had been waiting for an excuse for a long time; yes, Morldron was an idiot, but he was one of them, one of their own. He would never have robbed anyone, let alone while pretending to be their friend and smiling as he did it. Shabwan hadn't been involved but a fair number of the locals had beaten Hull to the ground before taking all the money from his unconscious bulk. Hull had left town the next day never to be seen again and the pub was now owned by Sooie, Kayleigh's father. The father of the source of Shabwan's misery.

'No, no magic he could ever do would be as good as that!'

They both laughed again, talking to Anika was easy; it made him feel secure.

'No, this magic was, well, I couldn't really understand exactly what Georgie was saying, you know how he is, bless his heart, but from what I understand he was...well it sounds a bit silly now.'

'Go on, what was he doing?' eagerness was pouring out of her eyes now.

'He was making cows fly.'

Anika was temporarily stunned. Clearly she'd expected this answer slightly less than the cows had expected the initial treatment.

'He was doing what?'

'Yeah I know, and not just hovering but actually sending them up into the air. Georgie said one of them hit a bird.'

Anika was laughing now.

'No! Why the hell would he do that?'

That wasn't the point and they both knew it. Mordron's insanity was well known, no news of what he had been doing, up at the barn, would really have surprised Anika, but making cows fly! Despite the fairly pointless nature of it (one could even perhaps argue extremely pointless) it was very impressive. After Hull's departure Morldron had often been heard claiming that he had deliberately started the fire in the pub. Anyone who could be bothered to listen would hear him bellowing and boasting of how he'd, 'used fire to banish the community of their foul scourge.'

Few could be bothered to listen and even fewer believed. The fact was that Morldron was a joke; his command of magic was ridiculously weak. Anyone who had traveled anywhere outside of San Hoist had seen real wizards at work and had seen the striking contrast between their craft and Morldron's.

'I've never seen that preaching old fruit cake as much as turn a tadpole into a frog and your telling me he can send cows up into the air.'

Ankia still looked shocked but lines of interest were creeping their way into her face, like little tributaries.

'Apparently so.'

The sound of wood creaking and giving way drifted over from the stage, puncturing the little bubble of conspiratorial intrigue that good gossip always creates.

'Ye gods this year will be the death of me. Bye Shabs'

Anika flashed him a tired yet happy smile as she set off to rectify the damage.

No one could have known then how much damage there would be to rectify before the week was out. So much of it would be irreparable.

6.

Shabwan watched Anika bustle over to the stage and begin reprimanding the sheepish looking boy who had lingered, unable to leave the scene of the crime. Now that their little chat was over he felt the familiar wave of misery descending upon him. Such had been his life for the past few months; short periods of distraction and relief only making the ever patient pain all the sharper and deeper when it returned. It always returned.

He had never been the type to get down. The Gods knew his parents wouldn't have stood for it. His mother had been an amazing woman, her philosophy had been that any misery could be turned around and sent packing with a swift boot up its arse. She'd raised him well, better than well and he missed her so much. He wondered if she could have made him feel better now, probably, he thought and suddenly felt the need to blink a lot.

Shabwan left the Plaine feeling about as bad as he could ever remember feeling. The little spark of optimism which had poked its vulnerable head out from behind the thundery wall of misery might as well never have bothered.

Chapter 3.

Sunday, six days till Laffrunda day.

1.

Vericoos felt much more himself the next morning; no doubt Shabwan would have been jealous if he'd known. He got up and had breakfast, a delicious feast of cured meat and fried potato, troweled lovingly onto his plate by the voluptuous Mrs. Creedy, patron (as she described herself) of The Daring Ferret guest house.

'So, you're obviously here for the festival?'

'Yes.'

Of course it was best to lie. Vericcos knew small communities; gossip was spread like manure and just as carefully, besides, why on earth would anyone believe the truth.

'You been before or is this your first time?'

Gods, this woman was brain numbing. She was like a fly, grinding sand paper on a blackboard while a baby screamed. Vericoos wondered for a moment why he'd come up with such an abstract metaphor. He didn't know but he was glad of it.

He needed to act….what was that word?... *personable.*

Not that coming up with bizarre multi barreled metaphors was a one way ticket to personability, but it was an indication of the presence of the more human side of his nature.

He needed to become known in the community as a nice old traveler; a little gone in the head perhaps. Here for a good time over whatever they called this festival that everyone seemed absolutely obsessed with.

'No this is my first time, but I'm so excited I could burst!'

This seemed to make her happy. It made Vericoos feel like a little bit of him died; a little bit more of him. He hated the mind numbing nature of non magical company but it was a fitting tribute to his arrogance that he could be proud of a performance while detesting everything it stood for.

'Well, you won't be disappointed, I can promise you that much.'

I wonder if you really can promise me that, said the voice in vericoos' mind for even though this woman clearly had the cranial capacity of a common forest squirrel it would still be nice to believe that she had just had some kind of premonition. Six days he had, until this wretched affair and in that time he had but one objective: to get better acquainted with the young man he had seen in the square. Much better acquainted. He was, after all, going to ask rather a lot of him.

'Did you know this is the fortieth year of Laffrunda?'

First things first, he needed to leave this room.

2.

Twenty minutes later Vericoos was outside. His guesthouse was on the north side of the town, which was only ten minutes walk from all the other sides of the town. This place was small but rich in character. The buildings all had a sort of misshapen quirkiness to them, like no one had really understood how buildings were held together but had held such a strong belief in the finished product that it hadn't really mattered.

The town was essentially a large crossroads centered around the plaine and the square. From above it might have seemed like someone had marked a big 'x' on the ground. Morldron's cows might have made such a comment if they were capable. The main road, which lead to the north of town, the one upon which Vericoos now stood was quite wide and dusty. There was a fair amount of traffic coming and going, a lot of which seemed to have something to do with the festival. Vericoos, from his slightly elevated position (the town was set at the base of a very slowly rising hill), could see straight through the square to the south bound road which lead to a small but complex maze of rickety, houses and inns. Beyond this accidental micro maze lay the ocean. The great Crantic was kicking up quite a swell. Vericoos could see lines of surf, beautifully stacked in neat rows almost as far as the eye could see. These lines of deep blue were gently marching their way toward the shore in perfect formation, held to attention by the light offshore breeze, on arrival at the end of their mammoth journey they lost all their dignity and crashed, with an explosion of white froth, into the rocky pier which protected the small fishing cove of San Hoist.

The other road that passed through town, the one that ran from east to west or west to east, depending on where you were going or how much of the local produce you had sampled, was slightly narrower but pretty much the same as the one Vericoos stood on. This road ran parallel to the coast for a long way, connecting many of these little fishing and farming communities, it also lead back to Paigndeen and the ale house where Vericoos had ended the lives of four unfortunate farmers not two days previously.

He could only hope that word of that scuffle wouldn't reach San Hoist, *that* could make things difficult. He couldn't imagine Mrs. Creedy giving him such sizable portions of fried meat and potatoes if she knew about that little skirmish. Mind you, he thought, it would be a miracle if anyone in this town could think about anything except for this wretched festival for more than five minutes. He doubted that even news of the use of *real* magic would interest them; or that any of them would understand what it meant.

Ah magic! Vericoos, as he so often did, took a moment to enjoy the feeling that he only got from that one place.

What a lot of problems it had caused him; and yet, the opiate-esque grip it held over his very soul had never once relinquished. Not even for a second. Once you'd held it, even once, it was more addictive than any drug, something that would no doubt interest the vast majority of this colorful little community. Vericoos held it, not like in the old days of course, he knew that. But he held it all the same and since that very first moment of realisation, his life's path had never strayed far from the pursuit of greater knowledge and command of the ultimate raw energy. Who was he kidding? It had never strayed *at all* from that path.

Vericoos was, at this present moment and as he'd quite rightly guessed, the most powerful magical entity on the planet, he had risen with the crest and fallen to the deepest darkest depths, and now he was the only survivor of that time, the time before the dip (or, as we should probably call it in the interest of accuracy, the latest dip). But, he reminded himself, this was no time for singing his own praises. For even with all his skills, knowledge, experience and power he was still powerless to achieve his aim without the help of another.

He should really find out his name.

Like any other junkie, the old man could sniff out the source of his beloved poison in any of the most dried up hovels of the world. This town held no real joy for a magic head, nowhere did any more, but this place really didn't. When you had spent your lifetime, which was to anyone else many, many lifetimes, completely absorbed in magical energy you could sense its presence, it sat like a layer over all your other senses. Like swirling water color paint on glass, magic sat between your eyes and your brain, between your nose and your sense of smell, between your skin and your touch. It was like a film over reality but it was so much... so much *realer* than reality. Vericoos couldn't sense a lot of it about here, that was certain. But he could sense a bit, and this little leak, this little vibration, so small as to be laughable, even depressing, still reeked of possibility, of endless suggestion and mystery. It was coming from a wooden mill, five hundred yards or so up the hill from the north road. A place that the locals sometimes referred to as 'the barmy barn'.

To say that the buildings of San Hoist were rickety was an accurate description, the only problem being that one would then feel that they needed to find a newer, much stronger word for this mill. A calamity perhaps. A wooden disaster held together by tenuous magical links created by someone who clearly knew a little of what magic could do and ignored a lot of what it couldn't. There was something about this place though, something interesting.

'Who dares trespass on my property?!' Came a booming, theatrical voice from somewhere within the mill. Vericoos didn't need to be a sorcerer to realise that the owner of the voice had magically amplified it. A thin figure emerged from the gloomy doorway clutching a crudely carved staff; clutching it like his life depended on it.

'Well speak or be damned, you won't be the first to have suffered my fury, nor will you be the last!'

It was possibly the least threatening thing that Vericoos had ever heard. The man stood in front of him was all knees and elbows, a big bony bag of bad coordination. He was wearing a loose fitting purple gown which somehow still didn't disguise the general knobbliness of his figure. His voice would have sounded at home on the stage coming from a very fat fellow wearing makeup and comedically proclaiming the tragedy of his existence. Vericoos wondered how much effort it actually took to keep up a voice like that all the time, it must be very wearing.

'Calm yourself old fellow I'm a friend, just a traveler here to enjoy er...Lafrwona festival.'

'Lafrowna...ha,' Morldron spat. 'I assume you mean Laffrunda my good fellow...LAFFRUNDA!'

As he said this last word he threw his arms apart and arched his back. There seemed, to Vericoos, absolutely no reason for this behavior, and the intended dramatic effect was lost when Morldrons staff came into contact with his own head. The deranged wizard was so surprised that he dropped his staff which began firing off tiny balls of red light, burning the surrounding foliage to cinder. Morldron eventually managed to get his hands back on his staff and cool it down. The staff owns the man, thought Vericoos, in much the same way that this festival owns them all.

'Oh...er...'

Morldron wasn't quite delirious enough not to be embarrassed by this turn of events, and he looked back rather sheepishly at Vericoos, who hadn't moved an inch while any of this went on.

'So...er...you're a traveler you say. Where might you have traveled from?'

'Oh you know, here and there, East and West.'

'I see,' said Morldron.

There was something wily about this old character, despite his obvious insanity. He, unlike the rest of the village, wasn't fooled by Vericoos' jovial tone he'd adopted since arrival. He saw deeper, he saw his eyes. No one else had looked into his eyes; you didn't usually see them unless Vericoos wanted you to. There was certainly no need to arouse any unnecessary suspicion in this old fox. He may not be taken very seriously but talk spills equally as viscously from any vessel, and a few conspirational words in the pub, even from Morldron would spread faster than the endless supply of bunting that was being put up.

'Listen, to tell you the truth my friend, I'm actually something of a magic enthusiast.'

Morldron's manner changed instantly, all suspicion fell out of his gaze, down towards the still smoldering grass.

'Ah well I see, then...' the thespian element returned to his voice. 'You've come to the right place for I am the wizard Morldron.'

Vericoos didn't respond. It felt strange being shouted at from point blank range. It didn't matter though; Morldron was gathering steam like a wheezing old train, clinging desperately to frayed and buckled tracks.

'If it's a magical service you seek...well my boy, (Morldron was coolly ignoring the fact that Vericoos looked older than death) that can be arranged...for a price.'

He whispered these last words and drew his cloak up around him. Vericoos hadn't lost so much of his sense of humor that he didn't have to stifle a grin.

'Well actually, it was just a demonstration I was after. You know there seem to be very few (ahem) wizards in this part of the world and I just find the whole thing so fascinating. Could you just show me something, anything?'

Morldron didn't reply he just looked straight into Vericoos eyes and then, in barely audible tones, uttered a single word:

'Behold.'

Vericoos actually let out a little grin this time but Morldron didn't see it, he had spun round towards the milling cows in the field and waved his staff in a wide arc which, to the trained eye, drew a beautiful fusion of pinks and purples in a smoky blur. One unfortunate bovine was flung a good fifty feet into the air. Vericoos caught a quick a glimpse of its stupid startled eyes. It rose surprisingly gracefully, hovered for a second and then began to plummet. Morldron's intention was clearly to catch it, he brought his staff in a kind of upward flick, as if he were catching a pancake rather than a ton of very rare beef. Sadly for the cow, his efforts weren't enough and, although the creature slowed slightly, it crashed into the floor with bone shattering force.

'Ah, er…oh dear!'

Morldron began waving his staff around in some kind of bizarre attempt at a healing ritual, if he'd have looked around he might have noticed the expression of shock which, for the briefest of moments, hovered over Vericoos face. He would have also seen the sorcerer's hand move slightly and a tiny ball of white light fly from his spindly fingertips, under Morldron's waving arm, into the cow. The cow would be fine. It would live a long and happy life, surprising everyone with its good health. Unfortunately however, it did not grow old gracefully and in its later years there was much unsavory behavior which the other cows found hugely embarrassing. Some of them even left the field and moved into the next one (quite a strong statement in bovine society).

'Ah there we go,' said Morldron as the disgruntled animal hauled itself to its feet. 'Easy really, simple healing spell.'

He turned back to Vericoos and, for a moment, was completely gone, so wrapped up in the garbled burbling of his own mind that he temporarily ceased to have any existence outside of it. Then some part of him remembered that he was meant to be showing off and he returned.

'Ah, er...yes (ahem) well there you have it.' the booming tone of the pantomime dame was back. 'A little taste my good sir, of the wonders of the magical world. Now you must excuse me.'

Morldron began scuttling back to his front door.

'Just one more thing.'

Vericoos waited, Morldron had his back to him. He hesitated, sensing the change in the newcomer and the sudden danger. He didn't want to turn around. One of the cows, not the one who would eventually become known, amongst his peers, as Josh the improper philanderer (cows are cleverer than people give them credit for), took a loud and noisy dump.

'Yes?'

Morldron finally looked round; Vericoos drew a smooth arc in the air, his longest finger glistening with the same light as the evening sun. Morldron's eyes immediately glazed over.

'A few questions.'

3.

Many miles north of town, the three riders, biggest, middle and smallest, were thundering along a dusty road. Their stolen steeds exhausted but frightened enough to keep going; for now anyway.

'Stop!' yelled the middle one, they all stopped.

'We need to eat.'

Agreed. They all knew it. The littlest one got down off his horse and began unpacking his pans from his bag. He seemed suddenly to grow more focused and looked up at his two companions,

'Where...are we?' the other two looked at him, then they looked at each other, distant recognition began to hurtle towards the front of their eyes, sudden understanding.

'We...'

They suddenly jerked and the glazed expression returned. They quickly and methodically began to prepare dinner. They ate without a word and then fell into a dreamless sleep.

Somewhere, a very long way away, their controller sat on a rock. The possession was going well, they were showing very little resilience, sometimes when they were especially hungry or tired they seemed to remember. Maybe this was when they most missed their old existence. The comfort of your wife's arms in a warm bed after a hearty meal was perhaps a memory that clung on harder than most; like a limpet and, to the controller, equally as pointless. What he, like so many powerful men, would fail to see was the importance of the tiniest little things in life.

The resistance they showed was, however, getting less and less. Soon he would have them completely.

As men they had been farmers, simple folk but strong physically. Now there was very little of that left, they belonged to another and once he had them, once he had them *completely*, they would be deadlier weapons than their simple minds could ever possibly have conceived. The controller moved from one uncomfortable position on his little rock to another. Not long now. Not long at all.

4.

Vericoos hadn't realised how late it had got. The sun had melted from yellow into deep red and was setting over the ocean. He had found out an awful lot from the wizard, who had turned out, against all the odds to be a most observant and knowledgeable fellow. Morldron would now be lying in his bed with no recollection at all of the tall stranger who had visited him that day. The tall stranger who was now walking with an even springier spring in his step, he'd even thought about whistling to himself but had then thought better of it. Vericoos knew how to get Shabwan (for such was the young man's name).He knew exactly how to get him.

He was going to get his key.

Chapter 4.

Monday. Five days till Laffrunda day.

1.

'Nah boy, not a chance! You're not spending another day moping about. We're going pari fishing. We should have gone last week but you've been such a miserable git!'

The words were harsh but the look wasn't. Coki was Shabwan's oldest mate and didn't have a malicious bone in his body. People sometimes mistook his niceness for weakness and were almost always punished. He was a strong and pathologically fearless young man.

Coki's handsome expression changed from kind mockery to more genuine concern.

'Look mate, you have got to start getting over her, she's not the be all and end all. There'll be others. When did you become a person who'd miss the opportunity to go out and make stonk?'

Leeham and Lewhay, Shabwan's other two closest friends laughed at this, they were stood further back. Shabwan could imagine the briefing before they'd arrived at his small cottage. Coki and Lewhay bickering over who was going to get to do the talking. Leeham would have been more than happy to be left out of it. He was a true mate, but not a huge fan of talking endlessly about things.

Lewhay must have reluctantly agreed that Coki could try to lift Shabwan's spirits, *this time!* The two had an intensely competitive relationship and even something as undesirable as attempting to cheer up a depressed friend would have had both fiercely debating why they could do it better.

Shabwan couldn't help but feel a bit happier, their laughter was completely justified; he'd always been the trail blazer when they were experimenting. While Coki could shovel untold amounts of whatever they were taking into his body for horribly long periods of time, Shabwan would be the one to get tragically screwed, almost irreversibly so on occasion. He loved the stonk and its sister drug the stonkette, two secret recipes known only to the four friends, which also just happened to function as their livelihood within this small community which loved nothing more than altering it's consciousness a bit.

'Listen, there's no way that come Saturday the four of us aren't going to get on the stonk together OK? It doesn't matter what else has happened in your life or how bloody sad you are, we aren't having a stonk-free Laffrunda.' Shabwan was smiling now; Coki could win anyone over, it would be pointless trying to resist.

'And if you're doing it with us, which you definitely are! Then you're definitely helping prepare it with us, OK?'

Shabwan gave in, bittersweet temporal relief washing over him.

'Yeah right, course I'm coming.'

Leeham and Lewhay cheered at this, it was nice but at the same time it made Shabwan feel stupid and embarrassed. How had it come to this? He was the one who usually supported the group and had, on occasion, held the whole thing together and now here he was, being dragged out of bed with so much difficulty that he was getting cheered. Still the idea of stonk did get him excited. It was their masterpiece, the four friends most closely guarded secret and a nice source of income.

It had all started when they had heard tell from Morldron, of all people, that a certain type of fish was said to multiply the effects of hallucinogenic mushrooms tenfold.

'A very rare and dangerous fish,' he had muttered. 'Not one you boys could ever hope to see.'

He was only right on two counts, it was dangerous and it was a fish. It certainly wasn't rare; there were hundreds of the things which fed just off the granite reef about two miles out from San Hoist harbor. No one fished them because they were killers, nasty poisonous little sods with two spines on their head which they used to administer their fatal toxins. Not a nice way to go.

Shabwan and Coki had been especially obsessed with the prospect of discovering this fish of Morldron's and had experimented with almost every form of local sea life until Coki had the brainwave of trying the Pari. It would make perfect sense after all; they were brightly colored, moody and extremely dangerous. All characteristics one could associate with something which was coursing with a hallucinogenic accelerator. Or so Coki had claimed, Shabwan had been fairly sure that this was all nonsense but it had turned out to be absolutely spot-on, something Coki still regularly gloated about to this day.

They decided on their various different duties on the walk down to the cove.

'I'll wrestle it up.' Shabwan stated.

He didn't need to look round to know that his friends had all exchanged glances.

'Are you sure Shab?' asked Lewhay.

This annoyed him, they'd dragged him out of bed to come here and now they were gonna tell him what he was and wasn't allowed to do. This wasn't the only reason he was annoyed though; there was another, a much more permanent fixture. Something which had irritated him for as long as he cared to remember.

For deep down Shabwan knew, had always known, that they were all just, ever so slightly...*better* than him. All a little bit better at just about everything. His role in the group had always been clearly defined: the funny one, a title that, by itself, was no issue. But Shabwan was well aware of the fact that he'd always striven so hard to make people laugh, on account of his feelings of general inadequacy when compared to the others. A little slice of jealousy for the superior physical prowess of the others; be it in sport, fishing or fighting, had been protected in the harbor of his being from the crashing waves of common sense and logic. He knew that it had come as a surprise to many when he and Kayleigh had first started seeing each other.

One of the others would have been a more obvious choice.

'Yeah, I'm wrestling it today.'

No one said anything; Shabwan's presently unpredictable temperament wasn't something anyone wanted to risk exciting. Coki was the first to break the slightly awkward silence, 'Yeah, OK cool, Shab's gonna wrestle, you two are on pike and I'll be bait. Simple.'

It wasn't simple. It was never simple.

Paris were little gits, they hunted in packs, one of the bigger members would spear the prey and the others would circle around, enclosing the victim, waiting for the poison to take effect so they could slowly nibble away at their prize. When Shabwan and Coki were little, (Leeham and Lewhay had moved to the town when they were a bit older) one of their friends had been killed by the Pari. It had been a freak attack. It was very rare for the fish to come close into the shore, but sometimes when there was no swell and the sea was glassy calm they could be seen zipping about below the surface. Evil little scouts about three feet long, thin and narrow, fading from a bright orange head to a lime green tail. This made them easy to spot which was a blessing in more ways than one.

It had been five years since the boys began trying to catch the Pari. Their early attempts had amounted to very little; mainly just Coki throwing sharpened spears into the sea and completely missing everything except salt and water. They had experimented with nets for a while but with less success than the spears. After a whole summer of fruitless attempts Lewhay had come up with the idea of bait; human bait.

While all the time they had spent watching the fish hadn't lead to an actual catch, it had lead to a fairly comprehensive knowledge of the Pari's behavior. It seemed that the big ones would patrol the edge of the shoal, waiting for a nice big fish to kill so that the others could break out of the tight ball that they swam in and feed. Even while this was going on the bigger fish would return to patrolling duties, they seemed to act as both scout and security. On this evidence, Lewhay devised a theory. If the rest of the fish only came after a biggie had successfully poisoned and incapacitated its prey, then it stood to reason that, if they were to lure said biggie away from the shoal then it would be a one on one battle...hopefully one they could win.

Coki was all up for it. He jumped into the water on a hot mid-summer's day, about twenty feet away from the swirling shoal of shimmering orange and green. The original plan they'd devised was to position themselves in such a way that the Pari would have to swim near to the boat to get to Coki; near enough to spear.

This idea was flawed, almost fatally so.

The scout Pari easily avoided their spears (It hadn't tried to avoid them, they had all just missed by quite a large distance) and headed straight for its meal. Cool menacing eyes flashed at Shabwan, Lewhay and Leeham as it broke the surface just beyond their reach. It was only thanks to some very quick reactions and a huge pile of luck that Coki avoided the twin jet black spines that protrude from the fish's ugly nose.

As they dragged Coki back into the boat, the Pari made its second pass, this time one of its prongs actually grazed his ankle, but mercifully it didn't penetrate the skin. Coki was always joking that he had nine lives and Shabwan suspected that this was one of the few occasions where he genuinely believed he'd lost one.

They had been shaken up for a while after that, but Coki, ever the motivator had kept their eyes focused on the prize.

'Imagine how good it'll be. Just imagine!'

They'd eventually agreed to try again and, when they did, it was Leeham's turn to come up with a suggestion,

'If it does what it did last time and comes up to the surface before attacking I reckon I could jump onto it and catch it with my arms.'

It wasn't unheard of for Leeham to make a boast or two and this idea was been greeted with much mockery. After a while however, when no other ideas were brought to the table it was agreed that they would try. Coki was keen to act as bait again (those who aren't like Coki will never understand the simple pleasure people like him get from risking everything) and Leeham would jump on the fish as it passed. Simple idea and, as it turned out, absolutely brilliant! The Pari attacked Coki in almost exactly the same way as before and Leeham, timing his jump to perfection landed on the fish and wrapped his arms around its narrow body. The Pari, like all fish can't turn its head (bless them!), so its deadly prongs were utterly useless, although they were constantly hovering just inches from Leeham's face. Once the fish was restrained, Leeham, the triumphantly smug hunter, was hauled aboard while still holding his prize. Shabwan and Lewhay dispatched it quickly with a knife and collected its blood in two glass jars which belonged to Leeway's mother.

They had found their technique.

The only thing left to do was to find out if they'd got the right fish. It was too horrible to imagine that after spending an entire summer hunting these horrible little murderers that they would find the blood completely useless.

They needn't have worried.

Prior to the stonk and stonkette revolution there was no money to be made in San Hoist from drugs. The climate ensures that mushrooms grow throughout the year so they're always in plentiful supply. No one would bother to buy them when it's a five minute walk to fields where they're in natural abundance. The boy's primary motivation had been to sort themselves out with a fresh new source of fun but, as they brewed it up for the first time a rather attractive idea occurred to them. If this fish blood did what Morldron said it would, then they would have quite a product on their hands; one that people would almost certainly be willing to part with a bit of cash for.

That night was one of the best. The blood didn't just multiply the effects, it enhanced all the good bits to levels they'd only dreamed of, while simultaneously eradicating any feelings of nausea, confusion or anxiety. They were in another world that evening, flying through a forest of thoughts, ideas, laughs and hugs. The world was all colours and music, the drabbest bit of wall looked like an intricate kaleidoscope of rustic beauty, every loose bit of rubbish in the road had an intricate and fascinating story attached to it. They knew and understood everything; universal comprehension apparently equally as attainable in both the pebbles beneath their feet and the stars in the sky.

Then the next day they had felt like what dogs do. Really, really bad, but it had been so, so…*so* worth it.

That day was also the last time any of them had to worry about money for, as they had quite rightly suspected, stonk (as Leeham, as the original captor, had been allowed to name it) sold. And selling proved a hell of a lot more comfortable than sweating out their summer days in the fields or fishing through the vengeful winter storms.

Four or five Pari hunting trips a year kept them in supply and gave them enough to sell so that all four could live comfortably. They'd nailed it. Life had been so good...*was* so good. If only Shabwan could pull himself out of this little rut then all would be back to normal. That was the shared consensus of the other three. Shabwan didn't want to return to how it was. How could he when so much had changed?

One thing they'd found was that to preserve the blood you had to mix it with salt, lots of salt. This was fine and worked well. The only thing was that the salted version wasn't quite as good as the raw product. The blood kept for about a week before it needed salting, so once you got a new fish you only had a week of full strength stonk. Normally they were quite happy doing 'the salt' but Laffrunda was special. For Laffrunda only the best was good enough; they wanted it raw, and the raw stuff was *not* for sharing. It was a nice feeling to see the whole town in a confused state of happy delirium thanks to your product but even nicer if you've also got an extra special batch that makes you have just a little bit more fun than everyone else. That was why they needed a fish today; if they could mix tonight then it would be just about perfect on Saturday, and if a certain member of the group could perhaps crack a smile or two then good times would be had by all.

Just over an hour later they were all sitting in their small rowing boat headed out towards Pari reef. The atmosphere was good now, all laughs, excitement and reminiscing about previous stonk expeditions. To the casual observer they were four young men without a care in the world. Nothing else was said about Shabwan being the wrestler but he knew they were slightly uneasy about it. With Lewhay or Leeham you just couldn't imagine them missing the fish, with Shabwan, well...you kind of could.

Heartbreak has a tendency to make people a bit pig headed. Such is life; it seems that the brain likes to rub salt into the souls wounds. Wrapping a bandage of arrogance and stubbornness around the vulnerable individual so as to further alienate them from those they need most. Shabwan knew how dangerous what they were doing was and he knew that the most talented person should be the wrestler. Coki wouldn't let anyone else be the bait, such was his way, but Shabwan could have just settled for being a pike man (so nicknamed in honor of the epically rubbish original attempts at spearing). It was still a very important and skilled job: hauling the wrestler back into the boat without letting yourself or anyone else get pronged. He was a good pike man, he and Lewhay were a good team, but today he wanted to be the wrestler and no one was going to change his mind. His friends love for him was such that they wouldn't question this, they knew he would try his absolute best and they'd just hope like hell it was enough. Coki, although he'd never admit it, quite relished the idea of a bit of extra danger.

The talking died out as they took up there positions, it was time to focus. They all knew what to do, but they were also soberly aware that they were still risking Coki's life for a bit of fun. Hell, a bit of fun they already had stockpiled!

'Ok everyone ready?'

Brief nods.

'Let’s have it.' Coki yelled as he jumped in.

Shabwan stood balanced on the small boat with his hand on the rail, his head felt clear and good; which meant no thoughts of Kayleigh. He could make out the bright orange of one of the patrolling Pari about twenty feet away, had it seen Coki...yes! It changed course and began to swim towards him, becoming brilliantly clear as it neared the surface. It would breach just before it attacked, god knows why they did that, Leeham thought it might be something to do with getting air in with the poison. Shabwan waited, the fish was just a few feet away on its deadly trajectory towards the calm, smiling Coki, gently treading water just to the left of the boat, the fish had almost breached, Shabwan could see its steely grey eyes, just a couple more moments, *don’t* rush it!...he jumped.

For a horrible second he thought he'd missed, the fish had sensed him and pulled out of the breach at the last minute, there was a horrible moment of nothing, as he crashed through the cool surface of the Crantic, and then Shabwan felt the slippery body against his chest. He brought his arms together in a bear hug with a quick snap, just the way Leeham had taught him, and the fish was held tight. He kicked his legs to bring himself vertical in the water, he could feel the Pari straining but he knew that he had him; the thin black prongs were a good six inches in front of his face, absolutely stationary, completely useless. He looked at Coki, adrenaline and happiness rising in him like a warm mist. He wanted to shout and scream he didn't have a care in the world! Then he noticed Coki's expression, it was an expression he wasn't at all used to seeing on that face. His friend was terrified.

'SHAB, THERE'S ANOTHER ONE!'

Was it Lewhay or Leeham, he didn't know, the world seemed strangely slow all of a sudden. The noises of the sea were crystal clear, the swell slapping against the bow of the boat, the gulls and the breeze. He could hear someone shouting something; it seemed foggy and far away, completely at odds with the noises of the sea. There it was, the other scout, it was the biggest he'd ever seen and it was coming straight at him. They are protective little gits, he thought and for some reason this made him feel like laughing. The fish was only a few feet away now, he was dimly aware of the screaming of all three of his friends. What were they on about? He supposed it probably didn't matter all that much anymore, he was, after all, going to die...DIE! The word suddenly seemed to wake him from whatever trance of acceptance he'd fallen into. Without really being aware of what he was doing he jerked his catch towards the oncoming scout he was aware of a moment of tension and a feeling of something giving.

He was still alive but probably only for a little while, he thought. The poison was in him and would soon reach the important parts, then he'd be a meal for the nasty little shoal. He wondered if they were on their way over yet. He wondered why he wasn't feeling any pain. Maybe the poison numbed it, perhaps these little gits gave you a merciful ending...or perhaps...There was a sudden flurry of movement, Coki had grabbed the other fish and had snapped it into the wrestler position, although it was putting up quite a fight. I'm not poisoned, was the first clear coherent thought that Shabwan remembered when he thought back to it later.

'Get on the boat!' Coki's imperative penetrated his confused train of thought. How had this happened? He wasn't poisoned, but it had stabbed him. No… It *hadn't* stabbed him! Suddenly everything became clear. Shabwan, who'd never included quick reactions or coordination in his list of good points, had shown almost impossible levels of both. In what would have been some of his last moments he had somehow managed to put his own catch up as a shield. The fish had stabbed its fellow scout.

'Shab, get in the boat!'

He better had he supposed.

A few moments later, thanks to some beautiful hauling by Leeham and Lewhay they were all four back in the boat. No one was talking yet. Lewhay was draining the blood but he'd already filled three jam jars to the brim.

'Chuck em back in for God's sakes,' said Leeham. 'We've got more than enough.'

It was a good idea, there was always danger with the spikes; they didn't think that the poison died when the fish did. Lewhay chucked the two dead fish overboard, they floated for a second, staining the surrounding water, then sunk away.

'Bloody hell!' Shabwan spat, his chest heaving.

He looked round at the others, all six eyes looked back at him, glistening eyes, overwhelmed with relief. Then they started laughing and they didn't stop for a long time. Nothing's funnier than the realisation that someone's alright after you had thought otherwise.

That night they mixed a big batch of shrooms with the fresh blood and hid it safely away. A Lafrowda to eclipse all others was now on the cards and some of the most well-deserved rest of their lives beckoned. As sleep took them into its welcoming bear hug the last thought that would have occurred to any of the four was that everything they'd done that day had been watched by another. In a guesthouse in the north of town a bird flew in through the open window. It skittered about on the floor for a moment and then turned into Vericoos. What an interesting day, he thought.

Chapter 5.

Tuesday, four days until Laffrunda.

1.

The three riders were thundering along the road getting ever closer to San Hoist. Such was his hold that they were making much better time than could ever have been anticipated. Their controller was in high spirits, stopping Vericoos had preserved, not his sanity but perhaps his will, for God knows how long. He had thought of nothing else and now, for the first time, he truly believed he was going to succeed. Surrounded by the most horrific scenery imaginable he smiled. His thoughts reached Vericoos, who, by way of contrast, was lying in bed in a small but tastefully decorated room in the little guesthouse with the annoying hostess.

'You feel confident?'

They weren't words as such, but had they been that would have been what they sounded like.

Vericoos felt none of the smug comfort he had so enjoyed last time he'd conversed with his adversary, now he felt anger. And, as they both knew all too well, all anger is born out of fear. Time, like the vicious turncoat it is, seemed to have switched loyalties.

'Just remember that I'm the one who's up here, I AM!!'

He shouted these last words, temporarily a madman, completely out of control. This scared him more than anything, but it was not a fear that we could hope to understand, not a fear which, like ours, had any founding in mortality or happiness.

'Erm...hello is everything alright sir?' inquired the ever irritating voice of Mrs. Creedy.

'Yes, yes I'm fine.' Vericoos readopted his jovial, traveling tones. 'Think I was just having a nightmare.'

'Oh, er...OK', no belief there, but never mind, he had much bigger problems. He had four days until the three got here and he needed Shabwan, he needed the boy to leave with him. No more skulking and spying. He was going to make contact today.

'Do you want your breakfast now sir?' One way or another, he only had to endure four more days of this woman. That, at least, was a blessing. Even Vericoos couldn't have known that beyond the weekend no one would ever have to 'endure' the voice of Mrs. Creedy again.

2.

'Come on you lazy git!'

Leeham's voice, deep and warm, seemed to be coming from somewhere. Shabwan drifted into consciousness, he'd been having a really bad dream but he couldn't quite recall it.

'Get out of bed!'

Leeham was apparently outside.

'OK, calm down.' Shabwan shouted back his mouth hoarse and dry; he took a sip of water and tried again. 'I'm coming.'

Ten minutes later, Shabwan and Leeham were bowling down the road towards the square. Today was going to be a busy one, yet despite this, Shabwan was feeling the best he had in ages, even better than when he'd got the fish. The world seemed a lot lighter, both in terms of brightness and the weight on his shoulders. The sun was out and seemed to have his proverbial hat on, and by God did they have a lot of customers to visit.

Back in the days when they originally began pedaling their wares they had needed to be careful. For While San Hoist was a small and very community minded place, it wasn't devoid of scoundrels and, while very few people in the town would want to get on the wrong side of Coki, there were those who would have believed they could steal from him and keep their identity secret. They couldn't have had that.

Lewhay had devised a simple method to avoid any unnecessary confrontation, it was the kind of system that, while not revolutionary, would've had most business owners in a state of perplexity; they would keep their prices modest. The Gods knew they could produce enough of the stuff and there was an endless supply of custom; they could sell it as fast as they could produce it. The thing about scum bags, Lewhay had pointed out, was that they're generally lazy, if they sold it to them at a price they didn't mind paying, then they'd be unlikely to try and take over their business interests. This had worked very well thus far. They made a lot and sold a lot and they tried not to get greedy. They were also, despite what you may think of drug dealers, a moral bunch, and an eye was always kept on those they were selling to. If someone was doing too much stonk or neglecting family or work in order to do it, they weren't allowed to purchase anymore. This hadn't happened much but on occasion people had gone a little far and Shabwan and the others had never sold to them again. It was a good system.

The build up to Laffrunda was always their busiest time. Those who did stonk regularly wanted a good batch in their pockets and those who didn't do it regularly almost always wanted to do so on Laffrunda day, it was very traditional. And so Shabwan and Leeham's trek around town took them to pretty much everywhere, from the slightly poorer end all the way up to the biggest houses to the north. They were welcomed in, given countless pies and drinks and filled their pockets with clunky, crudely fashioned currency.

'You seem a lot better today.' Leeham started.

Shabwan could still hear a note of apprehension in his friend's voice. It was fair enough; he'd been a real idiot lately. His quick temper must have been a lot for the boys to deal with, although they'd never shown it.

'Yeah I do feel real good today actually, got a bit of Laffrunda spirit.'

'And a pocket full of money.' They both laughed.

'Let's get the others and go to the pub.' Said Shabwan.

Leeham looked at him, this time with mock apprehension plastered all over his face. Again, it was fair enough. Shabwan knew he'd been melodramatic in his avoidance of The Star and it had annoyed the others.

'The pub!' You sure you're ready?'

'Piss off!' laughed Shabwan. 'Let's go and get mullered, we can certainly afford to.'

The inn was absolutely rammed that night. Sooie, like the four boys, always made a lot of money in the week leading up to Laffrunda. Unlike his predecessor Hull, he was an open and kindhearted fellow, with a beaming, ruddy face. He always had time for a chat with even the most boring of drunks and generally wouldn't serve those who had had one too many.

Yes, the Star inn was a quality establishment, especially on nights like this and nothing was going to sabotage Shabwan's newly found good cheer. Of that, for the first time in forever, he felt quietly confident.

3.

It seemed to Vericoos, sitting alone in the corner that, despite the ridiculous number of ale houses in San Hoist, the whole town had contained itself within these four walls. He had been sitting there for about an hour, his keen observational skills working their way around. The Star had a long central bar serving two rooms which were separated, but only by the narrow foyer which made up the entrance. It was more like one big room really, although the little foyer did, at present seem to be serving as some kind of generational barrier.

Along with his traveling cape Vericoos was also wearing an expression of curious innocence (that's curiosity and innocence combined, not an unusual expression of innocence). Those who noticed him looking round the room (not many) supposed he was just another old traveler, Laffrunda attracted them like bored youths to stonk; a tired reveler who hadn't yet lost his appetite for a good old fashioned celebration. Imagine how differently they would have felt had they known that this nondescript old gentleman had learned more of their little town in the last hour than most of them would learn in their whole lifetimes.

In the area where the younger inhabitants seemed to dwell, there were three groups of males, Shabwan and the boys having not yet arrived. two of the groups seemed to be on good terms but the third was different. Something had happened there, something bad. Yet it seemed that the original source of the conflict was no longer present, this was clear from the way they diligently avoided eye contact and indeed completely ignored each other's existence. It was as if the young men, sitting on the other side of the room had retained their hatred of the others but lost whatever it was that had caused the conflict in the first place.

There were also two bigger groups of young women (richer and poorer it seemed, although with a slight crossover). The evening was still at the stage when shyness was segregating the young people of opposing genders. Indeed, as a spectator of the pub's noisier second room you would be forgiven for thinking that some law forbade communication between the two. The young women were sprawled across two large tables that would later be moved to form the dance floor, and the young men were sat at three separate tables which adorned the walls.

Vericoos sometimes found it difficult not to see things as battles...when you've had so many it becomes tricky not too, and as he looked upon the town's younger men and women, he couldn't help but be reminded of conflict. Rather than the room seeming like some kind of predatory enclosure, however, it seemed more as if the young men were the vulnerable ones, like the larger inner circle of feminity might swell out and engulf them, robbing them of their little masculine fortresses. Thankfully for everyone, this silly pretence would be hard to keep up once the drink started flowing and would be lost completely once Sooie moved the two big tables away so that the dancing could begin.

The middle aged folk were harder to quantify; they tend not to stick in groups like younger folk. What Vericoos did notice, however, and what surprised him a great deal, was the huge number of couples that there were drinking together in this place. Every Inn he had passed through on his long and arduous journey to reach San Hoist had been dominated by men. The differences in the range of establishments he'd seen had been huge; he'd seen every kind of ale house there was to see. But, while the surrounds, the decoration and the music changed, the customers did not. The inn was where the *working* man came after a hard day and, in reality, *all* men consider themselves to be *working* men. Even those so privileged that their day to day lives would turn most green with envy, still see their obligatory duties as work.

Any routine in a man's life, especially that which involves interaction with someone or something he might not care to interact with, is seen as something which is his God given right to have an escape from. It doesn't matter if it's being buried for twelve hours in the deepest mine or entertaining other visiting members of your highly privileged family, any time a man has to routinely delve into something he doesn't wish to do he feels entitled to his break. Hence the inn: a place where men, who have always failed to notice the equal if not harder work put into life by their wives and girlfriends, come to be away from them and relax. Sure there were young girls there, single girls, eye candy for the tired worker, but women of middle age were noticeable only by their absence. Here in San Hoist these women held their own, drinking equally as much if not more than the male folk and making twice as much noise.

Vericoos liked this.

One of the things that had always mystified him the most about the human condition was the way the opposing genders treated each other. You see this, even more so than anywhere else, was where the magic and non magic communities differed. It's not that hard to understand when you think about it; it all comes down to strength.

Societies, no matter how advanced they become, always lean unfairly in favour of the strong. The patriarchal structure of Svin had evolved out of the man's role as the hunter in more primitive times and his superior physical strength had always apparently been enough to justify all kinds of oppression and mistreatment towards, as he saw it, his *opposing* gender.

In the community of magic, physical strength is about as valuable as a batch of unstonkified mushrooms in San Hoist. It is *talent* which is the true currency and women are equally as *talented* as men. Therefore, in the time before Vericoos became the last of his kind, there had, within the ruling classes, been no hierarchy between the two sexes. There was a great deal of hierarchy between those who had magic and those who didn't, but within the former, superiority was defined only by *talent*. Thus, as Vericoos looked around The Star and saw a rare little society where the women and the men communicated and existed as equals he was reminded of a better time. He was also reminded of her.

There was another thing which surprised him, something you definitely didn't need to be Vericoos to notice, and that was San Hoist's ground breaking love of inebriation. Vericoos had never been a great lover of drugs or alcohol, always preferring his much rarer and harder to come by vice. But that didn't stop him from being very impressed when he'd seen how Shabwan and his friends made their money. He could now see their huge customer base.

Having followed them for the whole day, riding the warm thermals that coiled above the harbor, he'd learned so much about the four young men. He now felt very confident about approaching Shabwan and had a strong inkling that he was going to get his chance tonight. His inklings were rarely wrong.

4.

An hour later Vericoos was growing bored of making his observations, there wasn't really a lot to know about this town. They seemed a well meaning bunch on the whole and they loved their festival more than their crops and fish. This wasn't too bad a quality Vericoos supposed; pleasure over sustenance, but he wondered if they realized how it was affecting their children, or if they were simply in denial.

While Shabwan and co. clearly thought they were morally sound in their business ventures, Vericoos had suspected, and now knew, that their product was having an effect on this place, a deeper effect than they realised. The younger folk had stopped their experimenting with the weird and wonderful ever since they'd realised that they could always see Shabwan, Coki or one of the others and get what they needed, each and every time. They were doing this a lot but Vericoos didn't think they were doing it half as much as their parents. How any one in this town ever managed to plow a field or catch a fish was a miracle and raising children is infinitely harder than either of those.

None of this was of any real concern to the old man. But that didn't mean that it was without value. Information is power and anything that related to the young man, sitting not twenty feet away from him was worth storing. The fact that Shabwan was clearly someone who cared about others meant that the effects of their product on the community would be something Vericoos could use against him if he had to. He hoped it wouldn't be like that.

In the sea of nameless people, who he regarded very much as one body, there was one *individual* who did concern him: a beautiful girl sitting at one of the large tables. Vericoos had known that this was Kayleigh, who he'd heard about from both Morldron and the boys themselves, the moment he'd stepped into the bar. His first thought had been that she was worth being depressed over, not conventionally beautiful, but so full of confidence that the world seemed to light up around her. He knew how people fell for girls like this and it was in a big way. They broke your heart the worst because, unlike with other girls, you felt like you'd found something truly special. Something different to what everybody else had, beauty feels all the more brilliant when you feel that you're the only one who regards it for what it truly is. You see beyond the superficial into the very soul itself. Not that you felt superior or smug, you'd be far too in love for such negativity.

The years that Vericoos had lived and the arts which he had completely devoted himself to had left him a strange contradiction of a character. One could be forgiven for thinking that, to have understood how Kayleigh could make a man feel, he must be able to relate to those feelings, perhaps even have felt an attraction to her. This was not the case, Vericoos studied humans in the way that humans passionately study other species; although he shared not the interest that drives people to spend their entire lives looking at caterpillars in some forgotten part of a forgotten wood. And yet, he was very, *very* good at it.

The reason that Vericoos had this edge over even those who spend their entire lives focusing on one low functioning species, was certainly not because of any kind of interest in his subject, or that he had been blessed (or cursed) with more time to hone his skills, it was because he had the memory.

Those who have spent entire years lying on the damp forest floor watching Huami lizards mate and form little societies may be able to learn everything about their behaviour patterns and endlessly study what they hope might be signs of emotions within the little purple reptiles but they will never, no matter how long they do it, ever have *been* a Huami lizard.

Vericoos was still, to all physical intents and purposes, a human, but his mind had become so much more, and wasn't it (As pretentious the rhetorical once asked) the mind that truly made the person, not the shell in which they live? Hermit crabs will trade their shell for a better one and, we can only assume, never think of the old one again. It's hard to imagine hermit crabs reminiscing about old shells, saying how they should have never moved, how the new bathroom leaks and the walls have dry rot. It seems much more prudent to imagine that they move happily onwards (I've always thought that they look like very optimistic and forward thinking animals). We could perhaps liken Vericoos to the hermit crab except for the fact that he would happily change so much more than just his shell. The old sorcerer had lost all ties to the human form such a long time ago, that he could barely remember it happening.

He could still remember why it happened though.

Since then, if it had better served his quest, he would have happily dropped this weak old body and moved onto something else. He still hoped that the opportunity might come along. He could change himself in to a wide range of creatures for limited amounts of time but to actually take on a new form was a far more complex process.

Therefore, what made Vericoos so adept at reading people and their societies was that he still had the memory of what it was like to be one of them. Imagine how much our lizard observer could learn if he were allowed, just for a day, to enter into the mind of his little subjects. Then you would have someone who was the tiniest little bit like Vericoos. Someone who, when they looked upon the males as they flashed their orange frills in a display of dominance, would remember exactly what it was like to own one of those frills and want nothing more than to exert a lovely bit of dominance.

An unimaginably perfect blend of subjectivity and objectivity.

5.

Shabwan would perhaps have felt a bit disconcerted by how well a total stranger could appreciate how he felt, but ignorance is bliss. And at this present moment Shabwan is blissfully unaware of Vericoos' existence. In fact, it is safe to say that, at this present moment in time, young Shabwan is still a couple of hours away from the most important encounter of his life. His days of jumping on fish, an art so recently mastered, are about to come to an abrupt end. Soon, the idea of jumping onto a fish which could so very easily kill you if you were to mistimed your leap by as much as a second will seem like a safe and enjoyable pastime.

Around San Hoist the air had a strange feel to it. Those who were inside the Star's granite walls remained oblivious. Even if they'd been outside, the vast majority of them had already consumed far too much ale to be picking up on subtle changes in something as typically unchanging as the air. Indeed as our four friends turned into the square not one of them passed comment on it either. They were too busy talking to think about the strangely effervescent nature of that which filled their lungs.

Morldron was different though.

As the old Wizard crossed the square he felt something which he hadn't felt before…Well, perhaps that wasn't strictly true. He had been feeling the increase for a while now. It seemed that almost every day his powers grew. But what he was feeling now wasn't the slow trickle that he'd become acclimatised to. This was more like a wave. The old man looked down at his hand, and what he saw there was perhaps the most surprising thing he had ever seen.

6.

Spirits were high among the four friends, the town had been supplied with stonk and their work was done for the week. Next week would probably be a bit quiet one; folk usually needed some down time after the festival. Shabwan's success with the Pari seemed to have completely returned him to his former good humor and he'd been holding court to the other three all the way to The Star but as he got within hearing distance of the place he seemed to shrink slightly. The others noticed. Of course they did. What none of them noticed was the terrified look on old Morldron's face as he bundled past them, moving much quicker than usual.

'You alright?'

'Yeah, yeah of course.'

It was all that needed to be said, they all knew Kayleigh would be in there and Shabwan would have to deal with more than just a fleeting glance of her. They knew he wasn't alright, not really, but he was willing to do a damn good impression of someone who was.

'Mate...screw her!'

Coki delivered the first word so tenderly that it sounded like some heartfelt advice was about to follow and the contrasting expletive seemed all the funnier for it. They all laughed and without another word walked through the heavy wooden door of The Star.

Jax and Ozki, two local musicians, who would be gracing the rickety wooden stage come Laffrunda day, were getting ready to perform. There was a lively atmosphere inside the inn, everyone was in good pre Laffrunda spirit and the four boys were greeted with a great many claps on the shoulders as they made their way to the bar. They were always popular, but at this time of year even those who generally disapproved of stonk required their services. Coki reveled in it, smiling and waving to everyone in the bar, shouting silly greetings. He might have looked like he was showing off, enjoying being the heroic dealer who could supply to all; the robin hood of intoxication, robbing nature and giving it to the needy. Leeham and Lewhay, at least, knew better: If Coki made enough of a scene as they arrived, he would keep Shabwan distracted, stop him from looking over to the large group of girls in the middle of the second room. If Shabwan was watching Coki he might not make eye contact with a certain one of these girls and the night might not be over before it had begun. The three boys were certainly to be commended; they had done a lot of this kind of thing of late.

7.

Vericoos smiled, as the boys entered the pub. He wasn't at all surprised to see how loved these four were, those who can alter the mind usually were. But it wasn't just this, Coki was a charmer the likes of whom he'd seldom seen and the other two had a quiet confidence and likeable manner. The whole bar seemed to want to greet them, all but one; she was suddenly looking awkwardly at the floor. Her former table captivating confidence extinguished, leaving a slight haze in the air where before there had been brilliant light. Vericoos knew that this was the dangerous part; young Shabwan might even turn and leave if he saw her and his mood took him the wrong way. Luckily he didn't and he made it to the bar, where he was immediately bought a drink and soon had a smile on his face. He was diligently avoiding even looking towards Kayleigh's half of the room but he looked like he was going to stay.

8.

Jax and Ozki played a wonderful selection of upbeat and folky melodies, held together by the clapping and foot stamping of the increasingly raucous crowd. Coki had taken to the dance floor and had that glint in his eye which meant that he was going to do everything in his power to go home with someone that night. Leeham, Lewhay and Shawban all sat at the bar, drinking fast and hard. The segregation in the young men and women which Vericoos had noticed earlier had all but gone, washed away by a tide of reasonably priced booze. Now everyone was up, dancing, drinking and trying (with varying degrees of success) to become better acquainted. The girls from Kayleigh's table were all up and dancing with members of the four different groups of boys. The richer girls had dropped the pretense of class they had held earlier and were now teasing and taunting their way around the room. There were probably going to be a lot of drunken walks to the nearby and infinitely more private fields tonight. Kayleigh had remained at her table with one friend. Seeing Shabwan had clearly rocked her, Vericoos supposed that this was the first time he'd been in here since the split.

9.

'How you doing son?' Sooie inquired of Shabwan, laying a sour smelling drink in front of him. 'Try this one. It'll make your eyes go funny. Not like that stuff that you boys sell of course, which reminds me thanks for my delivery. I don't suppose you'd fancy sharing your recipe with me?'

Sooie smiled, he already knew the answer.

'We'd have to kill you I'm afraid.' Shabwan grinned at him.

They'd gotten on really well when he'd been with Kayleigh; it hadn't been the usual tense affair one finds between a father and the boy violating his daughter. He knocked the strange smelling liquid back.

'Eugh, mate that's horrible,' Sooie smiled again. 'Yeah made it myself. Doesn't taste great, does it?'

'Nah but I think I can feel it already.' Shabwan coughed.

Sooie went off to the other side of the bar to serve Mrs. Creedy.

'He's a good old boy.' said Leeham.

'Yeah I miss him almost as much as I miss her.'

It was the kind of joke people make at emotional times, when you feel like you have to try and make everything funny to avoid the alternative; the kind of joke that makes people uneasy.

'Oi...none of that tonight, alright'

Lewhay was a bit drunk now and slightly more aggressive with it. Shabwan found drunken Lewhay frustrating and entertaining in equal measure but he knew that at present he was getting good advice. Lewhay was always good for advice no matter what state he was in.

'Yeah, yeah I know. I'm sorry.'

'None of that either, no cowshit apologies, we're on it tonight, just be yourself, relax!'

More good advice Shabwan supposed. The truth was he was actually feeling pretty good. There had been a couple of moments when he'd almost forgotten she was here. He still wouldn't look around, not yet anyway. Maybe another glass of that horrible sour stuff...

10.

They know how to drink, thought Vericoos, and unfortunately this meant drinking *together*. He needed to get Shabwan on his own, that was the key but unfortunately he was locked in with the other two. He was going to have to wait this one out for a bit longer. Approaching him while he was with the others would be no good at all.

11.

'Let's go and dance?' This suggestion told Shabwan that Leeham must be truly screwed.

'Yes mate I'm all over it.'

Lewhay loved dancing, what he lacked in skill he made up for with an innovative attitude.

'Yeah cool,' said Shabwan, 'I'm just gonna get another of those sour things then I'll be right there.'

His two friends looked reluctant for a minute, as if they'd much rather he came with them right now.

'See you in a minute.' Said Shabwan, a bit more forcefully.

Off they went over towards the bouncing figure of Coki, who was now surrounded by a group of giggling girls.

12.

Vericoos jumped to his feet. Shabwan was, temporarily at least, alone.

Time to act.

He began pushing his way through the crowded bar towards the slightly unbalanced young man. He was almost there when he himself was pushed aside by a small yet strong female who was sharing his path through the crowd.

13.

'Nice one Sooie.'

Shabwan threw the sour liquid down his throat, hoping that as little as possible would touch the sides. Had he continued looking at Sooie he would have noticed that the barman was looking slightly over his shoulder and mouthing something which looked a bit like 'not now!' Right, time for a boogie, thought Shabwan, he turned around and found himself looking straight at Kayleigh. His heart felt funny; suddenly he was rushing with nerves and anger. He felt raw. As if it was the day they'd broken up rather than all this time later. She was looking at him, her cute little face, easy to read (well easy for him), he knew she wanted him to say something, something which would suggest that things were OK between them, some lighthearted little greeting which would suggest that they could have a future as friends. How could he give her this? Why should he give her this?

'What?'

His tone was so aggressive that it immediately disgusted him, she recoiled, hurt. She was a strong person but she knew how much she'd hurt him and wouldn't get angry herself. He wished she would.

'It's just...it's nice to see you...I thought maybe we could sit down and have a little talk…If you'd like?'

He could have handled it if she was a bitch, it would be so much easier. She was just so unrelentingly lovely so rational and thoughtful. These qualities radiated out from her from her face, her stance and even her voice. She stood there, just wanting friendship, while completely understanding why this might not be possible. Her simple kindness reminded him of everything he loved, everything he missed so much and wanted more than he could ever express.

'No I wouldn't like that!' her faced twitched into what might have been anger but she controlled it. Shabwan hated to see it, once the anger fizzled away there was only sadness, the sadness hurt the most. Without another word he pushed past her and stormed out of the bar, knocking Mrs. Creedy's drink straight down her front as he went.

14.

Perfect, thought Vericoos, he couldn't have planned it better himself and that was saying something. He waited for a couple of seconds, so as not to make it too obvious, then he followed Shabwan outside.

15.

Shabwan was going to cry, he knew that already and he hated himself for it. Few things are as soul destroying as having your new found liberation and freedom snatched away from you. Just when you felt you might have escaped form your bonds of depression and self loathing, just when you thought you might be becoming yourself again, you are reminded of how tiny the distance you've come actually is. You're reminded in the harshest way that you are, in fact, not in control at all. The tears had come and he really wanted to get away from this place, he needed to be by himself. He wanted his mother. Shabwan was so wrapped up in these drunken thoughts that he barely noticed the tall thin stranger until he almost walked into him.

'Rough night son?'

The voice was warm and kindly, it didn't suit the body, it might have suited the face, he didn't know. The face was hidden under a hood.

'Listen,' said the tall figure. 'She's really not worth it, trust me I know. In fact I know more than you can imagine. Although, I wouldn't want to appear arrogant. '

Shabwan's grief was fast becoming anger, he was drunk as hell and he didn't need this old git.

'For example...what if I was to tell you I know exactly why you're here.'

The skinny old man took off his hood and looked directly into Shabwan's eyes.

'I know why you were born, I know, shall we say, your purpose and most importantly I know what you need to do.' The voice was no longer warm and friendly. It was clinical and measured...frightening.

'You don't know anything about me old man.'

Shabwan was feeling unsettled by all of this, he now wanted more than ever to get away. Away from the inn, away from the boys, away from Kayleigh and away form this weird old man. He began to walk away, pushing past Vericoos as he went. The old man pushed him backwards, gently but very firmly.

'You don't want to walk away now Shabwan, this I promise you.'

Shabwan tried again a bit harder and was pushed backwards, this time he almost fell. Sod this! He thought and pushed the old man hard in the chest. Just as he did this Coki, Leeham and Lewhay came out of the front door of The Star. They saw Shabwan push the old man; they also saw how the old man didn't move so much as a muscle. He stood there, still as stone, while Shabwan was projected through the air, as if he'd been thrown by three men, and landed painfully in a crumpled heap. They ran, as one, towards the lean figure in front of them. This time he did move, but only a little: he raised one hand in a smooth arc.

In front of the charging young men the air moved. It was as if a huge metal blade had swung through it, yet there was nothing there. Only a still calm which suggested that anything which had occupied that space a moment before wouldn't be as attached to itself as once it had been. They had stopped running, they looked at the thin old man, his face was calm but his eyes were blazing a cold blue steely light. He turned and was gone. They looked at each other unsure of what to do. Shabwan's groan brought them back to themselves.

'You alright mate?' Coki asked as they pulled him to his feet.

'Euuurgh, what happened?'

Shabwan was pretty dazed but seemed alright Leeham, Lewhay and Coki exchanged a dark look.

'I dunno mate but I think that we've just been pretty lucky.'

Chapter 6.

Wednesday three days to Laffrunda.

1.

You could tell it was very near now. The town was awash with color. Bunting hung like ivy wherever it could and in some places where it couldn't. In the plaine, Anika's lights had finally been erected and the stage hadn't collapsed for a record period of time. Laffrunda was nigh. The people of San Hoist who previously had just *seemed* as if they talked of nothing else, now actually didn't. Dozens of traders with their market stalls had arrived from various towns throughout Corne and the town's inns and guesthouses were completely full. Not one of the inhabitants or visitors of San Hoist

had the slightest suspicion that there were three other guests riding their way. Three guests with very little on their minds, very little indeed.

The controller was still sat on his rock; there was nowhere else for him to go. He was safe here but he didn't know for how long. They would come eventually, they always did. He was exhausted, the process of controlling is mighty draining, but his purpose was far too great to give up on. He was happy with his progress as well, the three hadn't shown any signs of memory or recollection for some time and he was finally confident that they were his.

Truly his.

They rode hard and fast, stopping only when their bodies began to show physical signs of exhaustion. The controller needed to keep them battle ready. They had a big fight ahead.

2.

Shabwan had heard the term hangover banded about throughout his life but he now knew that every other reference he'd heard had been a false one; the only true hangover ever to exist was the one he was currently experiencing. His head felt like someone had sliced it down the middle and then banged the two bits repeatedly against each other, before crudely sewing them back together. He was shivery and had a vile taste in his mouth. He poured himself a glass of water, had a sip and grimaced. You know you've gone too far when even water tastes nasty.

More troubling than the hangover was the hazy collection of memories, lingering just around the edge of his peripheral consciousness. Poised they were and ready to strike a devastating blow by revealing their true form. They were vague but felt extremely important. The only thing he could really remember with any clarity was the eyes and the way they'd flashed as he'd pushed the old man. Even as he thought about this another memory lurched out of the mist and grimaced nastily. The eyes were troubling it was true but there was also the tension, the inhuman solidity. He might as well have tried to push the church over.

He shook himself; it was probably all in his head. He had been absolutely screwed and pretty upset...oh God!! He'd forgotten about Kayleigh, oh no, no, no...what a shambles! He rolled over and attempted to get back to sleep, he'd probably feel better later.

He didn't but he went out any way. Nothing like a brisk walk his mum had always said. He walked up to the square keeping his head low, he didn't think anyone had seen him getting battered by some skinny old man, but you never knew and he wasn't in the mood to have the piss taken out of him; he might react badly. After about an hour of aimless wandering he got some food, a pastry filled with root veg and gristly mince beef and sat in the middle of the square a safe distance away from the inn. Even the faint smell of alcohol was still enough to make him fear for the newly replenished content of his stomach.

'I feel I owe you an apology.'

The voice mad him jump so severely that his fears almost became a reality. He didn't need to turn his head to know who owned it.

'Last night was an unfortunate misunderstanding. Please believe me when I say that I am nothing but a friend to you.'

'It didn't feel like that when you threw me through the air.' Replied Shabwan.

He had apparently been startled into bravery.

'Again I can only offer my apologies. I am after all a very old man and when one begins to feel vulnerable one is more inclined to defend oneself a little...shall we say overenthusiastically.'

Shabwan looked the old man up and down. He was wearing a full length traveling cloak with a hood which was currently down, revealing his very old very bald head. His long thin nose seemed to hang all the way down over his mouth, creating a most interesting profile. He also, Shabwan noticed, had an awful lot of scars, this in itself wasn't weird; a lot of old men had been involved in the battles. He'd certainly heard enough stories from the old timers in the pub to last him a lifetime, maybe even the lifetime of this old chap, he incorrectly supposed.

The thing about these scars was that they weren't immediately obvious or perhaps even immediately visible. It was as if you would notice one, a thin blueish line, and then your eyes would begin to follow it into what seemed like a whole web of scars, crisscrossing the old mans face like a large spiders web, but as soon as you noticed how many there were you lost focus and suddenly none were visible. It was like having a real mild hit of stonk and trying to force the hallucinogenic effects rather than appreciating them.

'You'll have to accept my apologies also,' said Shabwan. 'For I don't think I can believe that you feel vulnerable.'

Vericoos smiled at him.

'You're not stupid.'

'Who are you?'

'That's not important right now, what's important is you.'

Shabwan felt equally as confused hearing this sober as he had last night.

'What?'

'Listen I don't expect you to believe me right now, nor am I going to tell you everything right now, but I'm going to tell you what I hope is enough.'

Normally such cryptic horse muck would have annoyed Shabwan. He'd never liked melodrama, despite being more than capable of producing it. There was, however, something about this man, something he'd been too drunk to realise last night, something that caught your attention and which made you believe.

'OK then, tell me.'

There suddenly seemed a lot more tension than before, the air in the square seemed still and silent, the shouts coming from the plaine seemed distant and hugely unimportant. The only thing which mattered was listening to what this old gentleman had to say.

'Firstly let me tell you my name, its Vericoos.' Said Vericoos (somewhat obviously).

'Shabwan.'

'Yes I know, believe me I know a lot more about you than just your name and it's an absolute pleasure to finally get to talk to you.'

'How long have you wanted to talk to me for?'

Shabwan, in spite of himself, suddenly wanted to know everything. His hangover a distant memory, he didn't really know or understand what was happening but he could feel the importance of it. It was in the air, creating a little bubble around him and his strange new acquaintance.

Vericoos smiled; it was working. He knew how impressionable he could make himself once he was alone with someone. Magic was a very practical tool after all. He also knew that as much as he could create this little bubble of enchantment, where all his suggestions would fascinate and entice the listener he couldn't take complete control of Shabwan's mind, not without ruining him. Not without turning him into nothing more than one of the three monstrosities that were heading this way even as they spoke. No, he would have to rely on what he dubbed his 'sphere of influence'; a phrase which usually isn't meant to be taken literally.

'I need you to come with me, away from this place, Shabwan, I need you to leave right now and come with me. I can explain everything else on the way. You need to know that you must do something; something so important, not only for you and me, but for everyone and everything that you've ever known.'

3.

Shabwan was of stronger mind than Vericoos had thought; he was already starting to look conflicted. You see the thing about the sphere of influence was that if you didn't completely convince someone while they were in it, they could suddenly realise that they were being tricked. Shabwan was showing all the signs that some part of him, some deep subconscious part, was fighting against Vericoos. If Vericoos couldn't persuade him quickly then the game was up.

On the other hand, he thought as his grin drew lines across his dry old face, he might not need to. If he stopped now he would leave Shabwan unconvinced perhaps, but overwhelmed with curiosity. Leaving it now, while he still had time and allowing Shabwan's natural curiosity to do his work for him was eternally preferable to Shabwan realising that Vericoos was exerting some kind of magical control over him. There was, he reminded himself, still time.

'Anyway,' said Vericoos, arriving at a decision. 'Have a think about it.'

Shabwan's eyelids flickered for a second, whatever way the internal conflict was going, it was over now. He looked up at Vericoos who was now standing, his eyes wide with amazement.

'Erm...'

'I bid you a fond farewell', the voice had returned to its former jolly naivety, 'and a very happy Laffrunda.'

Shabwan didn't say anything, he only stared.

4.

As he walked up the north road back towards his guesthouse Vericoos was actually whistling, although he couldn’t for the life of him remember what tune it was. It hadn't gone perfectly, if it had, then the two of them would already have left San Hoist. Vericoos had suspected that Shabwan was too strong of mind for his sphere of influence to have forced an immediate decision without severely damaging him. Nevertheless, he had seen the look of wonder in the young mans eyes as he'd got up to leave. There was no part of Shabwan which had consciously suspected that magic was afoot and now all he would be left with was a sense that he had been given a great opportunity, a unique and glorious chance to be someone...in a way nothing could be truer.

It was clear that the boy had never been one for ambition (a lifetime as a stonk dealer had obviously seemed a fine prospect to him), but Vericoos was confident that his use of the sphere had been so cunning that the boy who once could have happily settled down forever in that tiny little place would now be infatuated with ideas of adventure and exploration, even though he really knew nothing of what was being asked of him. It would nag at his brain like depraved sexual desire, only so much more potent. The brief envelopment within the sphere may not have lead to a decision but, thought Vericoos, it had certainly changed the young man; changed him for the better...at least temporarily. It wouldn't be long now, till he made his decision, the *right* decision. The only threat came from those other three (and of course the other three as well). Even as he thought this, however,

Vericoos, exhilarated from his recent magical work, felt an upwelling of confidence. Let those boys try and talk him out of it. He knows what he wants and what he wants is the sun, compared to the candle flame of this backwards little town.

With regards to the other three...if they ever arrived, the time for talking would have long since finished.

5.

'Shab...Shab...SHAB! You still drunk mate?'

It was late in the evening and the four friends were sitting in the, now beautifully decorated, plaine. Coki had been relaying an anecdote but Shabwan hadn't been listening. He didn't really feel like he'd heard anything since his exchange with Vericoos. All other noise was tinny and distant compared to those warm and meaningful words. They were the only words that had ever really meant anything in his life. Nothing his friends, his parents or even Kayleigh had said held any meaning because none of them knew. There was only one person who knew...

'SHAB!'

He was dragged out of this pleasant sea of thought, back towards the surface. This annoyed him; the only place he wanted to be now was in his own mind. In the warm shallows *below* the surface, where, if he ever needed to look above at the real world, it was happily distant and distorted.

In his mind, he knew that his life now had a path, a reason, and it was one which was more important than these three idiots could ever comprehend. Bless their tiny minds. Still he supposed he should still interact with them a little. It would be a shame to act impolitely. He reluctantly breached the surface. That which had been blurry and distant before now looked clearer, realer, more...annoying.

'What?'

'What the hell's wrong with you?' Coki seemed irritated. He always was if he didn't think people were enjoying his stories enough.

'Nothing's wrong with me, I'm great mate...I'm so good.'

There was something truly unsettling about the way he was looking at them. When someone changes completely it's one thing, but when the differences are so subtle...well, that's quite another. The differences in Shabwan that his friends noticed were so subtle as to be almost unnoticeable, yet still the overall effect yelled and screamed at them like some demented banshee.

Confronted with this strange behavior, the other three had, quite correctly, assumed it had something to do with the old man, they had also, quite incorrectly, assumed it was something to do with what had happened the night before. No one had raised the subject yet but they all knew it was coming. They weren't cowards but none of them had slept as well as usual last night, and not just because they were projecting Sooie's home brew out of their bedroom windows onto the dusty streets below.

'Er...so you not too sore then?'

'What do you mean?'

Coki didn't know if Shabwan's airy and distant manner was annoying or scaring him more.

'I mean you got flung about ten feet through the air by some guy, who looked like he should have died about twenty years ago,' Coki looked sour. 'And I for one wish he had.'

Shabwan suddenly seemed more awake but none of the others noticed, they had all held off from talking about what had happened for long enough.

'Yeah right, old git.'

'That was pretty nuts though...I don't really know what he did, can you guys remember it?' Lewhay asked, still unaware of the new change which had come over Shabwan. He was no longer looking distant and dreamy, but instead looking from Leeham, who had called Vericoos an 'old git' to Coki who had said he wished he'd died, with absolute venom in his eyes. It was a dark look, one which might move to inflict actual physical pain. A look none of them would have said they'd ever seen on him before.

'I'd like another go at him,' said Lewhay. 'See how he fares without his magic or whatever the hell it was.'

That seemed to have done it; now that all three had got involved Shabwan had found his voice.

'What the hell is wrong with you?'

They all stared wide eyed but then Coki's eyes began to narrow, either his surprise was less than the other two or he was just happy to have a reason for a confrontation with Shabwan and wasn't too bothered what it was about.

'There was nothing wrong with that old man, don't you see? Oh God how can you not? He's the person I've been waiting for. He's the person we've all been waiting for. In fact he's the only one who can save us all and I'm going to help him...'

This should have been really funny, but it wasn't. Shabwan seemed too deranged for it to be funny. He was looking at them all in a new way now, a way that surprised them even further; he was looking at them with pity.

'I will try and save you I really will. I will try and save everyone.'

'How?'

There were so many questions that needed asking, Coki just seemed to have picked one out of the hat.

'I don't know.'

This *was* funny. Lewhay snorted a little.

'Well you might have some trouble then mate.' all three of them chuckled at this.

'DO YOU THINK THIS IS FUNNY?'

Shabwan flung himself at Lewhay and grabbed his shoulders. Lewhay hit him. It was more of a reaction shot than anything, not too hard but enough to send him rolling down the bank. He got up and charged, a manic and ugly look distorting his face, it was frightening. This time Coki was on his feet, his sinewy arm drew a smooth and very fast line in the air and connected with a soft 'clock!' at the bottom of Shabwan's jaw. Shabwan was unconscious before he hit the floor, indeed it seemed for the briefest of moments as if he was perfectly horizontal in the air, he looked almost graceful, moments later as he crumpled onto the grass of the plaine he looked less so.

'What the hell was that about?' asked Coki, not expecting an answer.

They all just looked at each other.

'We need to get him home, maybe he took some stonk on the sly and was just having a bit of a bad one.'

Lewhay's suggestion seemed highly possible and made them all feel a lot better. It could be that the combination of being battered by an old man and seeing Kayleigh had put their friend in a pretty bad place and he'd taken a devious dose of stonk to try and get himself through the day. Often when the mind is dark then the trip is even darker.

'Yeah that must be it.' said Leeham, a worried look still hovering over his face. 'Let’s get him to bed.'

Chapter 7.

Thursday. Two days until Laffrunda.

1.

They all stayed at Shabwan's that night. They wanted to be there when he woke up. Sleeping at his was kind of nice in an emasculating way that they'd never admit to each other. It reminded them of being younger and being looked after. They'd all spent a lot of time there as youngsters when his mum was alive. The house felt nice and cozy, the thick rock walls kept in a lot of the heat in the winter and blocked most of it out in the summer. The wooden kitchen top and table had the comforting look of a family home, one where many a huge meal had been prepared and shared. Shabwan's mother had been notorious for feeding an astonishing amount of people out of her tiny kitchen. Stews, soups and casseroles, all lovingly made in large quantities, would be handed out to pretty much anyone in the vicinity, and she'd loved every minute of it.

Shabwan lived here alone now but if you knew where to look, as his best friends did, then you could see how he'd carefully and heart-breakingly maintained some of his mum's favorite things exactly as she'd always had them. Her terracotta pots were still stacked in exactly the same way and her knifes all stuck in a wooden block in a fashion which looked haphazard but which they knew was how she'd always liked to keep them. It was no secret how much he missed her and they suspected that if anyone did anything to damage these two subtle little shrines then the outburst last night would seem very tame compared to what would follow.

'I wonder how he's feeling.' said Leeham. 'That was a sweet punch.'

'Haha yeah, I feel a little guilty about that.'

The other two knew that he felt *a lot* guilty about it, but then Shabwan had lost it in quite a big way. He was normally the type who, when he'd had too much, would tell you how much he loved you till the point when you were bored. Physical violence against his mates had been a nasty surprise.

'Do you, er, reckon he'll be pissed off?'

Coki sounded uncharacteristically sheepish, normally he would defend his actions to the hilt even if he knew they were wrong, and this time they all thought he was in the right.

'Nah; he probably won't remember. We can just tell him he fell over.'

They laughed but the atmosphere was still uneasy. They all wanted to believe that Shabwan had just hit the stonk last night. It could have happened, it definitely *could* have happened, but he had acted so strangely. Even within the remit of massively powerful hallucinogens there are conventions and behavior patterns that, when you get down to it, don't really differ that much from person to person. While what's going on inside their heads is open to infinite possibilities and variants the outward behavior of the stonk head is usually very easy to spot. It's something about the head movement and the eyes which usually gives it away. Shabwan's actions last night hadn't looked like those of a stonk head, even a stonk head in the midst of a really bad time. They had looked like something...different.

'Morning!'

They all jumped, they hadn't heard him come down the stairs.

'Er...how you doing mate?'

Coki was a far cry from his usual confident and boisterous self. He wasn't the sort to feel good about using his fists, especially when it had been against one of his best friends.

'Yeah, would probably be a lot better if you hadn't banged me out.'

Shabwan held his pretense of seriousness for a few moments more, and then his face split into a huge grin which instantly caused him to wince from the pain. They all fell about laughing, they had their mate back. Whatever had happened last night could probably be put down to a number of things, things that one day they should probably talk about. For now it was enough that Laffrunda was just around the corner and they were four again.

As Shabwan sat down to join them for breakfast it was as if none of it, the encounter outside the pub, the business with Kayleigh, the brawl last night, had ever happened.

2.

They're buying it! Thought Shabwan, savoring the rising euphoria. Yes this was the way for sure, if he simply pretended to be who he used to be, that ridiculous, selfish fool of a boy, then they would cause him no more problems and then all he needed to do was find the old man.

He was just glad that Coki's punch hadn't knocked his new found sense out of his head.

3.

Three hours later they were sat in the square enjoying the beautiful summer sun. The banter was good, all was well. Only one of them noticed the tall figure watching them from some distance.

'Let's go to the pub.' said Shabwan. 'I could use a drink for my jaw... oh, hold on there's Ellarus.' The town's drunken doctor was indeed bumbling his way across the square. 'Maybe the useless old codger can help.'

His friends looked at him quizzically.

'Well he is a doctor; mum said he used to be a good one before the drink took him. Maybe I can get him to remember. . I'll meet you three in the pub, get me a drink in.'

They went off, only Coki looked back. Shabwan waited until they were through the door into the darkness of the pub then he got up. He didn't even bother to pretend he was headed towards Ellarus; instead he went straight to Vericoos. The old man was stood, mostly concealed behind a tree which passed its days at the corner of the square. It was, coincidently, known as the watching tree, although no one new why.

'So, you're ready?'

Shabwan only nodded. Now that he was back in the presence of the object of his obsession, words seemed hard to find. It was like looking for Vericoos' scars.

'We must leave now.'

Again only a nod, Vericoos, ever humble, couldn't help but inwardly congratulate himself on what a fine job he'd done on this young man. Yet still all was not well, he could still feel that same troublesome strength of mind, that same unconscious or subconscious resistance rising up in Shabwan. What was it? Love of his home? His friends? Perhaps the memory of his mother or the love of that girl in the bar? Probably all of them, he concluded. Anyhow, there was no time for that, he needed Shabwan and he was staring, quite literally, at the best opportunity he could have ever hoped for to get him out of here unnoticed. If he could just squash this last tiny bit of resistance, then they'd be long gone by the time his friends even missed him. Vericoos extended his sphere engulfing Shabwan once more, he kept it mild; to damage his subject's mind would spell the end.

'I don't know if I can go without saying bye.' Shabwan was saying, it sounded like sleep talk.

Gods damn it thought Vericoos, if he changes his mind now he'll be lost to me for good. It was too much to hope for that Shabwan's second immersion within the sphere would leave him with the same rapt infatuation as the first time. The further he pushed it without getting the young man on board, the greater the chance of an unwanted epiphany. Magic is greater than we can comprehend, but the human mind is not without its own mysteries, perhaps equally as incomprehensible as the raw power that flows from the earth. The old sorcerer was far too arrogant to appreciate the irony of his most subtle and brilliant craft being at its most vulnerable as it faced something he deemed both unworthy and uninteresting.

'Yes, yes you can. You'll see them again, you'll see them all again. But if you don't leave now every last one of them will die.'

He'd won!

The distant, glimmering fire of resistance died in Shabwan. It was replaced with another fire: the raging inferno of desire to do as Vericoos bid and the desire to do it now. If Vericoos had, at that moment, asked Shabwan to get down on his knees and perform the crudest of favors he'd have found himself most satisfied.

Instead Shabwan said the two words that Vericoos had longed to hear ever since he'd first laid eyes on the lumbering young man:

'Let's go!'

His eyes were bright and childlike, full of excitement. Vericoos was about to respond when Coki's fist, still sore from its use for the same purpose the previous day, slammed into his mouth almost breaking his jaw.

'Not so solid this time eh?' Coki yelled, and he had a fair point.

Vericoos had been flung against the tree by the blow and now lay in a crumpled heap at the bottom. Leeham placed a well measured kick into his Ribs and Lewhay followed with a harder one. Vericoos coughed and spluttered, he could taste blood in his mouth. How had he let his guard drop so much? Three drug dealing fishermen had just outsmarted him, and worst of all Shabwan was shaking his head like someone waking up from a nightmare. Everything was lost, truly everything.

'What they hell were you doing to him, hey? Trying to hypnotise him up all nice, so you could sleep with him or something?' It seemed odd to Shabwan that Leeham would use such a euphemistic description of the primal act at a time like this.

Vericoos was so angry he considered killing them all, Shabwan included. If they only knew the damage they'd just done.

Shabwan was really starting to return to the cold light of reality now. Vericoos must have pushed him too hard in his eagerness to leave. He had been so busy congratulating himself on the quality of his work that he'd failed to finish it properly and at what costs? A few more seconds and it probably would have worked anyway, but thanks to Coki's, not so subtle, interruption, Shabwan was now becoming all too aware of the trickery and he wasn't looking at all happy about it.

The other three moved back slightly, so it was just Vericoos and Shabwan. Man on man, so they incorrectly thought

'What were you doing to me?' His tone was steely, like the colour of the sea in the deepest of winter, his eyes looked like the clouds that create said shade.

Vericoos said nothing, the game was up. Shabwan moved to kick him, he could have stopped him, he could have disintegrated them all with the slightest movement of his hand, but he didn't. Instead Shabwan's foot hit him hard in the ribs. He felt a crack and tasted the bitter, irony tang of blood in the back of his throat. Another kick, Vericoos' anger was reaching breaking point, he might as well kill them, everything was lost anyway, what difference did it make if they lived or died? He extended his hand beneath his robe, instantly feeling the magic rush there, away from where it was healing his ribs and jaw. He held it there, for a second; a handful of death. Then he had a thought, a moment of clarity so crystal that he wondered how he had ever let himself come so close to this point. Shabwan's third kick hit him square in the mouth, everything went blurry...

Chapter 8.

Friday, Laffrunda eve.

1.

Anika didn't like the eve. Sure the buildup was stressful but it was fun. She loved watching the town come alive. It was an old and tired metaphor but one that couldn't give more accuracy to the awakening of the Host. At the beginning of the festival week, little scraps of colour would begin to appear like little shoots, the odd banner in a window or extra flowerpot. More and more of these would, as the week went on, spark into existence, like little flushes of green in early spring. Then the bunting (To Anika's eye the creepers) would begin to reach out between all these little splashes, joining and cross pollinating them till the little flashes of colour became big bushes, engulfing houses and streets. Then came the lanterns, these were always added later in the week as they could be ruined by rain, not that there had been any chance of that this year. The lanterns were white, made of paper over twigs which were twisted by the town's children into all sorts of interesting shapes. The finished products cast a beautiful glow over the rest of the décor. They were, to Anika the little white blooms on a great bush of cloth and colour that meant that the organic side of the festival had come to life and that the time for her to get everything sorted was terrifyingly imminent. Anika loved watching all this, loved supervising it, until the eve.

During the week if something goes wrong there's always more time, there's always another day. Not today. Today, 'another day' becomes 'tomorrow' and 'tomorrow' becomes 'laffrunda' and realisation dawns that actually, there is no more time. Things need to work and they need to be organised and they need to meet both these criteria right bloody now!

And by God's there was still so much; the arguments over who would run shifts in the beer tent had turned into small civil wars. The stage, despite showing early signs of promise, was still falling over whenever it felt like it (although sitting down like a grumpy camel might be a better image) and the schedule of musicians was, of course, being chopped, changed and viscously bickered over. The musicians were always the same. In advance of the festival they would always be so relaxed, 'yeah I'll play whenever you want.' then when the day was near it was all, 'erm actually I think my set would go better after his and I don't want to play too early, my set is really orientated around the dance floor.'

Then there were the parades.

These involved the younger children of San Hoist and were perhaps the biggest logistical nightmare that has ever existed in any world, ever. It's amazing how much work goes into getting small children to stand in a line and carry things. Any adults that lay off the stonk and the booze for long enough to try and help with the parade always find themselves turning to said vices very shortly afterwards, usually leaving the younger members of their family to roam free for the day and vowing never to help with anything ever again. Ye gods, there was *so* much to do. Still, Anika had to admit that the preparation had gone a lot better than usual and things did have a way of coming together once the day was upon them. Happy coincidences and strokes of luck were what Laffrunda was built on and Anika had every confidence that tomorrow would bring a great barrow load of these, just like it always did.

2.

Several dimensions away, the controller had quite different ideas. Last night, upon feeling Vericoos' failure, he'd almost gone into spasms of ecstasy as the sense that all was lost rang out across his hideously purple sky. So linked to each other were they, so un-severable was the connection that bound them, that the controller's whole world had contorted with Vericoos' agony.

He had considered releasing the three there and then. They would have died instantly of course, but keeping them was draining him. Then, right at the last moment, he'd sensed something else, a little glimmer of hope; a nasty little worm of optimism crawling through the great apple of his victory. No, he said to himself, no, no, no. The time for their release was not yet upon him. Instead he would keep the three and he would finish what he'd started. They were, after all, only a day away now and still had plenty left to give. Vericoos had lived far too long anyway.

'This time tomorrow, Vericoos my old friend, will be the end, properly this time, I only wish I could be there to see it.'

He sat on his rock, dehydrated, starving, on the brink of death and laughed like a maniac.

3.

Anika could see Shabwan, Coki, Lewhay and Leeham crossing the plaine, they were laughing an awful lot about something. She did like those boys. It would be nice, for all four of them, if Shabwan could stop being such a little drip about Kayleigh. Still young love is glorious and terrifying in equal measures and for every soaring high there is the inevitable stagnant trough. The boys headed off across the square towards The Star; she could still hear their laughter as they went through the welcoming doorway. This time next week she would be able to do the same thing; enjoy a nice quiet and completely stress-free pint, but definitely not tonight. Instead, she looked back across the plaine at a million and one unfinished jobs completely failing to notice a lone figure was sitting, wearing a long traveling cloak.

4.

'Mate I just want to talk to her tonight alright?'

'No it's not alright you idiot, remember how last time you tried that, you almost got led off into the hills by that weird old goat.' Said Coki.

'What's that got to do with me talking to Kayleigh?'

'It was a joke, but just listen for a minute. It's a miracle that we've got you back in one piece. God knows what that old git had planned for you and despite the fact that you've been a limp squid for the past few months I'm still exceptionally pleased to have you back.'

'Thank you.'

'But now I've got you back I'm going to warn you of something.'

'What's that?'

'That you'd *better* be on good form for Laffrunda. We set out this week to get you back to your old self and have a big...no, a huge weekend and it feels like everything that could have happened to stop that happening has, but yet…here we are.'

'What's your point?'

'My point is that if you go and talk to her, there's every chance you'll regress to the same winging little nit you were a few days ago, who I only marginally preferred to the raving nutter who tried to attack Lewhay the other night.'

Coki's crinkly smile always smoothed over the harsh points of his words.

'Yeah OK point taken. Look... thanks for everything mate. You've been amazing.'

They had a hug, quite a tender one. It had been an emotional patch of time and also they were on the 'stonkette'.

If it seems like this tale is bound up amidst the world of drug taking then I must apologise, but I have to add just one more to the cocktail. It has been mentioned in passing at certain points but it is now time to give it a little more space. Stonkette was a brew Lewhay and Leeham had created. It was simple enough to make but, like the catching of the pari, it was the product of a huge amount of trial and error. The basic premise was to boil up a load of stonk with wheat and sugar, two things which, like the mushrooms that made up the bulk of the product, were readily available in the region of San Hoist. This process, for reasons best known to mother nature, removed all the hallucinogenic qualities and increased the potency of whatever it was which made you so chatty and happy. They had never divulged, not even to Coki and Shabwan, exactly how they had come across this unlikely recipe but everyone was happy that they had. Stonkette was the perfect drug for a night at the pub, dancing, chatting and hugging all coming naturally as breathing and any ill feeling or dislike instantly dissolving into a garbled and meaningless, yet highly satisfying conversation. Tonight was for Stonkette, tomorrow was for both forms of the mushroom based drug. It was a tried and tested, complete satisfaction guaranteed, technique for Laffrunda enjoyment.

The Eve passed without much incident, it was packed to the rafters in The Star with some local percussionist banging out a one hundred and eighty beat per minute mix of eclectic and wonderful rhythms while Sooie, leaving

Kayleigh on bar duties, played his huge double bass over the top. The beer, the stonk and the stonkette flowed freely. Even Anika (contrary to all her earlier predictions) managed to get in and enjoy a few drinks and a bit of a dance. Coki took her by the hand and spun her round and round and round until she collapsed in a dizzy tired heap. The vibe was nice, pure excitement about the day to come. Of course none of them could have known or would have ever pictured in their wildest nightmares, what it would bring.

Death, while being the only true grantee, is also often quite a shock.

Chapter 9.

Laffrunda Day.

1.

Ah, Laffrunda! No one from the city could ever truly comprehend the focus of the rural community on the party. You see the district of Corne lies to the far south of the country of Svin, little towns; farming, fishing and mining towns, stretch out across its long thin arm. San Hoist is as big as any settlement within a hundred miles. Very few have ever left and none have ever made it as far as the inner cities, or desire to. This far corner of the land is about as far removed from urban life as anywhere on Svin, something Shabwan will eventually come to learn. When he does reach the stage of his journey which exposes him to the wonders of the cities, he will marvel at the huge amount that there is to see and do. The bright lights and dingy cobbled alleys, the brothels and the clubs, the hundreds upon hundreds of street vendors and performers will all excite and mystify him. Yet he will always maintain that those in the city, those who are so exposed to all different kinds of entertaining sins on a daily basis, will never understand the community wide commitment to a good time of a small town whose day has come. That day is today, Laffrunda day.

2.

Anika had enjoyed all of three hours of uneasy sleep when she was dragged into an exhausted state of consciousness by a combination of panic and relief. It was today, whatever would happen would happen, whatever would go right would go right and whatever would go wrong...well, it's not as if anyone would be in any fit state to notice. She got up and went to the window of her little cottage (she only lived a few rows up from Shabwan in the more congested and confused southern side of San Hoist) the weather was beautiful, that was a good start, a rainy Laffrunda piled its own set of damp challenges to the top of her already teetering stack. The sky was the kind of light blue that you only get in the middle of summer; she could hear the sea gently washing into the wall of the harbor. She loved the rhythmical swashing of the waves, on any other day it would probably have sent her back off into a happy cocoon of unawareness, but not today.

She walked through the square towards the plaine, the only people around seemed to be the market stall traders who were setting up, a whole host of mouth watering smells brushed past her nostrils but she was too busy to let any of them actually enter. It was a strange kind of calm, which almost made the rapidly approaching chaos tricky to imagine. She arrived at the plaine and was pleased to see the majority of her volunteers already sat on the freshly cut grass of the plaine. They all looked absolutely hanging (it had been one to remember, if only they could! In The Star last night) but they were *there*, if not in mind then at least in body.

'Ah...my lovely group of volunteers.'

They all shuffled their feet and a few even managed a small smile. Anika could be menacing, albeit in a kind of friendly maternal way, but enough to make you feel a bit frightened when your hangover was so bad you were shaking. She gave them all their instructions; they were mostly young lads with no money for beer who knew that Anika would reward her volunteers accordingly. They would work through the morning and the afternoon, keeping everything running relatively smoothly until Anika released them into the early evening. By that stage things just seemed to run themselves and if they didn't, well…worse things happen at sea.

The first job for Anika's 'willing' helpers was to organise the children's midday parade. This was how Laffrunda always began; with three hundred or so fresh young faces, poking out from home made costumes, stomping from the East side of town to the West, carrying a huge range of weird and wonderful banners and sculptures. There was usually some kind of loose theme (this year it was sea creatures, last year it had been farm crops, you get the idea), although it seemed that many of the children didn't like to be bonded by such constrictive categories and chose instead to bully and pester their parents until they had transformed their offspring into multi coloured dragons, snarling monsters or beautiful princesses.

As the parade began to take shape, Anika, who was stood on a crate bellowing through a makeshift megaphone, noticed that some of the children had indeed embraced the aquatic theme. She could see a few dolphins, some mermaids and even a few pari. She could however, also see a young boy completely covered in some rusty metallic and not completely safe looking material, a donkey and one plump young girl who seemed to have come as a wardrobe. Those adults responsible enough to be sober at this point in the weekend (depressingly few), were helping distribute the banners and sculptures amongst the ranks. These small masterpieces were lovingly made every year by a team of local artist who, unlike the damned musicians, never asked for anything in return and Anika was eternally grateful for their efforts. The parade always looked wonderful.

Half an hour later, the parade was almost ready for the off. Anika had yelled herself hoarse but she had managed to get the children into something which resembled order. The children themselves were a sea of color; the nautical and the obscurely fantastical all in perfect harmony. Above their heads they held the banners and paper-and-stick sculptures, at least a hundred, Anika guessed. The banners showed a range of things but mainly they portrayed all that gave San Hoist its soul, the sea, the field, the harvest (perhaps ironically, no one seemed to have made one for stonk). There were also a smattering of banners made at home by the parents. Some of these, created by those within San Hoist who held onto delusions of grandeur showed crude family crests, although Anika was pretty sure that the vast majority of these had been invented within the lifetimes of their pretentious seamstresses rather than having any kind of historical relevance. Others were completely indistinguishable, just shapes and colors, and one banner near the front, held by the same plump girl who was wearing the wardrobe costume seemed to simply show a potato. Anika could only speculate as to why.

'OK everyone! Can you be quiet please?'

she'd already asked this five times and didn't hold out much hope for any success this time. The children, who were all vaguely in the right position ten minutes ago, had trouble remaining still. This wasn't so much of a problem with those just carrying a banner, but when someone from the team of eight children carrying the huge twig and paper dragon, decided he wanted to find his friends who were fifty feet away, complications arose. Anika's megaphone, if it had become suddenly aware of such things, would have wondered why it was emitting phrases like: 'can the dragon move back please?' and 'can the giant squid get back behind the little turtles?'

'QUIET!!!'

It would have been shocked out of such a thought pattern by this latest blast of sound. That was better, thought Anika, the general hubbub of excitement and bickering, clowning and crying died down, she could, at least, hear herself think.

'Thank you! Right I think we're about ready for off, aren't we?'

The question was about as rhetorical as it gets. If anyone had dared to answer her they'd have probably found themselves with a megaphone sticking out of somewhere unpleasant. The megaphone in question, already perplexed with it all, would probably have given up at that point. In the short time since it had been foolishly granted hypothetical consciousness it had been shouted at and thrust somewhere it had no desire to be. This would surely be too much for anyone or anything to bear, wouldn't you agree?

Under Anika's instruction the band, a mixture of fiddlers and percussionists began to play an annoyingly catchy but charming piece of music (da da da da, da dum dee da dee dum dee da, you know the one) and the parade began to move forwards... slowly.

Anika smiled, the first parade was off and with it the day had, at last, begun. The first one was always the hardest. While the midday children's parade was a case of one exhausted chief and a swarm of energetic Indians, the evening lantern parade was made up of more drunken adults, single mindedly determined that their way of doing things was the best, than you could shake a banner at. The lantern parade was an all chief affair, and signaled the time when Anika could finally relax a little after an exhausting day.

3.

'Come on I wanna see the parade.'

Shabwan had awoken feeling slightly worse than Anika's crew of helpers but he'd dragged himself out of bed none the less. He'd also cooked breakfast for the other three who had slept on the cold tiled floor of his kitchen, this apparently being preferable to stumbling another two hundred feet or so to reach their own houses.

'You're lazy gits, all of you.' He had said.

The other three had silently but gratefully forced Shabwan's eggs and bacon down their throats. None felt like eating but it was a necessity if they wanted to begin another heavy day immediately after a heavy night. Which they did.

'Are you alright Coki?' Shabwan inquired in a mocking tone of voice as if he was addressing a four year old who had had a tumble.

He knew his friend felt terrible but his competitive nature would override almost everything else.

'Nah mate I'm fine.'

He wasn't but he would pretend to be until he was, Shabwan turned to the other two, 'How about you guys, we could go back to bed if you wanted. I'll give you a cuddle, even if you are ugly.'

Shabwan's goading was annoying, the other two felt like getting up and slapping him, but they knew he was only trying to get them out of the house and into the festivities. And who could really blame him for that?

Twenty minutes later they were out of the house and heading up towards the square. There were people *everywhere*; Laffrunda drew them in from miles around. Some of those present had been up at the crack of dawn and walked the entire way. The four boys came off the side street on which Shabwan lived onto the main track that lead from the harbor up to the square, they were instantly engulfed in the huge crowd of people, every man woman and child in western Corne seemed to be trying to get to the square in time to see the midday parade go past.

'Eugh, I hate crowds.'

They all nodded at Coki's proclamation. They didn't normally mind large numbers of people but, hungover in the baking hot midsummer sun, the last place they wanted to be was in a crowd. They managed to elbow their way into the square and get four upsettingly hot ciders from a stall manned by one of Anika's volunteers. The pasty young man looked as if he was unsure of how he was going to stay on his feet for the next few hours, let alone serve people drinks and collect money in return. The world of economics wasn't somewhere he wanted to dwell for longer than necessary.

They drank the ciders quickly, if you managed to ignore the first few sips you stopped feeling sick. When the pints were finished they were all in much better spirits.

'First one down,' Coki smiled. 'Always works a treat.'

It was true. The first drink of the morning after a heavy night of stonkette and booze was always the hardest to get down, but it was a fairly instantaneous tonic. Their hangovers forgotten, the four friends were up and ready, not one of them spared a moments thought for their violent encounter with Vericoos the day before. All that lay ahead of them was music, fun and madness, maybe even sex if they were really lucky. Laffrunda was a notorious time for casual pro creation. Babies were certainly not the intention of this activity, but nine months after the festival (midway through the earliest quarter of the spring) there were almost always a string of new children welcomed into the world, not many of them the result of planned family extensions. These had become know, somewhat unimaginatively, as the Laffrunda births. Coki had had a few near misses in this fashion. His Laffrunda success rate was something he was irritatingly proud of. His three friends couldn't remember the last festival when he hadn't ended up in an intimate situation with the new and very temporary love of his life. The surrounding fields were his (and everyone else's) arena of choice, but on one memorable occasion, Shabwan's mother's bed had become the unfortunate victim of Coki's eagerness and poor sense of direction. They still laughed till this day at the memory of a naked Coki being chased up the main track by Shabwan's mum as the terrified girl, equally naked, fled in the opposite direction.

They watched the children's parade go by, it looked amazing; from the toothy grin of the huge stick-and-paper shark, which led the way, all the way to the giant San Hoist banner at the back. The latter got a particularly large cheer from the already fairly merry locals and a few friendly boos from some cheeky 'out-of-towners'. Shabwan saw an exhausted looking Anika walking along beside, the huge dark rings around her eyes didn't dull the twinkle within. She was clearly beginning to enjoy herself. She caught Shabwan's eye and waved, the four boys cheered, they wanted her to know how well she'd done. She beamed back and then instantly had to turn and separate two children, a jellyfish and a pari who had begun fighting. The pari was just one member of a whole shoal. Funny how so many children were dressed as them.

'They're kind of beautiful I suppose aren't they?'

'What are?'

Lewhay looked slightly bothered by Shabwan's question.

'Pari, I guess I'd never really thought about it before, but they are kind of beautiful.' Shabwan said.

'You know that one of them almost killed you earlier this week?' Said Leeham.

'Yeah I know,' replied Shabwan. 'But it's the beautiful stuff that hurts you the most.'

His three friends groaned and glanced at each other. Shabwan grinned broadly at them.

'I'm joking, that was the old me talking.' He laughed.

4.

Half a day's ride away came the three. And by all the Gods they looked terrible. The magical hold of possession seemed to have removed all of their humanity; all they'd retained was the shape. Their skin had gone the elusive blue of Vericoos' scars and they seemed to prickle with little flashes of purple energy. Their faces had become flatter and shapeless, their eyes black holes, so dark they barely even seemed to reflect. Where once there were noses now there was nothing, where once there were mouths now there were horrible reptilian slits.

They had needed food last night and their packs had offered nothing. Instead they'd killed an unfortunate family of traveling performers who were on their way to Laffrunda and had eaten them raw. Their final nourishment complete, they hadn't slept but had just ridden, three humanoid shapes, the mysterious blue of their skin in stark contrast to the dull farming clothes they wore, thundering along the final leg of their journey. The controller hadn't moved for a while now, to look at him you would think he was dead. In reality he was far from it, in some ways he had never been so alive. His state of concentration was so perfect that he had almost ceased to think, he only felt and urged. If he did think it was only in swirling images, himself... free, Vericoos...dead and, of course, the God.

5.

They were laughing, imagine that. Just a few short days later such a memory would seem as if it had never happened yet here they were, the four of them laughing away as if things couldn't be better. They were on their way to watch Jax and Ozki perform in the plaine. The pair always provided an uplifting and melodic performance, perfect for kicking off the musical side of the festivities. The laughter was at Coki, who'd tried to demonstrate a dance move he had seen Shabwan doing the night before, one that Shabwn would have been more than happy if no one had ever remembered. His sartorial tribute had come to a premature end as he'd tripped over and almost taken out a sausage stall. After much apologising to the enraged vendor, they had been on their way and now the fear of being separated by a meat cleaver had passed they were freely enjoying Coki's stupidity.

'That's what happens when you take the piss out of me: fate intervenes.' Said Shabwan.

'Yeah clearly, I thought that guy was going to kill me the way he was waving that knife around. He could have just fed me one of his sausages, would have probably been quicker.'

'Yeah we'll see about dancing later tonight anyway.' Leeham laughed.

They all sensed that another half joke, half serious boast was not far away and sure enough, 'Cos I'm going to be rewriting the rule book!'

They all laughed again, the thought of Leeham dancing with any grace or timing was funny enough. It was made even funnier by the fact that he thought he was good at it.

'The band sound really good; have you heard of them?'

'Yeah the dead gypsies, they're supposed to be amazing.' replied Lewhay.

'Yeah I can't wait,' put in Shabwan. 'Johnny Fergus said he saw them when he went away for a bit last year.'

'You're going to be tripping so hard by then you wouldn't care if it was just me up there and a set of maracas.' said Coki.

They all laughed again, it was probably true.

Jax and Ozki played to a packed plaine. Most people were sat around the edge relaxing, although a few early casualties of the boys produce were already skanking around in front of the stage, looking more like they were trying to summon some ancient god than enjoying a nice afternoon in the sun with a bit of music.

'There's always some who get on just a little bit early.' Said Lewhay, although this was hypocritical as the boys had all got a good few ciders down them in the short time they'd been up and had just had a few little hits of stonkette too.

'What time do you think we should, ahem...begin.'

'I don't know, let's just watch Jax and Ozki for a bit then maybe go back to mine and sort it out.'

Shabwan's suggestion was greeted with general agreement; the stonkette was good as was the cider but there was only one substance that they were really thinking about today.

It would perhaps be easy to look over from our part of the universe and judge both the boys and the people of San Hoist harshly for their lax attitude to consumption of mind altering substances. They certainly come across as a right carefree bunch, a lot of whom seem to have very little commitment to family or work and a great deal of commitment to getting screwed. We must remember two things however: one, that their world is very, very different to our own and two, that all that the four friends have really done is create a new way of doing what humans love best. They don't profit from violence or robbery, they profit from selling people a good time. Are they really any different from those who pioneered turning grapes into wine or first smoked tobacco? And if we consider all the evils those industries have done in our own world, then we'd have to say that Shabwan and co.'s fairly ethical attitude to the supply of their product should at least give them the benefit of the doubt.

Or maybe not. It's not really my place to say. It is, however, perhaps important to acknowledge that our own prejudices against the practices of our four friends and those who inhabit the little town of San Hoist might be bound up in arbitrary systems of legality which govern our own world and have no place in the world that Vericoos has so long inhabited. If that which grows from the earth makes you feel good and there is no system in place which tells you that using it to enjoy yourself should be punished then why the hell wouldn't you enjoy it? You just have to hope that one day you grow up enough to realise that the important thing in life is balance. There are lots of things you can take to enjoy yourself but there is also so much more to life as well. Most people come to realise this with age; a few, unfortunately, don't.

But enough of this horrifically pretentious overstepping of the narrative mark.

Let's, instead, return to a certain plaine somewhere in the western arm of Corne, a certain plaine, which will very soon be under great threat, but which is currently playing host to two musicians and an expanding dance floor (can you call it a dance floor when it's on grass, I'm not sure, anyway it was expanding).

6.

Jax and Ozki had moved from the more folky and balladesque numbers into their preferred faster and better known songs, a mix of sea shanties and field songs all reworked and put to a stomping beat. The change in style had been marked by a huge number of people hauling themselves up from the warm carpet of grass and crowding around the stage. The stonked out druids and lost souls were now joined by all and sunder. The whole town seemed to be moving to the rhythm. Only one man wasn't enjoying himself, one lonely figure stood, not in the carnage of the plaine, but down by the coast, watching the gentle summer swell lapping at the shore; contemplating.

Coki, Leeham and Lewhay were starting to feel pretty good, so they kept telling Shabwan every five minutes or so. Such was the effect of the stonkette, it loosened the tongue and if there was a gap in the conversation, people tended to fill it by describing how much they're enjoying themselves. Times like these call for movement. The stonkette rushes around your system at quite a rate and, while it's enjoyable to sit around letting your mouth spill out all sorts of nonsense, movement eventually becomes imperative.

Shabwan and his three friends rose to their feet and all but ran towards the stage, Shabwan noticed how many beautiful colors there were in the world as he went, he also noticed how peoples faces looked slightly different, it was hard to focus on any individual part, they eyes especially. Soon, after some friendly elbowing, they were at the front of the crowd.

Shabwan yelled to Ozki and Jax, 'Go on boys....yeeeeeeeeeeeew!'

They both grinned back at him, they'd remained sober thus far in order to perform their set and consequently the hyperbole of these bug eyed lunatics was not without its comedy. They themselves would be joining the brigade soon enough though.

Given a group of four young men, you might assume that one would be able to dance. With regards to our present company you'd have assumed wrong. They weren't just not very good at it, they were bad. Bad is definitely the word you'd use if you were to look upon the four figures now lurching and jumping about the place. All of the movement, the shambolic movement that resembled someone falling off a cliff while remaining vertical, seemed to happen off the beat, and with no sense of anything that resembled timing. The boys remained happily oblivious to these observations. A lot of fun was being had and none of them, except perhaps Leeham, would have cared if anyone were to point out how badly they were doing. It seemed that nothing could interrupt the euphoric flow of movement into which they'd entered...

7.

Vericoos looked at the sea. He could just fling himself in right now, save himself the trouble. He dismissed this thought as quickly as it had arisen. Even though all was lost he wouldn't shy away from his impending fight with the controller. There was no prize anymore, not without the boy, but there *was* savage revenge. He could smash the three foul creations, which drew ever closer, through the dimensions until they met the very man who controlled them, the very man who had robbed them of everything. No matter how badly the magic had taken them, Vericoos was pretty sure that they'd seek to destroy that which had ruined them, even if they were only doing so on the most basic of instincts.

The controller had won; no doubt about that. The feeling of bitter disappointment still physically hurt Vericoos like a knife in his side but, even in defeat, he doubted that sending these things back from whence they came, to kill his old enemy once and for all, would leave him dissatisfied. It was a small consolation, the final wooden spoon in their great battle, but it was one Vericoos would fight for. He would fight as hard as he had ever fought.

It was these emotions which the controller had mistaken for optimism; these emotions which had lead him to believe that Vericoos still held onto some hope for his quest. Since they had opened the connection there had been very few occasions when they'd misunderstood one another. They were usually accompanied by disastrous consequences.

Vericoos had flirted briefly with the idea of having one last attempt at persuading Shabwan, but he'd decided, very swiftly, against it. He knew a lost cause when he saw one. The feeling of excitement and disbelief which he'd known, oh so potently, when he first laid eyes on the boy seemed like a distant memory.

How had he failed? Had he been over eager? Probably. Gods he could have waited till after this cursed little festival. He could have left town and met the three on the road and destroyed them before anyone in San Hoist had even been aware of their existence. Then he could have got to Shabwan when he was hungover and weak and those other three meddlers, especially that Coki, were asleep in their beds. He'd have had no trouble persuading him. As it was Shabwan's guard would be up, and the moment he saw Vericoos his mind would begin to protect itself in ways its simple owner could never hope to comprehend.

The boy was popular too. Vericoos fancied that, were he to wonder into the town today and be seen by those who knew him or had heard of him last night in the pub (for the boys had doubtlessly thrown that tale around till it was sore), he would have a serious problem on his hands. They'd always remember the year they lynched the creepy old magician wouldn't they? These cursed drunks and users. Vericoos vowed that if this were to happen, he would take the whole damn town with him.

A lot of questions had flown around his brilliant mind since he'd arrived in this town, but now there was only one left. One that, as it would turn out would make all the difference to everything, one that would be a matter of life and death but mainly the latter... Where?

8.

'Where have you been all day?'

Shabwan really hadn't expected this. He'd been having a lot of fun and, for the first time in oh so long, hadn't even thought of Kayleigh. Consequently, when she popped up at his elbow his heart did a little skip and temporarily became the only part of him moving in time with the music. She was so beautiful it was untrue, despite his slightly blurred and overly mobile vision he could still appreciate the soft curves of her face, her big eyes and her full lips.

'I've been...around.'

His attempt to sound cool and distant sounded false to both their ears and as they met each others eyes they both knew it and laughed. It felt so good to be near her again, the stonkette flowing through his veins seemed to flow faster and truer. His brain felt warm and fuzzy, words escaped him.

'Jax and Ozki always know how to kick things off, don't they?'

They were talking normally now and Shabwan was glad of it, he didn't mind that he wasn't fighting it like before. He still loved her, loved her so damn much! As their eyes met again it seemed as if her very essence was seeping into his. As they stood there they connected. There was no need for words they could just stand here and be...

'Shabwan...you OK?'

Apparently she didn't feel quite the same and the reality of her question snapped Shabwan back from the little introverted heaven he was allowing himself to be smothered into. He laughed briefly at the memory of his former thoughts. Such was the way with stonkette, one minute the voice in your head seemed like it was spouting indisputable gospel, the next it'd be gone, fading out like the hum of Jax's guitar at the end of a song, and you'd move on, into the next set of ideas and dreams. These would follow the same pattern; beginning their short lives like crystals, ringing out over the sounds of music and the muffled humming of your brain yet, all too quickly, they would dissolve and be swallowed up into that same fuzzy buzz.

'You're off it already aren't you?'

She didn't mean this literally, off it described his mental state whereas he himself was most definitely *on* it.

'Yeah!'

That was all he could really manage, that and a big beaming grin. She smiled back.

'I think I'm getting there,' she said, her eyes gleaming in a way that suggested that she was telling the truth. 'Listen Shab, can we have a talk, I mean if you can talk, I just really think that, you know...we should.'

She laughed at the structure of her own sentence; her mouth seemed to be beating her brain in the race to inebriation.

'Yeah...yeah that'd be wicked.'

Both Shabwan's brain and mouth had beaten hers hands down, but at the sound of her suggestion he felt a stirring in his loins and the air felt cool in his lungs. Was there still a chance with her? Was there something? Even if there wasn't they could surely still have sex. It was Laffrunda after all. The last tiny wisp of his rational mind, which had, up till now been holding on...just for the sake of it really, shouted out to him. You shouldn't be doing this today, don't let this get in your head...WAIT! He ignored it, useless rationality; there was no place for it today. How did it expect him to get anything done? He would talk with Kayleigh, they would sort things out and everything would be back to normal, everything would in fact be better than it had ever had been.

Now, most of you probably think that Shabwan is about to make a huge and very unfortunate mistake. You'd be absolutely right but where you might be slightly wrong, however, is in your reckoning of *when* this will occur. It is perhaps bitterly ironic that the day Shabwan was forced to make a decision which would affect the lives of everyone everywhere he was also battling to do the same thing in his own tiny little universe. So much lies ahead for our hero and yet in his own addled head, as the laffrunda sun gives the plaine a golden glow, the world seems only to exist in the smallest of units. In the space beyond him and her, there is nothing and with regards to time? Well, the next five minutes is all there is, or at least all that matters.

'Sit here.'

Kayleigh had found a good spot up on the raised banks of the plaine. There wasn't a lot of room in between all the people; some of them had already passed out. Shabwan sat down, a little bit too close to her, she didn't flinch or move back but instead leaned in towards him, he felt the stirring again, this time a lot stronger, he pulled his legs up so as not to reveal the embarrassing bulge.

His heart was beating fast, fast and hard. It reminded him of how it felt when he was plucking up courage to try and kiss her for the first time. He'd been sober then, alas not the case now. Now the whole world was the bubble in which he and Kayleigh were contained, its perimeter hanging just a few inches above their skin, he was acutely aware of everything within this space; all the distances between him and her, and all the points of contact (he liked these). The outside world was still there and, in one sense, he was very aware of that too; but in another, he probably wouldn't have noticed if the whole thing had exploded right then and there.

'Shabwan I've been thinking, real hard about things and...'

She stopped, on this moment all things hung. Shabwan 's confidence, just moments ago an indestructible wall building itself bigger and bigger, faltered. She was going to tell him that she just really wanted them to be friends, that she missed his friendship and wished they could talk more. God's he'd misread everything, he suddenly felt more sober than he'd done in hours, the dark sobriety only a slightly hallucinogenic reality can offer. Her lips hadn't moved yet, neither had her eyes, wow it had been a long time. Why wouldn't she just say it? Say it and dash his happiness all across the grass. He felt tears welling up in his eyes but felt no shame, this was too dark for shame. He'd retracted into his own head so deeply so quickly that he barely heard her saying it.

'You were right.'

She smiled at him, he was plunged back into the here and now (well, sort of). This was too much, could she mean...?

'I just didn't think it was worth it at the time...I mean you were a an idiot about a lot of things and I just felt it wasn't worth the fight... at the time but now, I don't know, these past few weeks have just...oh I've missed you.'

He didn't move, he couldn't move, his mind was all just one wave of hope rushing towards a single point, a make or break point. She misread this...

'You don't want me back...I was prepared for this, I mean, yeah I know you've had a hard time since and I hurt you a lot , which I'm so sorry for...I just want you. I'm sorry Shab.' she got up to leave, he grabbed her arm.

9.

He'd always remember that kiss, her lips felt so soft and beautiful he feared that they would melt, yet at the same time all he wanted was for them to melt into each other, so they could be eternally united, never again apart. His head felt clearer now, the basting he'd just given his poor brain seemed to have flushed the main part of the stonkette out of it. He'd been off his head a bit ago, when they'd left the dance floor. He hadn't really realised but then, you never do until after. They kissed for a long time, he was split in two, one part of him burned for physical reaffirmation of their love; he feared his loins would explode at any minute (not something he'd have wanted to happen in a crowded plaine, especially not on Laffrunda), he wished everyone here would vanish into thin air and he wouldn't mind if he never saw them again, if it meant that he could gently peel off her clothes and...

The other part of him just wanted to sit here for ever, to prolong this unexpected moment, a moment that a big part of him still feared wasn't real, for as long as was possible. They could just kiss until they had to stop, for eating or perhaps sleeping, but not until it was absolutely necessary either way. In the end she made the decision for him, she took him by the hand stood up and led him out of the plaine.

'Wow... Look!'

Coki grabbed Leeham by the shoulders, he was shaking his hips with such mal-coordinated vigor that he needed to be restrained if they were to have any kind of conversation. Leeham followed the line of Coki's point with some difficulty, when his eyes had sufficiently adjusted he could just about make out two figures weaving their way through the crowd out of the Plaine, one of them looked like Kayleigh the other one was...

'My God...Lewhay, Lewhay!' it took even more effort to get Lewhay to stop dancing but between the two of them they managed it and everyone within a ten foot radius suddenly felt a bit more comfortable.

'What?' this one syllable word seemed to roll out of Lewhay's mouth, ridiculously long and drawn out 'wuuuu hat'.

'Shabwan just left with Kayleigh.'

No response, just a minor shake of the head and then he was back to his dancing. There would be no getting anything of worth out of him for half an hour or so, best to leave him to it. Leeham and Coki on the other hand suddenly felt a lot more clear headed.

'What's he doing?'

'Dammit! She's gonna mess him up so much. Surely she could have gone somewhere else for a lay. That Bitch!' Coki's anger levels rose and burst out of him; people all around took a step back. 'She's gonna hurt him all over again.'

Leeham nodded gravely.

'What should we do?'

'Nothing.' Coki was truly angry now; he spat this word out like it tasted bad.

'He's gotta learn himself, we've helped him through this and it's been a damn long slog and if he's gonna just get with her for a one day thing which is gonna make him feel infinitely worse, then he can get over it without my help next time.'

He didn't mean it but he wished he did. Leeham was just shaking his head, only Lewhay seemed like he wasn't that bothered as he spun a startled fellow dancer around in a hazardous pirouette. After everything they'd gone through with Shabwan to reach this point they couldn't believe he was just going to go and have sex with her. What better way to sabotage your journey to recovery than reminding yourself in a haze of stonkette of what you miss and what you'll only ever have again on a very temporary basis.

10.

For Shabwan, what his friends may or may not have thought of his actions was a very minor concern. There was little room in his head for anything other than her. He was less 'off it' now but he still didn't trust that this was really happening. She lead him by the hand away from the plaine, they walked past the stalls in the crowded square, past the Star and down a little path which lead to a field, home only to a few cattle (not the ones Morldron had so recently granted the temporal gift of aviation to). Kayliegh stopped here, she turned to Shabwan, he opened his mouth to say something but she kissed him before he got the chance. They slowly sunk to the floor, Shabwan felt the same way he had when this had first happened all those months ago, the burning desire to run his hands over every flawless curve of her body but also the fear, the heart fluctuating fear that one wrong move might shatter this perfect dream into a million pieces. She sensed this, it wasn't difficult, every muscle in his body was tight and stiff and his hands were trembling.

'Hey...look at me,' she pulled his head forward so his eyes were near to hers. 'It's fine, don't be nervous...we've done this before after all.'

After that it was easy. She lay beneath him and he lifted up the pretty summer frock she was wearing and pulled it slowly over her head, savoring each new part of her that was revealed under the hot summer sun as he did so. She lay there naked, her body inviting him in. He too removed his clothes and she drew him into her, they made love slowly, almost for the entirety, they only sped up when they both sensed the end and then climaxed together; her soft moans becoming louder and louder her body becoming rigid, just for a moment, and then releasing. Neither of them said anything for a while, they both just lay there, the remaining stonkette in their blood was washing over them anew, mixed with the glorious euphoria of lying, post orgasm, with someone you truly love. Nature seemed to rise up around them, hugging them into its golden green glow, they felt part of the very earth on which they lay, part of the blue sky above them, even part of the stupid bovine creatures who had wandered over for a look, gormlessly chewing their way through endless grass.

They kissed for a while longer, her lips soft, her tongue caressing his, then the kisses became hungrier she ran her hand down his chest towards his midriff, he raised one of his hands and cupped the perfect orb of her left breast, his middle finger drawing little circles around the edge of her nipple and then sliding onto its little peak, her breath became deeper as he did this, soon they were making love again, much more violently this time. They were so exhausted when they finished that they both slumped straight into sleep.

Shabwan awoke twenty minutes later, his initial moment of confusion diffusing instantly into warm feelings of recollection. He looked to his left, Kayleigh was lying on her back, her eyes closed, her lily white breasts rising and falling ever so gently. He could let her sleep for a bit, but there were so many questions and as quickly as the warm feeling had entered his stomach it was replaced by one of fear. The stonkette seemed to have all but washed out of his brain, he had a little bit of afterglow but it was tinged with a sense of paranoia and unhelpful waves of nausea.

'Kayleigh.'

She stirred a little. He stroked the left side of her face.

'uuuuuum.'

Half yawn, half acknowledgment, her eyes were still closed.

'Kayleigh,' he said again.

'Yeah?'

She was at her most lovely when she was just waking up, he'd always said so. To him she was at her most beautiful when her eyes were all puffy and she had that slightly dazed but happy look she always wore as she came into the world. Again she sensed that something was wrong, she was so good at it. It had been both a blessing and a curse when they'd been together. She was so sensitive and had always known when he was upset. Unfortunately he'd often needed to hide his reasons.

'What's the matter?'

These words frightened him, they'd preempted so many of their big fights, so many times when all he'd wanted to do was just snap out of it and he'd found himself unable to, then frustration and anger would take over...

'I'm just...I just, want this to be real,' he always found it difficult to get the first few words out then the rest came easy. 'You know, it's Laffrunda, and you're quite wasted, which is fine I love it when you are, but...I just, I don't want this to be for one day or some kind of sympathy vote or just a mistake or...I don't know...'

He trailed out and looked down at the grass, she'd waited for him to finish and now wasn't saying anything. Shabwan, who could bear it no longer, looked up. Kayleigh was smiling although there were tears in her eyes, the same way she'd looked when they'd made up after the first few arguments, when it had still seemed like they'd actually resolved things. Before it all changed.

'Shabwan, I know what you're thinking, but I promise, I'm quite sober now and I've wanted this for a while, I've just, not really known how to say it or when to say it and I know I should have told you sooner, but please, please believe me when I say that I want you,' she wasn't one for romantic gestures, or a fan of drama, so these next few words told him beyond all doubt that she was serious. 'I want you...totally and completely.'

The tragic thing was that Coki and Leeham were completely wrong; Kayleigh meant every word of what she said.

11.

'Where the hell are they?'

Coki was in a blind rage now, storming about the square throwing cider down his neck and bellowing Shabwan's name, he was attracting quite a few funny looks but as of yet no comments. He looked dangerous.

'Look, they're probably having sex right now.' Lewhay was in a better way than when we last saw him, although he'd refused to leave the plaine until Jax and Ozki had finished their third encore and he'd spent five minutes telling them how much he loved both them and their music. 'Do you really want to find him at such a time?'

Leeham laughed, Coki spun round looking daggers at them both.

'If he's gonna blow us off to spend Laffrunda with her then that's fine, but he's going to tell us to our faces.'

Leeham and Lewhay exchanged slightly nervous glances as Coki turned away and continued his erratic searching.

'Shab…SHAB!'

12.

They were completely naked now. The amount of magical energy running through their bodies had burned through their clothes; it was burning the horses upon which they sat, although they had almost as little will as their riders now. Their blue skin wasn't so much skin anymore but a kind of mist, occasionally you might glimpse a bit of something solid, but not often, you'd be more inclined to notice the lightning like flashes which seemed to be holding their shape together. They were a lot more magic than human now, dangerously so; three time bombs, full to the brim and almost completely out of control...Almost.

He couldn't hold it for much longer, but then, he wouldn't have to.

13.

Kayleigh hadn't spoken much for the last twenty minutes. He was talking more than enough for both of them; promises and plans mainly. Things were going to be different, that was they key message, it wasn't a subtle one either. He'd said those exact words at least fifteen times. She didn't mind, she loved his emotional rambling. He'd built up quite a momentum as well, best to let him tire himself out a little. He stopped eventually and then beamed at her, well aware of how much he'd been talking, how much of it was nonsense and how none of it even mattered anymore because they were together again. This thought brought on another sharp realization: shit! The boys…

'Kayleigh…listen, you know that I would happily lie in this field with you for the rest of my life, it's just Coki and the boys, we're meant to get on the stonk later...well, now really, and I think that they might actually kill me if I'm not there. Leeham and Lewhay might be happy to just do it in some kind of metaphorical way but I reckon Coki would want to go whole hog.'

She laughed, he'd known she would understand, she'd always appreciated the importance of spending time with your friends, it was he who'd had the problem.

'Yeah of course, I wouldn't want to disrupt the Laffrunda tradition. I think Coki would have to find twin spikes to put our heads on.'

'Haha, yeah.' He replied and they kissed again.

He didn't really want to leave. For a second he actually thought he wasn't going to, that he would instead stay with her, that they could just hide away for the day and that he would make his peace with the boys some time in the distant future, when it became safe to approach Coki once more. Then he thought again; his mates deserved so much more than that. They had, after all, been with him through all of this and, his newly sober state of mind curtly reminded him, they were probably gonna be pretty angry with him anyway. He'd have to make them believe that this was for real otherwise they were going to have trouble enjoying a pleasant trip. If you're going to do a lot of strong hallucinogens with a group of people then the last thing you want is bad air between you. It will inevitably get staler and staler until it eventually became poisonous. No, he needed to find them, and find them soon. His relationship was back on and the levels of happy delirium coursing through his veins would have been enough to make him jam a live pari into his chest, if that had been what she wanted. But still, even through all this, he was uncomfortably aware that he was on the cusp of losing, or at least severely hurting, the three people who, after the girl lying next to him, were the most important people in his life.

14.

'There he is!'

Coki wheeled round at the sound of Leeham's voice and saw him instantly. Shabwan was coming towards them from over by the pub. He was looking sheepish but this didn't cover the glow that seemed to radiate out of him.

'So...' Coki began, the word ringing with rage.

Shabwan took a great risk and cut him off.

'I know what you're going to say but please, just let me say one thing before you start.' Coki nodded, he looked like he'd rather just punch him.

'We're back together.'

He might as well have said that the sky was coming down. Or that they would soon be fighting for their lives.

'Really?...What!!?'

Coki looked like this was all too much for him. Shabwan wondered if he'd already ruined his mate's Laffrunda beyond the point of repair, he hoped not…everything suddenly seemed a bit realer than it had before.

'Yeah, I know, I know it's messed up. But she says she wants me back and you all know how much I still love her.'

Shab,' said Lewhay tenderly. 'Are you sure she meant it?'

'Well, I though she might not but she seemed pretty adamant. She said she's been feeling it for a while and that she just hadn't found the right moment and anyway that's probably…definitely true…because…well I haven't really given her any moments have I?' He tried to keep the defensive tone out of his voice and almost succeeded. It's always amusing when people try to sound carefree by busting out a great long spiel that would never have any place in a natural conversation. Such longwinded and unnatural bursts of confusing dialogue only ever seem to crop up when the perpetrator has mapped out exactly what they want to say in advance and in their attempt to sound uncontrived they only ever seem to achieve the opposite.

In spite of the obvious premeditation and babbling nature of this rant Leeham and Lewhay still seemed fairly convinced by it. They were such relaxed characters; they didn't really care too much about what Shabwan did or didn't do, especially today. They both absorbed this new information with considerable ease and felt that the situation was now resolved. It was true that he might have the wrong decision but that was something that they would learn in the fullness of time. They both felt that more than enough of their favorite day of the year had already been spent on this high drama. Enough was enough…especially when a big steaming mug of foul tasting stonk was poised just around the metaphorical corner to take your mind to places which were a whole lot more fun than this one.

It was different with Coki as Shabwan had suspected it might be, and it was fair enough. Coki was the one who had spent the most time with him; had sat up all night talking to him about it when he was so depressed that he hadn't eaten all day. He was the one who'd counseled him and, as is often the case with counselors, he'd taken Shabwan's pain on as his own. In advising his friend to forget all about her and encouraging him to see her bad points and the positive reasons for their not being together, he'd sacrificed his own friendship with her. Now she was back and Coki couldn't help but feel confused and alienated by this. Shabwan had confided everything in him over these last couple of months and he'd given him so much in return now without even a thought in Coki's direction he was back with her, he knew he probably should be happy for him but...

'Do you two wanna catch us up in a bit, we'll go to Shabwan's and start getting everything ready.'

This was a welcome suggestion from Leeham; Coki and Shabwan needed to talk.

They walked in silence for a little while, Coki still looking dangerously angry. They didn't have any trouble getting through the crowd; people seemed to be naturally giving them a wide berth. Shabwan finally plucked up the courage to break the silence, which was cutting through even the raucous hubbub of the square.

'So, erm, maybe we should talk about this before we go stonking.'

'Yeah we should.'

'Right, erm, do you wanna start.'

Coki didn't even acknowledge this, he just plowed straight in. His words had the calmly measured feel of those which had been rehearsed, however briefly, in order to prevent something regrettable being said. Coki, despite his anger wanted his message to be clear and heartfelt. He also wasn't above a little guilt tripping.

'It's not for me to tell you what you can and can't do, I know that, but just remember how much she hurt you. That's all I'm saying.'

It wasn't all he was saying, there was so much more, but it didn't need saying; they both understood it. Shabwan's guilt was a lot stronger now (Coki had, of course, been successful), his after-relations buzz was fading slightly and the colder reality of how he'd made his friend feel was right in his face.

'I know it's a big risk, I know that, I just really feel that it's a worthwhile one, and had it been another day, any other day I'd have definitely talked to you about it first.' The lines in Coki's brow relinquished a little. 'It was just ...Laffrunda, you know how it is.'

Coki smiled a little at this but then frowned as he was reminded of his other cause for grievance.

'Yeah you're right, it *is* Laffrunda.'

'I know,' Shabwan was on a roll now; he found it much more difficult to stop talking than to start. 'And I know that that's probably why you're feeling this annoyed but you know that I would have never missed this afternoon,' Coki looked at him sceptically. 'It's true. Do you know how tempting it was to stay with her?' Coki opened his mouth to reply but Shabwan didn't let him. 'Very tempting, that's how, but I wouldn't have ever done it because ...because this afternoon is more important.'

Coki smiled, a lot more genuinely this time, he knew that Shabwan didn't mean this; that girl was everything to him and while he loved his mates and was, for the most part, a good one in return, they had always taken the back seat to Kayleigh. This said, just the fact that Shabwan had said it showed that he understood and was sensitive to Coki's grievance. There was too much history between the pair for this to continue, especially with what they had ahead of them.

'Alright then you idiot, I forgive you.'

The sun was already two thirds of the way through its daily mission and they needed to get a move on, Lewhay and Leeham were probably putting the finishing touches to the brew by now.

15.

'They're not here! Well has anyone heard anything?'

Anika was addressing her crew of helpers, although she was reluctant to give them that title, the amount of help that they'd actually been was debatable. Thanks to their incompetence, she'd ended up having to single handedly coordinate the children's parade and later in the day she'd seen that the plaine bar, the source of most of the festivals income, continually under staffed and at one point completely un-staffed. The gods alone knew how much alcohol the locals had helped themselves to in that short window of time. She'd found the three boys who were meant to be working the bar sleeping behind the tent and after banging their skulls together in all three different combinations, she'd sent them back to work. Admittedly, since then things did seem to have gone a bit better but then came this latest piece of news, delivered by the short straw-drawer who now stood before her, an uncomfortable distance in front of the rest of the little tikes. She cast her eyes to the heavens momentarily and vowed for the thirty fourth time that day that this would be the last year. She didn't mean it. At least…she didn't think that she meant it. Had it been up to Anika, this would not have been the last Laffrunda...Sadly it was not up to her, it wasn't up to any of them.

'So you're telling me that no one knows anything about the whereabouts of the dead gypsies?'

They all shook their heads.

'They're meant to be staying in The Star but Sooie hasn't heard anything.' one brave soul volunteered.

This was bad news. The dead gypsies were one of the most famous traveling bands in Corne, it had been a lot of work for Anika to secure them for the festival and there would no doubt be a lot of very angry and disappointed people if they didn't show up.

'They were meant to get here last night.'

The young lads shifted their feet uneasily. They had a shared feeling that if Anika were to loose the plot now her wave of anger would no doubt wash away those who lay unprotected in its immediate vicinity. She eyed the disheveled group, they were looking everywhere but at her, she would have to choose one at random, funny way to have to hand out a death sentence.

'Payine, go and get your fathers horse and ride out along the northern road, there's a chance they could still be on the way, when you find them come back straight away and tell me, also tell them that they need to be here in six hours, I don't know if the concept of time will really mean anything to that bunch so you might have to get a bit creative with your explanation.'

Payine was looking up at Anika in horror, having worked through the hell of his hangover all day he had believed his ordeal to be almost over. Now he was being sent out on horseback on this baking hot summer's day to find and hurry along a group of musicians whose attitude to inebriation would make the residents of San Hoist look like a nun's convention.

'Why me?' He inquired, a question that he would repeat to himself a few hours later with his last conscious thought.

'Because I said so,' replied Anika in a harsh tone that, under different circumstances, she might have come to greatly regret. 'And because you were napping when you should have been working and because you lost the festival money.'

He could have pointed out that he wasn't the only one who'd done this but then he caught sight of Anika's eyes, tired yet burning. He felt conflicted; every part of his brain was screaming at him to stay, he could run away now and then spend the rest of the day hiding from Anika. She would probably even forgive him at some incomprehensibly distant point in the future. Had be gone through with this hastily hatched plan, he and Shabwan, in some other reality perhaps, could have shared a bet on whether Anika or Coki would have been the first to offer some forgiveness. Instead, like Shabwan just a few minutes earlier, he fought against his impulses.

'OK,' he said. 'I'll er…go now?'

'Yes you will.'

There was such an air of unquestionable finality to this statement that Payine doubted any living being could have disobeyed the command. He went to get his fathers horse and was soon riding out of town along the northern road.

No one from San Hoist ever saw him alive again.

16.

The three were very close now. He could sense *them*, rather than just his old enemy's knowledge of their location. They brought with them a nasty poisonous quality that, to his well trained eye, was already swirling about in the San Hoistian air. Vericoos hadn't heard anything from the controller that he could classify as language for some time, but he could, as ever, sense his will and the will can say so much more than words ever could. It can paint pictures and write songs so beautiful, deep and descriptive that they would take generations upon generations of mortal work to complete.

Ever since they had forged their initial connection and first discovered true communication, they had been aware of the ultimate futility of language. Not that they did not see the beauty of the spoken and written word but they also saw everything that it was not. They saw how, once you could truly communicate, you became (or should have become) the envy of anyone who had ever tried to paint a picture with words. Not that any of these fools had any concept of what the communication actually entailed, which was ironic in a sense because for most of them it was what they truly desired.

Vericoos and the controller saw how poets and writers sculpted every last vowel to try to create an image of what they held in their minds, something that their readers could draw from, could interpret and be touched by…and they saw how they failed. True communication allowed one access to another's mind as if it were a blank canvas, yet so much more than a blank canvas: an enormous multi dimensional space, in which one could paint with everything that the other had ever experienced and if they hadn't, well you could show them. Show them in such a way that they would never have any doubt of what you meant. Emotion and memory trailed through this space like effervescent watercolors tweaking and complementing images that had more depth, colour and purpose than the naked eye could ever perceive.

Imagine that most mundane of questions: where did you grow up? Apparently an essential part of any stuffy dinner party (the horrible kind where someone is trying to get a group of people who don't know each other to enjoy each other company against their wills, not the kind that Shabwan's mum used to host). The normal answer to this question would be simple…insert name of town, plus description of area here, and agreeably this is probably enough information for the majority of circumstances, especially the aforementioned dreary social occasions. Now imagine that for some reason you needed to say more, more than you ever possibly could. Perhaps, against all the odds, one of these dinner parties- where someone you didn't particularly like had invited you saying: 'oh you *muuuuuust* meet so and so- turns out to be the occasion where you meet the love of your life. Imagine you know it right then and, gazing across the table into the eyes of the person you know that you were born to spend eternity with, you hear them ask that same question…'Where did you grow up?' Suddenly there aren't enough minutes in the universe. You want this individual to understand every last little thing about your first rickety old house. You want them to *taste* the way the air tasted when you looked out of the window and saw it was going to be a sunny day. You want them to *hear* the anxiety you felt in the dark and experience the relief as your mother alleviated it. You want them to *feel* how different your bedroom looked when you'd experienced both triumph and disaster. How full the kitchen was with her and how lonely it was without her.

But there aren't enough minutes. There could never possibly be and as the relationship goes on and seemingly every topic is talked to death with the hunger than only two newly aquatinted love birds can produce, you may one day come to a point where you *feel* that you have told someone everything about the house where you grew up or your job or any other trivial thing…but have you really?

Imagine that you could…imagine that you could convey every little thing that you'd love to convey in those first blissful moments with someone. Imagine that they could experience everything you experienced. Fear all you'd feared love all you'd loved and then a whole lot more and imagine that they could have all this, not slowly delivered over a lifetime spent together but in the briefest of moments. Then you would be imagining true communication; a thought both beautiful and truly terrifying. Something which only the biggest of egos would have seen in the way that Vericoos and his then friend had seen it. True communication had defined the very nature of their relationship and it was only fitting that it was here so pertinently, so close to the end.

Vericoos knew that the old git must have almost killed himself by now and the Gods alone knew what state these things would be in when they actually arrived. Would they still have their human form? Vericoos didn't know. Maybe he could go and have a look at them, better the devil you know and all that. Yes, that seemed a good idea. He could also take a look at the route they were taking here, see if there was anywhere that leant itself to an ambush; not a form of attack he had any great love for but this was a fight unlike any other, one that he must win at any cost.

He moved his hand, which a moment later was his wing and set off.

17.

Their Laffrunda tradition hadn't changed a bit since the conception of their two products. They always did some stonkette to watch the midday bands then brewed up the stonk proper for the afternoon. Then come the evening and the final performance (Anika always seemed to manage to get something special) they would return to the stonkette, more out of necessity than anything else, they just needed something to keep them going.

Leeham and Lewhay had indeed finished the brew when Coki and Shabwan arrived back at the cottage, they could smell the foul earthiness of it before they'd even opened the front door. Five minutes later they'd all drank a cupful and were walking towards the cliffs, for what they were about to experience you didn't want to be around a crowd; that was, in fact, the last thing you wanted. They would instead sit down on the cliffs, just the four of them, and enjoy.

Half an hour later we would have trouble recognising our four friends, they were lost to anything that you would call conventional sanity. Coki was in the process of explaining to the group, amidst a fit of giggles, how the grass was making itself into little arrows, which would point them along the next stage of their journey,

'They're leading this way!' He yelled and then collapsed into laughter at the sound of his own voice.

'I love the sea.' put in Leeham, the irrelevance of his comments had been a continued source of amusement to Lewhay and Shabwan and this was no exception. In the last ten minutes, apart from informing them of his love of the ocean he had also proclaimed that lobsters held on to things while others wouldn't and that eating and drinking weren't that different, once you got down to it. He had a point.

They continued along the coastal path overlooking the harbor which was close to where they had caught the fish responsible for their present condition. It really was a beautiful day. The sea looked incredible and would have done even without the stonk. With it, the whole world was one big incomprehensible mass of swirling fizzing colors, although to Shabwan it still seemed that he could tell what was real and wasn't. It was almost as if there was a translucent sheet sitting in front of his eyes, warping and transforming everything into fascinating beauty, yet still leaving untouched a certain level of the natural. Almost as if the stonk knew and respected that which must be there while still giving it a whole new and in many ways improved design.

They were pretty much at the peak of it now, and walking was abandoned for a while, they lay in a field looking out over the sea. All four of them were talking but not one sentence linked to anything any of the others had said, their mouths were simply spewing out the nonsense that was flowing through their brains. Conversation (if you could call it that eventually faded into giggles and the odd burbled bit of almost language. Yes, it was probably safe to say that they'd reached the peak; but the highest point of the mind is also the closest to the edge and while it is awfully fun to teeter along that thin line you wouldn't want to fall...There be dragons, as someone once said.

Later Shabwan would remember very little of that time, but let us try, difficult as it may be for those of a sober mind, to share some of his experience with him. Who knows it may prove to be helpful later on...

He knew he was still there, although he didn't really mind either way. The important part of him was there and that was what mattered, although 'no' chimed in another voice, a laughing jesters voice cruel and kind in the same impossible way. She is what matters isn't that what you've always said ISN'T THAT WHAT YOU'VE ALWAYS THOUGHT...at this moment Kayleigh's face appeared in front of him and was then broken into a million pieces, he saw her eyes flash just for a moment before this happened and then all the little pieces of her fell upon him like rain, this was nice but then another new voice came through, cold and hard, this voice definitely wasn't bothering to go through his ears to reach its target ...'she's broken into too many it said...three is what you want, only three but then you'll learn that soon enough.'

'No I won't' Shabwan replied defiant, and then laughed at his own seriousness, instantly forgetting the sound of this strange voice and its odd words. There were more images now, he could see the grass and he could see the sea, although they appeared to have swapped colours and textures for the time being. The waves broke earthy and that didn't seem good. Then the sea spoke to him, it was trying to warn him of something... how funny, he thought and barked like a seal. Then a Pari, not the same as the Pari's they had caught but jet black flew up into the air and yelled something it sounded like, 'don't leave, you mustn't leave....barrrrrrr boo!' What did a stupid fish know, he had no intention of leaving, not now, not ever, he had his lady back and he had his friends with him, his best friends. Just as he thought this they all four stood in front of him, Kayleigh in front and the other three behind her. What a lovely four, he sang in a ridiculous melody...He liked seeing them but then he had a sudden strange realisation. While the four figures were seemingly grinning kindly at him, as soon as he moved his focus away from one of theirs their expression would change into snarling malice, he kept trying to catch them out but found he couldn't quite do It, nevertheless it unsettled him. He wanted them to go so he could talk to the sea again, tell it there was no need to worry, that he would look after everyone and everything...Three! why was that in his head again, his three friends maybe, even as he thought this the cruel and cold voice returned, 'ah if only twas them' tis you that must become the three.' This was both confusing and discomforting and Shabwan was beginning to feel strangely aware of himself, He didn't want this, he wanted to get lost again, wanted the stonk to take him so that there was no longer anything to worry about...it did. He was soon flying above himself, not very far, he could still make out the whites of his and his three friend's eyes...couldn't he? It didn't matter, he couldn't really fly anyway so he wasn't scared of losing himself. It was more like he was swimming through the air; it was delightful dee dee dee dee lightfull. He looked down at himself, all seemed well there, well almost everything ...There was Coki then on his left Lewhay, then on his left Leeham then on his left Shabwan, then on his left...Shabwan again and on this new Shabwan's left...yet another Shabwan. How very curious he thought, still not to worry he had wings now and without a further though for his three separate forms lying on the luscious green grass (or was it a wave) he took to the sky proper...

He'd been having such a great time, swooping and diving about the place that he hadn't realised there was someone else up here with him, someone he knew, but form where he couldn't say. They were speaking to him, 'the boy is dead and he won't be the last...' what did that mean? Why were people trying to spoil his fun? He flew down towards the town, swooping over the crowded plaine, savoring the sound of guitar music on his keen birds ears, he was glad to be free of that voice, it had been a right nuisance... he supposed he'd better be getting back to his body again, his wings seemed to be getting tired and also...ceasing to exist. He made haste back towards the cliffs, pursued all the way by the sounds of the bloody voice, 'THREE' it shouted, 'there will be three'. He could see his body now, his bodies, he corrected himself, which one was the proper one? He knew the answer to this and for some reason it really bothered him, 'all of them...' As he flew towards them he began to panic, which one should he go into...he needn't have worried as he dived they began to get closer and closer, merging...they were merging... just like the grass around them merged together to make the field (or did it make a wave?). Just before he plunged into his own chest, for now he only had one again, he heard one word, colder and louder than anything he had just experienced...

Shabwan opened his eyes, wow! That had been intense. He tried to cling onto the memory of what had just happened but found it very difficult. There were a few fleeting images, birds, grass, knifes...knives, why knives? It felt important but he couldn't say why. As he lay there the memories diffused and swirled away, soaking into the ground around him; the place where they had come from and where they now belonged. Out at sea the waves, made entirely of water, crashed and broke.

18.

It took them an hour to get back up to the plaine. They were feeling pretty ropey and were desperately in need of a hit of stonkette. An evening of hard dancing beckoned, but there was no way they could approach it without some serious help. They had talked fairly enthusiastically about what had happened to them, or that which they could remember. Leeham claimed to have been inside a bush, learning how it worked, Lewhay said he couldn't remember anything although he was pretty sure he had had a good time, Coki had told them little, he seemed to have been hit pretty hard and was taking a little longer to recover. Although his grin told them that, whatever had happened, he'd been enjoying himself. Words would come back eventually.

Shabwan had offered what he could remember, he thought he might have been able to fly but wasn't sure. He didn't tell them about the feeling of uneasiness that had crept into his gut, a feeling that he had just been told something desperately important and that he should really try and remember it. Not a nice feeling and one that unsettled him so much that even the thought of seeing Kayleigh again wasn't really making him feel any better. First time for everything, he supposed.

19.

As mentioned before, it takes a lot to surprise someone of Vericoos' age and experience. Nevertheless, he had, just a few moments ago, been about as surprised as he could ever remember being. Having been made painfully aware of the intellectual and metaphysical capabilities of his, apparently erroneously, selected 'one', the last thing that he'd expected was to find that Shabwan, or at least some part of the young man, had joined him as he soared in his eagle form over the ever diligently advancing forms of the three. The current progression of events left little time for speculation but even if they had Vericoos doubted that he would have arrived at any kind of conclusion. How in the name of Poaieror's great green trousers had the young man departed his own physical form…such things were truly *not* for the likes of him. He could not know at this point that the answer to this question would have such huge ramifications.

Vericoos had watched emotionlessly as the three rode down on the young man from the hoist. The poor fellow stopped his mount in the middle of the road, completely transfixed, and just stared straight at them. To his credit, the controller had bellowed a few warnings at the boy from whatever resemblance of a mouth the three had left but he hadn't altered their course, maybe he couldn't any more. The young man's horse had clearly possessed a stronger survival instinct and had bucked him off and run to safety. The boy just sat there, watching until the three sets of pounding hooves sent him off on the next stage of his journey. Watching this Vericoos wondered if the controller had indeed completely lost control of the three and whether they would now just bear down upon San Hoist to whatever ends. The death of this young lad certainly supported this idea. Senseless death of the young wasn't ever something that appealed to his old adversary. For a moment he was convinced that the controller had finally lost all control, but he was wrong.

They had sensed Vericoos and they had stopped. They gazed up at him, blue steam rising form them much more violently now, the white lightning flashes which made up their shapes were blazing several times a second. Vericoos was hardly surprised that they'd stunned the boy so; even he'd hardly ever seen the like. Maybe he should just fight them, have it out here and now, to whatever ends. Then he thought again...the same thought that had stopped him killing the boys as they'd assaulted him in the square, although then he had not realised the true potential, yet now he saw it…By God's how had he *not* seen it? Now that he did it seemed so evident, what infernal curse had limited his thinking so?

He flew like he'd never flown before back towards San Hoist.

There was perhaps one last chance.

20.

'Ah there you are, where the hell have you been?'

The lead singer of the dead gypsies was clearly not used to being spoken to like this.

'We've been down the coast,' he replied 'it's such a beautiful time of year we just thought we'd have a bit of a camp out man, you know get back to nature.'

'Well don't you think you could have at least come and told me you were here?' Anika almost shouted this.

'Wow, calm down lady we're here and that's what matters.'

She shook her head, she would get nowhere with these people.

'OK, well you're on in an hour, *perhaps* you'd like to go and set up.'

'Yeah, yeah cool, don't worry we know what we're doing.'

Anika left them to it, bloody musicians; all ego and no sense. Still they would put on a great show she was sure of that. For the first time in the day she began to relax. The lantern parade was taking shape nicely and the band was getting set up. Her job was almost complete and this year had been another great success. Perhaps even the greatest.

21.

Shabwan and Kayleigh watched the lantern parade together, hand in hand, everything was beautiful again now. While the thought of seeing her again hadn't been enough to alleviate his anxieties, the reality had been. The nagging and confusing thoughts, which had threatened to ruin his evening, had been well and truly buried.

After the parade the four friends and Kayleigh made their way to the front of the stage. The Dead Gypsies would be on soon and they had all just done a huge load of stonkette in a 'death or glory' style last stand. Hopefully it would enable them to dance till the last beat faded away and then carry their fatigued minds and bodies to some after gathering or other, where they could eventually let unconsciousness welcome them into its forgiving arms...That was the plan, it had worked in the past and was certainly showing no signs of failing this time.

'I can't wait for this.' Kayleigh was saying.

'Yeah right it's gonna be amazing!'

Coki had his arm round her, all was forgotten. All was back to normal.

They danced like maniacs to the furious ever evolving sound of The Dead Gypsies, all manner of deep twisted melodies and raucous beats drove the crowd into a tautologously wild frenzy. An hour later as they crashed to the end of their second encore it was all over. Shabwan felt delirious with happiness and pretty ready to pass out. The Plaine began to empty. People were leaving in a variety of different states. Some looked like they knew roughly what their name was and where they were meant to be going. Others did not. Some weren't leaving at all and looked like they wouldn't be able to for some time. Shabwan, Kayleigh and the others made their way towards the back of the plaine and eventually found, amidst the crowd of ambling zombies, a patch of grass big enough for them all to sit on.

'Ahhhhh, that was nice.' said Leeham.

His sweaty face was beaming and his eyes were still glinting although they were beginning to look like they might roll back into his head at any stage. Just at that moment, which was, interestingly enough, the last time they would all be together, Anika came running up, looking extremely worried. At first they didn't notice the panic in her eyes and they greeted her with a congratulatory cheer. She ignored this.

'Have any of you seen Payine?'

'Nah, not all day,' responded Shabwan. 'Anyone else?'

They all shook their heads, Ankia looked like she was about to burst into tears.

'I sent him off to look for the band, hours and hours ago. He rode out along the north road, I kind of forgot about him, what with everything else going on and now no one seems to have seen him. I don't think he's come back.'

'I'm sure he's fine, he was such a state in The Star last night I wouldn't be surprised if he's just asleep in a bush somewhere.' Said Coki with some difficulty and much slurring.

His attempt at comfort didn't seem to have any affect on Anika,

'What! If something's happened to him...'

She set off at a trot across the plaine, towards a hot food stall which was doing a roaring trade.

'He's blatantly fine, bless her for worrying though.' Said Lewhay.

They all nodded in agreement, they doubted any serious harm had come to Payine. He must have just succumb to the midday heat and found somewhere to sleep his woes away. Shabwan looked around the plaine, maybe he could find him now. It'd be nice to put Anika's mind at rest and there was every chance that Payine had returned and blended into the heaving mass of people. As he gazed around, trying to focus his blurry eyes something caught them, something which made his heart flutter but in a much more unpleasant fashion than when he'd lain in the field with Kayleigh.

'Shabwan...Shabwan? You alright mate?' Asked Coki.

He wasn't, but before he could tell them why they heard a scream.

22.

Vericoos knew Shabwan had seen him and that was all well and good. Perfect, in fact. His mind was cold now, but his body burned with fury. He opened the last internal gates and let it all come forth. The magic began to glow under his skin, the scars suddenly perfectly visible crisscrossing his face and arms, the air around him prickled, and a light blue mist began to rise from him.

It was time.

23.

Shabwan had been looking the other way when it happened, but the sound of the scream was enough to make him turn. A fraction of a second later, the hot food stall exploded, the fire they were using to cook the sausages was flung into the cloth of the roof which instantly caught. The unfortunate man who'd been working the stall didn't even make a sound as he was consumed in the growing fireball of his own business.

The terrifying and incomprehensible cause of this diabolical commotion became visible as it clattered through the debris: three riders flashing, steaming and vaguely human shaped had hit the stall as they'd jumped the wall of the plaine. Shabwan and the others watched with absolute horror as Anika, who had just moments before been speaking to the five young people who were so proud of what she'd achieved that day, fell beneath the hooves of their steeds. She seemed to fall in slow motion and then a flash of scarlet, roughly where her head must have been sent and icy spear of dread through Shabwan's heart. As the riders came to a halt there was an eerie moment of silence where everything and nothing seemed to be real. Then the screaming started, a petrifying cacophony spilling from the mouths of hundreds of people who had just, in the briefest of moments, been exposed to the fragility of life and learned the true vale of their own.

At least ten people, it seemed so strange to Shabwan that his brain would count at a time like this, seemed to have been killed as the three had jumped over the wall and charged through the stall, their burning bodies lay scattered around the flaming wood and cloth, Shabwan could still make out the words, Sari's saus... clinging onto the frame. Those who were left in the plaine began to exit it with as much speed as they could manage; some were trampled as hundreds of people all tried to force their way out of the two small exits at once. The smart ones just jumped over the banks.

The three riders were stood stock still, the last of the flaming wreckage of the stall dropping around them. Shabwan was struck by how weak the flame looked next to those hateful flashes. Like most men, he had an unhealthy obsession with fire. He loved to peer into its white hot heart and could do so for hours, and like most he also naively believed that he could control it. A ball of fire, greater than Shabwan had ever seen, had just swallowed up a huge wooden fixture as if it were nothing, yet here was something so much more dangerous. These malevolent flashes of power that seemed to bind these beings together, like some razor sharp wire frame, had all the terrifying, destructive qualities of the hottest element but there was nothing about them which appealed to you. Where you might look at a flame and be somewhat mystified by its beauty you would look at these flashes and feel nothing but cold fear and repulsion. They're evil, thought Shabwan; they're not of this world. As he tried to come to grips with what he was seeing he was struck by the peculiar notion that you could throw all the fire in the world at these three figures and they would not so much as blink…

24.

They hadn't moved a muscle. They still sat exactly as they had before, simply unable to take on board the hideous events that were unfolding around them. An age passed shortly followed by another one. Then after generations had come and gone, after pyramids had been built and then eroded into dust, they found their voices.

'What the hell!'

'What's going one?'

Someone screamed.

Luckily for them, the three riders seemed to have little or no interest in them. They were instead advancing , much more slowly now, on the hooded figure who stood at the other end of the plaine, the only figure, in point of fact, who was putting no effort whatsoever into leaving the great green amphitheatre.

They passed quite close though, and as they did Shabwan saw their horrible mounts, bleeding and burnt they were, crazed bloodshot eyes looking wildly in every direction as if they had absolutely no idea what was driving them forwards.

One thought, more than any other, seemed to be dragging itself laboriously out of the tangled wreckage of his exhausted and drug addled mind: they'd killed Anika! Anika who'd made this day year in year out, Anika who had been a great friend of his mums, Anika who had children and a husband and who had always, always had time for him. They'd killed her...

25.

Vericoos was pleased to see that the majority of the townspeople had made themselves scarce. He needed room to work. He was equally pleased to see that Shabwan and his little crew had stayed. He drew back one hand, one glowing white hand, hotter than all the forges of the earth and flung a ball of light into the middle of the three riders. It landed between them and for a second nothing happened...Then there was more light, as three lime green tubes shot out into the chests of the riders and seemed to latch onto them like bizarre fishing hooks. The riders stopped their advance, their bodies convulsing and twitching, they seemed momentarily incapacitated and yet no less dangerous. The ball had caught them though and now it was pulsing its malevolent energy along these bright tubes. There was a hideous screeching noise and the three began to vibrate, and by the Gods if the world them around didn't vibrate along with them… Their heads seemed to swell and the slits that must have been their eyes disappeared completely. It seemed as if the battle may have already been won, Shabwan felt a tiny upwelling of hope, barely distinguishable amongst the turmoil of shock and fear than seemed to have him paralysed. But then, just as the riders looked on the point of exploding, the lime green tubes retracted then the white ball faded, glimmered desperately for a second and then died.

Vericoos looked up, for he had been forced to his knees by the effort of maintaining his assault and now saw that which he already knew; said effort had been in vain and everything, yes absolutely everything had been lost.

For a second there was no sound or movement from the three; then they began to laugh. At least, that's the only thing it could have been, although surely no living soul had ever heard such a sound before. They began their advance on Vericoos, who was struggling to stay on his knees and clearly had no hope of rising any higher. The laughter was piercing his skull. His brain finally accepted in linguistic form something which Vericoos' subconscious had known ever since he had felt the last of his strength fail along with his deadly enchantment:

He was about to die at the hands of his old adversary.

It was a fitting end, the only way he'd ever really believed that he would die and he'd be dammed if he gave the controller any more satisfaction than he was doubtless already getting from it. The three raised their hands as one and dark red energy pulsed and swirled between their fingers and, with a sense of dread the likes of which he had never known, Vericoos understood what they really had in store for him. He'd been so foolish as to assume that the controller would be so merciful as to grant him death.

'No...' He said. 'No...please.' It was the first time he had ever begged.

He closed his eyes, so as not to let the controller look at them as he went. This was it, he would soon never again hear the noises of this world, never again hear any noise of any world that he would wish to hear. He tried to savor the last few moments. He felt oddly peaceful...almost whimsical, not an emotion he had dabbled much with during his time on this earth but one that would apparently assert itself during his last seconds. What, he wondered, would be the last things that he'd hear? He wasn't going to let the old git see his eyes but with his ears, he could drink up the last little bit...soon he would want to take nothing at all from his surrounds...He could hear a girl screaming, it sounded like... 'NO!'

26.

The controller stood on his rock. It was the first time he'd stood in as long as he could remember, he was surprised he even could. He had drawn himself into the three for this, the final moment. He couldn't allow them to administer the ultimate punishment without being there, albeit in some incomprehensible cross dimensional way. He raised his arms, feeling them join with those of the three, he wanted, no he needed, to feel Vericoos extinguished, to feel his life force crushed beneath his own hands and then he would send him to that unimaginable place...the red place.

A split second later he would have succeeded, but then a deep gash appeared, as if by magic, in the side of his chest and he screamed.

27.

'No Shabwan!'

Kayleigh was trying to yell but her voice seemed weak and distant. She watched as the boy she loved ran towards the burning wreckage of the stall and selected himself a sharp piece of wood, his movements were quick and mechanical as if everything he did had somehow already happened. He ran back towards the three and as he did so she caught a glimpse of his eyes, there was little there that she recognized and not for the briefest of heartbeats did those suddenly hollow pupils flitter away from their target. Shabwan rounded the three and plunged his makeshift sword into the chest of the left hand rider.

28.

Shabwan felt the wood pierce something but it definitely wasn't skin. He'd never stabbed anyone before but still he knew. Everything stopped; all the noise of the distant screaming people, the noise of the fire and the mad demonic laughter. The void it left was even more unpleasant. The three things weren't dead, or maybe they were but they certainly weren't any less dangerous for it. And now they were looking straight at Shabwan.

29.

The boy had saved him, it was unbelievable and yet strangely predictable at the same time. Of course the boy had saved him, now all he had to do was return the favor. With all the force that remained in his body Vericoos brought his arms together and swung them in an upwards curve, they whistled through the eerie silence and when they reached the zenith of their arc...

30

Coki didn't remember much but he remembered the light, such a brilliant light he felt that everything must be lost, surely this was the end, or at least some kind of end, there could be nothing left after light like this. Then it was gone and everything *was* left, well everything except those three riders.

Shabwan lay on the ground. The old man was next to him, dragging himself laboriously to his feet. Coki ran over to join Kayleigh at his friend's side, he seemed alright. A little shocked, but alive.

'Are they gone?' Shabwan was asking.

'I think so...I think so.' Kayleigh was hugging him and sobbing.

'Unfortunately they are not gone.'

The old man was up on his feet, looming above them, it was strange that, just moments ago, he had looked so vulnerable. Coki had a strong urge to try and kill him, which seemed odd considering what had just happened.

'I'm afraid I've only banished them temporarily, they'll be back very shortly.'

'What do we do?' asked Leeham, who was helping Kayleigh get Shabwan up. He, like Shabwan seemed to have found some trust in the old man. Vericoos, in turn, completely ignored him.

'Shabwan, you must listen to me and listen well, these things are here for you and I and us only. They will tear this little town of yours apart until we are both dead. Do you understand?'

'Why...why me?'

'We don't have time!'

The strength had returned to his voice, it seemed the old man healed quickly.

'We may only have one chance,' he continued. 'We must draw them out.'

Shabwan looked at him dumbfounded, never had he held less affection for the term 'we'.

'If we can get them out in the open then I think I can take them, but you must come with me, if they sense you've remained here then they will kill you and everyone else.'

No one said a word, they couldn't, Shabwan looked at Kayleigh; she shook her head, her eyes wide and pleading. So much had happened in such a short amount of time and now this…

'Alright, I'll come.'

No force on earth could have made him meet her gaze as he said it. Instead he diligently stared at the scorched earth around his feet, there were some other muffled noises of protest, he assumed from his three friends but they didn't matter. There was only one path for him now and it lay not with them.

The next thing Shabwan was aware of was a strange shrinking sensation as if his whole being was being pulled into the tiny point just behind his navel and then, for the second time that day, he was airborne.

31.

As promised by the old sorcerer, the three riders returned shortly after. Vericoos' spell, rather than killing them as Kayleigh and the others had so fervently hoped, had apparently dispersed them across the ground like some bizarre sowing of a ploughed field, and sure enough, within a few minutes, they began to rise up again.

As Coki watched in fascinated horror, the whole plaine began to steam, light blue steam it was, like some tiny gnome fog, or perhaps a normal fog viewed from miles and miles above the earth. The smoke or steam or whatever the hell it was began to flow, like water, back towards the site where the three had last stood whole. Then, once enough of the foul stuff had congregated the flashes of white lighting, which had apparently given these things the remnants of their human shape, appeared once again and began, like some deranged potter, to whip the smoky steam back into shape. It was like watching a spider that spun not web, but lightning and rather than trapping, it was molding, nay even creating. As quickly as it had begun, this diabolical spectacle, from which he could not peel his eyes away from no matter how hard he tried, was over and the three stood whole again.

Without even a glance in Coki, Leeham, Lewhay and Kayleigh's direction they climbed astride their horses, which had for some inexplicable reason hung around, and began riding. They exited the plaine and began riding out of town along the eastern road. Their mounts no longer seemed capable of much though and they made their way at little more than a trot, a far cry from the devastating gallop which had brought Anika and Payine and all the others lives to such a tragically abrupt end.

32.

Shabwan landed hard and immediately threw up. His body and soul had been put through far too much for one day and still there was more fighting to come. Vericoos pulled him up off the ground by his collar.

'No time for that,' he was saying. 'We need to be ready.'

'What do you mean, we?'

'I mean I. But I need you to make yourself scarce. Go and get in that field.'

Vericoos pointed over behind them and Shabwan willingly obliged. He could have happily lain down on the cold night grass and passed out at that point, but he had to see. He crouched down by the gate at the entrance to the field and stared at the silent moonlit silhouette in front of him.

33.

'We need to follow them,' Kayleigh was shouting at the boys. 'Come on! What's wrong with you?'

She was right; they had to go. They set off together at a run. They couldn't see the riders anymore, but once they got away from the lights of the town they could make out an eerie light blue glow that was easy enough to follow.

34.

The controller was bleeding fairly heavily from the wound in his side; he would not last much longer like this. The only thing now holding his creations in existence was his own power and that was on the brink of failure, this needed to end soon.

35.

Vericoos waited patiently, it wouldn't be long now. He had transported them just a short way out of the town, to the nearest point where there was enough room, enough room to attempt the impossible. Sure enough, not two minutes later the three, pre-empted by their eerie blue glow, entered the field from the road and began charging towards him. The controller seemed to have somehow managed to convince their horses into one final effort; the poor beasts must have been craving death.

Vericoos stood, his palms held level in front of him, the glistening whiteness of his skin pointing directly up at the heavens...

36.

Shabwan watched as the three riders thundered towards Vericoos, the old man wasn't moving a muscle, for a second Shabwan wondered if he was going to move at all, maybe this was all some bizarre sacrifice, maybe he was meant to die here, maybe he'd done too much stonk and none of this was real. Then Vericoos threw his arms upwards over his shoulders and every unbelievable thing that Shabwan had seen that day, stonked up or otherwise, paled into insignificance.

Behind the three advancing riders, the earth, the very earth! Rose up like a vast wave, the noise of the soil and the tearing roots was immense. The huge earthy swell peaked, pitched and broke over the three. Vericoos stood between Shabwan and this great explosion of grass, roots and earth, his arms raised and raw white light emanating from his entire body. The land had become the sea in an attempt to smother the unwanted evil that was stalking about on its surface.

The three, even in the face of this new devastating energy, were not willing to give up without a fight and as the ground tried to close itself up, chomping down again and again like some great mouth, light blue misty arms tried to wrench it open and the lightning flashed more vigorously than ever. For a horrible second Shabwan though they were going to escape, but then with a soft squelching sound the earth sealed itself shut. For a moment the last few wisps of disembodied mist swirled in the air and then vanished forever.

37.

Shabwan ran to Vericoos who had fallen again.

'The others are coming.' The old man spluttered; he seemed dangerously ill.

'Yeah we'll help get you back to town.'

'NO!' Vericoos grabbed Shabwan by the scruff. 'Don't you see...they will come again,' a horrible dawning realisation began to take hold of the young San Hoister. 'We have to leave right now.'

'Shabwan!'

He could hear Kayleigh's voice. They were on the road just outside the field.

'We have to leave now... please.'

Vericoos was right. Shabwan knew it and hated it in equal proportions. It would be so much harder if he were to see them, if they were to try and persuade him to stay, could he resist? He didn't think so. With tears streaming down his face he nodded.

'Alright.'

Half a second later they were gone.

They landed on a hill, somewhere to the north of town. Shabwan could still see the orange glow of the fire and the column of black smoke, visible in the glow of the full moon. They sat there for some time not saying a word. Vericoos was healing himself while Shabwan silently wept, after a while he spoke.

'Just what is it that you want from me exactly?'

'You Shabwan?' The old man sighed heavily. 'It's really quite complicated.'

Shabwan looked at him and suddenly, despite the obvious deadly power of the other, *he* was the more dangerous of the pair.

'Simplify it.'

The imperative was barely more than a whisper, it was a tone Shabwan had never heard come from his or anyone else's mouth before. Vericoos looked at the young man who sat before him, the young man who had just sacrificed everything and said seven words.

'I want you to kill a god.'

Shabwan looked at him for a moment longer, hearing but not hearing. Then he was unconscious.

Book 2.

The Unlikely Hero.

Chapter 1.

Payinzee.

1.

They had to travel on foot; Vericoos was very clear about that. Apparently the amount of magic he had used recently had been an enormous risk and to use any more would be suicide. He did look strange. The scars which Shabwan had once found it so hard to focus on now bulged out of his skin like varicose veins and his eyes, although still brilliant, now seemed to have been sucked backwards into his skull.

Shabwan hadn't slept at all well since leaving San Hoist. He was visited every night by upsetting visions: Anika's head exploding in a flash of brilliant scarlet, the three riders, all blue smoke and lightning and Kayleigh. Every time he closed his eyes he would see hers; red, puffy, tearful...not understanding. It had been three days since he'd seen her but it might as well have been a lifetime. The decision to leave, taken so quickly and with such momentary conviction had sealed off that chapter of his life. There was no going back now.

Vericoos had been quite clear on that point as well.

There was hardly any conversation. When Vericoos had told Shabwan what he wanted from him (the words were as uncomfortable night time callers as his visions: *kill a god...kill a god...kill a god,* they would chant until he was too exhausted to listen anymore), Shabwan had felt like a candle had gone out in his head. Where there should have been interest, where he should have wanted to know every last fact about what was coming, there was only a hollow, echoey space where the thoughts of what had been lost bounced around, never quite settling down. He didn't know how he was meant to kill a god or why a god needed killing or the answers to any other of the million other questions which he should have cared about. All he knew was that he couldn't go back and that was all that really mattered.

His silence came of little surprise to Vericoos. The boy had been through a lot after all. He was, in point of fact, glad that Shabwan was so wrapped up in himself; it was all that was keeping the boy from realizing how weak he'd become. So much of what was to come would require Shabwan's faith in Vericoos' power; if he knew how little of it he had left, at least for now, then...

'Where are we headed exactly?'

Vericoos started, this was the first sound he'd heard come from the boy in quite some time, apart from the moaning at night.

'We're going to Hardram. Have you heard of it?'

The boy's blank expression told him the answer.

'It's quite a place', Vericoos said, but it was clear that his young traveling companion didn't want to hear any more. The little spark of interest had been extinguished before it could become a flame. He turned away from Vericoos ' gaze and lowered his head. The sorcerer wondered if he would keep up this stony silence all the way there.

They had a long way to go.

2.

Nothing much changed for a week. They walked at the same slow pace (which, unbeknown to Shabwan, was a pace which was nearly killing Vericoos); they stopped and ate, catching whatever unlucky wildlife they could. Then they made a little fire and slept. Since his question about where they were heading, Shabwan hadn't said another word but his night time shouting and moaning had become worse and worse.

They were traveling along the northern road, which lead away from San Hoist, the same road upon which the three had ridden into town. This road would eventually begin to swing to the North East and would take them to the forest, then through the mountains it would become little more then a track, though if all went to plan they wouldn't need to walk it.

'We need horses.' The second time Shabwan spoke it was clear that his mood had not improved.

'Erm…Yes of course…I, er… I wasn't sure if you could ride or not.' Replied Vericoos.

'Well I can,' came Shabwan's sharp retort. 'And forgive me if I've got this wrong but it seems like we would go a lot quicker on horseback, seeing as we *can't* use magic and all.' The sentence was stacked to the rafters with malice, venom and all the blame that Vericoos hadn't been at all surprised to sense that Shabwan was laying firmly at his door.

'Yes, it would seem to be an excellent idea.' Replied Vericoos, keeping all but the faintest wisps of irony from his voice. 'Perhaps at the next town we can get some.'

This was going to be a problem. The combination of walking miles each day and pretending that he didn't find this difficult was taking all (and then some) of Vericoos' remaining strength. He had used so much of his magical energy in his last battle with the three that he had damaged, almost beyond repair, the thing that he loved and needed above all other: his *talent*. For now, it is safe to imagine that this term will be as confusing for the reader as it will be for young Shabwan when he first comes to hear about it, but rather than the author undertaking a garbled and badly worded explanation of it at this juncture we will instead wait and let Vericoos explain in his own words. I'm sure that he'll be more than happy to oblige. There's nothing he hates more than an unnecessarily bulky word count, especially when it interrupts an already struggling narrative.

His body was now relying on its physical reserves and these were not in the least bit plentiful. He needed rest, real rest, and he needed to get somewhere where he could replenish his magical stockpile. More importantly, he needed to do all of it without the boy realizing that any little thing (let alone the vast actuality of the situation) was wrong. If that were to happen it would spell the end of everything he had ever fought for. Gods he was getting sick and tired of things spelling the end, if it wasn't one thing it was invariably another. Shabwan was already so angry with him for making him leave his home and those that he loved…if he were to appear as some weak old man rather than the vastly powerful sorcerer who had crushed the three...

Still, the boy must have been impressed by what he had seen. The magic Vericoos had used in a field just to the west of San Hoist had little precedent. Vericoos himself hadn't really believed it would work but by Gods it had. As weak as he felt now, Vericoos could still savor that gloriously brutal climax over and over again. Indeed, every night, once Shabwan had lain down and begun his nightly chorus of misery, Vericoos would lie there for hours recalling and relishing the moment, as the tons of earth and twisted roots plunged down upon his enemy.

He remembered also the struggle as the controller had forced everything he had left through the dimensions and how for the briefest and most terrifying of seconds Vericoos had thought that he had succeeded after all. Despite the savagery and power of the earthy wave it had looked like the three riders would prevail, that they would wrench themselves out of the gap where the earth was trying to re seal itself. Had they done this it would all have been over. The wave that had robbed them of their unwanted existence and the controller of his last chance had robbed Vericoos of much also, had the three escaped from his most beautiful yet terrible creation then he doubted he'd have been able to so much as raise his hands to plead mercy. Then they would have sent him there, to the red place.

Still he reminded himself, no need to dwell on what might have been. He was alive, although being forced to fly again so quickly, in order to get Shabwan away from his friends had almost been the final nail in his coffin. That night he had gone to sleep wondering if he would wake up again. Thanks solely to magic Vericoos had lived far longer than he should have and as he lay on the hill overlooking San Hoist, he thought that this inhuman preservation, which he'd enjoyed for so long, may have finally come to an end.

Luckily he'd been wrong, but he was still dangerously low; running on fumes he might have said if he had any interest in fuel, and it was absolutely imperative that the boy did not become aware of this. He needed to regain enough strength to convince this sulky teenager, who apparently was the most important (non magical…of course!) person who'd ever lived, that all was well, until they reached the forest. There he would be able to find the one thing that would bring him back but until then he would be in grave, grave danger.

3.

It was another two days of silent walking before they arrived at the nearest town. It looked only slightly bigger than San Hoist, thought Shabwan as they entered, and infinitely gloomier. Whereas San Hoist had that sort of rickety charm which gives places so much character and intrigue, and encourages travel writers to come up with literary brilliance like ‘loose yourself (and your sense of direction) wandering the maze of cobbled streets for hours on end’ this place just looked barren and uninteresting. As if it had been created for no other reason than…well, what?

The houses were all uniform wooden dwellings, set in rows leading off from the road which passed directly through the middle of the town. The further you walked down the dusty main road the more you became aware of how little geometric difference surrounded you. There was something *too* symmetrical about it all; that was the problem. It was as if someone had laid the town, like a trap, on either side of the road, ready to lurch in upon the unsuspecting traveler. Shabwan couldn't have said why he had such a bad feeling about the place, for him it was just a feeling. Vericoos, on the other hand, knew exactly what was wrong; they would be fortunate indeed to make it out of here alive.

It was amazing that the boy couldn’t even see the big black house.

They went into the first inn they came to. As they entered Shabwan felt a short but savage stab of homesickness as he thought of the Star. It didn’t last long though; The Long Woman had about as little in common with the warm glow of Sooie’s establishment as it was possible to have.

The moment they entered silence fell over the cramped and dusty room. Vericoos had become very used to this in the various inns he had visited throughout Corne. This, like so many others, was a place for locals and despite the fact that it sat on the busiest road in this whole region, any stranger would always be welcomed in with the same frosty treatment.

The patrons of the bar all had the same downtrodden look to them. Clearly they worked hard; harder than they wanted to. The town of Payinzee, for such was the name they had seen written in oddly grand letters on the wooden sign at the entrance of the town, was completely surrounded by flat farm land. It stretched as far as the eye could see and looked baked, like a giant cookie; the kind Anika used to bake. This summer had been one of the hottest in living memory (people always say that, don't they?) and the crops had suffered as a result. It was common, in these small communities, for a bad harvest to lead to low morale, but there was something else at work here. These people didn't look like they were simply worried about the winter’s food supply.

'Good evening', said the barman, who was, what you might term, a menacing figure. He loomed over the polished wooden bar at them, his many scars and one good eye moodily illuminated by the few weakly burning candles that sat on the dark mahogany.

'What can I get you...ah, gentlemen?'

The barman glanced from side to side as he said this, making brief eye contact with the patrons who sat on the dirty stools. There were a few sniggers; clearly the barman had just made a joke. Vericoos looked around. If he hadn't ruptured his *talent* he would have had some fun in here. As it was it was, probably best to just be polite. Shabwan was looking useless too, he hadn't said anything since they'd arrived in town and didn't even seem to realise that he was in a bar, let alone that they had become the focus of the moody looks of some pretty drunk and fairly burly farmers.

'We'd like a room for the night.'

'What, together?' replied the barman and the sniggering became outright guffaws, the wheezy, obnoxious laughter of a group of men of a certain age. Vericoos pretended he hadn't noticed although he was becoming increasingly uneasy. If these men decided to increase their enjoyment by giving the newcomers a bit of a kicking then Vericoos would be powerless to defend either himself or the useless, sulky little man who was stood next to him; too wrapped up in his own problems to venture out of his own head. Oh woe is me! Thought the sorcerer, bitterly. Shabwan truly did not know he was born and would soon, in all likelihood, miss his own death if he didn't sharpen up.

'No, no two rooms would be much better, if that's possible.'

'Are you sure? It gets cold at night, you two could snuggle.'

The levels of hilarity hit the roof at this stage, it seemed like the whole bar, including the crude furniture and mahogany foundations, was laughing at them. Vericoos seethed silently. How angry it made him that such a situation was a threat to him, and worse, a threat to his mission. Had he been himself he would have smashed this humorous fellow's head into the bar until he had the level of silence he required. Then he would have given them all one of his terrifying little speeches, he'd have loved to have watched their stupid grins fall away leaving only terror in their wake. As it was...

'No, two would be preferable thank you.'

The barman had had enough fun it seemed. He grinned at Vericoos and handed him a set of keys.

'Room two...and you,' he passed a set of keys to Shabwan. 'Room four.'

Shabwan said nothing, he just absentmindedly reached out and took the keys, but the barman didn't release them. Shabwan was so distant that he didn't realise what was happening so he just pulled harder. The barman tightened his grip.

'What do you say?'

'What?' Shabwan replied like someone waking up from a dream.

'I said, what do you say?'

The bar was completely silent now. All eyes were on Shabwan and the set of keys, like a tiny little rope in a tug of war. They glinted a little in the dirty candle light.

Shabwan glanced at Vericoos; the old man was not looking at him.

Shabwan yanked the keys hard but not hard enough, just when it felt like they had slipped from the thick ugly fingers of the man he was apparently in some kind of competition with, they were snatched back and, before he knew what had happened, Shabwan's head was pushed down against the bar. He could feel the sticky beer gluing his cheek to the wood and wondered, somewhat whimsically given the apparent seriousness of the situation, if he'd be able to raise his head up from the sugary goo, even after this ugly stranger had released him.

'You want to die tonight little boy?'

As depressed as he was Shabwan *didn't*. The gravity of the situation was dawning on him (*finally!* Thought Vericoos). This was not a good place and this bar was probably the worst part of it (*wrong*! Thought Vericoos). These people wouldn't mind kicking him until he was a bloody mess and then either dumping him back on the road or dumping his body in the river. It wouldn't really matter to them (*precisely*! Thought Vericoos)

'I'll ask you one more time...What do you say?'

'Please' said Shabwan, his voice sounding weak and small. Why wasn't Vericoos doing anything?

'I can't hear you.'

'Please!' said Shabwan again, hating himself for it.

'There you go then.' The barman let him up and then threw the keys in his face; then he lowered himself in a mock bow.

'Have a most pleasant evening gentlemen.'

The vicious guffaws followed them all the way up the creaky stairs.

4.

He felt uneasy as he lay in bed that night. what would Shabwan think about the fact that he hadn't intervened? At the height of his powers he could have read the boys mind from miles away, as it was he couldn't even 'hear' him through two thin wooden walls (although his thoughts had been clear enough in the bar, fear always broadcasts the loudest). If he were lucky, the boy would assume that Vericoos had been testing him, or punishing him maybe for letting his guard down. If he was unlucky...the boy's will was hanging by a thread anyway it wouldn't take a lot to break it. That wasn't the only thing that stopped Vericoos sleeping that night, however; he knew what was wrong with these poor, poor people.

5.

Shabwan lit the little candle by his bed, dreading the inevitable calling of the things he'd seen and the people he'd left. He thought of Coki, Leeham and Lewhay and how angry they must be at him, how confused. He tried to console himself with the fact that he was keeping them safe but it did little to comfort him. Then he thought of her, it always came back to her in the end. Her smile, her eyes, her voice...

6.

It was a beautiful morning but this was not the place to enjoy it. The blazing sun seemed harsh and unforgiving; its dry heat wavering off the dusty road, the fields around the town burned a dull orange. As Shabwan looked through the dusty window of his room upon the barren landscape he missed the sea, he thought of the noise of the waves and the fishing trips with his friends. Then came a knock at his door, for a moment he feared it may be the barman coming to give him a good morning beating but then Vericoos spoke.

'Shabwan, open the door.'

His voice was full of urgency, it was frightening. He opened the door and Vericoos entered.

'What's the matter?' Shabwan inquired.

'What...the matter...oh nothing,' said Vericoos, 'I just…we need to get some horses and get a move on.'

'Yeah, I agree.' Said Shabwan.

There was an uneasy silence, he knew something was wrong with but he couldn't quite put his finger on it.

'Well then,' said Vericoos. 'let's be off.'

They walked down the main street together after paying an extortionate amount of money to the grinning barman. All the while, as he was handing over the money, Vericoos could feel Shabwan's eyes burning into him. He sensed the curiosity and the dawning comprehension. This young man had had everything, his whole life, taken from him, and he'd done it because he'd trusted Vericoos. This unlikely trust had been forged instantaneously when the terrified boy had watched Vericoos crushing the three into the very earth on which they stood; now it was wavering severely as he watched that same person handing over a large sum of undeserved money to a man who had treated them with both rudeness and violence. The two acts gave off very different message and it would only be a matter of time until the boy realised...

They'd asked a fair few people and had always gotten the same response; no one wanted to sell them a horse, no one even wanted to speak to them but the few who did were very clearly not willing to sell them anything. The people of Payinzee hurried about the place, they didn't seem to look up or even acknowledge each other. Shabwan found himself thinking of ants.

'This is useless,' he said to Vericoos after yet another person ignored them and this time it was the sorcerers turn to remain silent. He was looking down at the hot dusty earth of the northern road and seemed not to hear Shabwan, 'I'm going to ask this guy,' Shabwan said.

He had seen a very drunk man, all beady eyes and beard, sitting on the steps of what seemed to be a shop, although it was almost identical to the wooden dwellings which surrounded it. The man was singing loudly and tunelessly and Shabwan suspected that, while he may have little in the way of useful information, he would at least talk to them.

The old drunk was singing the same line over and over again in a variety of different ways, each as ear-bendingly bad as the last, 'We used to be freeeeee...we useeeeed to be free...oh how we used to be so...freeeeeeee.'

It was truly horrible. Although it seemed to Shabwan that people were giving him a wider birth than was necessary. He looked harmless enough, and yet people seemed to hurry past him even quicker than they'd been walking before. Some of them even crossed the road.

'Good afternoon…' Shabwan began.

'arrrrrrrr and what do we have here? A traveler...what an honor. Many pass through but few stay and fewer still talk to old Marty.'

'Er, oh right', said Shabwan.

The old man's eyes were flicking around, never focusing on any one spot for too long. 'Those who do', continued Marty, seemingly unaware that Shabwan had spoken, 'would learn a thing or two, a thing that'd make them turn back if they had more wits that withies, if you know what I mean?'

The question startled Shabwan, not because he didn't know what Marty meant but because as Marty asked it, his eyes, which had been hitherto spinning about all over the place, like a couple of circular dies with only one black spot, suddenly locked into position completely focused on Shabwan's. The effect was quite amazing; he felt like he'd never been looked at quite like this before.

'Erm, yeah I do' he lied, and the old man burst into laughter before launching into another verse of his 'freeeeeeee' song. Shabwan waited a few moments for him to finish and then asked, 'Do you know where we might be able to lay our hands on a couple of horses?'

This apparently was the funniest thing the old man had ever heard, he rocked back and forth, spitting and coughing in between raucous bellows of laughter which would have stood out, even in the inn at which they'd stayed.

'Horses for courses that's what ye wants and that's what ye'll get... if you speaks to Lomwai that is. Lomwai he do control everything that gets bought and sold round here...wahay!', at this old Marty threw back another great gulp of whatever was in the dirty bottle he was carrying and fell backwards onto the stairs. From the disgusting snores he began omitting Shabwan assumed he must have fallen asleep.

'Well, that was actually kind of helpful,' said Shabwan. 'We just need to find Lomwai and buy a couple of horses and we can get out of here, supposing of course Lomwai exists. I assume you've got more money?' Vericoos nodded but said nothing. Shabwan couldn't be bothered with finding out what was wrong with him. He imagined that the old man wanted to get out of this horrible little place just as much as he did and all they needed to do to accomplish that was find this Lomwai. One thing was for sure: Shabwan was determined to do it today. He definitely didn't want to spend another night at the inn.

7.

Unfortunately but not unsurprisingly, however, they couldn't find anyone who would tell them where to find Lomwai, they tried all three of the towns inns and several shops and were always greeted with looks which told them they needed to leave and stop asking questions,

'God, I'm really starting to hate this place.' said Shabwan.

Vericoos only nodded and looked gravely back at the floor. The old man was being *worse* than useless. For someone who'd been so keen to get Shabwan on board and get on with their quest or mission or whatever you wanted to call it he now seemed very reluctant.

'I'm going to ask this woman,' said Shabwan. 'Excuse me, miss! EXCUSE ME!'

Shabwan almost had to scream this into the woman's face to get her to stop. She was carrying a depressingly small basket of vegetables.

'Yes.' her voice was weak and timid and, while she glanced up at Shabwan, she wouldn't make eye contact with him.

'Do you know where we can find Lomwai?'

Shabwan hadn't seen the other's reactions to this question as close up as he now saw the woman's, but if he had he would have seen that the same flash of fear that darted across her tired old face had been equally as present in all of them.

'No, no I don't know anything, I'm sorry.'

She tried to hurry past him but Shabwan moved to block her, he was getting really bored now.

'Look, just please tell me where he lives. We can give you some money.'

This seemed to get her interest but she still looked very scared. Vericoos didn't seem to have noticed that Shabwan was even talking to her. Shabwan marched up to him, he was starting to get just as annoyed with the old man as he was with everyone else in this horrible, dusty, dried out little place.

'Give me some coins.'

Vericoos looked blank for a moment and then dipped his scarred hand into a little pouch that he kept round his neck. It emerged with two large gold coins. Shabwan grabbed them and showed them to the old woman. The eyes which had found it so hard to focus on Shabwan's face now looked like they'd have to be physically prised away from the two glinting objects he held in his hand.

'Come on. Where does he live?'

Her eyes flitted from the gold coins to Shabwan and then back again; he nodded encouragingly. In one swift movement she took the coins from his hand and pointed over his shoulder. Then she turned and hurried away in the opposite direction from the one she'd originally been heading.

Shabwan looked to where she'd pointed and almost fainted with shock; how the hell hadn't he seen it before? It was completely at odds with the dull symmetry of the rest of the town and now he looked at it...well it was the only thing here that you possibly could notice. Glinting in the harsh summer sun was a great black house.

8.

While everything else in Payinzee was single storey, apart from the inn where Vericoos and Shabwan had enjoyed such pleasant hospitality, the black house stood three tiers high. It loomed menacingly over the eastern side of the road and Shabwan suddenly understood why the whole place had seemed like a trap to him earlier. But...could he have known of this place without, in fact, seeing it? It seemed impossible, so impossible! But then so did so much.

The roof of the house rose into an ornate silver point and below it rested a huge balcony, the purpose of which was clear; observation. Whoever had built this monstrosity wasn't content just to own Payinzee, they also seemed to want to be able to watch it; all of it. The scuttling, frightened citizens all made sense now; once you realised it was there you couldn't help but feel that the great balcony was just waiting to lunge over the top of the uniform wooden shacks and crush you where you stood. Shabwan marvelled that he had spent a whole day here and not even glanced in its direction...

'It's enchanted,' said Vericoos as if reading his thoughts. 'It can't be seen until someone tells you where it is, however I get the feeling that *it* has been watching us for some time.'

'Who do you think lives there?' Shabwan asked.

It was a relief to hear the sorcerer speak again but his manner was still hugely unsettling.

'Who do you think?' replied Vericoos and Shabwan realised that he had known the answer ever since the ornate black monstrosity had first revealed itself, or at least its visual form, to him.

'Lomwai.'

'Full marks!' Vericoos looked gloomily up at the balcony. 'Something tells me that we may have trouble acquiring horses from him.'

Shabwan agreed. There was something horribly ominous about the house. Now that his eyes had adjusted to it, he could make out lots of silver décor, standing aggressively out from the jet black of the wood. He could also make out orange flames licking up the walls although the wood itself didn't seem to be on fire. The house sat over Payinzee like a huge black predator, or perhaps more like a leech; gently sucking the lifeblood out of the place and feeding its own swelling belly. Shabwan's earlier thoughts, that had likened the inhabitants of Payizee to ants, now confused him much less. They were living in fear, sat beneath a hostile queen who could reach down and squash anyone who lingered, or became unproductive, for too long. *So the house is the queen, the people are the workers...that just leaves the soldiers.*

This didn't seem the time to be smug but Vericoos had a detestable lofty air about him as he said:

'Did it not seem strange to you that every house in this town is identical?'

'Yeah but...'

'They've been built by magic,' he glanced around him at the strange little dwellings. 'I would imagine that, in happier times, all of these homes were much more personal to their owners, but at some stage, some very recent stage, the whole lot have been levelled and these have been built in their place.'

It now occurred to Shabwan that Vericoos must have been able to see the great black house since their arrival, yet he'd said nothing.

'Why would anyone have done that?' he asked, already knowing the answer.

'Control,' Vericoos replied, simply. 'Remove people's concept of identity and they're much easier to control, much easier to imprison. This is a dark place.'

Shabwan felt a lurch in his stomach. The man he'd seen summon up the very earth, just a week ago, was frightened. Only now did he see the strange mood of his companion for what it was. Fear, after all, is one of the great levellers. Everyone has their point at which they are broken and when that happens, they all become very, very similar. *Magic or not,* thought Shabwan.

'We should leave.'

'I fear it may already be too late.' replied Vericoos.

9.

'Come forth, come forth!' came the icy voice. Suddenly every door in the road flew open and out poured the people, those that lived directly on the road were soon joined by those who lived in the rows behind. They lined up neatly and silently, Shabwan caught sight of the barman with whom he'd failed to get off to a good start with last night; he no longer looked threatening. He, like all the others, stood noiselessly, looking straight ahead.

Shabwan and Vericoos were now enclosed within a gauntlet made up of every man, woman and child of Payinzee. The trap's been sprung, thought Shabwan. For, as unthreatening as the barman and all the others now looked, he was certain that no escape would be permitted to him and Vericoos. He looked around for the source of the voice but couldn't see anyone; it had sounded like it came from everywhere. Then, without warning, he stood before them; tall, impressive and dark. His thin, yet prominent, eyebrows sat over a pair of the greenest and most viscous looking eyes Shabwan had ever seen. His lipless mouth was curled into a sneer of pleasure.

'What do we have here?' His voice was cold and high but it rang with excitement.

Shabwan was at a loss for words. The whole situation was exceptionally strange and it had happened so quickly that he only now sensed how much danger they were actually in. The on looking crowd looked terrified too but it was a dangerous terror. Again Shabwan felt the strong sense that, if the owner of the black house were to give the word, he and Vericoos would be torn limb from limb, as easily as if they were the brittle dried out corn that adorned the landscape. Vericoos was saying nothing; he was busy looking down at the floor.

'Well?' The man, who could only be Lomwai, looked from Shabwan to Vericoos. 'It seems a couple of challenger's have entered our midst. Wouldn't you say so?'

There were a few reluctant cheers of agreement from the assembled crowd.

'I said wouldn't you say so?'

This time there was a much louder cheer although it still sang of misery. Lomwai held one hand up to the sky and dark green flame rolled upwards from his fingers. When he spoke again his voice was much heavier and deeper.

'Is that what you want; to challenge the great Lomwai in single combat?'

Shabwan knew that there was no way they had done anything to suggest this. But he supposed that Lomwai had decided that this was the way it was going to go the moment he spied them from his voyeuristic balcony. They were going to be slaughtered to massage the ego of a maniac; to keep his subjects in check.

'We do not wish for any such thing, we only came here to buy a horse...'

'SILENCE!' roared Lomwai and Shabwan felt a horrible jolt of fear and a sick lurching in his stomach as he saw Vericoos fall instantly into silence. He couldn't understand it; while it was obvious that he was in the presence of someone of magical skill he could feel how superficial and vain this skill was. Lomwai held the community in fear but Shabwan, even with his massively limited knowledge of magic, could sense that he didn't have any real power (*Any real talent! Corrected an alien voice in his head)*. The house, the voice, the green flames, it all just reminded him of Morldron, albeit a saner version who looked like he enjoyed killing and enslaving. The magic he had seen Vericoos perform could have swallowed up this whole town and spat out nothing but the bones, it could have shattered Lomwai into a million pieces before the magician (*That's right the Magician! Came the same strange invasive voice, the source of which he did not know or understand*) could have even raised a hand. So why the hell didn't he just do it? Why didn't he just do them all a favour and then they could get out of this hellish place.

'So two challengers have entered my town, and what must be done about this?'

A few of the townspeople mumbled something.

'I SAID, WHAT MUST BE DONE?' As Lomwai bellowed the sky over the road darkened and the same flames that Shabwan had seen licking up the walls of the great black house now rolled over the roofs and walls of all the buildings that surrounded them, people were screaming.

'Why don't you leave them alone you git?'

The screaming stopped. Everyone turned. The flames went out. The old man whom Shabwan had spoken to, not ten minutes earlier, was on his feet and lurching towards Lomwai. The magician looked momentarily surprised but as the old drunk got nearer, his face took on a look of malicious pleasure. He was about to have some fun.

'The rest of this town might be too cowardly to tell you, but I've had enough. You murdering swine!!'

Old Marty was in range and he swung the now empty bottle he was carrying at Lomwai's head. For an excited second Shabwan thought it would connect but instead, at the point of contact with the magician's cranium, it stopped dead. Marty looked at the bottle, confusion etched all over his bright red face. Then the bottle began to glow, a bright lime green. It twisted and contorted until it began to grow features; *human features!* Shabwan watched with horror as it took on, not only the same malicious grin, but the same malicious face as its creator.

Marty opened and shut his mouth like a fish, then the bottle jumped in the air. It hovered for a second, spinning round and round until the glassy face became a blur. Then, just when it seemed that the bottle would never come down, it plunged itself into the same mouth which had drunk its contents. Shabwan saw Marty's eyes, wide with fear, as the bottle, still whole and still glowing, wriggled and pushed its way into his mouth and then down his throat. He spun on the spot looking around with eyes pleading. He opened his mouth and the sickly lime green light could be seen illuminating his few remaining teeth. There was a cracking noise followed by a stomach turning squelching; Marty opened his mouth again, the lime green light was gone, replaced by dark crimson as blood flowed freely out over the old drunks chin. He looked up at his killer, his last look one of strange acceptance, and then fell face down in the dirt.

Shabwan reeled, he had still got the same feeling of superficiality as he watched these events unfold, there was no real power here, not like he'd seen, but he also saw how deadly it was, how evil. A few of the people in the crowd were crying. He could hear the wails of little children and their parents attempting to shut them up without being noticed. The hideous oppression of it all clawed at Shabwan and the feeling was back, the same feeling he'd felt when he'd seen Anika fall. A feeling, he'd assumed, would only flow through him when those he cared deeply about were hurt or threatened, now he was beginning to know different...For the first time since leaving the place and the people he loved so much, he felt in control…Time to act.

Vericoos knew that it was too late and he now saw how stupid he had been. He had sensed, as soon as they'd got within sight of the town that something was amiss. Then shortly after the black house had drawn into view and his fears had been confirmed. He'd racked his brains for reasons not to go to Payinzee but had been unable to come up with any that wouldn't expose his weakness. Since they'd arrived he'd been hoping that they would be able to keep their heads down, get whatever horses they could lay their hands on and be gone. It seemed crazy that he'd worried so much about the boy realising that he was weak, surely that would have been preferable to this. Despite all Vericoos' skill and power he was about to become easy prey for someone infinitely less *talented.*

It was happening again.

'So you two, care to choose your weapons?'

Now that there was no chance of escape, Vericoos could stop pretending to be a frightened old man. His last hope had been that humility may make them seem unworthy targets but this hope was long gone. Lomwai had sensed that Vericoos was of magical quality as soon as he'd arrived in the town and, since that moment, battle had been inevitable. Vericoos had been surprised, as he stood there, at how much young Shabwan had learned. Listening to his companions thoughts he was pleasantly surprised to find that the boy understood that this magic was of little real power and that he also saw that this made it no less deadly when combined with the malice of its controller.

The increase in flow was much faster than he had suspected, he wondered how little time had passed since this guy was just another magician who people saw for help with building, farming and remedies.

Not long at all, thought the sorcerer, not long at all.

'I want you to know that you are going to win today, but believe me when I say that you cannot kill me and one day I will find you, in this dimension or any other and when I do I'll make you plead for death.'

Nice simple threat, straight to the point, thought Shabwan. Unfortunately it seemed as if the old man was also admitting that they were going to lose. Shabwan didn't want to lose.

'You'll die first.'

This was the quietest thing Lomwai had said, it was the first time he had addressed them directly rather than prancing and preening about in front of the crowd. Vericoos stared unflinchingly up at Lomwai who held his hands out in front of him, lime green light began to flicker between his fingers; deadly light.

Vericoos was ready, he couldn't believe that they had fallen so early in their quest but he would be damned if he gave this disgrace upon humanity a moment of pleasure from his demise. He locked his eyes with those of Lomwai and thought only of the moment when they would meet again. Shabwan would die here but he...

Something caught the corner of his eye, something moving very fast.

Shabwan had had about enough. Vericoos, the hypocritical old git, seemed ready to give up on everything right here but he wasn't. And, he thought seething with an anger he could not have imagined ten days ago; *he* didn't even really know what they were doing.

He acted without really thinking. In between where he stood and the corpse of Marty lay, was a rock, a nice simple rock, he picked it up, pulled back his arm and flung it with all his might at Lomwai.

The rock smashed into the magician's mouth, shattering his teeth. He rocked backwards, eye lids fluttering, only the whites visible. Then Shabwan was upon him forcing him to the ground; he grabbed the fallen rock and beat it repeatedly into Lomwai's skull, he had never killed before but still he felt no remorse as he saw the life blink out of the green eyes. He smashed the rock down one last time.

10.

Shabwan and Vericoos were enjoying the fifteenth drink. All fifteen had been heartily slammed in front of them and the idea of payment for the privilege would have been considered insanity. The inn was unrecognisable from the place they'd stayed last night. Where there had been cold, mocking laughter from burly, threatening figures there was now real laughter, the laughter of relief, and not just from the men. The whole town was in there celebrating.

'So, he'd always lived here?' Shabwan asked.

'Yeah as far as I can remember,' replied the same barman who had flung the keys at him the night before, who now seemed to have appointed himself Shabwan's best friend. There were several others listening all of them hanging off Shabwan's every word and laughing raucously at his every bad joke. That's right, Shabwan was making jokes! His transformation over the last few hours had been almost as dramatic as the townspeople's.

'But then last week he was in here telling everyone how he was now in charge of the town. We all thought he was drunk and a few people laughed at him, eventually he stormed off. No one thought anything of it, he'd always been all right you see. Offered his services if you had the right money.'

Shabwan nodded, he felt somehow like he already knew the story.

'Then the next morning was when it happened.'

There were some dark things muttered in the surrounding group.

'What happened?' Shabwan caught Vericoos' eye as he said this. The old man was watching him and didn't seem the least bit drunk despite the endless alcohol they had consumed amidst the celebrations.

'I'd just opened up, I remember, then suddenly there was that horrible voice you heard today, you know they high one, it shook the bar it was so loud. It told us we all had to assemble in the main street, course most of us went out there just out of curiosity, but there were a few who didn't come. Either they were asleep or too hungover or ...too young.'

The bar seemed to get a lot quieter as he said this, for the first time that evening there was something other than celebration in the air. 'And then...well, there was all this green and orange light and a hell of a noise and then, well if you hadn't been there you wouldn't have believed it...all the wood was just up in the air.'

'All the wood?' asked Shabwan.

'Yeah from the houses, they never used to be in lines like this and they used to be a lot nicer, but once he did whatever he did, every plank of wood rose up out the ground and then they came down as they are now; all in these damned lines. Then once they'd settled he allocated them to people, course people were scared then and they did what he said and it wasn't till after that we discovered that those who'd still been inside...well...'

'They died?'

'Yeah that's right they died. Thirty two in all...thirty two! And one of them was John's little...' The barman trailed off. The man, who could only have been John, began to cry.

'Since then he's been sat up in that big black house, no one even knows how that got there, and if he saw people talking or not working or just doing anything he disliked he'd flame them from up on that balcony.' A new storyteller had stepped in as the barman attempted to comfort the now weeping figure of John.

'Since then we've just had to work, we were still allowed to come in here but only after he'd watched us working all through the day. We couldn't believe it when you showed up. We thought people must know about what was going on but you two seemed completely oblivious.'

Shabwan met Vericoos' gaze again, there was so much he wanted to ask. As much as he was enjoying himself as the celebrated champion of the townspeople, he couldn't wait for the crowd to disperse so he could finally speak to the old man.

'Yeah, and we're sorry for how we treated you as well.'

The barman was back in.

'No it's fine I understand,' Shabwan thought of the people he had lost and how it mad him feel. He could forgive the barman and all the others for their behaviour.

'So when did it all happen?' Shabwan was amazed that just over a weeks journey away from San Hoist such a thing had been going on and he'd known nothing about it.

'Oh...erm five or was it six days ago.'

Again Shabwan looked at Vericoos, the old man was silent as he had been for most of the night, but Shabwan saw much in his expression. The dejection and misery, within which he'd been imprisoned for the last week, seemed a long way away now, the adrenaline of the day was still gently washing through him along with all the foul local bitter he'd drunk and for the first time since leaving San Hoist he wanted to know. He wanted to know just what it was they were doing.

That and the answers to a hundred other questions which were now burning through his brain.

11.

They left Payinzee the next morning, the townspeople came out and made the same gauntlet they had made yesterday only this time it made Shabwan feel warm and happy rather than morbidly terrified. Vericoos watched his companion waving and smiling as they left, leading their new horses (very good mounts; the townspeople had been eager to express their gratitude) along the northern road. How lucky the youngster was; that his first kill had been such a just act, there would be many more and some of these would not seem to have such a purpose. The boy had shown no signs of remorse as yet but that would come. It always did.

Once they were out of sight of the town (although not the plume of smoke which was rising from the big black house which now contained Lomwai's corpse) Shabwan looked at Vericoos as if challenging him to say something. The boy clearly wanted him to speak first. But how to begin? Where on earth could you possibly begin?

'You can't ride, can you?'

That would have to do then.

Finding a starting point is always a difficult task for anyone: be it someone trying to craft a story, or a couple looking for the necessary point to focus on so as to justify just when they began to get so damn annoyed with each other. When there is so much to say, finding those first few words before the floodgates open has baffled so many folk into silence and therefore preserved said floodgates, never with good consequences. For this reason, the fact that Shabwan chose to begin with Vericoos' inability to ride was perhaps equally as logical and constructive as starting at the very beginning.

Vericoos shook his head, no doubt equally as bored as you, dear reader, with all this nonsensical musing about beginnings.

'The magic you did in San Hoist, it almost killed you didn't it?'

He nodded.

'Is there anything that can restore you?'

Was the boy smarter than Vericoos had given him credit for? He couldn't rule it out, although he had very rarely been wrong about anyone.

'Yes there is.'

Shabwan nodded as if he'd already known the answer and had just been awaiting confirmation.

'Well then we need to get it then, don't we?'

He grinned at Vericoos, who was surprised to see that a momentary glimpse of something (was it…affection?) crept into the smile. This was all turning out to be most confusing.

'Luckily for us, the only place we can get it lies directly on our path.'

'That's good.' said Shabwan.

They travelled in silence for the rest of the day. It was clear that Vericoos was struggling immensely and Shabwan couldn't have the old man talking himself to death before he'd found out what he needed to know.

Chapter 2.

Nightmares and Magic.

1.

Night had fallen when they set up camp just off the northern road. It was warm and balmy and there was very little noise, after what they had just been through the calm took a little while to get used to. Shabwan, who had undertook the first leg of the journey with an air of complete and utter indifference now found that he burned with questions. The thrill of the battle had not yet left him and the grateful faces of the people of Payinzee kept flashing before his tired eyes; infinitely more pleasant than the faces of his friends and loved ones which had haunted his sleep only two days ago.

Where were they going? That was one question. It was no more important than any of the others but it seemed like a logical one to ask first. In his excitement Shabwan had forgotten that this was the only one he had, in fact, already asked. He had a very limited geographical knowledge; having never ventured far from San Hoist. When he had, he'd travelled along the coast, not to the North as they were now. Even though Payinzee was only a week's walk away from his home town he'd rarely even heard people speak of it. San Hoist was a very self contained little community and Shabwan, like most of its inhabitants, had never had a great desire to travel anywhere he didn't need to. This was to be his first big journey and now he came to think about it, he imagined it would be just that...big.

Perhaps even through the forest and over the mountains.

Shabwan had always heard people use this phrase and never taken much interest in its meaning. It was generally used when people wanted to give the impression that something was an unfathomably long distance away. He smiled as he recalled Coki telling him that his chances of getting with Kayleigh were: 'through the forest and over the mountains.' Then the wave of familiar sadness descended over him again. Although now it was different. Something had happened to him in Payizee; he had changed.

Before his arrival in that terrible place, the only thing which had driven Shabwan onwards was the memory of the three riders and the knowledge that, by following Vericoos, he was keeping such danger from ever reaching his friends and his love again. Since the battle with Lomwai however, he now felt something else driving him on, something fiery in his blood. The change was so intriguing, so all consuming, that it was, for the most part at least, keeping the realisation that he had become a killer from his door.

As amazing as it was to admit it to himself; he now wanted to go with the old man. Indeed if Vericoos were to tell him that he was going to go on without him and kill the God himself, would he even return home? He didn't think so. Not now that he had experienced a little taste of what the journey was offering him. It wouldn't be possible to just turn away. The thoughts of his three friends and of Kayleigh still weighed his heart down like lead, but he now understood clearer than ever that he couldn't go back to them. Not until it was done.

2.

Shabwan looked over at his companion. The old man had fallen asleep already. Dammit! He wouldn't get any answers tonight. He hoped that Vericoos would be all right, the Gods knew what he'd do if he wasn't. He still knew nothing of what he was meant to be doing aside from the one line of explanation he'd been offered on the hill overlooking the fiery glow of San Hoist. He would just have to make sure the old man survived until they reached wherever it was that he could recover. Then he would be more than capable of looking after himself.

Shabwan supposed he should sleep, but even the thought of doing so seemed ridiculous: 'through the forest and over the mountains'. The bizarre cocktail of new feelings and emotions he was experiencing kept him awake for most of that night. He saw things too; he saw his friends but he also saw Vericoos, he saw himself walking through the gauntlet of newly liberated and cheering people and thought to himself, 'there could be so many more'. He saw Lomwai's face exploding as he heaved the rock onto it again and again, then he saw Kayleigh...

They were walking together as they always had done, through the fields, and he was explaining to her what he had to do; she looked sad.

'But why?' she was saying, her beautiful voice floated into his ears, caressing the lobes gently.

'Just because I have to that's all.'

She looked puzzled now, and there was something different about her something he couldn't quite put his finger on. She looked beautiful any idiot could see that, but when he'd looked at her he'd always thought that he saw what others didn't, an extra layer of beauty, an aura...whatever you wanted to call it. This wasn't exactly missing just different, and he didn't like it. He also didn't like the way she was showing him no understanding, couldn't she see how glorious his victory would be, how the residents of Payinzee would soon become the residents of the entire world, the republic of the free. All praising the one who had killed the god.

'I love you.'

She said it so simply and sweetly that it completely interrupted his train of thought.

'I...'

Now the sadness was back, he needed her, she was more important than anything, she alone.

'I love you.'

As he spoke the words she began to warp and change. The same steam he had seen rise from Vericoos, before the battle in the plaine, now began to rise from Kayleigh, only it was jet black. She writhed and screamed in agony, he tried to grab her and hold onto her but he couldn't; every part of her which he touched turned into the same black steam and her cries became harsher, more desperate.

Then it was no longer Kayleigh who stood before him, he backed away terrified; where she had been the black steam was now swirling into a new shape, one which was being bound together by thin bolts of green and orange lightning.

'No...No...NOOOOO!' Shabwan screamed, and then with one final green flash that burned his retinas, Lomwai stood before him. His mouth broke into a grin that was larger than his face; and not figuratively, his mouth was actually expanding outwards beyond the confines of his jaw and cheeks and razor sharp teeth were poking their way through the gums. He advanced on Shabwan, whose legs were suddenly bound by lime green light. He was going to die, the magician was going to eat him, those hideous teeth and that huge gaping mouth would consume him in seconds. He closed his eyes...

He opened them again, he wasn't dead, but Lomwai was standing over him, his great teeth now visible for what they truly were: Pari spines.

'You've got some now haven't you my boy?'

Shabwan could only stare back up at the hideous monstrosity that had replaced his love.

'How does it feel? No more importantly how does she feel?'

He began to laugh manically and then they were spinning, spinning through the air, and they were joined by everyone that Shabwan had ever met, he saw his mum, Vericoos looming threateningly over her and he saw Anika her head crushed and bleeding. Then he saw Coki, he was being stabbed by someone wearing a cloak and hood, Leeham and Lewhay were trying to help him but they couldn't. He began to scream, he screamed louder than he'd ever screamed but it wasn't his voice that he heard but...

'Wake up!' Shouted Vericoos.

Shabwan jerked awake, the horrific images that had been flowing through his mind evaporated but the feeling of fear and dread in his gut remained; as real as stone.

'What...What's the matter,' said Shabwan, he didn't want the old man to know what he'd been seeing.

'You were screaming in your sleep.'

Shabwan couldn't detect any mockery in Vericoos' voice but he still felt ashamed. He didn't want him to think that he suffered from childish nightmares. Yet even as he thought this he knew that it had been so much more.

'I've made us some breakfast.' said the old man, and Shabwan didn't know if he was more relieved that the subject had been changed or that Vericoos was apparently now well enough to hunt. The smell of roasting rabbit caressed his nostrils and the feeling in his gut eased. For Shabwan, like so many young men, food was the greatest of all healers. Some people think it is time; these people are wrong.

'Ah! That smells amazing.' replied Shabwan and a few minutes later they were ravenously devouring the unfortunate beast. Once they'd finished breakfast Shabwan began to feel troubled again (OK maybe time is better, but in the short term give me food any time). He couldn't find any room in his own head to escape from what he'd seen while he slept. Last night's questions, which had seemed so overbearing and important that he could hardly wait for the morning, now seemed minor and insignificant.

'You were right to kill him,' said Vericoos, and Shabwan wondered again if the old man could read his mind.

'He was evil, perhaps not always so but he was drunk on power. You saw what he had done to that place with your own eyes and you punished him accordingly.'

Shabwan could only look down at the rabbit carcass which now lay on the dusty earth, he knew that Vericoos was about to answer one of his big questions but he cared little.

'I know that you don't care and I also know what you saw last night.' Said Vericoos, abruptly ending any doubt Shabwan might still have had about his mind reading abilities.

'What you saw was a pitiful attempt at revenge by the magician that you killed. I would imagine that as he sensed his demise, he put his last efforts into leaving you something that would haunt you. It was no more real than that ridiculous flame that he seemed so fond of rolling up the walls and if you treat it as otherwise you're a fool.'

Vericoos' cold tone was melted by the reassurance of his words.

'But I saw...'

'I know exactly what you saw, as I told you. Do not think of it again. If you take one piece of advice from me take that one. Although I recommend that you do take a few more as we venture onwards.'

Vericoos was smiling again, it was an odd effect, ugly yet beautiful. Shabwan relaxed. Of course that was what had happened, while he didn't understand it, it made perfect sense. The whole vision, nightmare, whatever it had been, reeked of Lomwai's vein, superficial and nasty power. A petty attempt at revenge indeed.

Now Shabwan felt strong again, as he had the night before; strong and curious...

'Would you like to know why he was as he was?'

Shabwan nodded.

'Did you perhaps sense a difference between what I did down on the cliffs and what Lomwai did in that town? I mean a difference beyond the superficial' asked Vericoos. He had the good manners to make his eyes seem questioning despite already knowing the answer.

'Yeah, I did...' Shabwan was lost in thought for a moment. 'What you did on the cliffs scared me; it scared me so much that I couldn't move. It was as if the whole world obeyed your command and if you wanted it would do *anything*.'

Vericoos nodded, his eyes gleaming and a thin smile across his lips. Shabwan's first thought was that it might just be pride in his own work, nothing like job satisfaction after all, but it seemed like there was something else here. Something he didn't quite understand.

'What Lomwai was doing...it just felt nasty. Kind of petty really, almost as if, for all the visual spectacle he had created, he didn't really have any power. I had very little fear as I faced him.'

Vericoos nodded again, this time looking more like a proud grandfather observing his grandson's first attempts at fishing, albeit minus any of the warmth that this image conjures up.

'You've understood much, much more than I expected, but there was one thing that you failed to understand. You see, Lomwai did, in fact, have a huge amount of power, what he lacked was skill.'

Shabwan regarded Vericoos quizzically.

'But, moving the whole town around, building that big black house, does that not require skill?'

'Not a great deal,' responded Vericoos and Shabwan suddenly thought of Morldron's cows.

'There's more of it around now isn't there?'

The same unsettling gleam was back in Vericoos' eyes,

'Yes, more and more, although that doesn't entirely explain our green and orange friend. Unfortunately we must get on and I feel that walking and talking may prove too tiring. But tonight I will tell you about magic.'

3.

They made slow progress that day. The fact that they now had horses was slowing them down rather than speeding them up. Walking along the northern road they passed by a couple of small villages and one or two guest houses. The scenery stayed much the same; the ploughed fields were the red of clay while the grass still looked strikingly green, despite the relentless heat of the summer. Anyone who saw the two travellers thought nothing of it; just two men, one old, tall and thin one young, broad and dark, leading two horses along with them.

They walked all day and continued for a couple of hours after the sun had gone down. Shabwan kept asking Vericoos if he wanted to stop but the old man merely shook his head. The effort of walking was visibly taking it out of him yet he still seemed not to want to show it. Then it dawned on Shabwan...What it was that was *really* driving the old man, at least for now.

Shabwan had experienced a couple of episodes in his younger life where his drug taking had danced on the thin line between recreation and necessity, and courtesy of his father, he was no stranger to the outward signs of physical addiction. He wondered how it had taken him so long to realise that he wasn't looking at someone who simply couldn't bear to show weakness. Instead he now saw, not the powerful sorcerer who had moved the earth to save him, but just another addict who found every moment he was separated from his vice of choice a living hell.

It was strange to regard Vericoos in this new light. Obviously there was a large part of the old man which was stubborn and proud and would not enjoy showing weakness to anyone, let alone someone like Shabwan. But now there was this new part too: the addict. The part of Vericoos, perhaps the most human part, which would drag itself along until his very last breath, endlessly searching for what it had lost.

Shabwan was conflicted. On the one hand, this new realisation greatly increased his empathy with the old man; it made him seem more human and exposed the fact that he too had lost something which hurt him. Not as much as Shabwan but still something. Then on the other it made him hate the old git; they were supposedly off on this monumentally important quest, one which Shabwan had sacrificed everything for, and yet, to the old man, it was not the most important thing. As much as he might care about their quest, and even about Shabwan (strange as that thought was), there was something else on his mind, something which, until it returned, would seem more important than anything else ever could. And, thought Shabwan, as he felt a strange pang in his guts, he'll sacrifice absolutely anything to get it.

4.

By the time they made camp the full moon was looming over them, its big impassive white face couldn't care less for anything that had transpired or was yet to come, yet still it saw all.

Vericoos made a fire. Shabwan couldn't help but be entertained by the look in his eye as he made it using conventional methods. Clearly it had been a long time since he had been forced to do so and the process wasn't exactly filling him with happy memories. The old man scowled at the wood and flint as if it were they who had robbed him of his magic.

Once the fire was made and Shabwan had caught a rabbit, they settled down to eat. Shabwan watched as Vericoos took out a little bag that hung around his neck and sprinkled some herbs over the poor beast, the same mouth watering smell that had awoken him that morning filled his nostrils. He ate ravenously, for they had not stopped for lunch, but this wasn't the only reason that he finished his meal in under two minutes (normally it took him at least four); It was finally time for answers.

'Lets start with Payinzee shall we?' asked Vericoos. Though the question was completely rhetorical, it wasn't as if Shawban was about to say, 'no, let's not, let's start with your childhood. How was your relationship with your mother?' Not that he would have wanted to, but it's always nice to illustrate these things. If we only ever talked about what did happen then where would we be? I once had a friend who would only ever discuss that which had happened. He would never hypothesise or wonder about anything, claiming there to be no point. His is another story, and not one that ends well, let me tell you.

So instead of bowling into a pointless Freudian analysis of his travelling partner Shabwan just nodded. He hadn't spoken a word but the old man knew what he wanted and, of course, would have done even without his mind reading abilities. This made Shabwan think of something, 'Hang on. Do you not need magic to read my mind?'

'Very, very little,' replied Vericoos, 'alas it is all I am capable of at the moment, the very easiest and most basic form of magic is still at my disposable but all else...'

The old man looked bitterly into the fire as if its presence was a constant reminder of his current predicament. Shabwan thought of an old fisherman to whom they had stopped selling stonk. He had been using it far too much and had not taken kindly to being blacklisted, but they had been adamant and had never sold it to him again. It had worked (unfortunately sometimes these things didn't), he had sorted himself out and returned to the sea in order to support his family. The old man had, however, always had a certain look to him after that. A look of pining and longing, a look that Shabwan saw now, a look that seemed even more yearning and desperate in the flickering light cast by their weak and non magical fire.

'Anyway where was I?' Said Vericoos. Apparently he'd been just as lost in thought as Shabwan.

'The man you killed, Lomwai. He wasn't much different to a fellow I met in San Hoist by the name of Morldorn.'

'What?' Shabwan snorted with laughter, he couldn't imagine anyone more different.

'You think it's funny? But I do not speak of personality or appearance, I speak of *talent*.'

Shabwan laughed again at this and Vericoos began to look annoyed.

'Not talent boy, *talent.*' If you heard him say it you would understand the difference, it wasn't so much in the pronunciation (although there was a difference, think *taaaalent*, rather than talent) as in the look. However, once you'd heard it once (or maybe seen it) you'd never confuse the two again.

'Sorry, sorry it's just Morldron didn't have any talent really. He was completely useless.' Shabwan was apparently slower on the uptake than most at this juncture. Ironic when this particular piece of information would come to have such a strong impact on him.

'So you say, but I fancy that '*was*' is more important in this claim than you realise.'

Vericoos looked at Shabwan as if challenging him to laugh again. He did not. Instead he thought of the conversation he'd had with Annika in the plaine. God's it felt like years ago.

'Well...there were rumours that he had got a bit more powerful but no one really listened to them. I mean did you say that you met him? He was completely insane.'

'Oh yes,' replied Vericoos 'and I fancy that he'd never done so much as turn a hallucinogenic mushroom into a more powerful hallucinogenic mushroom, but with regards to *talent,* he had, a similar amount to our deceased friend.'

Shabwan was starting to feel confused, why was Vericoos making jibes about their stonk business? And what did he mean *talent?* He said it so ominously and deeply that it seemed almost ridiculous.

'What do you mean?' asked Shabwan, eloquent as ever, and was surprised to see that Vericoos looked pleased.

He had seemed so proud of Shabwan's level of understanding yesterday, and now he looked equally as happy when he was completely lost.

'I can see I'm going to have to make this simple, so let us start properly. What would you call me?'

This question seemed a far cry from making things simple but Shabwan answered anyway, 'Vericoos.'

'Yes very good that's my name,' the old man was really starting to enjoy himself now. 'But what would you say that I am?'

'A magician,' Shabwan replied, truly lost now.

'Aha wrong! Completely wrong! Do you think a *Magician* (Vericoos pronounced the word as if even saying it tainted his palate) could have brought the very earth crashing down on his foes? Do you think a *magician* could have lived as long as I have? Do you think a *magician* could...?' Vericoos stopped, as if surprised by his own words.

Shabwan was relieved; the old man had seemed as mad as Morldron and Lomwai rolled into one for a moment.

'So what are you then?' he asked.

'I, my boy, am a sorcerer.'

Shabwan just stared blankly at Vericoos, and this truly *did* annoy the latter. He had delivered the line in such a way that it would have been more fitting for a huge bolt of lightning to split the sky immediately after. But instead all he got was this gormless young man staring back at him. And to think he'd shown such promise yesterday.

'But I thought that sorcerers weren't real, I mean I've heard loads about them in old stories and stuff and how they lived in flying castles and everyone was terrified of them. I always thought that they were what mothers told their children about to frighten them.' Vericoos was looking angry now, but Shabwan didn't notice. 'For example,' he continued. ' There's this one story everyone always tells in San Hoist about this guy Nortune, who gathered up the whole sea in a huge bag and threw it over this city where people weren't obeying him.'

'Nartune.' said Vericoos.

'No Nortune,' replied Shabwan, 'apparently he used to live on a huge magical ship and wage war and terror from the sea.'

'His name was Nartune,' said Vericoos. 'And he did have a magical ship.'

Shabwan looked at Vericoos, comprehension of the impossible dawning on him.

'Did you know him?' He asked.

'Know him,' laughed Vericoos. 'I killed him.'

The boy looked completely perplexed. It was going to be a long night. Shabwan had hit the nail on the head with his evaluation of Vericoos' paradoxical attitude towards his level of understanding. It had been so much easier yesterday. Yesterday he'd just been able to sense things. He felt like, without actually thinking too much about it, he had gleaned a great deal of knowledge and understanding from the events that had taken place in Payinzee. Now, in the cold light of day (or the weak light of a fire) it was much more difficult to get your head around stuff, especially when the old man opposite was telling him that he'd killed someone who Shabwan thought only existed in folklore. Imagine if you were in the pub one night and someone was claiming that they'd killed humpty dumpty…or something similar.

'How old would you say I am?' he asked, 'and don't be afraid of being rude.'

'Erm...ninety one.'

Vericoos laughed at the precise nature of the guess.

'No, not quite, I am in fact, probably closer to two thousand and ninety one.'

This was greeted with the blankest expression yet, as Vericoos had suspected it might be. He could say more but it would be better to wait and let Shabwan's intolerably slow brain tick this over for itself. Eventually it did, although the moon had visibly moved in the sky in the time it had taken.

'The stories about the sorcerers are true?'

'Well I imagine a lot of detail had been lost and a lot added but essentially they are true yes, just very old.'

'And you are a sorcerer?' Vericoos felt he'd been perfectly clear on this point but apparently further classification was needed.

'Yes, I am.'

Perhaps now they could begin.

5.

Shabwan was reeling again. It was a feeling he was beginning to get used to. The body only has so much truck with being shocked, after a while it just becomes bored and any new information, however mind-blowing, in fact fails to blow the mind and is instead treated with a forlorn casual indifference. To suggest that the mind reels is to suggest that it is like a spool sat atop a sewing machine, and like any spool, it can only reel so far. Unlike a spool however it cannot be changed; although that metaphor has no relevance whatsoever at this juncture.

What does have relevance (thank god!) is what Shabwan was thinking. And this was, that every young boy and girl knew the stories of the sorcerers (see it was worth the wait, bet you're glad of our little detour into the minds innermost workings now, aren't you?). But they were legend, folklore, children's stories, weren't they? The man who sat before him, who had, admittedly, done magic which Shabwan would never have dreamed possible, was claiming to have known these people, and to have been alive three thousand years ago. It didn't make any sense. It would be a bit like you're drunken aunty, one Christmas, telling you that she used to roll with Buddha, God and the Easter bunny back in the day (which mine actually did once).

'So magicians...' Shabwan felt he was beginning to grasp at least something of what he was being told, despite the narrator's blatant disregard for continuity.

'They're what remains, that is all; tiny insignificant magical vessels. When I was young Lomwai would have been nothing more than a common street performer.'

'There were magicians when you were young also?' asked Shabwan.

'Oh yes,' replied Vericoos. 'Pathetic failures, little better than those of no magic,'

'So why have they survived when sorcerers haven't?' Shabwan asked.

Vericoos was taken aback. Although, like with Shabwan's reeling mind, this was something else he was learning to expect this from their conversations. Explaining something to Shabwan was like driving a cart down a muddy road, with the wheels sticking, almost fast then suddenly, without warning, the cart would make a terrific hair point turn as the boy got his head round something.

'Why do you think that sorcerers haven't survived?'

'Well it's just obvious isn't it...you're the only one.'

Shabwan didn't know how he knew this but he felt like he'd known it since the moment Vericoos told him he was a sorcerer.

'I'm...not quite,' replied Vericoos and again he waited, reading Shabwan's thoughts, waiting for the cart to pivot once more.

'There's another?'

Vericoos nodded encouragingly.

'He was the one controlling the three riders? The one who killed Anika?'

Vericoos nodded again and the boy lowered his eyes into the fire, the flickering flames made them look dangerous... murderous; the same eyes Lomwai had seen before he saw no more.

'Where is he?' Shabwan asked; his tone noticeably different, his thoughts infinitely darker.

'He is a long way from here. His only contact with this world is through control, as you saw. If it's of any consolation to you he is in a place worse than you could ever imagine...The worst place.' Said Vericoos, and then thought to himself, well...almost.

'So you and he are the only two sorcerers left,' said Shabwan, 'and magicians, who are weak and useless are the only others who have magic?'

'The only other humans.' replied Vericoos and Shabwan looked at him questioningly, 'we'll get to that.'

'So why was Lomwai able to do all that stuff, I mean I know I said I could feel how superficial and weak his magic was but it was still a lot more impressive than what Morldron used to do and it seemed like he would have been capable of a little more than street entertainment if he'd have lived in your day.'

'Ah well, you see our friend Lomwai was an interesting case.'

Shabwan snorted; it was as if Vericoos was telling him about an interesting herb or type of wood, not a man who had killed and enslaved people. *Who was murdered* said an unpleasant little voice in the back of his mind.

'There were two things happening in that village with regards to Lomwai, one of them is happening everywhere and I believe you touched on it earlier.'

Shabwan thought back.

'There's more magic now isn't there?' he asked, an expectant look in his eye, no, more than expectant, excited. This troubled Vericoos.

'Yes, the world is flowing, it has happened before and always with disastrous consequences, but with any luck you and I will be able to stop it.'

Shabwan was tired now, he craved sleep but still he yearned for more information. He hadn't thought of Kayleigh once since Vericoos had started talking.

'Me and you?'

'Yes, that is, shall we say, the secondary goal of our quest, you see in time every magician on the planet will become like Lomwai, that is to say they'll have the same amount of magic and that, as you've seen with your own eyes, is something that must be avoided. '

'But,' said Shabwan. 'If the 'world is flowing, as you called it, then surely the magicians will already have the same power as Lomwai.'

'Ah no...You see there was another thing that you must understand about Lomwai, and in order to do so you must first understand how *talent* works.'

Shabwan once more fought off the temptation to laugh at how Vericoos pronounced the word.

'There is one key difference between a sorcerer and a magician,' continued Vericoos, 'the magician is born with no talent, they strive endlessly until they are able to harvest a little of the worlds natural power and cast the most basic magic. Their *talent* is made completely from scratch, forged from toil and grind but will never amount to anything of real power. Sorcerers, on the other hand, are born with *talent.* They have within them, from the moment they are conscious, the ability to harvest, not some, but all of the world's natural power. The *talent* that resides within them has to be nurtured and trained but ultimately there is little that it cannot accomplish.'

Shabwan nodded, comprehension, at least of this part, was etched all over his face in the firelight.

'You've broken your talent, haven't you?'

'Yes,' replied Vericoos, 'almost beyond repair, but thankfully not quite. Perhaps ruptured would be a better word.'

'So that was why you were acting so strange when we were in Payinzee?'

'Exactly, Lomwai could have killed me very easily and...'

Vericoos stopped suddenly; he'd almost said the one thing he must not say.

'And what?' asked Shabwan.

'And our quest would have been over before it had begun.' (Good save! he congratulated himself)

Shabwan looked thoughtful.

'You could have told me.' Disappointment was painted all over Shabwan's face. Clearly the boy's mind had smoothed over the details of how he'd been behaving the week before they reached Payinzee.

'I realise now that I could have done,' lied Vericoos. 'But at the time I felt that you were afraid and on the verge of abandoning me at any moment. If I had shown my weakness then you might have fled back home and everything would have been lost.'

Shabwan looked even more disappointed, and perhaps a little angry, yes there was definitely anger there...

'I've left everything, my whole life, my friends, the girl who I love...everything. And you thought that I would just walk out and leave you?'

'I can only hope that you forgive me,' replied Vericoos, suddenly wondering if he'd understood less than he'd thought. 'Please understand that I too am weak, and our prize is so great, our aim so important, that we cannot fail. If I didn't trust you it was only because I didn't know you. I have since seen what you are made of and I promise you that my trust will not waver again.'

Shabwan still looked disgruntled, but his curiosity soon engulfed his ill feeling towards the sorcerer. He was also dimly aware that he'd just been complimented.

'So Lomwai was a really powerful magician?' he asked,

'Yes, but not solely because of the flow, that would have increased his powers but only to the level of your friend Morldron.'

Shabwan laughed, as in his minds eye he saw the image of a confused cow, suddenly soaring twenty feet into the air.

'What was different about Lomwai was that he had absorbed all the excess energy that was expelled after my little piece down by the cliffs.' Vericoos' eyes misted over but only for a second, you could have blinked and missed it. 'You see I travelled much around this area before I found you and I'm fairly certain that Lomwai and Morldron were the only two magicians within reach of the magic I performed.'

'But you said you had never been to Payinzee.' interrupted Shabwan.

'Yes but I've been almost everywhere else, and trust me, I've got a sense for these things. What happened to Lomwai was different; indeed I'm not sure it has *ever* happened before. In the past when the flow has increased, magicians have found that the slow nature of this increase has meant they could do more and more magic, yet their *talent* remains the same size. Because there is more magic pulsing out of the earth they can do that which they've always dreamed. But as I said, *normally,* this is a slow process, one which comes on gradually and therefore some of them at least, don't go mad with the power.

'What happened to Lomwai was that he had become aware of the gradual increase in his powers and had probably been trying more and more magic, gaining confidence and feeling more important. Then suddenly the energy from my spell would have hit him and he would have absorbed some of the power. By no means all,' Vericoos, looked very sternly at Shabwan as he said this. 'But still a lot more than he could ever have dreamed of possessing otherwise. '

'That's what sent him mad?' Shabwan asked.

'I believe so, he had probably always been of little status within his community, much like old Morldron and suddenly he had all this power and...well, he saw an opportunity for change'

'So as the flow increases,' said Shabwan. 'All the magicians will become like Lomwai?'

'Well we cannot say for sure,' replied Vericoos, 'but it is likely that at least some will and Payinzee will become a model for towns and cities all over the country and that's before they start fighting each other and the real trouble starts.'

'But we're going to stop it.' said Shabwan and the lack of a question mark was potent in the cooler night air. He's getting it alright, thought Vericoos.

The young man, who now knew so much more, could barely keep his eyes open. There were so many questions still to ask but only one that was important now, one that he needed to know the answer to; for if it was a yes he would drag his exhausted body off the ground climb onto his horse and ride straight back to San Hoist.

'Has Morldron become like him?'

Vericoos slowly shook his head and Shabwan felt a sense of relief, as strong as he'd ever known.

'I'm afraid that Morldron was too close to me when I cast the spell, the excess power will doubtless have killed him.'

Shabwan was too tired to feel sad; he was numb, his brain swimming with all the new information. Without saying another word to Vericoos he rolled over and fell asleep.

Chapter 3.

San Hoist again.

1.

They had decided to bury them all together. It seemed to make sense. Nine had been killed on Laffrunda night. Nine lives brought to a sudden and unexpected end all within a few seconds of each other...all but two. Morldron had been found later, everyone had assumed that he too had been slain by the three, despite the fact that his body had been found a little way along the Eastern road and all the others had lain around the wreckage of the hot food stall. And of course there was Payine, whose body had been found by his farther the following day.

Once the three had departed on their last ride, the residents of San Hoist had returned to the plaine and there they had found the bodies. Those present would never forget the scream as Anika's husband Telly had first seen his wife. He had collapsed onto her, cradling her ruined head in his arms, dry sobs racking his throat raw; it had taken them hours to persuade him to leave the body.

Of the others who had died; six had been from San Hoist, including Mrs. Creedy who had played host to Vericoos for the week leading up to the tragedy, the other three had been visitors, although all had come with family who had remained in San Hoist to bury them. The idea of travelling home with the bodies was too much to bear. As was the idea of six separate funerals; San Hoist had been rocked to its very core by events that no one could believe let alone understand, six beloved (yes even Mrs Creedy and Morldron were beloved) citizens had lost their lives and the idea of six individual ceremonies…well, it wasn't going to happen.

Four people had been hit harder than the others, for they had suffered a loss which was as incomprehensible as the arrival of the three, but as yet they seemed to have been the only ones to realise it had taken place. In the grief that followed Laffrunda, Coki, Leeham, Lewhay and Kayleigh had spent almost every minute together; the loss of Anika had hit them all hard but the further loss of Shabwan...that couldn't even be explained.

They were sitting together on the hill to the north of town, almost exactly in the same spot that Shabwan had wept just over a week before. San Hoist had remained uncharacteristically lush and green this year, despite the baking summer, but since the festival the grass had turned a dirty brown colour and the orange, clayey earth of the ploughed fields looked even uglier. From here they could still make out the dark black ring of grass that had been scorched by the flaming stall, the site of the death of a close friend and the beginning of the confrontation which had somehow robbed them of an even closer one.

Beyond San Hoist, over to the East, they could see the field, the field which looked like any other but which they all knew had done the impossible. They may have doubted that it had ever happened if it weren't for the fact that, while the fields around it had been baked an even lighter shade of orange by the hot sun, this one field was bursting at the seams with, not just grass, but all manner of flora that had never been seen in this part of the world before. This was where they looked now.

'Do you think his body is still under there?' Lewhay asked the group.

Despite the fact that they'd talked about nothing else since it had happened, this one question still hadn't been broached, but now, on the day of the funeral, it seemed only right.

'I hope so,' Kayleigh instantly replied, 'then he will have had a burial.'

In Corne, none but the richest were given a burial. Certainly no one of Shabwan's status would have ever been laid to rest below the surface of the earth. Kayleigh put her head onto Coki's shoulder and began to weep; she'd been weeping a lot. They had decided not to tell anyone about Shabwan, not yet. For one thing, with all the general fear and disbelief they did not want to frighten people more, by telling them that another San Hoister had been swallowed by a huge wave of earth which had risen out of the ground and moved like water. They would tell them when the time was right, people would probably notice his absence soon after the funeral was over, but until then the grief was theirs.

'I will never understand why he went with him,' Lewhay continued, his voice cracking and tears beginning to roll down his cheeks,' why didn't he stick with us...we always...'

He trailed out and Leeham put his arm round his shoulders. None of them understood anything that had happened that night, and they didn't think they ever would. There was only one thing that was for sure; he was gone.

They walked back into town fifteen minutes later; they didn't want to be late.

In honour of Anika's roll in the festival they had left all the Laffrunda décor as it was. Some people had claimed that it was too much of a harsh reminder of what had happened but Telly had put his foot down, saying that his wife had loved Laffrunda as much as anything and would want it to be part of her commemoration. The effect was a strange one; as among the colourful fabric, the plants also hung, they hung out of the side of their pots and down form their baskets; dried out and brown. The organic life had perished while the soul of the festival lived on. Usually this was the way of things; whether the festival would truly survive, however, was another matter.

The Plaine was packed full of people again. The stage had become a funeral alter, Harro the priest stood waiting there, in front of the stage was the pile of wood that would soon become an inferno. The bodies of the unfortunate lay on carts which were lined up in the square. Sooie was moving around them now, handing out shots of strong sour alcohol to the friends and family members who were preparing either to push the carts or to march behind them in the solemn parade. The town only had one funeral cart (normally that was enough) so others had been drafted in. It was a difficult sight to behold; the tired foundations of the festival, still blowing slightly in the uncomfortably hot summer breeze, providing the backdrop to so many tear streaked faces. Telly's intentions had been good, but the effect hadn't been; the visual element of the town served to remind them all so vividly of the tragedy that it was going to be hard to celebrate and remember those who'd been lost. Not that it ever would have been easy.

The carts of the three visitors who had died were integrated with the others, they had died as San Hoisters, even if only for the day, and the town felt strongly that there should be no segregation at the ceremony. Morldron's cart was second to last and was being pushed by Sooie, Lewyah and Coki. Leeham and Kayleigh were helping push Anika's cart further towards the front.

Coki found himself overcome with emotion as he pushed next to Telly. Anika's head had been covered with a sheet with flowers on top, her hands were folded on her chest, her husband had one hand on her shoulder and the other on the cart, his eyes never left her, tears were rolling down his face and silent sobs were shaking his burly frame. Coki could think of nothing to say to him, or to Anika's two children (only five and seven years old) who walked alongside their father holding hands, trying their best to be brave for him.

It all suddenly seemed too much; the intense grief of the whole situation coupled with the grief that was, as yet, only theirs. Yet still Coki felt glad that they hadn't said anything; somehow it was better that Shabwan's death remain completely absent, rather than his empty cart be pushed along with nothing to offer back to the earth. He's already been offered, thought Coki and tears overcame him again. In front of him he could see Kayleigh's shoulders shaking.

Eventually the entire procession entered the plaine, there had been some argument as to whether it was crass to burn the dead in the same place that the tragedy had occurred but Telly, along with many others, had argued that the plaine had been the site of such happiness for all nine that it was the most natural place to return them. Once all the carts had been pushed into position, in a circle around the unlit fire, and all the pushers had sat down, the ceremony begun. Funerals in San Hoist were very simple affairs; a song or two was sung a few words offered and then the dead would be burned, returned to nature. They were not an atheist community, some believed in the old religions and some even believed that the gods still inhabited the earth 'through the forest and over the mountains', but it was a private belief that they held, not one that was openly celebrated. Their lives were governed by nature; the way the sun and the rain treated the crops and the way the wind shaped and crafted the sea; that was what could give or take away their happiness. As nature watched over them, they in turn watched it back. They didn't necessarily believe it to be divine as such, but conscious? Most certainly. So when the time came for a San Hoister to take their longest nap, they were given back to that which had given them so much.

Kayleigh couldn't wait for it to be over. She knew that, for now at least, her thoughts should be in the plaine. This was the 'giving back' and it was highly disrespectful to not take this moment to remember the time she'd spent with Anika, They had been very close and she'd helped Kayleigh a lot when her and Shabwan had first...But her thoughts were not with Anika, they were with him.

Like Coki she still felt glad it was a secret, she didn't want him here, even though physically he wouldn't be. She didn't want him to be given back with the others, he was more important...as soon as she'd had this thought she felt disgusted with herself, like she was letting Anika down, and Payine (who she'd always liked) Gods even letting Morldron down. It was strange that they'd found his body as they'd returned to the town, they were sure they hadn't seen him on the way out but then maybe they'd missed him. They'd been in such a hurry to reach Shabwan.

The songs and speeches went on for a long time, in a San Hoistian giving back anyone who wants to has the right to stand up and speak about those they've lost. Today there were a lot of people who wanted to. While the four friends found it hard to hear people talk about Anika (Telly only managed a few words but they were enough) it was Payine's father Duri who was hardest to hear. Duri spoke with heart wrenching dignity, holding tightly onto the banister of the stage and staring directly ahead, concentrating so hard on every word, determined to say his piece for his lost boy.

Once the last word had been said it was time for the burning. The bodies were laid across the wood in a line; it was going to be a huge fire. Virtually the entire town had spent the previous day gathering wood. Harpo solemnly offered the bodies to nature and threw a burning torch onto the dry timbers.

As Coki watched the fire rise up and begin to devour the nine bodies he felt a sense of relief, once this was over he felt he could truly start grieving for his friend. They had perhaps been selfish to keep his demise to themselves, perhaps as a San Hoister and a victim of the same tragedy he should have been commemorated with the rest, even though his body could not have been. They just couldn't face it, they were still having trouble believing that it had happened and the thought of explaining it to everyone else...No doubt the others would be angry, accuse them of wanting a private ceremony for their friend, people say funny things in times of grief. And if they did, he'd kill them, he thought savagely to himself.

The flames were roaring now and the bodies were hardly visible; instead he could just make out silhouettes of bright light bearing a more human form than the timber surrounding them, it reminded him uncomfortably of how the three had looked. He dragged his mind back into the moment; he wanted to say goodbye to Morldron, to Payine and to Anika and this was his chance.

That was when it happened...

Suddenly the fire changed, the flames slowed and almost stopped. Instead of ferociously roaring up from the bone dry timbers they were now rolling lazily and silently through the air. It was beautiful, hypnotic but also terrifying. Yet, no one screamed, there was no noise at all. It had seemingly all been sucked into the fire. Nothing moved except for the flames, all eyes were fixed on the same spot. Then, finally, something else moved.

Kayleigh wondered if she'd gone mad, everything that had happened since Laffrunda must finally have got the better of her. Reality was lost and she was not sorry for it, perhaps there would be less pain this way. Then she realised that she couldn't have lost her mind, or perhaps if she had then everyone else in the plaine had too, because they were all looking at exactly the same spot: the spot where the flaming corpse of Morldron the magician was dragging his body out of the fire.

He made no sound, there was no sound.... that was, until he spoke. The voice was crystal clear, but it was a voice none of them had ever heard before. It belonged to a man called Lubwan, but we have hitherto known him as the controller. The words sailed effortlessly through the soundless vacuum in which the people of the hoist now seemed trapped, and later, when they discussed what had happened there wasn't one word of debate about what had been said.

'He is alive...if you want to find him you'll have to go through the forest and over the mountains.'

Morldron's corpse lay back down into the flames as if he were getting into bed after a hard days magic and the flames began to roar again, the sound of them rushing back into the plaine, as if it had never left. No one spoke until the fire had died down and the nine bodies were nothing but ash.

2.

They had been given hope, a slim, terrifying, incomprehensible hope, but that was all they needed. They avoided going to the pub for the wake, where the poor residents of San Hoist would be discussing this latest horrifying turn of events and trying, in vain, to celebrate those who had passed.

They would leave notes, that would be easiest, Kayleigh could leave them with her dad at the pub, he would understand and could be counted on to distribute the notes to the rest of their families: simple messages of farewell, much easier than real goodbyes, the kind of goodbyes that would stop you leaving. All they had were some ancient words, which had been delivered in a fashion which they couldn't quite believe, but this was enough. Enough that the four friends (for in the belief of Shabwan's death Kayleigh had become just as close to them as her boyfriend had) decided to leave San Hoist the following morning. Kayleigh gave the notes to her father and explained what they had to do. He cried as did she but he was also completely understanding.

He promised to give the notes to Coki, Leeham and Lewhay's mothers the next day and had supplied four horses, one of which wasn't strictly his, for the journey.

3.

They now stood on the same hill that they had sat on before the funeral, the hill where Shabwan had taken his last look at San Hoist and they now did the same. The bunting was gone; it had been taken in straight after the funeral (even before people had gone to the wake) and the town looked as it always did, although slightly uglier and drier than any of them could remember.

Coki couldn't shake the uncomfortable feeling that the soul was being baked out of the place. He looked at the plaine, once the heart of the community, a heart that was now blotted with two big cancerous burns; one from the ceremonial fire which had returned the bodies to nature and the other from the site that had made the aforementioned necessary. His eyes were then drawn, as they had been every time he'd come up here since Laffrunda, to the one field of green...To his eyes San Hoist looked dead, something he would have never dreamed but that field...

Chapter 4.

Lubwan.

1.

We used to know Lubwan as the controller but this would now be inaccurate as he no longer controls; now he lies. Having said this, he has recently done something within the realm of control that no magical person would have ever dreamed possible. Vericoos earthy wave had been one thing, this...well it had been quite another. And like the wave, it has had a massively detrimental effect on its creator. Lubwan now lies next to his rock, a rock he had sat on for so long the shape of it was permanently imprinted into his arse, he is on the brink of unconsciousness but he can't allow himself to slip into it, as inviting as it seems.

His presence has gone unnoticed here for a long time, but the magic he has just used to re animate the corpse of that lowly magician must have been felt throughout the dimensions. It was safe to say that those things which inhabited this one will have most certainly felt it. And now they will be on their way; hungry things, and he has just revealed himself to be the most scrumptious morsel they could ever have hoped for. Despite this he still smiles to himself, Vericoos and the boy must fail and he has just achieved the unthinkable and managed to intervene one last time in his old adversary's plans.

Vericoos must have thought that when that great earthy mouth slammed shut, as well as consuming his three, it had also devoured any hope of success that Lubwan had been harbouring. And what was even better was that Vericoos' *talent* was at such a tragic low that he wouldn't even have felt the shock wave that just rattled through the dimensions. Every magical person or creature, from the lowliest human magician to the gargantuan monstrosities that Lubwan could now sense closing in on him would have felt it, every single one...apart from the one it was a threat to...perfect!

Chapter 5.

Explanations.

1.

The next day, they had to travel in silence again as Vericoos still wasn't strong enough to speak and walk simultaneously. He wasn't sure, however, that he'd have spoken even if he could have done. It was immensely gratifying to see the hunger on young Shabwan's face. The incessant desire for more knowledge was etched all over his oddly handsome features and this, for Vericoos, was good news indeed. The longer he left it the more curious the boy would become and, when the time came, it would be easier to make him believe.

For it was immensely important that the boy believed *everything* Vericoos told him; it would be crucial later on. Vericoos knew that there was no way that he could prolong his tale beyond that night, if he tried, Shabwan might kill him. The boy wanted nothing more than to hear what was in store for him. Indeed it now seemed as if he thought of little else.

The road changed little, it remained straight dusty and wide, slightly raised from the surrounding fields and due to the flat nature of the terrain you could see for miles around. Not that there was that much to see; dry farmland and isolated wooden dwellings, until...

'Hey, I can see them.' Shabwan shouted.

He was correct. You could, if you squinted very hard through the heat haze, make out the deep grey of the mountains and if you looked even harder, you could make out the lush green band of the forest, hugging their roots. They were well on their way now, given two more days Vericoos reckoned he would be able to ride and once they were on horseback the forest couldn't be more than a few days ride away. He looked at Shabwan and smiled, the hungry glint was omnipresent in the boy's eyes, as it had been all day. He knew that his companion was counting down the seconds until the sun would set and Vericoos would call them to a halt, then the tale would finally begin.

2.

The seconds did eventually decrease in number all the way down to the littlest one and then the one that is nothing at all, although Shabwan had almost stopped believing that they ever would. The sun had been creeping so slowly across the sky that he had feared it might stop. Fortunately it had continued its smooth arc and had reached the inevitable climax of its journey (although, of course, it didn't see it this way). They would not see it again until the morning and by then Shabwan would know so much more. Although the truth of what he would know would be another matter entirely.

It took an intolerable amount of time for him to find a rabbit. Every other evening his hunt had lead to the demise of one of the little creatures within minutes. They seemed to dwell near to the road for some reason. Surely they must have known this was a bad idea, they can't all be as stupid as they look. Shabwan laughed at his own train of thought; he wasn't really angry at the rabbits, in truth it was highly beneficial, that they lived in close proximity to the road. He was just venting his frustration anywhere he could; it had been a very frustrating day.

Eventually he saw two ears poking out of a small bush a bit further along. He picked up a rock and threw it at the rabbit. The rock seemed to dip unnaturally, like some unseen force dragged it towards Shabwan’s prey. It did the job though, the little creature moved no more and soon found itself being sprinkled with the contents of Vericoos little neck bag. Had it still been alive and somehow survived the further problems associated with being cooked and eaten it would have heard a story. A story told, like so many, by an old man to a boy...or perhaps a young man (it depended what mood Vericoos was in and if the narrator felt like he was using one word too much). The story took some time to tell, indeed by the time it had finished the rabbit had almost been completely digested, something which would have no doubt ruined its enjoyment of the tale even if, miraculously, all of the other misfortunes that had become it that evening hadn't.

While the old man told the story, the flames of their small fire sent shadows dancing across his face. Shabwan watched transfixed, for the first time since they had left San Hoist the old man's eyes had returned to their former encapsulating glory. His story went like this...

3.

When Vericoos and Lubwan were Shabwan's age they, like so many who end up as mortal enemies, had been friends. They met while attending the great academy of sorcery in the city of Durpo, a city which lay wrapped around the huge bay of Franko to the east of the mountains which separated Corne form the rest of Svin.

It was an amazing place, one where Vericoos and Lubwan, who had both been born and raised in the country, had always dreamed of going ever since they were small. In the normal run of things neither would ever have been discovered, there were many who had the *talent* who lived too far away from the cities and never stood a chance of making it to either of the great magical academies; Durpo or Hardram. For these two however, it had been different. It had been one of the things which first brought them together.

They had both lived on farms, Vericoos to the East, near to the border and Lubwan to the much colder North. Their early years had followed similar patterns of frustration and under appreciation. Both had realised from an early age that they were special; they had abilities, they had *talent* (although neither of them had known to call it that), but they had only been able to put these gifts to use within the realm of agriculture. Not the greatest arena for such things, I’m sure you agree. It had, however, been a tremendous help for their parents, who could now sit back and watch their eight year old son plough a field with a wave of their arm or summon the entire herd of cows into the milking parlour with a click of their finger, but for the two young boys, who would later become sorcerers, it was nowhere near enough.

4.

Until Vericoos was twelve, he spent year after boring year helping his parents on the farm, dreaming of the day he would be able to leave his small village and find a place where he would find others like him, people who could train him to be better. He heard stories, from the very few traders who passed through their village, of the city of Duro; a huge marble city, full of shining towers and winding cobbled streets, a city which overlooked a pristine bay where the water was crystal clear, a city of magic.

Vericoos parents were a selfish pair. Their son was far too useful on the farm and about the house to let him leave and pursue some hedonistic dream. His place was there and as long as it was, they could just keep on getting fatter and richer. Unfortunately for Vericoos his untrained command of magic had therefore been limited to the superficial; lifting crops out of the ground was infinitely easier than the sphere of influence, and therefore the young Vericoos could do nothing to change his parent's minds.

Luckily for him his talents had not gone unnoticed by others. It was true that few traders passed through the quiet village, but those who had, had often left with more than just grain and potatoes; they had left with tales of a young boy with power the likes of which they'd never seen. Now, people are not often prone to believing such ale-house tales; that is not until they are relayed over and over again, and soon people from the surrounding, larger towns began to take an interest in this young boy and what he could do.

One night, a travelling sorcerer by the name of Sonkai (Vericoos eyes misted over slightly as he said the name) had come to the town of Clax, only thirty miles away from Vericoos' village. Seeing a sorcerer so far away from the cities was quite a treat and that night, Sonkai was surrounded in the Farmer's arms pub, by a huge group of locals, virtually clamouring over each other to ask questions and get a better view of the story-telling sorcerer. After many a drink had been recycled through tired and abused old livers it was time for the locals to offer a story of their own.

They spoke of a young boy, a simple farming lad in one of the villages, who, according to all who had seen him, had enormous power; a boy only twelve years of age. Sonkai's initial reaction had been one of indifference. He was no doubt hearing the same kind of folklore you heard whenever you travelled to the more out-of-touch areas of Svin, but he was a polite fellow and listened with feigned interest.

That was until he heard something which changed everything.

'He can summon cows?' He asked. 'How exactly does he do this?'

The man who'd been telling the story suddenly looked a little bit frightened and a lot more sober; he didn't want to get any of the details wrong.

'Erm...well they say, I mean I've never seen it myself of course, but they say he...just clicks his fingers.'

Sonkai had retired to bed shortly after that. He'd heard enough to arouse his interest. A lot of magic could be achieved simply with a wave of the arm or movement of the finger, but, for reasons they weren't quite sure of, magic involving animals usually required some audible form. Like the click of one's fingers for example. Before leaving the next day he acquired the necessary information from the barman.

Vericoos would never forget seeing Sonkai arrive. He had never seen another person of magical quality before, yet as soon as the tubby sorcerer set foot in his parent's cottage he'd known that he was, for the first time, meeting one of his own. Sonkai had wanted to be introduced to Vericoos, but his parents had been unwilling; Vericoos had watched with fascination through the crack in his bedroom door as his parents demanded to know what possible business this stranger could have with their son. Vericoos supposed now that they too had realised Sonkai's intentions very quickly. Eventually Vericoos had been able to bear it no more and had emerged from his tiny bedroom.

He always remembered how Sonkai looked at him the first time he saw him, it was a look he'd never seen directed in his direction before; a look of respect.

5.

After introductions had been reluctantly made, Sonkai asked if Vericoos would perhaps like to show him what he could do. Vericoos' parent's initial forthright protests had now become barely audible mumbles; they had sensed the inevitability of what was coming. The three adults and one small boy then went out the back of the little farm cottage, onto the little wooden balcony which overlooked the surrounding farmland. Sonkai had smiled encouragingly at Vericoos, who for the first time in his life had started to feel extremely nervous; this might be his one chance to escape, to fulfil his destiny.

Literally everything was at stake.

As he waved his arm in a smooth arc and felt the warm tingling sensation, effervescent in his bloodstream, he prayed silently to himself that it would be enough. As the grain that lay before them rose up in a cloud and began to dance and swirl like a flock of birds, Vericoos concentrated all the energy he could muster as the grain made impossible patterns and mimicked the shapes of the clouds in the sky. He focussed every last particle of his brain and he held it for as long as possible. As the grain flitted back to its original housing he staggered and only just kept his footing. It was the strongest, most exhausting spell he had ever cast and now it was over, he couldn't bring himself to raise his eyes; because raising his eyes would mean meeting those of his judge. For his parents, he cared not, he had long ago realised that they had never wanted him to realise his true potential; a selfish act for which he would never forgive them. But for the squat newcomer who stood to their left...for him Vericoos felt everything, this was the one man who could save him from his mediocre existence, the one man who could pluck him from the cesspool and deliver him to his rightful place.

When he had, after what had seemed to his young mind more time than the world had any right to posses, plucked up the courage to look up, his fears had all been alleviated, for the expression he saw on the sorcerer's face was not one of disappointment, it wasn't even one of pleasant surprise, it was one of awe.

6.

There had been more arguing once they were back in the kitchen. Vericoos' mother, suddenly confronted with the reality of losing her son, had seemingly found a maternal side to her nature which had hitherto been absent. His father, who had always been more business minded, now saw a future where manual labour was once more a prominent part of his existence. Vericoos had hated them so much at that moment, he had never felt wanted or needed beyond his superficial uses in that house, and while he had never really craved affection from either parent, he had always been aware of its absence. Now they were about to lose him they were suddenly the perfect family unit, one that believed it was about to be torn apart by an uninvited and invading presence.

Luckily for Vericoos not only was Sonkai a skilled diplomat he was also good at reading what people wanted from life, and despite the wailing and the protests, they left the next morning; the 'distraught' mother and father mopping up their tears with the cloth of the bag of gold which Sonkai had left them (two days later this gold evaporated into thin air). Sonkai had offered no words of comfort to Vericoos as he had known that none were needed. He was a moral man and would never have removed a child from a loving family; but both sorcerers who left that small farming village that day, knew, with absolute clarity, that this wasn't what had happened.

In fact Vericoos would soon, for the first time in his life, join his true family.

The journey to Durpo had been one filled with stories; every night Vericoos would sit and listen, his keen eyes wide, as Sonkai told him tales of sorcery. Before Vericoos had even arrived at the capital, he learned much of the order of which he was soon to join; he learned how there was a huge distinction between lowly magicians and people like himself, people who had the *talent,* he also learned that when he arrived in Durpo his dreams were all to come true as he would attend the world's best magical academy, where he could hone his craft.

Every day seemed like a year to the young Vericoos and while he loved the time he spent with his old travelling companion, he could not wait to lay his eyes on the tottering spires of Durpo. He felt like he could see it already, felt like he could taste the enriched magical air that rose up out of the clear waters of the bay. Eventually, after almost a month on the road they had come over the top of a long slow incline and he had seen it for the first time...Durpo; the place that would be his home for all those years, until he was forced below. The place of his monumental rise to power, but not the place of his fall. The rickety shacks and cobbled streets of the outskirts gently rose into higher and higher buildings until, once you reached the area near the seafront, the towers began to rise up like great golden fingers reaching up towards the sun.

Three of those towers belonged to the academy of magic and it was there that Vericoos and Lubwan first met, as terrified new room mates about to commence their education. They had clicked instantly. Both had come from backgrounds where they'd been unappreciated, and both felt equally lucky to have been discovered. They soon found themselves top of all of their classes, continually wowing their tutors and driving each other into more and more challenging experiments, sometimes with near disastrous consequences. They graduated five years later, life was good, no, life was great.

But then the god had come.

7.

At this point in the story Shabwan's eyes widened; this was the piece he truly wanted to know and yet, at the mention of the word God, some small part of him seemed to shrink into a childlike state.

'You see,' said Vericoos, 'We all knew that the Gods existed, it hadn't been that long since they had departed the mortal realm. Some three thousand, or so, years before my birth, the Earth had still been their favoured residence and its inhabitants had been little more than slaves, that was in the time before Krunk of course.'

Shabwan looked blank, but Vericoos continued anyway.

'We knew that they existed and that it hadn't been that pleasant to have them around, we didn't know which dimensions they now resided in but we were happy that it wasn't ours. For one thing Gods despise magic...that is, at least, most gods.'

'Not the one who came down though?' Said Shabwan.

'No,' replied Vericoos slowly, 'not him.'

He seemed lost in thought for some time. Then he continued...

8.

The God came down on a Tuesday and he told them to call him Veo. He killed a few people that day; a number that they would eventually come to regard as low. He never explained why he'd come but they all knew what he planned to do...he planned to take control.

They all knew the legends of the time before Krunk; the time when the Gods had strode about the earth, using their human minions to fight their wars and to cater to their every need. Clearly the newcomer wanted to reinstate these old customs, although he planned to have an even better time of it than the Gods of old because, while there were many of them, he was going to be unique. No troubling wars or competition from other divine beings, instead just one ruler of all.

What he hadn't realised, and what was a hugely unpleasant surprise for him, was that the old Gods had lived on the earth during a period when there had been no mortal magic, and consequently he, unlike them, was fought. The sorcerers battled hard with Veo; it was a long and gruelling fight in which many, many lives were lost.

9.

Vericoos looked at Shabwan, who was still gazing back at him, enraptured.

'To tell you everything that happened in those years would take more time than we have, believe me. It is enough to say that they were hard and filled with tragedy; every time we would drive Veo away he would come back with new and more terrible foes, it seemed his obsession was with Durpo, it was the only place he wanted to control, but eventually he gave up and turned his attentions instead to Hardram...When he did, Lubwan stood at his side.'

Shabwan gasped out loud, he couldn't stop himself.

'My old friend decided to ally himself with our greatest enemy and together they took the city of Hardram killing so many sorcerers in the process that we were unsure even of the total number, but the effects were clear...the world was split. Hardram became a city of slaves, a terrible place where Veo and Lubwan ruled together. Durpo was ours, at least for the time being, we knew it would not be long until they came for us once more. Luckily, however, fate was on our side.'

'How could he turn against you? How could he do that?'

Shabwan was looking shocked as if he himself had been the one to be betrayed. Vericoos sighed.

'Power does strange things to people.'

This seemed to be all he was willing to say and he was silent for a long while as if absorbed in painful memories. He didn't speak for so long that Shabwan feared he had forgotten he was there.

'So you were saying about fate?' he prompted.

'Ah yes,' replied Vericoos, slowly returning to the moment.' Chance and circumstance conspired together and I'm doubtless that if they hadn't then you would not have lived your life as a free man; Veo would still be in power today.'

'But doesn't that mean that once we get over the mountains we'll be in his lands?' asked Shabwan.

Vericoos laughed, surprised at the division the mountains provided in the boys mind; as if they could hold back a God.

'No, no Shabwan. If Veo had remained at large then he would have taken Corne like he would have taken the rest of Svin. I met him on a couple of occasions in non violent circumstances, and believe me, no amount of power would ever have been enough for him. If he were in control just over those mountains, then he would be in control everywhere and you would be a slave.'

'So what happened then, if he's not over there then why do I have to kill him?'

The old sorcerer closed his eyes, as if summoning his full concentration, and then continued his tale.

10.

They had enjoyed a few conflict-free months in Durpo, but where there had been the chaos of battle now there was a tense, uneasy stillness. No one trusted this new period of calm, and while they had heard no word from Hardram for some time, they all knew what was going on there. Veo and Lubwan were building an army; one which would finally be able to take Durpo. Vericoos was, by this stage, the most senior sorcerer in the city and was therefore in charge of its defence.

He was less than optimistic about their chances; so far their victories had all come about from Veo's lack of understanding of magic. While the God's had their own divine power, it seemed that mortal magic remained something of a mystery to them. Perhaps this was why the old Gods had left when the kingdom of Krunk, the world's first great magical empire, had risen up.

Veo had attacked them in a dozen different ways, but each time they'd been able to drive him back and the reason for this, Vericoos knew just as well as any of the other remaining sorcerers, was that they'd continually taken him by surprise. Clearly, he was a vain being, and hadn't imagined that mortal power would be any match for his command of the elements, the earth and the beasts which lived upon it. Yet, each and every time he had found himself defeated. Driven back by powers he could not understand.

The next attack would be different, however. They were all sure of that.

With Lubwan by his side the God Veo would march out of the city of Hardram with his command of nature and his human slave army ready to deploy. He would march on Durpo and, unlike before, he would have a complete understanding of what he would come up against once he arrived. Not only would his second in command have told him what the sorcerers would use against him and how to defeat it, he would also be adding his own rather impressive arsenal to the attack.

This was what truly made Vericoos' blood run cold. Throughout the battles with Veo Lubwan had stood by his side, their equally overwhelming power had caused Veo's anger and frustration to bend the very ground on which the city lay time and time again, yet he could never win, or truly hurt the city, as they stood together.

Now they must fight.

Vericoos and Lubwan. There had been little to choose between them throughout their lives. Both had been awesomely powerful and had, against all the odds, come to graduate as the two most impressive students in living memory. Their fame spread well out of the cities, winding its way along little country roads and warming the ears of the patrons of quiet little inns up and down Svin. Now only one path lay ahead of them and if Vericoos couldn't stop Lubwan then the world would look very different indeed. Freedom would be a word only uttered, a memory fast becoming a dream.

11.

'But you did stop them, didn't you?' asked Shabwan.

He had been doing his level best not to interrupt but now found himself so tense and excited that he could control his mouth no longer. Vericoos looked a little annoyed; he was clearly, among all his other talents, a master of crafting a story and didn't feel that this had been the right time for his young companion to halt his flow.

'Yes I stopped them; I sent them both to places that neither of them could have imagined. The problem was that I had to send myself to one of them also.'

Shabwan, despite his annoying interruptions, was a fine one man audience. Vericoos was enjoying the way his sometimes-simple face was switching between, brilliant enrapture and gormless incomprehension. The latter of these now dropped back into view, leaving Shabwan's jaw slightly open. Vericoos looked into the fire again...

They had shared much through their young lives. That was the simple fact to which the earth owed its current state of liberation. Lubwan and Vericoos had experimented with so many different levels of sorcery that the bond of thought, which so often forms between magical companions, had become a permanent fixture. As friends they had liked it. They had never heard, even in the great legends of Krunk, of another magical pair who had had constant access to each others thoughts. They could communicate instantly with each other wherever they were, something which they had put to the test when either of the pair had been taken off on long ventures with their tutors.

That was how Vericoos realised that Lubwan was about to betray them...betray him. His old friend, his best friend suddenly, for the first time since they'd established it, shut down the connection. There had been many times, during their relationship that they had kept the contact to a minimum; when you were enjoying a nice evening with a young lady, for example, (Shabwan balked as Vericoos said this and was amazed to see a hint of red in the old man's cheeks-could he really be embarrassed) the last thing you wanted was your best friend inside your head. But even in these periods, when you would literally have had to force yourself into the others mind to hear or be heard, there was still something there. A little flicker which could, with a moment of mutual will, be opened up into a gaping chasm, through which all could be immediately shared. As was so often the case with magic it was the potential that you felt so potently, not necessarily the effects.

Vericoos would always remember that moment, the moment when he lost the person to whom he'd been closest. He had been walking along the city wall, pondering the best course of action in the wake of new information about Veo's actions, when the connection was suddenly shut. For a moment Vericoos stood there unable to move. Something which had been omnipresent in his mind for so long was just...gone and there could only be one reason why.

He tried with all his considerable might to drill open just the smallest gap so he could talk to his friend. So he could try and find some evidence which would tell him that, which he now knew must have happened, could not be true. Four days later a messenger, half dead, arrived at the gates of Durpo. He spoke little before he died but he told them enough. Lubwan and Veo had taken Hardram; the sorcerers had fought valiantly but ultimately it had been in vain. The combined might of the God and the Sorcerer had been terrible to behold.

'Terrible yet...beautiful...' Had been the last thing the messenger had contributed in this realm.

For days they had waited, scouts were sent out to the area surrounding Hardram, but none returned; in fact no traffic at all reached Durpo. It was as if all of Svin was under a deadly and silent siege; everyone was hiding from a foe many of them had never seen. Cut off from the rest of the world and with no news of Hardram, Vericoos had only one option; to prepare for battle. Any magician, however lowly, was given a crash course in dangerous offensive magic. The able bodied citizens of Durpo, men and women alike, were trained for combat. The walls were constantly manned and everyone remained constantly within them. The preparations went well and Vericoos had every faith that his people, for that was how he now had to think of them, were ready for a battle.

All of this: the preparations, the training, the willingness to spill blood (magical or otherwise) was the only way forward now for the people of Durpo, to use an old and tired metaphor it was their path. But this path...well, who knew if the old legends had any truth in them or not, but if they did...if they did then they were risking bringing the same terrible fate that the people of Krunk had suffered down upon their heads. This thought more than the others had kept Vericoos awake during the short periods of time he allowed himself for rest. For Vericoos knew that when the inevitable fight came to the walls, they would be risking precisely what some referred to as 'the end of the old world.' When so much magic concentrates in a small area, especially when so much of that magic has come from *talentless* sources...Well, no one knew what would happen and even fewer people wanted to find out.

If someone had told him a few months ago that he would ever risk this situation, Vericoos would have laughed heartily, opening up his mind so that Lubwan too could enjoy the ridiculousness of the suggestion. Now it was their only choice, if they didn't fight then their fate would be worse than that which the legends claim, became the people of Krunk. It depended what legends you believed of course, some of them claimed that a great battle, just like the one they were now facing had escalated, exploded outwards killing all who were there. Others, darker legends, claimed that the people had not died...they had been taken with the magic, when it had left. But taken where? Nobody knew. They all just gave the same dark look as they finished their tale, as if to say, 'its better that we don't know.'

All Vericoos knew was that the world of Krunk, the first great magical empire had definitely gone somewhere, they didn't just all get bored and wonder off, dissolving into dust as they went and conveniently leaving behind no trace whatsoever of the entire empire. No one knew what had happened for sure, but as the battle loomed there was a nasty feel of histories patient repetition in the air.

12.

It had been too long.

Those were the words most commonly spoken around the city, as people glanced nervously over the reinforced walls, as they scurried about the streets, too nervous to discuss anything but the impending. They had been waiting weeks. What on earth were Veo and Lubwan doing in Hardram? They couldn't possibly be waiting for Vericoos to bring the fight to them. Veo was too hungry, he had always wanted Durpo and had only settled for Hardram after it had become clear, even to his gargantuan ego, that he wasn't yet ready to take it. That was another thing that Vericoos had spent a long time wondering about; why, when Lubwan and Veo had originally formed their allegiance, had they not just claimed the prize that had been so long evading divine capture? It seemed curious that, when Veo had finally acquired the weapon he had needed, instead of exploiting the element of surprise, he had instead set off to capture a city he had hitherto shown no interest in. Vericoos had a few theories on the matter each as unlikely as the next.

He knew that when he laid eyes upon his new adversary, he would have to instantly fight for the kill, any hesitation against an enemy as powerful as Lubwan would be foolish indeed. Yet he wondered still, if he might get just the smallest of chances to speak with him, it was a ridiculous idea and a dangerous one. But there were so many unanswered questions. So much that he didn't and could never possibly understand, that he still entertained it none the less.

It was that night when he was lying in bed when it had happened. Vericoos hadn't slept in weeks but had been lying there staring at the same patch of ceiling he always did, when the connection, *the connection*, the one which he believed had been closed for ever was rammed open with a greater force than he'd ever previously experienced.

13.

'He spoke to you again?'

'No he did not. In fact, I believed he had no intention of opening that channel at all and it was in doing so that he gave me the one chance that I needed to destroy them both.'

The first light blue fingers of dawn had begun to clasp weakly onto the horizon, the sun had finished providing it's illumination to the stories of others and was almost ready to return to ours. Yet there was no sign of tiredness on the boys face.

'You see, what I saw, when the connection was reopened was a huge misinterpretation, not only did I misinterpret it myself, I was also unaware that the two I saw were also in the process of a great misinterpretation.' Shabwan blinked at Vericoos; *now* he looked tired. It seemed that while he still yearned for more, the patches he didn't understand, which Vericoos loved to weave into the tale, were beginning to take it out of him. 'Not one of us correctly guessed what was about to happen, it was only by the strangest of chances, and one that I still do not really understand, that things went my way.'

'What did you see?' asked Shabwan, as the first true sunlight of the day caught his face.

14.

They had always heard stories about the knife of the three. Every young sorcerer was told them and then told to ignore them. Such was the contradictory nature of a magical education. Vericoos had supposed that the tutors had believed that one day the young students would hear the stories from some other source and set off on a ridiculous quest to find the thing. Vericoos had never been much interested in it; he liked magic you could conduct with your bare hands, he was powerful enough and certainly didn't need implements to assist with his sorcery.

Still you couldn't live in the magical world without at least sometimes thinking about the knife. There were different stories but they all told roughly the same tale. One that started with a huge hole ('this,' Vericoos told Shabwan, 'should have been all the warning Lubwan needed. Never trust a story that starts off by trying to fill an unfillable hole.') The fact was that no one knew why, when Krunk had been such an epically powerful magical empire, none of its artefacts had survived. Certainly, there were ruins, and a few old pieces of literature that people claimed were from that time, but as far as magical implements went, there was nothing.

Even though Krunk had fallen an estimated two and a half thousand years before, it still seemed strange that nothing had survived. Especially because the relatively new school of thought on the subject believed it was exceptionally hard to destroy something which had been enchanted. Could time alone be accredited? Perhaps, but it was difficult to imagine, when you saw the keen edge of a magical blade or the beauty of an old cauldron, that such a thing would ever wither and expire. Even after the magic had left, surely the steel and wooden vessels which had once held its enchantment would have been preserved maybe not perfectly but surely at least somehow. It just made no sense that there was nothing...

15.

'I myself never gave it much thought,' said Vericoos, 'it seemed strange that such an empire as Krunk would have left nothing behind. No swords, staffs, armour anything. But what did it matter? The way I saw it we were on our way to building a new empire, one that could be greater than the one which people spent so much time hypothesizing about. Who cared why Krunk had left us nothing, when we could create it ourselves?'

Vericoos seemed to be getting angry, and Shabwan saw, just for a moment, a ghost of the young man; still idealistic and hopeful, yet full of frustration. He saw a young, forward thinking, Vericoos and found it easy to imagine, how one of the greatest young sorcerers of that age had hated the way in which people seemed more interested in looking back and speculating about that which they could never know, rather than developing and improving what they had.

'The only thing that interested the kind of people that told these stories more that what had happened to the magical flotsam and jetsam of Krunk, was the one piece that was supposed to have survived.'

Shabwan's belly grumbled loudly, and he glanced down at it as if to reprimand it for the interruption.

'There was supposedly one knife, a fairly simple thing, an instrument of subdivision. Do you know what that is?'

'You know I don't?' replied Shabwan, reminding Vericoos of how difficult it was to know who you were addressing when you spoke to this young man. While he was capable of showing all kinds of stupidity, he became mightily offended if you made any kind of assumption about his intelligence.

'Of course, I apologise,' replied Vericoos, looking amused. 'Subdivision is a very superficial branch of magic; while it is indeed possible to multiply yourself into replicas, your mind will always remain in one. It would be, as you will soon learn, catastrophic to divide the mind in such a way.'

'So you can make more of yourself, but only one of you controls them.' asked Shabwan, his eyes wide and glinting in the morning sun.

'Sounds interesting doesn't it?' replied Vericoos,' well believe me it isn't. The mindless entities which you bring into existence have such low intelligence and ability to function that if you actually sought to do anything useful with them you would find them much greater hindrance than help.'

Shabwan laughed, he'd suddenly been visited by an image of the Vericoos he knew, the brilliant keen-eyed one, barking orders at two dull-eyed and clumsy Vericoos' who were attempting some kind of menial task. He saw what the old man meant; there were much more efficient ways of getting things done. Although he added to himself; stupid useless expendable replicas would be great when Pari fishing. Although he doubted Coki would ever give up such a golden opportunity to put himself in mortal danger. For the first time that night (or day, as it was now) he'd temporarily lost his interest in Vericoos' tale, what made this even stranger was that he sensed that they were just getting to the most important part. He must be exhausted but he couldn't feel it, he looked up into his companion's eyes, hoping he looked apologetic and willed him to continue.

16.

There had been times when he and Lubwan had laughed about the knife; it didn't even sound that good to them. Those who believed were convinced that the knife had been the most powerful instrument to come out of Krunk and it had been this which had ensured its survival. Matthias, who'd shared a room with the two sorcerers in the academy, had been one such believer which had annoyed both Vericoos and Lubwan...

'You had another room mate?' asked Shabwan, he was surprised to feel an instant kinship with this unknown Matthias character, but almost immediately realised that it made perfect sense; it must have been hard for anyone to live with the two greatest students of the age, a massively amplified version of how he'd felt growing up with three friends who were always slightly better than him at...well, pretty much everything.

'Yes Matthias, he was one of the many who lost their lives in those conflicts...'

Shabwan was silent, the memory of his friends, which had been so absent of late suddenly seemed stronger than ever.

'Anyway, Matthias, like so many others, believed in the knife's existence and believed also that it had the power to do what no sorcerer ever had, to induce complete subdivision.'

'You mean, to divide yourself, properly...with your mind and everything?'

'Yes, they believed that whosoever plunged it into their heart would split, not into one controller and however many brainless replicas, but instead...'

'Into three prefect replicas?' interrupted Shabwan.

'Yes' replied Vericoos, eyeing Shabwan curiously. 'Into three.'

17.

That was the biggest shock of all once the connection reopened. Much worse than to finally have complete confirmation that his friend was indeed in allegiance with the God Veo, was the realisation that they had this knife, this legendary knife, and the Lubwan actually believed it was going to work.

They were stood in the great hall of Hardram which was empty apart from the two of them, it was a vast space but together they still seemed to fill it. The discussion was of their impending victory.

'I will use it here and then we will march. If there is any thought of desertion or disobedience still alive in my forces I will quash it with my sudden, ah... shall we say, omnipotence.'

They laughed together and then Lubwan asked:

'How many, divisions will you make?'

'I think just three for now, enough to excite and terrify our, ah, followers.'

More harsh laughter. Why had Lubwan not realised that the connection was open again? None of it made one grain of sense, then to Vericoos' absolute horror Veo took the knife and muttered, 'It's time.'

18.

He acted without a moments thought. He had never believed in the knife, not for a moment. But he had seen and felt Lubwan's thoughts all too clearly and he knew one thing for certain: Lubwan believed in the knife. His respect for the power and wisdom of his new adversary was enough that he went against his better judgment. If the knife worked then the battle for Durpo would not be a battle, it would be a massacre... Before he even realised what he was doing he was in the air, flying faster than a speeding arrow, the air around him twisted and melted, suddenly full of colour.

19.

Vericoos paused for a moment and looked at Shabwan.

'Will you hear what happened when I reached the great hall?'

The question surprised Shabwan; why would he have listened to all the rest and then not wanted to hear the end? Why would anyone not want to know the end?

'Because Shabwan, what I'm about to tell you is the most important part of all. It's really the part where you come in to the tale and I need you to understand every last word.'

Shabwan could feel tiredness creeping over him, lulling him into a blissful sleep on the uncomfortable dusty ground. He drove it away, all the comfort in the world wasn't worth missing this.

'Tell me,' he said, and Vericoos did...

20.

It had taken so little time for him to reach Hadram that, as he smashed through the doors of the great hall, Veo hadn't even begun to raise the knife. Vericoos landed on his feet, skidded and stopped just short of the God.

'Ah wonderful,' cried he. 'Our guest has arrived.'

Vericoos thrust his hand outwards, palm facing towards Veo, intending to force the knife out of his hand and, if luck served, smash it into a billion pieces against the far wall. Before he could launch the spell, however, a force, like a tidal wave, smashed into his left; flinging him across the room like a rag doll. He crumpled in a heap on the floor, stunned and winded.

'Welcome Vericoos.' called Lubwan and another huge wave of power drove him against the wall again.

He was done for and he knew it, Lubwan had all but killed him, and as he lay there fighting unconsciousness, another horrible realisation began to dawn on him.

'Did you think that I'd opened up that channel accidentally?' Lubwan's tone was mocking and it seemed to be coming from somewhere far away.

'Who would have thought it?' Lubwan was addressing Veo now. 'The greatest sorcerer of our age fell for our simple little trap.'

Vericoos sat up and rubbed his eyes, his vision became clear again and the throbbing in his head eased off a little. Veo was standing about twenty feet away, his emerald green robe dancing around him; above it sat the expressionless wooden mask which Veo always wore. Vericoos had never understood the mask; the rest of Veo's image was all colour and shine; silver and white bangles jostling for position on his muscular arms, a cloak which seemed to be able to take on any colour it wanted, a dazzling silver breastplate and then...just a simple piece of wood with expressionless features carved into it.

'Yes, I did expect rather more of you Vericoos,' said the rolling deep voice from under the placid wooden mouth. 'I believed you wouldn't be tricked so easily, but Lubwan here assured me that you would come, and now look...you have!'

As Veo shouted this Vericoos felt a new force lift him and throw him across the room; no wonder we've been able to defeat him thought Vericoos as he crashed to the ground, our abilities are infinitely different. The force, which Veo had just flung him across the room with, was cold and hard, like being picked up and thrown by a huge metal trowel, had he not already been wounded it wouldn't have even moved him. The force Lubwan had flung him against the wall with was quite different...so much more beautiful, why had the man, who he thought he had known and understood, allied himself with this hateful form of energy?

Lubwan advanced again, his powerful muscular frame shaking, perhaps with excitement or maybe with pure rage. Vericoos recognised nothing about him.

'Wait!' called Veo, 'I want him to see it happen, I want him to see the three who will tear apart his precious city. Once he's seen you may do with him what you like.'

Vericoos couldn't tear his eyes away. Through the pain he rose to his feet, and for a moment and for the last ever time, he and Lubwan stood shoulder to shoulder, watching as Veo slowly but purposely sunk the dagger into his heart.

21.

Everything went quiet...Vericoos hadn't realised, in the chaos of his arrival, that there was a monumental noise coming from outside the great hall. It sounded as if the entire population of Hardram was getting ready for war, sounded like they were damn excited about it too. Then it stopped. Vericoos and Lubwan ceased, just for a moment to be aware of each other. Both of their attentions were focussed wholly and completely on Veo.

22.

The God was kneeling on the ground, one arm pressed on the floor supporting his weight and the other pressed into his chest where his hand was still clasped around the hilt of the dagger. The wooden block which sat atop his face was pointed at the floor; in that moment he could have just been another soldier who'd received a fatal wound, slowly getting ready to continue his journey. Then the noise returned with such vigour that Vericoos was surprised it didn't blow the tall stained glass windows in. He could hear men and women screaming and banging, horrible, primal guttural sounds. Hardram was no longer anything more than an extension of the being which knelt before the two sorcerers. The screaming citizens were not expressing their own emotions but those of their master. Like a vicious herd of animals they roared together, Vericoos could see none of them, but the fires out in the street were casting terrible shadows over the walls of the hall; people doing inhuman things, terrible things...

Then, with a small but very audible popping sound, one Veo became three. Vericoos would have thought that the pandemonium coming from outside the windows and the broken doors of the hall could get no worse but sure enough it did. Surely humans could not make noises like that. The three Veo's stood up and Vericoos knew then that it was all over. The stories of the blade had been true; the God had perfectly sub divided and could do so as much as he wished. Durpo and all of Svin were doomed. Vericoos tuned to look at Lubwan; he wanted one last look at his friend before the end, maybe in that one look he would be able to see why he'd done this, what had driven him to this ultimate act of destructive madness. As his eyes met Lubwan's he didn't really know what he expected to see, triumph perhaps...certainly not terror.

'My...my lord.' Lubwan's voice was weak and uneasy.

'Reeeeeeeeeeeeeeeeeeeeee! Hahahahahah!' The voice, no the voices, which came from the Veo, were indistinguishable from the threatening baritone Vericoos had heard just a few minutes ago.

Then the three Veo's began to spin and dance, the noises outside the hall, which before had been unified in their nature, now sounded shambolic; the horrible screams were still there but they were joined by laughter and even song it seemed. Before it had sounded like a huge flock were driving their noise against the hall in unison, now it sounded equally big but...different, weaker perhaps.

'Loooooooooooooooobwan!' One of the Veo's shouted this then fell over, he began laughing manically but soon the laughter became cries and then childlike sobs. Vericoos knew he should act, Lubwan was distracted and Veo had seemingly been massively weakened by what had happened. He should strike now, but...he couldn't. What was happening before his eyes was transfixing him. One Veo was now weeping and rolling from side to side, one was laughing manically, the other...He sensed his fellow sorcerer's actions just in time and managed to shield himself from Lubwan's attack. They did battle, raging from one end of the hall to the other, deadly flashes of light illuminating their shadows against the vast walls of the hall. Neither seemed to be able to get the upper hand until suddenly and without warning, one of Vericoos' attacks smashed into Lubwan's side, spinning him round a full three hundred and sixty degrees before he slumped to the floor.

Vericoos wasted no time, his desire to understand Lubwan's actions was gone. He could see his path clearly now, the only path. He summoned all his energy into a huge wall of power and launched it. It would have killed him then if the sorcerer hadn't managed to raise one hand and cast the ghost of a protective spell. As it was it smashed his through several pillars until he came to a rest at the far end of the hall.

Vericoos advanced on the three Veo's: the weeper, the one who was consumed with laughter and the other one… the motionless one. Vericoos was about to attempt magic he had no right to perform, but he must perform it still, whatever the risks...

23.

'You see, Shabwan, some spells you can perform if you have the power, but you cannot perform them alone. They require you to beg the help of the magic, and when you do that you are putting yourself at great risk. I could see it, I could conceptualise how I could contain Veo even if I couldn't kill him. I could see it as clearly as I see you now yet it was beyond my power. Beyond the power of any sorcerer who has ever lived,' Vericoos grimaced. 'I had to beg the assistance of the magic...something that I came to regret immensely.'

24.

It was silent, that was what was so strange about it, the noise outside had at first sounded like it was coming from a pack, a vicious group, all single minded in their intentions. Then it had sounded like chaos, like whatever had united this hellish mob had broken, and their will, while equally as destructive and terrifying, had been fragmented.

Now it was silent. But Vericoos could still feel them all, whatever they were, and now instead of noise there came an equally as oppressive and stifling air of tension. Like a million eyes were hidden just out of sight, terrifyingly surveying his every move. Did they dare to breathe? He didn't know. All his attention lay on the terribly subdivided God who lay in front of him. Vericoos still knew little about the blade, which now lay on the floor with not a fleck of blood upon it, but he felt confident he knew what had happened. The knife had attempted to do what those who believed in it thought it could. It had attempted a perfect subdivision, but instead of three clean and symmetrical cuts it had roughly hacked and chopped the divine being, with no real care or attention. Instead of being cut into perfect chips he had been mashed...

Enough of these thoughts, Vericoos told himself; it seemed ridiculous to fall back on a culinary metaphor at a time like this (he'd never cooked himself a meal in his life for one thing). But then, the behaviour of the three Veo's was making the situation seem a lot less serious, even with the hideously solid wall of silence coming from outside.

He thought of all that he'd ever been taught about borrowing magic, ignoring the bit when he'd been told it should never ever be done, no matter what, and then he borrowed.

25.

'I created a building,' said Vericoos. 'Sounds simple enough, only it wasn't like any building that has ever been or will be again. I believe people now call it the tri-halls.'

Vericoos waited to see if Shabwan would show his, occasionally present, gift of quick understanding. He didn't and Vericoos was glad of it.

'This building that I created had three rooms, one for each Veo I drove him behind the three doors splitting him forever in three, because, as you must have come to realise by now Shabwan, in using the knife he broke himself. He split his mind into three, the result being instant insanity and without his mind his divine power was little more than useless. Once I'd forged the rooms it took me seconds to get him inside and shut the doors.'

The sun was fairly high in the sky now and Shabwan's eyelids were fluttering, yet the eyes beneath them, pink and puffy, still cried out for more.

'As I closed the doors I cast an enchantment on them, it would have been risky for me to make it so they could never be opened. Such sweeping statements are easy to find loopholes in. You have to be very specific when using magic, especially borrowed magic. So I made it so that the three doors can only ever be opened by the same person, at exactly the same moment in time and with three separate wills acting on each door.' For a moment there was a flicker of something on the old man's face, something new. 'Do you see it Shabwan? Do you see what I did?'

The boy nodded.

'You'd have to stab yourself with the knife to be able to do it.'

Vericoos looked proud.

'Exactly,' he said. 'Sub division itself would not allow one to open the door as it would only be one will acting on all three handles. The knife is the only thing which would allow anyone to ever open the doors. I had made the blade the guardian of the room; should anyone ever want to release the Veo's they would drive themselves mad in the process and probably have no will left at all, let alone enough to follow the rigorous criteria of my enchantment.'

26.

The room was small, a circular tube with three doors leading from it. Vericoos stood in it now in the middle of the great hall. There was nothing physical behind the doors, not in this realm, the prisons that they provided the gateway to were a long way from here, but the only way to access them would be from this little circular room. Vericoos could feel the magic fading quickly, soon he wouldn't be able to defend himself. It seemed like a bad idea to leave this little gateway in the middle of the hall so, with the last bit of power available to him, Vericoos made it air borne. It flew through the roof of the great hall like a bullet and came to rest some fifty feet above it, spinning gently...

27.

'Which is where it still is to this day,' said Vericoos.

He looked at Shabwan as if to imply that he had finished but Shabwan knew that there was more, at least a little.

'So you imprisoned him in three bits. That little room above Hardram is the gateway to three different prisons in other dimensions, each of which contain an insane and weakened part of the whole being?'

'Exactly,' replied Vericoos. 'Pretty smart thinking if I do say so myself.'

'And no one can get into it unless they're willing to stab themselves with the same knife that put Veo in that state in the first place?'

'Yes,' Vericoos knew that Shabwan wanted to ask another question. The big question, but first he wanted to hear how it all ended. That and he probably wanted to delude himself for just a little longer. Ignorance is bliss, even pretend ignorance...

28.

Vericoos floated back down into the hall, his intention being to finish off Lubwan, once and for all. He was so exhilarated by his victory that he didn't even think about what was to come. As he floated down he saw the huge crowd of people who were outside, he had been right in his estimations of the amount. Surely this was every man woman and child from this city; he had never seen so many people. They were no longer screaming, nor confused nor silent, instead they were making much more natural and comforting sounds. Sounds of human beings, probably wondering why they were all stood outside the great hall and wondering what had happened to them. All of you are saved thought Vericoos, every last one, there's just one more nasty piece of work to attend to.

He dropped into the hall through the cylindrical hole his creation had made as it rocketed upwards. As soon as his eyes had readjusted to the strange light of the place he saw Lubwan standing beneath him. He expected the sorcerer to raise his hands and attempt a spell but he didn't. Vericoos floated down and came to rest on the ground, eye to eye with Lubwan.

'Why?' he asked.

Lubwan opened his mouth, what could he possibly say? Thought Vericoos, what can explain this? He never tried. Instead he screamed and threw both hands out in front of him deadly energy rushing out from them towards Vericoos' heart. He was briefly aware of a sensation of acceptance and then the spell stopped. It hung in the air between the two of them; a big blue pulse, throbbing yet stationary. Both sorcerers stared at it; there was nothing in the world, nothing that they'd ever heard that could explain this. Then, the pulses coming form the blue ball began to extend and take shape; they became arms, horrible bony arms and then, quick as a flash, the arms grabbed the sorcerers and pulled them into the blue ball...

29.

'What happened to you?' Shabwan asked, after staring at Vericoos in silence for over a minute.

'We were taken to a different place, a bad place. One I will not speak of.'

Shabwan nodded, now the story had reached its climax there was only one more thing he needed to know. Then he would sleep.

'I'm going to stab myself with it aren't I?'

Vericoos nodded, that slow deliberate nod that Shabwan had come to know so well.

'Yes you are.'

Then there was nothing.

Chapter 6.

On the road again.

1.

Vericoos could ride again. This sped things up a lot.

The countryside around them was becoming slowly greener and lusher and in the same way that the grass was beginning to spread over the dry earth, understanding of what lay ahead of Shabwan was beginning to spread through his mind. In the days immediately after Vericoos long story he felt exhausted, not just because he'd stayed up all night listening to the tale, but also because of the sheer weight of the information he had to digest. It was sitting heavily and uncomfortably in his stomach. He kept playing the images he'd forged while listening to the sorcerer over and over in his head. He was so involved in his own thoughts that he didn't even realise that they'd almost reached the forest.

The mountains were looming over them now; Vericoos could see why this whole region of the country viewed them as such an impassable barrier, they looked intimidating from this side. When approached from Hardram, which lay just at the foot of the other side of this same range, the mountains rose up slowly and gracefully. The towering peaks were still hidden in the clouds, but the climb up to them was gradual, it began with rolling green hills, which became rock slopes and then eventually snowy peaks. From this side, however, the mountains seemed to rise up almost instantly. They just grew out of the forest, like great thunderclouds rising above the horizon. There were few paths through the mountains that one would call safe, but they were there if you knew where to look. Once Shabwan became fully aware of the mountains ominous presence, he began to wonder if anyone from Corne had ever traversed them before. You certainly wouldn't unless you absolutely had to.

There was one bit of the story that Vericoos had saved for last, he had originally planned to tell the tale all in one go but it had taken longer than he'd predicted and when he'd seen the exhaustion is his companion's eyes he'd decided to save perhaps the most important piece until last. When they'd awoken late the next afternoon, Vericoos had considered telling Shabwan before they'd set off on their day's journey, but then he'd reconsidered. The boy had a lot to take in, perhaps best to let him get his head round what he already knew before whacking him with this most crucial part of the whole business. It was absolutely imperative that when the boy came to plunging the dagger into himself and laying his three hands on the three doors, that both his will and his intent would be completely focussed. Vericoos would be able to hold the boys sanity in place after he'd stabbed himself, if he got his power back that was, but so much of it would still hang in the balance. He would need to tell Shabwan this last piece of the puzzle soon, but not just yet.

That night they camped just outside of the forest, as far as Vericoos knew they didn't even have a proper name. People tended to call them an array of dark and ominous names like 'the forest of no return' and other such nonsense. As the sun set that night they sat in silence and Vericoos decided it was time. Yet it was his companion who spoke first.

'When I stab myself,' began Shabwan. 'What will happen to me?'

Vericoos looked Shabwan dead in the eye and when he spoke it was in tones of grave seriousness.

'You will be split into three like Veo,' Vericoos watched Shabwan closely as he said this. 'But unlike Veo, you will not loose your mind, because I will be there to hold it together for you.'

Shabwan nodded, and replied, 'Yeah, I guessed as much.' And Vericoos was interested to see how much the boys trust had actually grown in him.

'So will I be just three versions of myself then? If it works I mean.'

'Ah...no' replied Vericoos; the time was most certainly right. 'There is one last bit of the tale that I did not divulge to you when we spoke the other night,' he paused and glance up at the stars. It was a very clear night. 'Let me tell you what I saw when I stood in my completed chamber, as it rose up above Hardram, and perhaps we can discuss together what it may mean...'

2.

Vericoos felt the room shudder as it smashed through the ceiling of the great hall. Like a champagne cork fired out of a bottle. There were no windows in the room, just a hatch in the bottom through which you could enter and exit (this had not been part of his design), but Vericoos could still sense the upward motion. It soon stopped, however, and the room came to rest, spinning gently.

The room was unremarkable in appearance, stone walls, a couple of candles providing dirty light and three heavy set wooden doors, evenly spaced around the wall. The doors had no keyholes, only dull brass door knobs. Vericoos was about to open the hatch and depart this horrible foyer he'd created when he notice three things; three things which were in the room he had created but were not of his creation.

On each of the dull wooden doors, situated dead centrally, just above the knobs, were three metal plaques. Unlike the rest of the room, which was dull and unremarkable (save for the fact that it was floating some two hundred feet up in the air), these plaques were eye catching, Vericoos couldn't believe he hadn't noticed them until now. They were brilliant gleaming silver with jet black copperplate writing spelling out two words on each. Three of these six words were the same; the other three were all different.

One of them said: *The Conqueror*

One of them said: *The Trickster*

One of them said: *The Fool*

Vericoos looked at Shabwan; He could feel understanding beginning to dawn on him. He could also see that the boy understood the importance of this part of the tale. It pleased him immensely.

'The knife divided him into those things?' Shabwan was looking thoughtful and not the least bit stupid.

'Yes,' replied Vericoos. 'I believe so.'

He waited, watching intently, would the boy get it?

'Are you saying...' began Shabwan. That the knife chose to turn him into those three things, rather than just splitting him into three random bits?'

'It would seem so,' said Vericoos, he wanted to say as little as possible at this crucial stage. People learn things so much better if they feel that they worked them out for themselves rather than being told them.

'So,' said Shabwan. 'What do they all mean?' His brow furrowed. 'Does the knife choose three parts of you and then make you into them?'

'I believe so,' said Vericoos and then found he could hold his quiet no longer. 'I believe that this knife was a very strange creation indeed, its very difficult to understand why the people of Krunk would have had need of such a device, let alone preserved it in favour of all else.' Vericoos looked off into the dark forest, the home of that which could recover him. 'When Veo stabbed himself, he believed, totally and completely, that he would become three versions of himself, three exact replicas. As you heard from my story, the reality was quite different. Instead of becoming three beings, alike in thought and mind but all with the same level of independent skill and ability, he became three fragments of himself. When I first saw this happen, I took it that the knife had sliced up his mind any which way and what I was seeing was the consequence: three beings unable to defend themselves or string a sentence together. I would have continued to believe this until now, had I not seen those shining silver plaques. They changed everything.'

Shabwan had not looked up for sometime, he had always loved watching fire; he found it helped him concentrate. He also sometimes believed he could see things in the flames. Now he thought he could see Kayleigh and had a sudden troubling memory of her breaking into millions of pieces, and a cold voice...*Too many!*

'They told you that the knife had chosen to split the God the way it had?'

'Exactly,' said Vericoos, 'on some level which we can unfortunately never hope to understand, this knife has some sort of strange will, some ability to divide up a person...'

'As it sees right' interjected Shabwan.

'Yes, as it sees right.' This was amazing, the boy had shown time and again an uncanny ability to understand what, for so many, would be completely incomprehensible. Vericoos doubted that any of his three friends who had given the old man such a kicking that day could ever have got their heads around it.

'Three fragments.' Muttered Shabwan quietly.

'Fragments, yes but perhaps 'divisions' is a better word,' said Vericoos.

Shabwan looked at him strangely.

'Well...whatever, yeah. So when I come to plunge this thing into myself I'm going to be split into three parts of my personality or my soul or whatever you want to call it?'

'Yes,' replied Vericoos. 'But luckily for you I will be on hand to hold your minds together, I've spent a lot of time reading your thoughts of late, and I'm aware of how intrusive this must have been, but I hope you can see now that I've been making myself as familiar as possible with your mind, getting to know every little part of it so that when the time comes, I will be able to hold you together.'

'But my three minds won't be as my one is now?'

'Alas not, while all of this is speculation I believe that the divisions will leave you still very much yourself, but whatever divisions the knife has chosen to make will become the dominating forces within you. You will be you but without the ability to regulate and rationalise, whatever divisions have been made will be what drives those three Shabwans as they go through the doors.'

'Sounds like I will be insane to me,' said Shabwan, but he was smiling as he said it.

'I have no doubt that it will be an incredibly strange experience. But you will have a huge advantage over Veo, firstly you'll know what is about to happen and you'll have ample time to prepare for it. While this doesn't sound like a huge help, believe me it will make all the difference. And secondly, as I've mentioned before, you will have me in that room with you, focussing every jot of power that I have on holding those three minds together. I am confident that I will be able to do enough to allow you to retain a sense of who you are and what you must do.'

'And once I've finished?'

'Then I'll restore you to how you were before.' Said Vericoos, instantly and without hesitation.

Shabwan looked up from the fire. He fixed the sorcerer with a heavy stare, but said nothing.

'Perhaps now you see why I have had to search so far and wide to find you Shabwan. I knew from the moment I set out on this quest that I would need to find someone whose soul was, shall we say, compatible with mine. When you stab yourself it will take all the power I have to get you through those doors in any condition to fight. It will be the most difficult magic I have ever attempted and there is no doubt that it can only work with you.'

3.

It was finally starting to make sense. Shabwan had wondered and pondered so many times since setting out on the journey, why him? Why, out of all the great warriors that there must be, even in Corne let alone in the rest of Svin, had Vericoos come to San Hoist and snatched him away from

Laffrunda day. Why had he chosen a humble stonk dealer over everyone else in the world? It was because of some connection, some inexplicable connection, which would allow Vericoos to hold him together where he could hold no other. Perhaps I've just done the perfect amount of drugs, thought Shabwan. I've opened my mind up in just the right way to make this possible. It would be ironic if our little fishing trips were the reason that I, and only I, am capable of killing a God.

4.

'We'll probably never know why,' continued Vericoos. 'But I sense fates hand at work, even though I had been searching for you for some time, the chances of running into you, as I did, were still astronomically small.'

Shabwan nodded, it made about as much sense as anything else did.

'There's another thing which I've been thinking about a lot,' said Shabwan.

'Go on,'

'Well...Why have we actually got to do this? I mean if you have created this prison which has successfully held him for two thousand years, then why have I got to go in there now?'

There was no petulance in Shabwan's voice, you could tell that he truly knew his part now and he was determined to see it through to whatever ends; his question came with no intention of excusing himself from duty.

'Because Shabwan, my enchantment is finally failing…'

5.

Let us cast our eyes away from our two friends, just for a moment. Perhaps imagine that we could fly, with the agility of an eagle over the towering peaks of the mountains. Then what would we see? As the clouds thin and clear and the rock turns back to grass, we would see a city, a huge sprawling city which has long ago burst out of the confinements of its walls. These now act more as an easy way to get around the inner city, than as a guardian of its outskirts. It's a sign of the times perhaps, that defence is no longer needed.

Svin has enjoyed a long and illustrious peace with the North and the East; trade routes have flourished between Hardram, Durpo and places far beyond. There is a threat to the city though, and all who reside there can sense it, the threat comes not from the North or from the East, no army is coming here. The threat comes from directly above.

Let us enjoy for a moment, the irony that this one God, the only God throughout all the universes to have been imprisoned, is the only one who truly resides above the people.

Often with religion people are prone to gazing 'up to the heavens', when they wish to communicate with those whom they worship. People seem obsessed with the idea that the Gods are up there, just above the clouds perhaps. In reality the layout of dimensions and universes is far too complicated for this ever to be the case; there is no such thing as a world that would simply sit atop another one. No, the Gods are there all right, but the dimensions they inhabit do not obey any rules that people would like to attach to them. And so there is only one case where a God sits physically above the people and that is in the city of Hardram.

It looks like a big ugly cork, although it only turns, it never bobs. It sits perfectly above the centre of Hardram, the hole in the roof of the great hall has been repaired and above it is a statue of a man we might recognise if we got in a little closer...but then if we got in a little closer we would see some other things as well. People hurrying about the streets not saying a word to each other, empty markets and deserted alleys. People are frightened, why? Because they can sense that it is breaking.

None have ever liked its presence, hanging there in the sky; it's difficult to forget about the threat which it has so long housed. For even though he is divided people still fear him. They fear the stories of how easily he took Hardram the first time. How he made everyone who lived his slaves, will-less beings, incapable of anything other than satisfying the wants of their master.

If he came again, could they stop that happening? Once the enchantment finally breaks, will he be able to re-attach himself, as it were? The cracks began to appear in the little floating circular room over a year ago and they've been getting visibly bigger, occasionally from within them you see a flash of what looked like lighting, but usually there is just a deep red light, like the fires of hell, some of the more melodramatic residents of Hardram have commented.

At night it looks truly terrifying, so much so that only the bravest of the city dwellers will raise their eyes upwards once the sun has set. Eventually people began to leave and those who have stayed are wondering why they had done so for this long. Not that it would make any difference. If the enchantment breaks and Veo is allowed to forge himself back into one being, then no corner of this earth will be safe.

Chapter 7.

Through the forest and over the mountains.

1.

The next morning they entered the forest. Vericoos had said little although he had warned Shabwan to be on his guard.

'This forest is not safe.' He had said.

It wasn't the most useful advice Shabwan had ever received but you made do. Besides, there seemed to be no getting through to Vericoos this morning and Shabwan had an inkling as to why: they were getting close to whatever it was that would restore him to his former self. Soon he would have his magic back, and like any addict, the need became greatest when the prize was nearest.

He had asked Vericoos what it was they needed to do to get him his magic and the sorcerer had said nothing, only stared off into the trees. Shabwan had never really believed he would talk to him about it anyway.

Despite the apparent danger the forest was beautiful; it was difficult to keep your guard up in such an attractive place. The dark bark of the trees glistened with silvery strings of thread that seemed to be made almost entirely of light and the cool knee high grass brushed lovingly against your legs as you moved soundlessly through it. The foliage above their heads was so thick that the sunlight penetrated it only in long thin staffs of misty white light. There was a certain type of peace in here, the kind you could never get out in the open. Maybe this is how it lures you in, thought Shabwan, like a camouflaged predator that looks to its prey like a comforting shelter and then shelters it forever.

Vericoos didn't seem to be enjoying it one bit. He was marching on ahead, travelling almost as fast as he had while riding the horses that they'd set free at the entrance to the forest. Shabwan was surprised by the level of understanding and acceptance he felt for everything which had been said to him. It should have been a bigger shock to find out that he was apparently the only person in the world capable of ramming a knife into his own heart, successfully maintaining his sanity and then completing the fairly simple follow up task of slaying a divine being.

As it was, he just felt like he'd accepted it all in the same way he would have accepted any other logical and essential piece of information. From the sounds of things none of it was going to be easy or pleasant, yet he felt no fear. He would have perhaps even gone as far as to say that he was eager to get started. There were still a few questions floating round his head but, for the moment, he had more than enough food for thought. There was no way he would let Vericoos, the old junkie, avoid talking for much longer but, for now at least, he had enough to keep his mind well and truly occupied.

So did Vericoos.

2.

When it got dark in the forest it got truly dark and, for the first time since he'd entered, Shabwan began to feel a little intimidated by the place. Beyond the circle of orange that their little fire cast, there was nothing but the deepest black and some strange animal noises that, Shabwan was fairly confident, hadn't been there during the day. Vericoos spoke suddenly, taking him by surprise.

'We will reach the place where I can rejuvenate tomorrow.'

'Well that's good news,' said Shabwan.

There was something around that fire that night which had hitherto been absent. Something Shabwan thought he had left behind in the Hoist. For as he gazed at across the fire at the old man he felt, not only a sense of companionship, but a sense of friendship. The sorcerer clearly didn't want to say anything about where he had gone after the battle with Veo and Lubwan, but Shabwan was fairly confident that it had been no paradise. As far as he could tell, Vericoos had risked everything to save others and had paid a terrible price. Any of the wrongdoing he felt he had suffered in San Hoist felt infinitely easier to bear now that he knew that the sorcerer had been acting with the same good intentions he had shown all that time ago. He felt happy and proud to stand at the man's side, even if he had been being a bit of an idiot all day.

'So, have you been thinking about your three then?' Vericoos enquired, and Shabwan could see what an effort it was for him to think about anything other than the following day.

'Have you not been reading my mind today?'

'Not today.' replied Vericoos, and Shabwan believed him.

'Well yeah, I've been thinking of little else actually. Would I be right in guessing that you think that the knife chooses the three most prominent parts of your character for the divisions?'

'Yes,' replied Vericoos, 'Again it is pure speculation. I knew very little of the intricacies of Veo's character but from what I do know, it seems that the knife may well have acted as you've guessed.'

'Hmmm,' said Shabwan. 'So it's going to pick the three strongest or most evident bits of my mind and then those bits will be what controls me, well a version of me at least...'

Shabwan tailed off, it was true that he had been thinking about this all day, but it had been to no avail. It was such a bizarre concept to begin with that he found it very difficult to imagine. On top of that, it was so difficult to think about yourself in that way, such a strange form of something which people found difficult at the best of times: self evaluation.

'Would you like to know what I think?' asked Vericoos.

At first it seemed strange to Shabwan that he was surprised by the sorcerer having such a clear idea of what would happen. Once he had found out about the divisions, he'd assumed it would be his task, and his alone, to probe deeply inside himself, to try and ascertain what this strange and possibly temperamental object would do to him. But then…of course, it made sense. Vericoos had been listening to him thinking for a long time now and had been focussing as much energy as he could afford onto understanding Shabwan's mind, perhaps even his soul. When he eventually came to understand things properly he realised it had never been his job to try and work out what the knife would do.

'Since we've been together,' said Vericoos. 'You have, on more than one occasion, shown me that you are capable of extreme bravery and selflessness.'

Shabwan felt a huge upwelling of pride, he wasn't sure if he'd ever had a straight up, no holds barred, compliment from the old man before and he liked it. But there was more to come:

'Not only are you brave and can fight when called upon to do so, you are also unassuming and modest about both of these talents. Perhaps you never realised that you had them, I don't know. But if we are lucky, then the knife will pick this as one aspect of your character to divide. That particular Shabwan would stand an excellent chance when he goes on to battle Veo.'

Shabwan was feeling genuinely humbled, the old man apparently regarded him as some kind of hero. Unfortunately however his happiness was short lived.

'The second division,' continued Vericoos, 'I fear may not stand such a good chance of victory.'

'Pardon,' said Shabwan, and if you listened ever so carefully you could hear a bubble burst.

'Ever since I met you,' said Vericoos. 'There has been one thing which has been on your mind with more potency and intensity than any other. Can you think what that is? Perhaps 'thing' was the wrong word to use, it sounds somewhat disrespectful don't you think? How about...person.'

This was strange. Shabwan knew what Vericoos meant…knew *who* Vericoos meant, but he didn't know why the old man was now talking to him with such contempt. He seemed to have gone from valiant unassuming hero, to love struck teenager in no time at all. But then, that was exactly what the knife would do to him, he supposed.

'You mean Kayleigh.'

'Of course I do.'

It almost seemed like Vericoos was actually sneering now. A desperate junkie who has one more night to get through, thought Shabwan. It was at this moment that his companion seemed most human to him.

'Why don't you tell me exactly what happened between the two of you for I fear,' said Vericoos: Vericoos the human. 'That when the time comes, this is a part of you I will need to have a much greater understanding of. Your heart and mind are so full of this girl that it would greatly surprise me if the knife wasn't to do something with this.'

Shabwan felt horrified, it was a nasty idea. Couldn't Vericoos have given him a little longer to stew in being the hero before crushing him with this particular concept of a fragment? A *division* he corrected himself.

'Please,' said Vericoos, and his expression had softened; the wave of nastiness had apparently passed. 'Let me have your tale.'

Chapter 8.

Love and Friendship.

1.

Earlier, we departed from our two friends, only for a moment, to glimpse what lay over the mountains. Now we must let one of them carry us with him, as he casts his mind back just over a year and takes us to the happiest point of his life. A point when he could never have imagined that one day he would end up sitting in the forest below the mountains, so many miles away, relaying the events which were, for the moment, his present, to the most powerful sorcerer in the world.

Shabwan was with his mates, if you could call them that. Surely if people were your friends then they wouldn't take the piss out of you this much.

'...and then' spluttered Coki, through what was apparently an unconquerable attack of laughter. 'You started trying it on with that Maria girl...the one from Noree, the one who's here visiting her uncle. She was having even less of it than the others, but yet you still decided to bring out all your best lines... (He adopted a mockery of Shabwan's voice) "Care to join me for a walk in the moonlight"'

Shabwan grimaced, he hated Coki's ability to remember all the worst bits from the night before and remind him of it in cringe inducing detail. The best thing to do was try and not appear embarrassed, because if Coki thought he was getting through to you, he would really get the wind in his sails.

'Yeah well,' he started, desperately trying to think of some comeback that would both put his friend in his place and show that he didn't really care what he was saying...none came to him and his three friends howled with laughter once more.

It was pretty funny he supposed; he only had a few hazy recollections of bowling around the Star. It had been one of those nights where any female who had been unlucky enough to dither in his line of sight for too long had been treated to a leering and lecherous string of chat up lines. Unbelievably, none had taken the bait!

'Never mind mate,' Coki was saying. 'I'm sure your luck will pick up soon.'

Shabwan's friend winked at him, knowing full well that this falsely patronising tone would irritate his friend just as much as the harsh reminders he had been handing out.

'Sod off!' replied Shabwan, realising that this time, like most times, his friend had won.

They laughed again as Shabwan finally dropped his act of indifference.

'Mate, I was horrible last night, I hope no one else remembers it as well as you apparently do.'

Coki smiled and clapped and arm around his shoulders, he'd only really wanted to get Shabwan to stop acting so cool about everything and join in with the fun.

'Yeah, you're no good at pretending you're not embarrassed,' he grinned. 'You wanna take leaf out of my book.'

It was probably true. Coki was just as capable of producing embarrassing performances, but whenever his mates reminded him of them he would laugh harder than anyone. Shabwan was quite the opposite; he'd met up with his friends that day, hoping his actions from the previous evening would have been absorbed into the general hubbub of the pub. Apparently it had not been the case. He had instead stuck out like a lecherously sore thumb and was now paying the price. Every time Coki brought up yet another incident that he'd either completely forgotten or had a hazy (did-that-actually-happen?-oh-please-God-let-it-not-have-actually-happened) recollection of, his insides squirmed harder and his face turned a little redder.

2.

There was another reason why this latest string of actions was worrying him…what if she'd seen him? In fact it wasn't even really a question, she'd been working in there last night; of course she'd seen him. He felt like punching himself in the head, although that probably wouldn't help his hangover. This would be a devastating blow to his already very slim chances. So slim as to make Leeham look fat, they were, and the sight of him slobbering over countless horrified women in the Star last night must have shaved a few more precious pounds off. He didn't talk much that day; he couldn't wait to be alone.

As he lay in bed that night, all he could think of was her. It was so strange how quickly and aggressively these feelings had come on; that was how he knew they were so right. He hadn't told anyone the way he felt about Kayleigh, even his closest friends. They would think it was weird.

He didn't really even know the girl but that didn't stop his stomach clenching every time they made eye contact. Feeling like this wasn't something he'd experienced before either and there were certainly parts of it which scared him, scared him a lot. A few weeks ago, he'd been happily trundling along through life, not a care in the world. Well...that wasn't entirely true; he still missed his mum so much that it felt like a lead weight was constantly sitting in his stomach, but he was getting by. Now he had this to deal with; near obsessive feelings for a girl who he had only spoken to on a few occasions. Still, it didn't feel that bad...quite nice actually.

The other mad thing was that he actually wanted to do something about these feelings, something beyond the superficial haystack romping so championed in this part of the world. In the past, he'd had a few half serious things with girls but nothing which he'd ever chased; something the misogynistic part of him had always been fairly proud of, and it would always be his lack of enthusiasm which would lead to the inevitable moody parting of ways. This time it would be the level of enthusiasm which would likely terrify the poor object of his desire. He'd spent an agonizing couple of weeks battling with the idea of confiding in his friends but always something had held him back. That was another reason he knew this was serious.

3.

Three days later they were in the Star again. His friends had been in for the last two evenings, but Shabwan had felt too embarrassed to set foot in the building. The thought of the hilarity of Coki's taunting being enjoyed by the congregation of the Star was a strong deterrent. There was also a pull though, she was there. And as much has he feared that his antics the other night had put her off forever, he still wanted to see her.

'Maybe it hadn't been as bad as all that,' went the kind of ridiculously optimistic thought that those recently smitten often find themselves suddenly gifted in producing.

It didn't help that the first person Shabwan saw upon entry into the lion's den was Maria, the one from Noree. She looked at him as if she had rarely, if ever, seen anything worse and flinched when he smiled weakly at her. God he must have been a nightmare that night, best just to keep his head down as much as possible and get through the evening. Hopefully he'd suffer as little embarrassment as possible.

The bar was fairly quiet that evening, and unlike on Laffrunda eve, when we last joined Shabwan in this venue, he didn't have to fight his way through to the bar. Consequently Sooie saw him as soon as he entered the room and bellowed an ominous, 'Ah...here he is.'

Shabwan's stomach lurched; one of the women hadn't been Sooie's sister, had she?

'The young casanova returns!'

This was greeted by huge roars of laughter, a great deal more that the relatively quiet room should have been capable of producing.

'Nice to see you again Shabwan, I was worried we may have lost you.'

Shabwan grinned, a little more confidently now. It was strange that being publicly humiliated made you feel less embarrassed; things were better out in the open after all. At least he now knew where he stood: Everyone had seen and everyone had found it really funny. It was also a relief, because if he was being openly mocked and humiliated then his behaviour couldn't have been too dreadful. Had he done anything really bad, then dark glances and silence would have been his reception, to which this was infinitely preferable. That didn't mean his cheeks weren't burning though, and that was before he made eye contact with her.

She was just so lovely, that was all there was to it. Everything about her was amazing. As Shabwan's heart leapt into his mouth and he felt his eyes bulging he feared that his presence alone would somehow betray his feelings. Was it possible that the way he looked at her, or even the way he stood in the room (feeling more than ever like there was a spotlight shining on his head) could give away everything he felt for her? Of course it wasn't, if it was, then why would she have returned his nervous grin with such a beautiful twinkling little smile of her own? Surely if his eyes, or any other part of his shameful self, could give away the extent of his desires, then she would have responded by fleeing the premises.

'What are you drinking Shabby?'

'Er...what?' Shabwan replied to Sooie's perfectly reasonable question.

Damn, how long had he been silent for, it felt like everyone in the pub was looking at him, but that didn't matter because everyone in the pub included her.

'Erm just a beer please.' He tried to grin confidently at the barkeeper but felt he saw suspicion in Sooie's dark eyes as he turned away to fetch a glass. They picked up their drinks and sat down at the table by the window. Finally Shabwan managed to tear his eyes away from her and back towards Coki, who was regarding him with interest.

'You alright?' he asked. 'You still worried about what you did the other night?'

'What?' replied Shabwan, equally as gormless as when he'd addressed Sooie, his anxieties about how the patrons of the Star would treat him after his recent antics felt like they were a million miles away now. Had he ever cared about them? It didn't feel like he had, not since they'd made eye contact.

Half an hour later they were still sat around the table by the window, although Shabwan was now sitting with his back to the bar, behind which Kayleigh was working. Much as he burned to be able to glance at her it was easier to concentrate on what his friends were saying when she was out of sight. He didn't feel ready to share this with anyone just yet and it would only be so long before one of his so called chums noticed his repetitive fleeting looks.

He could still feel her though, and it was sending him barmy. Just knowing that she was there, that she might even be looking at the back of his head with, what he barely dared believe was, the same interest she had shown when they'd first seen each other.

'...what do you think?' Lewhay asked.

Apparently Shabwan hadn't been doing quite as well at acting nonchalantly as he'd thought, as he now found that he had no idea what Lewhay was asking him.

'Would anyone like another one?' he asked in overly jubilant tones that made all of his friends, especially the disgruntled Lewhay, look at him quizzically. They all mumbled and nodded; he didn't really hear what they said. His mind was already over by the bar, where it was desperately trying to arrange words into some kind of order. Ideally they would sound relaxed, just like any other fellow addressing an attractive girl. That would be the ideal, Shabwan thought as he turned to face the bar and saw her there looking at him. A quick re-evaluation of his goals became an immediate necessity; just getting a sentence out was going to be something of an achievement.

'Hey Shabwan,' she said as he reached the bar. Apparently when making eye contact with someone makes you feel like you might fall over, to hear them talk to you and say your name can be quite a shock.

'Erm...hey.' he said.

'How are you this evening?'

He didn't notice the question as much as he noticed they way she lent on the bar when she spoke to him, the way her face was suddenly closer to his.

'Yeah I'm good.' he replied, 'and you?' it wasn't exactly stimulating conversation, but he'd got this far without either blurting out that he loved her and that he wanted to spend the rest of his life with her or running away. And this he would take as a victory.

Another half an hour had past and it had been *so* much better than the last. Shabwan was sitting again but this time he wasn't sitting with the three increasingly drunk young men by the window. No siree. He was instead sitting at the bar, on a tall unbalanced stool, talking and gazing into the eyes of the wonderful creature who now sat on the stool next to him. Kayleigh had finished her shift, it didn't need both her and her dad on a quiet night like this, and she had decided to come and join Shabwan for a drink or two.

The conversation was actually going well…amazingly well! Although, Shabwan later came to realise, perhaps not quite as well as all that. The reason for this hyperbolic interpretation of the goings on stemmed from Shabwan's participation in one of the great male traditions. The tradition we all mock when we see our friends embroiled in, yet we all take part equally as fervently ourselves.

The fine art of the over-read.

That's right, you all know it, the practice of allowing the mind to paint the most idealistic pictures based on the briefest and often bleakest of stimuli. The bragging to our friends that a girl is most definitely interested because she put her hand on our leg or fluttered her eyelashes. The romantically smitten male knows no bounds when it comes to letting his imagination run wild with all sorts of hopeful fantasies and it was into this, not so exclusive, club that Shabwan was now ploughing head first.

To him it seemed as if the impossible was speedily becoming a reality. How could it be that she was acting like this if she didn't feel at least a tiny portion of what he felt for her? She was a lovely girl, renowned for being so, she definitely wasn't some trollop looking for a night of fun, so surely that must mean that all these little touches and eye glances could only be a display of romantic intention.

The best kind of romantic intention, the kind that can deliver one to the promised land beyond the hay bails.

When they eventually came to be together, they had laughed at Shabwan's interpretation of that first night.

'How could you have read into it so much?' She had laughed, 'I liked you a bit, but I was just being friendly.'

He always knew that that wasn't completely true; she'd felt a bit more than that. But her initial feelings hadn't been of the gargantuan proportions that his had; that was for sure. For her it came later, and by then, the same part of Shabwan that they had affectionately mocked together was well on it's way to ruining the whole relationship.

4.

They talked and talked that evening, Shabwan barely even looked over at his friends once. He barely looked anywhere apart from at her. He was dimly aware of the noise from the window table increasing but he did not look over, not until she went off to powder her nose.

'Ah so you've chosen to join us then.' Shabwan was taken aback by Coki's harsh tone, he looked from Lewhay to Leeham and saw the same look upon both their faces, don't push him! They wordlessly implied.

'What's the matter?' asked Shabwan.

He knew that he should heed his friend's warnings but at the same time he was fairly certain that he'd done nothing wrong and definitely didn't deserve this response. Coki gestured with his head over towards the fireplace and Shabwan immediately understood.

It was a testimony to how much he'd been wrapped up in Kayleigh's words that he didn't, until now, notice the lary group who were sitting around the fireplace. They were no strangers to Shabwan; a group of farmers whom he had grow up playing with. But who now, thanks to an incident involving Coki and a girl, were his sworn enemies.

The funny part was, Coki had been completely in the wrong.

The alpha male of the other group was a young man named Por, a big lumbering brute who had a bright shock of blonde hair which sat over his handsome freckly face. Por had been going out with this girl Harriet for some time and by all accounts had mistreated her often. Sometimes the abuse had been verbal and sometimes physical. Por was not a popular man in the community, indeed his only real friends were the five others that sat around the table with him. Some people were polite to him out of fear and some just ignored him. Por didn't really care. He had never cared much what people thought of him and back in the bad old days when Tull had run the Star, it was rumoured that Por had helped him run his various schemes.

Shabwan and the others had always had a bit of a stand off with the group. They had never really crossed paths over any issue which could have lead to conflict. Although they had all known that when that day came, conflict there would be. And so it had come in the form of Coki's charming smile and winning ways.

The fling between him and Harriet had not lasted long. The problem had been a simple one; Coki actually liked her and was therefore unhappy just to be someone who she saw behind her boyfriend's back. Especially when her boyfriend was such a violent brute. He was, as he told her often, completely unafraid of the consequences of the two of them going public. Doubtless Por would try to kill him but he was up to the challenge. She had seemed for a while as if she would indeed leave her unhappy and abusive relationship but when it had come to crunch time, she had chosen Por.

5.

They all remembered the night well.

Harriet, for reasons no one would ever understand, decided that the pub was the ideal venue to confess everything to her boyfriend. Por punched her hard in the mouth, breaking two of her teeth. While the rest of the bar stood in shocked silence Coki ran over to help. Unfortunately he was on a pretty heavy dose of stonk at the time and found that his hand to eye coordination wasn't as good as it sometimes was.

The initial skirmish was broken up, although it took a great effort and the help of almost all present. The two fighters were dragged outside and held apart whilst Harriet screamed and sobbed. Once everyone was outside they began to get a better idea of what was actually going on; some of the men who had held Por back inside the pub, now understood where his anger was coming from and felt that he deserved a crack at Coki. Despite hating the man's guts, they wouldn't see him left without a chance to avenge this infidelity.

Coki scared Shabwan that night. Before going into the first confrontation he had screamed and raged, yelling at Por how he was going to, 'put him in the ground.' That hadn't frightened Shabwan, it was what came after.

As Coki was dragged outside he fell silent, no one could get through to him, his deep brown eyes never once wavered from Por. He just stared at him and stared at him, waiting for his chance.

It came of course. The men who were holding Por eventually had had enough and released him, those who were holding Coki let go of him upon seeing his opponent charge. A circle formed around the two brawlers, no one else intervened, nor would Coki or Por have wanted them to. This conflict was to be settled one on one.

Por won.

He was the only person in San Hoist to be able to claim such a feat. Coki fought hard and landed a couple of devastating elbows to Por's huge jaw but it wasn't enough. Eventually his bigger adversary wrapped his arms around Coki's legs and dump tackled him onto the ground. Coki banged his head hard, momentarily dazing himself, and Por seized the opportunity, pounding his fists over and over again into Coki's face.

Again it had taken a great many of them to restrain him. The man was in a blind rage by now, shouting and howling like an animal. Eventually his five friends, the ones who he sat with now, dragged him away. Shabwan remembered being upset by how tenderly Harriet looked at Por, even as he was dragged off with her other lover's blood dripping from his knuckles.

Nothing upset him more that to see abused people still laying all their affections on the source of their misery.

6.

Coki had been hurt, not terribly but badly enough. It took him a while to recover. All the same, as he lay in his bed eating soup, he talked of nothing else but revenge. As soon as he was up again, he assured his mates, Por would pay. They knew he meant it as well. But they also knew that the decision that Harriet had since made had hurt him deeply.

What they never knew until he told them some months later, was that she came to visit him one day, as he lay in his bed, and pleaded with him to end it. While she couldn't leave Por for him, she could equally not bare to see them hurt each other. She assured him that her love for him was real and if he returned her love he would end the feud. So he did. At the time they hadn't really questioned why he suddenly changed his mind about seeking revenge. They'd been quite relieved if the truth were told and from then on there had been an uneasy peace between the two groups.

Por remained with Harriet, but if the rumours were true he had become even more abusive towards her. He and Coki never even looked at each other. Their peace seemed to rely on a mutual ignoring of the others existence and it continued this way for some time. The boys knew that Coki was still upset about Harriet and hated the impotent position she had placed him in by asking that he seek peace. Someone he loved was being hurt regularly, right in front of his eyes and he had been told that if he loved her he would allow it to continue.

You couldn't blame him for being upset.

7.

'What's going on?' Shabwan asked.

This time he *was* looking directly at Coki.

'That gits been making comments all night, I swear if he says one more thing then...'

"Ere Coki,' Por yelled. 'We were just reminiscing about fights we'd had in the past, I was saying that the one I had with you was a bit like the ones I used to have with my sister.'

Raucous laughter echoed around the room, it was quieter now. People had sensed that something wasn't right.

'Of course,' Por continued, now staring directly at Coki. 'I'd know all about how it feels to hit a woman.'

That did it.

However much Coki liked the girl didn't matter any more. The truce was at an end. It was only out of respect for Sooie and the other customers that Coki didn't pick up a chair and break it across Por's fat head then and there. Instead he just said one word, a word dripping with cold hard anger.

'Outside.'

The fight had been similar to the last one; it had happened in the same place, with a similar group of people stood around watching. There had, however, been one major difference...

8.

Shabwan was amazed by the strength his friend still had after that brutal burst of energy. Even though all three of them had a good solid hold, Coki was still bucking and jolting them every which way.

The fact that his opponent was a bloody mess on the dusty earth outside the Star certainly didn't seem to suggest to Coki that the fight was over. It took them almost an hour to drag him home, every time they would give him a bit of slack he would try and run back up to the square.

Harriet had arrived shortly after the fight and had screamed at Coki, 'You monster! What have you done to him?'

It was as if he hadn't seen her.

Once they got him into his house he calmed down considerably. It was a funny transformation to see a man go from murderous rage to being worried that they might wake up his mum; but it was one that Coki went through none the less. Once he was sat down he fell asleep quite quickly; physical and emotional exhaustion were apparently stronger than the hate and rage which had driven him moments before. Shabwan stayed there to make sure he didn't leave again but he slept soundly, as he slept he wore a thin smile.

The next day they had gone for a walk together, just Coki and Shabwan. The other two had gone home the night before (and would later report that Harriet and Por had already left town, they would, apparently, not be seeing them again) Shabwan had had a feeling his friend would want to talk once he awoke. He was right.

'I feel better for doing it.' Coki was saying.

'Really?' said Shabwan.

'Well yeah, I mean I know that she said that she didn't want me to do it, but in saying that she kind of left me in this horrible limbo.' Coki sighed. 'I was never going to be able to have her and we were never going to even be able to have a friendship so at least this way I got to give that sod a kicking he'll never forget.'

'Yeah you did that all right.' Laughed Shabwan.

Coki grinned; it seemed that he was telling the truth.

Often, Shabwan supposed, it was just better to decide on a course of action and follow it through. The finality that you get from doing so is often better than living a life of wondering and waiting. Coki would probably never speak to Harriet again and he'd lost any chance he had; the kind of chance many men would have spent all their lives waiting on. But at least now, he had his revenge. Shabwan knew his friend well and knew that he would sleep a lot easier at night from now on.

'So,' Coki was saying. 'You and Kayleigh…'

He grinned cheekily. Shabwan was startled; in truth the events of the night before had been dramatic enough to push Kayleigh out of his mind. This said, the moment Coki mentioned her name, everything he had been feeling prior to the confrontation came flooding back to him. He didn't really know what to say. Would Coki understand if he told him how he felt about her? It was probably best to censor it. A little bit at least.

'Yeah she's pretty cool, seems nice...A very...nice girl.' he ended and Coki laughed.

'Ha ha, you can't try and play it cool now mate, I saw the way you were looking at her last night.'

Shabwan groaned, his worst fears had come true, he'd been too obvious. She had probably just been humouring him and now thought he was the biggest idiot on earth.

'She seemed to be looking at you in the same way though.'

Coki said this quietly and casually; as if it was probably of little interest to Shabwan who knew exactly what his friend was doing. Coki loved a little bit of gentle torture and knew that once he'd said this Shabwan would be bubbling over with a million excited questions. Coki also knew how much his friend liked to try and hide this side of his nature and how ultimately this always proved useless. Shabwan held his cool for all of five seconds and then blurted out a stream of words so fast that most of them were in-distinguishable.

'Really? You think she was looking at me that way? Well that was kind of what I thought but I didn't really know. I mean I thought I might have looked too keen and she might have seen me the other night and been put off. But there was body language. Did you see the body language? And there was flirting she was definitely flirting. Wouldn't you say?'

Coki smiled.

'Yeah mate, I would.'

Shabwan's heart leapt as if this confirmation from his friend had come directly from the girl herself.

'So seriously,' asked Shabwan, feeling a little calmer now. 'What do you think of my chances?'

Coki looked at him gravely and Shabwan's heart sank.

'Through the forest and over the mountains I'm afraid.'

Shabwan gawped at him, what did he mean? After all the other stuff he said. Shabwan felt misery wrapping around him like a cloak. Then Coki started laughing, that infuriatingly gleeful laugh he always did after he'd got someone good.

'Nah only joking mate, I'd say they were strong, although you probably want to get in there soon, I don't think you're the only one whose interested.'

These last words were supposed to be a casual jibe, just a bit of a giggle, but this was not how they came across to Shabwan. He now felt a desperate sense of urgency, unlike he'd ever experienced before. His earlier paranoia about coming on too strong had gone right out of the window.

Now he realised that those feelings he’d been so terrified would scare her off were actually a godsend. An attempt by his subconscious, in its infinite wisdom, to ensure that he moved quickly enough; before some other bloody opportunist got in there ahead of him. The thought of it made him sick, imagine seeing her with another man...It was just too much to bear. He would act as quickly as possible and tell her exactly how he felt, well...maybe not exactly.

9.

To prepare his plan of action Shabwan had come down to the cliffs, this was where he could talk to his mum.

Ever since she had died this was the place he came when he wanted to feel close to her. It was a beautiful little section of the coast path and one they had often walked together. On one side the sea rolled lovingly over the rocks which it had spent generations gently smoothing. And on the other, banks of lavender rose up sharply from the path giving both a beautiful smell and a feeling of absolute privacy. You were only half an hour's walk from the Hoist but you could have been the only people on Earth.

Just up from the shoreline there was one particular rock where they'd always sat together and eaten her lavish picnics.

This was where he sat now, it was strange to feel so excited and happy about something and yet at the same time feel the tragedy of your loss so much more potently. He could never wait to tell his mum about exciting new things in his life and this was no exception. Indeed, since her death, this was probably the time he had been most excited. Sitting here now though, he needed to do more than just to tell her…

He needed advice.

While, of course, he couldn't actually hear her voice, he sometimes fancied that, if he concentrated really hard, he could sense his mum's feelings. Rolling in like the waves below. It was here and nowhere else where he would hatch his plan. He would go through all his ideas and, if there was one that was better than all the others, he knew that his mum would let him know. And that, for Shabwan, was everything.

He thought long and hard, and he listened hard too…After what must have been an awful long time (the sun had apparently been keen to cover serious ground while he'd been thinking) things seemed a lot clearer.

Terrifying but clearer.

As far as he could see, the best option was to tell Kayleigh straight. There was no need to go overboard, but the signals he had received in the pub combined with Coki's encouragement had been incentive enough for him to decide that honesty was the best policy.

It had shocked him deeply to hear Coki say that he thought there were others who shared Shabwan's interest in her. Shabwan supposed that he'd been naïve to think otherwise; despite all his paranoia and lack of self confidence, there was a part of him which had definitely always believed in some kind of fairytale ending between him and Kayleigh. The idea that some other chancer might intervene before they could gallop off into the sunset together was a strange one.

Not a particularly pleasant one either.

So that part was simple enough: tell Kayleigh that he had strong feelings for her and was very keen to start a relationship, although hopefully in slightly more creative language than that. As he looked out over the calm sea he didn't feel any sort of a sense of approval from his mum but he didn't get any feelings of discouragement either. This was a good sign; this was the one place in the world where he was actually able to realise that something was a bad idea before it was too late. He would obviously have liked some undisputable sign that this was the right path, but right now… he was willing to take silence as confirmation.

The next question was how to go about telling her. Privacy would be a valuable asset. As Shabwan began to feel more and more clear-headed and confident of what he was going to say, he also began to feel that it would be a shame if his beloved were to miss even one word of it. Confidence with Shabwan was like a snowball on a shallow slope; it took a while to get going but once it did…well, exponential wasn't even the word.

She would be at the pub tonight, she had told him this last night. God so much had happened since then, so much time had passed. Time: full of endless opportunities for the hateful 'others', who Coki had described, to have whisked away all of his dreams. Shabwan shook these horrible thoughts out of his mind like they were water in his ears.

Perhaps he could ask her to step outside for a moment, and then he could lead her to the bench in the square where he could tell her everything. His stomach lurched at the thought of doing it so soon but at the same time he felt a rush of excitement, perhaps even a rush of providence.

An hour later, he was still sat on the rock (not that long in Lubwan's terms but in anyone else's: a fairly lengthy bit of rock perching). Anyone who might have happened to stumble across him might have thought he was some kind of lunatic. So deep in thought was he that he was quite openly and obliviously chatting away to himself. He resembled some stonked out old druid, perched above the sea mumbling a strange old prayer. This was no prayer though. It was a plan; a perfect plan.

Burning feelings of desire can do very strange things to people. If we take as a case in point our close friend Shabwan: we may presume that if someone were to show him, just a few short weeks ago, this strange version of himself that he has become, then he would have laughed at it and claimed it some kind of trickery. There was no way that he would ever end up like that (or maybe 'this'. Such things get a bit confusing with these bizarre imaginings). Yet here he was. Completely transformed and consumed.

She was the most important thing in the world. So much so that nothing else mattered; no other thought stood a chance of survival. And now finally, after playing out every different scenario in his head he had hatched his flawless plan.

In the beautiful naivety of his minds eye he had already seen how it would all play out. It was just a matter of realising it.

Interestingly enough, he never got the opportunity…or needed it.

10.

'Shabwan!'

A sweet voice cut through the trance he'd fallen into and he felt that increasingly familiar feeling of his heart skipping and stuttering. His perfectly sculpted words dissolved almost instantly, leaving behind a potent emptiness, in which nervousness settled like an unwanted squatter.

'Shabwan,' she said again and this time he looked up.

There she was, for of course it was Kayleigh. She was looking even more beautiful than in his mental picture of her (and that was saying something). The summer dress she was wearing floated around her in the soft breeze but occasionally clung to her body for a second, highlighting the perfect line of her hips or the soft curve of her breasts.

Shabwan gulped and closed his eyes.

11.

It was as if he had been drunk for the last few days and suddenly he'd sobered up.

All he had thought about was her, so much so that he'd actually marched down to the cliffs and hatched a plan, *a plan!* For the love of the gods what was wrong with him? He suddenly felt so damn foolish. Once he'd told Coki of his feelings, the inner passions he had been repressing for fear that, well...that this would happen, they had spilled outwards and completely consumed him.

Coki had opened the floodgates and suddenly Shabwan had become this hopeless romantic, the kind of person who went down to the cliffs to compose a speech designed to win his love...what an idiot! Yet even as he thought this to himself he felt bad; he'd come down here to talk to his mum, hadn't he? He'd certainly begun with good intentions but then he'd kind of dissolved into some weeping poet. And the best thing of all was that now she was actually here, none of it was going to be of any use whatsoever.

Like I said passion, especially the first big experience of passion, can do very funny things to people.

'Hey,' said Shabwan. His voice sounded high and unnatural, yet still proved useful for returning the narrative to the moment.

'How are you doing?' she asked, rolling the words out slowly.

She had her hands behind her back. He imagined she was winding her fingers together. She looked a little bashful. This simultaneously made her look even more beautiful than before and gave Shabwan a little boost of confidence. It was a good sign if she was nervous as well.

'I really like you...' he blurted, and in the history of all blurts it was a biggun.

Oh Gods, what the hell did he do that for. Was he even the least bit in control of what he said or did any more? It didn't seem so. Having narrowly avoided carrying out his original intentions, whatever they'd been (he couldn't even remember any more, but from the way he'd been acting he suspected that it had been something like turning up at the pub covered in rose petals and singing a song he had written called *Kayleigh is like a flower* or something equally as rubbish), he had now gone right to the other end of the spectrum and blurted out his feelings like an over excited child.

Damn that Coki, damn him all the way through the forest and over the mountains. For it was he who'd given Shabwan the confidence he needed to act like such a nit...

Who was he trying to kid? There was only one person to blame here.

He looked up into her eyes, dreading the look of contempt that he would doubtless find there. Apology was what this situation needed, any fool could see that, and by Gods there was most certainly a fool present. They had reached damage limitation time. Shabwan had dashed his hopes of a relationship onto the rocks below the cliffs but at least he could perhaps save a little bit of face.

He never had to.

When he made eye contact with her again he found that, rather than looking at him like the small child he felt like, she was looking at him and smiling. Better than that, she too looked nervous and excited.

'Erm...thank you,' she said and then giggled.

Then he started giggling too. It was an amazing feeling. While they had laughed a lot in the pub the night before, this was the first time that they truly laughed together.

'Are you always that suave?' she asked when the laughter subsided a little.

'Yeah, most of the time,' Shabwan said.

'There's nothing I like more than a man who'll just blurt out his feelings like he can't bear to contain them a moment longer.'

'The funny part is, I was actually down here planning how I was going to tell you.'

She almost collapsed at this point. He loved how easy it was to tell her things. Things which should have been mortifying embarrassing with her just…weren't.

'Was that how you planned to do it?'

'Nah,' he replied. 'But trust me what I just did then was probably better than what I was dreaming up.'

She beamed at him:

'You serious?'

'Yeah, I think I actually am,' he said and then they were kissing.

12.

The first few months were by far the happiest of his life yet now when he thinks back to them it is difficult to pick out individual events. Humans have a tendency to think in chapters and Shabwan was no different. It seemed to him that all the forces that governed the universe had conspired to bring them together, how could there have been any other explanation…?

13.

He was looking intently into the fire now and Vericoos sensed that this part was too painful for him to recall. Yet still he *needed* to know it.

'Perhaps I could read your mind, just for this part of the tale,' said Vericoos. 'If I do so, it will save you from having to recount this particular part.'

Shabwan nodded, he felt slightly ashamed as he did so. There was a sense of relief that was accompanying the story. As he relayed each line to Vericoos it felt as if a little more weight was lifted from his shoulders. But this particular part just seemed too painful. Better to let the old man read it in the same way he'd read so much else.

Vericoos opened up his mind to the flow of Shabwan's thoughts. Then he looked at the boy, meeting his almost accusatory gaze.

'Do you see?' he asked.

'Yes,' replied Vericoos, 'I believe that I understand.'

In a way this was true.

14.

Shabwan resumed his tale, it was much easier to talk about how it went wrong than when it had been perfect...

It came, as these things often do, as an equally big shock to both of them the first time it happened.

They had been together for some months and not one day in that time had been anything less than perfection. They'd fallen asleep gazing into each others eyes almost every night and woken up twice as in love the next morning. They'd taken stonk together and had unbelievable, mind blowing sex down on the cliffs. To Shabwan this had felt so special that he hadn't even spoken of it to his three best friends. They'd walked hand in hand along the beaches and swan in the ocean together. He'd even taken her to the place where he spoke to his mum, admittedly this had been where they had first kissed, but he had brought her again and this time he had told her the significance of the place. She had looked at him so tenderly as he spoke that he'd feared his heart might burst.

Throughout all this blissful time, the time that he had found himself unable to speak of and had conveyed to his companion through thought alone, there had never been a single bad word, never a moment of anger between the two of them. This was made all the better by the fact that they both felt they were holding nothing back. They could be completely themselves and never even mildly irritate the other. This could have continued for a long time, had Shabwan not let the ugliest part of his nature scratch its evil claws into what was otherwise perfection.

Kayleigh's best friend was Michael, had been ever since either of them could remember. Shabwan liked him and he trusted him: that was what made it all so weird. He knew that they were exceptionally close and he even felt mildly guilty about how little time Kayleigh was spending with Michael in the first few glorious months of their relationship (later Leeham would point out to him that he had never felt guilty about how little time he was spending with his own friends).

Shabwan and Michael had known each other casually from before and when he and Kayleigh had started seeing each other they had quickly become much better friends. Jealousy was a word that Shabwan had often heard his mother use when talking about his father but it was never one he'd given a lot of thought to.

That was about to change.

It was all in the body language. That was one of the last coherent thoughts he could remember having when he woke up the next day. He had been sitting with Coki, Leeham and Lewhay enjoying one of the rare moments when all four of them had been together. At the time he hadn't realised that he was to blame for this rarity. The night had been a fine one, they were all damn drunk, the jokes were flowing and life felt good...until suddenly he realised it. Saw it clear as day, how had he been so foolish? Kayleigh was in love with Michael! Why else would she have stroked his arm in that way? Shabwan sat there instantly seething. The noise of the pub seemed distant and muffled, not like his thoughts which were loud, clear and downright nasty.

She was doing it again; always touching him and with Shabwan sitting right here. Did she want to humiliate him in front of everyone? Later, when Shabwan had time to try and piece his memories together it always amazed him how jealousy so instantaneously modified his character. It did it so quickly and completely that he didn't even realise it had happened.

If he remembered how happy and carefree he'd been a minute ago, before he started feeling like this he didn't acknowledge it. In Shabwan's drunken world, this had always been the way of things. He sat there for half an hour or so, just looking at the pair of them together, every laugh he heard grated on him and all the dialogue that he couldn't hear over the noise of the pub was dubbed over, as he created worst case scenario after worse case scenario in his head. As he drank more and more it suddenly occurred to him that he should say something. Yes, that was the best course of action; hurt her as much as she was hurting him. Not that she cared, that was painfully obvious.

Eventually he got his chance.

After she had caught his eye a few times and winked or flashed him her beautiful smile and he in turn had either stared back stony faced or looked away, she came over and asked him if he was O.K.

'Why do you care?' he'd viciously responded.

'What do you mean?' she replied, clearly stung.

'I'm surprised that you've got time to worry if I'm OK or not, with all the effort you're putting into trying to screw Michael.'

She physically recoiled as he said this, but the effect was just as immediate on him as it was on her. The moment the words left his lips he wished he could grab them and haul them back in, or at least hurl them to the floor and stamp them out of existence. This, he discovered, as the emotion became a more and more prominent part of his life, was the cruel trick of jealousy. You would sit there stewing in anger, feeling oh so righteous, so deliriously convinced that you were being deliberately hurt and betrayed by someone you loved. Yet as soon as you voiced your opinion and saw the hurt on your loved ones face...well, that was the moment that you suddenly woke up to yourself. And of course by then it was too late; what has been said can never be unsaid.

What the hell were you on about? Your newly awakened head would suddenly scream. There was nothing to be jealous of. The combination of liquor and insecurity had lead you to fabricate some horrible reality out of nothing more than your girlfriend showing a bit of mild affection to her best friend; someone with whom she had the very definition of a platonic relationship. Why is it so easy to tell yourself this afterwards? It would be so much more useful before.

They sat there together for the rest of the night and she was amazing about it. She got him to explain how he had felt and why it had made him act like that. Then she assured him he had nothing to worry about, even though he knew this and believed it so completely. They made love as passionately as ever that night and spoke about it again afterwards. It was even easier in that euphoric state where you feely truly free from your inhibitions and able to speak without applying any censorship or even thought to your own words.

As they had fallen asleep the relationship had felt stronger than ever. He was still consumed with guilt for what he had said to her, but it had been so easy for them to put right that he felt almost glad it had happened. Surely it was just a one night thing, a weird bit of stupidity that came from nowhere and had been sent back there. Everything was amazing, even better than it had been before.

If only that had been true.

You see, as much as he didn't want it, something had been born in Shabwan that night. An ugly, horrible part of him had come to life; a part that he was powerless to either ignore or crush.

The ability to do so soon became what he desired more than anything.

He would always know he was in the wrong when he glanced moodily at her across the bar or when his mood suddenly changed. It was usually when her and Michael shared a joke or talked about something from the past that he didn't really know about.

He knew he was in the wrong when he would ignore her when she tried to catch his eye as she spoke with Michael. He knew he was in the wrong when he would ask loaded questions about what they'd been talking about. He knew he was in the wrong and he hated himself for it but for some bloody reason, some eternal flaw in his makeup, he still couldn't stop it.

Still at least he was pretty sure that he was hiding it from her. Yes he got angry and moody and was sometimes less nice to be around but he was pretty sure that she didn't make the link between this and his feelings of jealousy. His feelings that, even while he was having them, he knew to be completely irrational and have no founding in reality. He began to dread evenings in the pub when they would be in a big group and he would have to invent answers to satisfy the people who continually enquired:

'Are you O.K.?'

Because he *didn't* want to hurt her.

Nothing hurt him more than the memory of her recoil as he'd said those horrible words to her in the pub that night. If there was one act from his entire life that he was allowed to take back, that could be removed from the records forever then it would be that one.

Looking back he could never believe that he'd been so stupid as to think that hiding the problem, rather than dealing with it, was any course of action to take. Wasn't that exactly what his Dad would have done? He consoled himself by repeating over and over that he had done it for her. The problem was, not only had it been a bad idea in the first place, it also hadn't worked.

He'd been drunk again, why did he not make that link? That was the thing: when you internalised things you never got a good perspective on them and your own warped view on reality became gospel.

It happened just as it had before, only this time it was much more embarrassing. Kayleigh and Michael had been laughing about something, which, in Shabwan's drunken mind, could only have been a natural precursor to sex, when had anybody ever laughed for any other reason? Later that evening Michael walked past Shabwan on his way to the bathroom and Shabwan bumped elbows with him.

'Oops sorry Shab,' he said, even though he knew it hadn't been his fault.

Shabwan stared at him for a moment, not saying a word and then looked away. Michael carried on his way to the toilet looking pretty shocked. Up until that moment the pair had always got on really well and Shabwan had never exhibited to Michael any of the petulant aggression he was now overflowing with.

It was almost an hour and four drinks later when Shabwan marched over to where they sat and said, 'Sorry to interrupt guys, obviously you're having such a lovely time together and I'd hate to break it up, but just to let you know I'm heading off now.'

It wasn't what he said that made him cringe so hard when he thought back to it, but the way he'd said it. So infinitely petty and viscous, every word dripping with double meaning. It must have been bad for Michael but for Kayleigh...

Not that he worried about that at the time; instead he stormed out of the star convinced, momentarily…oh so momentarily, of the brilliance of his actions. This conviction wore off before he even got through the door but he did not go back. How could he? Instead he'd spent an agonizing few hours lying in bed, too ashamed to return to the pub, just hoping that Kayleigh would come round so he could try and make things right. She had come round but it had been very different to the last time.

'Do you think I don't see the way you are every time I and he have a conversation?' she screamed.

'What do you mean?' asked Shabwan although he knew perfectly well.

'All your little moods and your weird little glances, do you know how hard that makes things for me?'

She was crying now and he felt so terrible, much, much worse than the first time.

'I'm sorry,' he said adding his tears to hers. Although clearly there was as little place for them in her mind as there was for his apology.

'You acted like a complete idiot! Do you want me to have no male friends? Is that it? Because I won't ever do that Shabwan. Not for you, not for anyone!'

'I don't want that,' he replied and he meant it. But he knew how weak it sounded now that she'd pointed out how so much of his behaviour argued to the contrary.

He pleaded with her to see how sorry he was and eventually she yielded, although somewhat reluctantly. They made love and while it was a beautiful relief it was also horrible. He could barely bring himself to look at her. He felt humble and worthless and yet even for that he hated himself. He knew that by acting so pathetically he was making it hard, or even impossible, for her to be as angry at him as she had every right to be.

The next day they talked long and hard and she genuinely frightened him. It seemed she wasn't willing to stand for any more of it and there was a lot that had to change. No more subtle passive aggressiveness, no more drunken outbursts. But then she said something which had filled him with such glorious hope and the belief that he could succeed.

'I love you, and I want you to talk to me, do you understand?' suddenly there seemed to be more colour in the world. 'That was what made this hurt so much more is that you'd kept all this to yourself. It's OK to tell me that you're feeling really irrational or that something is bothering you, well...within reason,' she added. And he had to concede that she had a point considering how stupid some of the stuff which had bothered him was.

'But don't you see how sad it would be to lose this?' she said. Tears were shining in her eyes in the morning sun. 'You have nothing to worry about Shab but it's all up to you. Can you see that? You can make it or you can ruin it.'

And that day he vowed that he would make it and he meant it more than anything in his life.

15.

'She's an intelligent girl,' said Vericoos.

It was the first time he had interrupted all through the story, apart from when he'd offered to read Shabwan's mind. But it had been clear at that point that the young man was not going to continue.

'Yeah she is,' said Shabwan, 'unfortunately I am not an intelligent man.'

Vericoos looked at him.

'You are not the first, nor will you be the last to suffer from this problem, of that I am confident.'

Shabwan did not look up, he seemed to want no words of kindness, he had temporarily forgotten that he had found redemption for his actions and was completely absorbed in the guilt that still plagued him, even with all else that had happened...

16.

He did really well after that, even if he said it himself.

The incentive that Kayleigh had given him gave him the confidence to share what was happening with his friends. Coki, Leeham and Lewhay had all been of great help; especially Lewhay who had suffered from very similar problems himself. For months he didn't feel a single twinge of anything that even resembled jealousy. He apologised to Michael and found that he was very forgiving; nice fellow that he was. They even talked about it together, Michael offered him good advice on how to deal with it and Shabwan really believed he'd exorcised his demons.

Having nearly lost her, the next few months were just as euphoric as the first and blend into a similar happy blur when he tries to recall them now. He doesn't so much recall individual events but the feeling of warmth that sits in his gut every time his eyes flutter open and he sees her face through the blur of sleep or the way her voice sounds when she sings in the bath. When all life is that good the brain has no need to take in individual occurrences. It is just happy to be, a state that is very rare and is always very highly cherished by those who have had it. Even more so by those who have lost it.

He remembers thinking, as they walked to the star that evening, an evening which treated them with the first real spring sun of the year that things couldn't be better, he was with his best friends (a group who had been exceptionally tolerant of his neglect and who would soon be even more tolerant of his misery) and a girl for whom he had feelings of such proportion that he previously could only have guessed at their magnitude. The summer was on its way, they'd been doing stonk together all day and now they were off to the pub to celebrate, celebrate what?

Maintaining their sanity perhaps; it had been quite a strong dose…

The next morning he heard two words.

'It's over.'

He remembered the full stop at the end of that sentence just as potently as the two horrible words that had preceded it. The full stop which told him that this decision was final. It had been thought over, probably over a sleepless night where he had apparently lain there passed out.

His head was pulsing and his memory completely absent. There was something though: a sense of regret and dread which told him that, although he couldn't recall it, there was some horribly just and irreversible reason for what she was now thinking. Something he had done the night before.

The memory never came back to him but she had painted a good picture. Shabwan had apparently got very drunk very quickly. The effects of the stonk wearing off had left him feeling pretty hollow and depleted and rather than going home to bed as he'd been advised, even by Coki, he had opted to drink through it.

He'd begun to fall into the silent state of moodiness which only ever meant one thing and, of course, the beast had returned. Apparently it had only been on holiday. Even though Michael hadn't even been there, Shabwan had openly accused Kayleigh, in front of all his friends and whoever else was in the pub with a set of ears, of being in love with him. When she had pleaded with him to calm down he had pushed her; quite hard apparently.

Coki had slapped him hard round the face and sent him home, now here they were.

17.

Vericoos watched and listened with interest. Here it was; the act which had broken the relationship. It had been such a long time since he himself had felt anything like this for another person, yet the boy's story still kindled something deep inside him, the ghost of a memory. Still a million miles from, what one might term, empathy but something none the less.

'She ended it and there was nothing I could say to her. I pleaded and pleaded. I said everything I could think of but there was nothing I could do. I think it was because I had made her believe, hell made myself believe, that we were through it and that was what made it so cruel when it came back.'

His voice was hollow now, monosyllabic. Vericoos saw that the boy had finally lost the battle he'd been having since the story began with his tear ducts. They were now spewing forth their salty content which was streaming down the boys cheeks.

'She felt like she had to end it, I don't think she really wanted to, but she knew it was the right thing to do...The boys eventually told me I had to let it go and I did. I had completely given up on it, she wanted to be friends; she's just so lovely like that, even after everything I had done.'

'But you got her back?' said Vericoos as another faint ghost of an emotion stirred deep within his stomach. One he thought he'd never feel again.

'Yeah,' Shabwan replied.

And you, dear reader, know this part of the story very well although Vericoos did not.

Shabwan told him, as briefly as he could, for he still sensed that it was important for the sorcerer to know as much as possible. And, even though this part hurt him even more than recounting those early blissful months, he did not think to ask the sorcerer to read his mind again.

This part needed to be told.

Shabwan finished his tale and then looked up at the sorcerer, his face tear stained and blotchy. The old man was looking at him, wearing an expression that Shabwan had not seen before. Was it possible, that even with the monumental importance of the task that lay ahead of them he still felt a small amount of guilt for removing Shabwan from his love? Maybe even empathised with his pain?

'It was a good tale, and it was well told. I thank you for it, truly I do,' Said Vericoos. 'When the time comes, that, which you have just told me, may well prove to be the difference between success and failure.'

Vericoos began preparing his bed on the soft grass, tonight was going to be the most comfortable sleep they had had in quite a while. The dry earth that lay to the sides of the northern road seemed like a distant memory.

'But wait,' said Shabwan, he too was sleepy, exhausted even, it had been a long and emotional story to tell. But there was more to discuss. 'What about the third division, what do you think that will be?'

'I'm afraid that I have no idea,' said Vericoos and Shabwan felt his heart sink a little.

'I have been thinking, I really have, and nothing, as yet, has become apparent to me. We will have to hope that as we finish this last stage of our journey it will become clear to us both. I would not like to imagine us going into the god chamber unprepared.'

Shabwan didn't like the use of the term 'God chamber', it sounded respectful, like a church rather than a prison.

'So,' he said, feeling sleep begin to draw him in. 'We've got the unlikely hero, the romantic idiot and one other...I wonder what it will be.'

'Hmmm, yes,' replied Vericoos. 'I wonder.'

Book 3

The Fool.

Chapter 1.

Recovery.

1.

They slept, they both slept, and it was deep. The younger inhabitants of San Hoist used the word 'deep' to mean good and in this instance it was fulfilling both its literal and its informal functions. The sleep was deep and the sleep was good.

2.

Vericoos needed it so badly now. His tired old frame was beginning to waste away. It had been deprived, for too long now, of the *talent* which had kept it going for all these years. It shouldn't matter though, because tomorrow they would go to her. Then the final leg of the journey would be over before it had begun.

Once he had spoken with her, once he had claimed back what was rightfully his, then he would fly straight over these mountains and then there would be nothing, nothing to stand between them and the little room which was really so much more; a little room where Shabwan would be divided, a little room which was the gateway to the unimaginable.

Vericoos had been thinking these pleasant thoughts as he'd dropped off. He had, at so many points on his journey, felt like he was on the verge of failure: in Payinzee, in San Hoist and on a thousand other occasions before that. Now, for the first time, he truly believed that they were almost there. He had somehow, against all the odds, found this curious boy, dragged him along with him and kept him in one piece. The boy even seemed accepting of the job which lay before him; something Vericoos would have never believed when he'd first watched Shabwan amble across the square of the little agricultural community where he'd been born and raised.

Vericoos felt better than he had felt in a long time, and tomorrow, he would finally have *it* back. Around him the leaves trembled for a moment as if they were frightened of the thought of it.

Sleep had taken him like it had not taken him for years, the kind of sleep which takes hours to truly rise out of, and was there really anyone who deserved it more?

3.

In the darkness that surrounded their camp there were little noises. Strange sounds indeed they were; somewhere between a hoot and a grumble. These sounds were quiet and conspirational and seem to come from all around. They waited for a little while longer, so as to be sure that 'long and old' and 'slumpy', as they thought of them, were well and truly asleep. Then they began to move in, ever so slowly.

They would not need much time.

4.

Vericoos awoke and immediately knew something was wrong. He and the boy had become close in more ways than those of a non magical disposition could understand. Vericoos' mind fed off of Shabwan's in a way that he hadn't felt since he had forged the connection with Lubwan.

The connection had become so strong that he could have extracted the entire story of Shabwan and Kayleigh's relationship in a moment had he so chosen. The only reason he had not was because there was so much more one could learn from listening. Listening, not just to the tale but to how someone crafts it. The bits they choose to leave out and the bits they dwell on tell you so much about a person. And hadn't that always been his chief objective? To learn about Shabwan…to understand the intricacies of his very soul.

He'd needed to do this, so that when the time came he could hold the young man's sanity together and get him through the three doors.

Of course he wouldn't be able to do that at all if he didn't have Shabwan.

He knew that the young man had gone and he knew where. He didn't have to look at the empty patch of grass next to the embers of the fire to confirm this but he did so anyway. Some habits you never really loose and not truly *believing* something until it has passed down your optic nerve is certainly one of these.

Vericoos could save his cause; there was still time, but he could not do it without help. He would have to go and see her now. Leaving their humble pile of possessions where they were (and where they would forever rest) He rose to his feet and he began to run; an undignified run, a run of desperation. For time was something which had always been against them and now it was about to defeat them.

5.

There are very few places on Earth where there is a direct gateway to the magic and this is a damn good thing.

Even the most crazed and hungry magical minds have shivered at the thought of the magic flowing directly from the source. You see, even when the flow is strongest, the magic still comes from the world around you. It oozes out of the rivers, the sea and the trees at such a rate that it's a wonder that these vessels survive.

But still, it comes from *them.*

The thought of magic flowing directly from the source is a terrifying one; for no one, not even the stupidest (think back to Crid the leader of the 'front') would be so arrogant as to believe that they had any hope of channelling or controlling it.

But there are places where this happens, and it is to one of these places which Vericoos now heads. It will be dangerous that's for sure, there is every chance that the magic will just take him and suck him into some unimaginable place or that it will flow through him so hard and fast that it removes all traces of life from his tired old body.

It could do either of these things or, as he so fervently hopes: it may heal him. The outcome of our tale depends entirely on the choice the magic makes, but it is not only the choice of the magic.

It is her choice also.

6.

The forest was thick and dark now. There were no more thin fingers of dusty sunlight puncturing the thick canopy above. The only light, other than the dull green glow that seemed somehow to be everywhere, was coming from the strange, shimmering, gossamer that clung to the trees like spider's webs and the odd little floating silver things that looked to Vericoos like insects, but he couldn't be sure. He definitely didn't have time to investigate the wildlife.

7.

He could hear sounds, strange inhuman sounds. Like a hooting call of a gangly bird but then also like the grumbling of an old man, his accent so thick as to render his words incoherent.

Hooo... durpa durpa duapa it seemed to go.

How very strange thought Shabwan as he slipped once again into unconsciousness.

8.

Vericoos was not aware of how far he'd run but once he got there he realised it must have been an awfully long way. The foliage above his head had not only grown thicker it had also grown down. Now the leaves were only inches above his head, like the trees were reaching down to crush him.

He put these ridiculous thoughts out of his head, but still there was no denying that the forest was becoming more claustrophobic. When they had first entered them, Vericoos had been struck by the cathedral-like atmosphere of the place; the ceiling well out of sight and the trees widely spaced apart, like great pillars. Now the great forest had become more like a mine. Dark as hell, illuminated only by the blue thread and all these strange little silvery things floating about, like little glints of some metallic vein, disappearing off into the darkness.

9.

There was a burning stitch in the old man's side which threatened to rob him of his balance and leave him splayed across the lush forest floor. He had a nasty feeling that if this were to happen, the little lights, which seemed to have gained an interest in him as he ran and now hovered around him like flies around meat, would suddenly take a much greater and more threatening interest.

Indeed, as the trees stood even closer together the silver things were not his only concern. For the thin blue thread, which had until now been tightly wrapped around the smooth barks, now reached out towards him. It seemed that while he was running it couldn't get a grip but he feared that, were he to stop, or even slow down, he might find that the thin blue thread was much stronger than it looked.

He was becoming increasingly uneasy but at least there was no fear that he may lose his sense of direction. His destination burned in his mind and he doubted he could alter his course even if he wanted to. The last few weeks had been hell; the loss of his *talent* had been eating away at him, so much worse than addiction had eaten away at the old man to whom Shabwan and co. had stopped selling their stonk to.

Only his quest had kept him sane and now, once again, he was on the verge of losing everything. The same man who we once saw carry himself with such grace and dignity, now ran desperately through the wood, batting his arms at his own head trying to ward off what looked like fire flies. He was yelling now; hoarse cries they were, upsetting to hear.

10.

It was cold up here, and there were no trees. That was strange. He could hear the same strange noises he had heard before but now there seemed to be a lot more of them. Even though he had no idea what this strange language was, or from what creature's mouths it was spilling, he could still tell that they were arguing.

It seemed like he was being carried but he knew not how, perhaps being floated was a better way of putting it.

This time, just before he lost consciousness, he saw a pair of the greenest eyes he had ever seen, only for a moment. Then he smelt something sweet, like his mum's citrus tarts, and was asleep once more.

11.

Vericcos had initially only *suspected* that the only two things within the wood which provided illumination had some kind of malicious intent towards him, he now *knew* it. The thread, which had once looked to Shabwan so beautiful, was thread no longer, it was more like tentacles and it had begun to steam.

Twice Vericoos almost tripped as these blue vines lashed at his legs and arms trying to restrain him. They were stronger now and it was only his erratic momentum that was carrying him through them. The little silver lights were coming in closer now and within them he saw faces, malicious sneering faces, like the masks that he had so often seen actors wear, only these were alive. For a moment he tried to remember what else they reminded him of. It only took him a moment: that terrifying wooden mask that sat upon the shoulders of Veo.

He could hear a horrible buzzing noise now, a noise which could only be coming from the razor sharp silvery wings which were keeping these little horrors air borne. They began to dive at his face, cutting him, and Vericoos wrapped his arms around his head to protect his eyes, he would have to rely on luck to carry him the rest of the way; if he were to blindly trip or perhaps run straight into one of the trees; he would find himself wrapped in those terrible vines and then slashed to pieces by the nasty grinning little faces and their razor wings. It would be a slow and unpleasant way to go, that much he knew.

Then it was over.

Vericoos hadn't realised how loud the forest had become until they fell silent again. The hideous buzzing that had come from those deathly little faces had ceased, as had the horrible whipping and snapping noises which had been coming from those electric blue threads (had they ever really been thread?) as they'd tried to bind him. As quickly as the noises stopped Vericoos forgot all about them, for now he had uncovered his eyes he could see why all was so perfectly serene.

12.

It's quiet in here, thought Shabwan. Although there was definitely some dripping, he liked that sound though; it reminded him of something nice. The air was cool up here (up? How did he know he was up) and finally he seemed to have stopped moving. Slowly he managed to sit up, it was a lot of work as his eyes seemed to want to close again and his mind felt warm and fuzzy. He rubbed his eyes and then opened them.

Then he screamed.

13.

Vericoos stood at the entrance and had to fight off a sudden and almost overwhelming desire to fall to his knees. For the first time in as long as he could remember, thoughts of his quest were pushed completely out of his mind. It was just so...beautiful.

In front of him was a shallow lake, the water so clear that you could see the rock bottom as clearly as if there were no water at all. At the other end of the lake was the entrance. The mouth of a small cave about five feet across and seven feet high. Around this cave were little floating specks of light. Vericoos started as he realised that they were the same little specks which had just sought to attack and cut him as he ran through the wood.

Only now they were so different; the little faces which had looked malicious and menacing were now smiling at him and their razor sharp wings now looked more like those of a dragonfly; soft and delicate.

'Come...come,' they seemed to whisper. 'We mean you no harm.'

Vericoos reached up and touched his cheek where only moments earlier he had felt one of the little horrors draw blood yet as his fingers brushed the skin he found no cut or laceration. He began to walk into the little pool, not caring one bit for the dampening of his clothes. Another ten paces would take him to the entrance, to her.

His old mind felt beautifully clear for there was so much magic around here, so much glorious magic. For the first time in his life he felt pure power. It seeped into his every pore, filtered by nothing, not even by the air.

Indeed, it seemed that here it *was* the air because Vericoos wasn't breathing...

He neared the entrance of the cave, looking around him at the little welcoming faces. They looked at Vericoos from all around him and, even though they'd been attacking him moments before, he did not fear them. For now he understood they had simply been testing him. In the warm blur of his thoughts this was certain; it had been a trial to test his worth, to see whether he deserved to have his *talent* healed and by the gods he had passed. As soon as he entered the cave he would...

The little faces suddenly stopped dead still. Before they had been drifting around, aimlessly as insects, now they were still. Vericoos looked around at the little expressions and noticed that they had changed again, and not for the good...

14.

Before Shabwan stood the most ridiculous creatures that he had ever seen. They looked like little men. Tiny little men (how many of them must it have taken to carry him up here?) and they had so much hair on their faces that Shabwan could only see their noses sticking out. Great bulbous things they were. They were all naked apart from a little loin cloth around their waists. Shabwan made a quick guess that he must be in the presence of at least three hundred of these strange little things, yet all of them, to him, looked completely identical.

One of them spoke, and despite the growing fear in Shabwan's guts, the ridiculous sound of it still made him feel like laughing.

'Nwoooooooaaaah!' Said the little man.

The assembled oddities all nodded their heads earnestly at this and repeated the same odd sound. Shabwan could feel his senses clearing rapidly now, but this was doing nothing to alleviate his confusion. What did these little things want?

He could sense the danger of the situation, serious danger. His way out of the huge cave he was in seemed to be blocked by even more of these things. Yet they had not harmed him, not yet at least. And now, ridiculous as it seemed, they were apparently trying to communicate with him.

It was only then that he realised that his earlier estimate of three hundred had been incredibly off the mark. He had only taken into account the ones directly in front of him.

There were lots more.

As he looked up he realised that the cave he had entered was in fact a vast chamber. Its top must be somewhere up there in the darkness but Shabwan could only guess as to how far. The only light was coming from the top of the narrow slope in front of him. *The exit!* Thought Shabwan.

Running in a circle around the edge of the chamber was a thick rock ledge, on top of which were built what looked like tiny little houses, and in front of these houses stood so many more of these strange little creatures. Shabwan had a brief attempt at guessing some kind of number and then gave up. His brain wasn't designed to think in those kinds of quantities. He'd needed to stifle his laughter a few moments ago. He didn't feel like laughing any more. Fear was gripping him far too hard.

15.

'Die!' they all said together in one horrible hissing voice and as they did the razor edged buzzing started once more.

They flew, as one, towards Vericoos, who was only now realising what a fool he had been. He'd been right to think that these things had been testing him but wrong to suppose that the test was over.

He had no physical strength left and no *talent* either, which meant he was surely done for. He consoled himself with the fact that he would die in the most beautiful place he had ever seen. How many people got to say that? He thought. And it was then, just as he was making his final peace and bidding the world a fond farewell, that his hand moved.

It reminded him of when he was young; when he had first begun doing magic out in the fields behind his parent's house. In those days his magic had been erratic and wild, it had seemed to jump out of him whenever it could and sometimes he had felt powerless to do anything other than watch. That had been the start and apparently, this was to be the end.

Only...it wasn't!

Excitement filled him as he felt it again. His *talent* was still gone, possibly for ever. But that didn't change the fact that the impossible seemed to be happening. That right now, in what he thought was to be his last second, his hand was full to the brim with that which he had come for…

Quick as a flash he opened his palm and the little faces with their razor wings which had been but inches from Vericoos' own, were suddenly halted. Better than that, they were vibrating uncontrollably, their expressions now of pain and perhaps even fear. Vericoos closed his fist once more and the magic was gone. It had been a momentary thing but it had been enough, he relished the soft plopping sounds as one by one the little faces, or masks or whatever they were, hit the gloriously clear surface of the pool.

They didn't look menacing now, far from it, Vericoos thought with the savage glee which always followed a victory, especially a seemingly impossible one. They were moving still, not dead it seemed, but perhaps wounded; swimming around under the glassy surface, their wings seemed to have become fins. Their faces were all upturned and all showed exactly the same look of wounded pride and fear.

They look like petulant children who thought they were running the school and have just been shouted at by their teacher, thought Vericoos. As he strode through the water, confidently now, the little things did all they could to get out of his way.

Vericoos had passed his test, well his first one at least. And in doing so he had experienced a little flash of what he was there to reclaim. The cave ahead of him reeked with that glorious potential. The air was thick and syrupy but not sickly...far from it. As the old sorcerer entered the cave he felt no fear.

Although he most certainly should have done, for the events which would eventually be the undoing of his entire quest were about to be set in motion.

Such is life.

16.

Shabwan was amazed that he'd ever mistaken this place for a cave. It was more like an underground city. What he'd thought was an exit, through which sunlight was flowing from the outside world, had turned out not to be nothing so inviting. It was, in fact, some kind of little church which was emitting a light remarkably similar to the evening sun. Shabwan could see no possible source for it.

His original assumption, upon waking up, had been that these little things had dragged him through a cave door into the gateway to their world. Now he realised that he was actually right in the heart of it. Whatever entrance he passed through to get here he must have passed it some time ago. This massive tubular catacomb had to be the central area of the city, for everything else seemed to lead away from it.

There were all the houses adorning the massive ledge which wound its way upwards but between these houses were gaps which, Shabwan now saw, were streets that must lead off into other parts of this underground kingdom. There were dozens of these just in the part of the chamber Shabwan could see. The Gods knew how many more there were up there in the darkness.

The things had been trying their very limited line of communication with him for some time and although they were having little success with Shabwan, it seemed that they could communicate very well amongst themselves.

Hoooo...durpa durpa durpa! Was all they seemed to be able to say yet apparently this was enough. Shabwan had only been awake for a short period of time, yet he fancied that he had heard this incredibly simple linguistic pattern used to convey a huge range of different meanings. The range of tones, pitch and speed they applied to the four words, if you could call them that, seemed to be where the secret to their language lay.

When they tried to speak to Shabwan it was always in the same incomprehensible drone as before.

'Nwoooooooah' or 'sttttttoooooooo' seemed to be the most common. At first this had just seemed like madness but as time went on Shabwan was beginning to get the idea that these were their attempts at human words. It seemed the only logical explanation, although what place logic had down here he didn't know. He guessed that their mouths, or beaks or whatever the hell they had under all that hair, were only made for producing that one sound, and anything else gave them great difficulty. The Gods knew they were trying though. It seemed that they really wanted to make him understand something before they killed him.

It was as he was having these morbid thoughts that he heard a new word, one that they hadn't tried before and one that, unbelievably, he understood.

17.

'Welcome Vericoos.' said a voice which was just as beautiful as the little lake outside.' I see you got through my little messengers all right.'

'Show yourself.' said Vericoos in tones that were far from warm.

And she did.

Before him, completely naked, stood Sheeba one of the appointed guardians. She was more beautiful than any human woman he had ever seen and he knew, as she began to walk towards him, that she would grant him physical possession of her if he asked. But sex was the last thing on his mind. She had so much more to offer him.

'You know why I have come.' he said.

'Of course I do,' she replied. 'Ever since you burst back through and shattered my little enchantment, I've been expecting you.'

Vericoos felt his confidence falter. She knew! Of course she knew. It was her and her kind who had frozen it in the first place after all. Her and the rest of her kind who had ended the existence of the sorcerers, even though the magic had still flown. How could he have been so stupid as to think she wouldn't have realised he'd broken their enchantment.

Whether she was angry about it or not was difficult to say. It was clear, however, from her lazy tone and the confidently slow way she was descending the pearly steps which lead up to her dwelling, that she was in no hurry to complete this little bit of business.

'Why don't we have a sit down.' she suggested.

Vericoos reluctantly sat down.

'How do you like my garden?' she asked as she sat down next to him on a bench which, like the steps, seemed to be made out of pearl.

He liked it a great deal.

You may remember that a certain field on the outskirts of San Hoist now blooms with a selection of flowers that you probably wouldn't be able to find anywhere else on the planet, no matter how hard you looked. Unless, of course, you looked here. Sheeba's garden boasted that same shock of unnatural nature only a thousand times more...more what? Thought Vericoos. The garden was beautiful, that was for sure, blooms of every colour reached up and danced in the glittery, pearly light that seemed to come from everywhere. The electric blue gossamer which had clung to the trees, and almost to Vericoos, was here also. It hung down from the ceiling not unlike the bunting which had decorated the town from which he had removed young Shabwan.

Yet for all this beauty there was danger also; in the same way that the little silver faces had been pleasing on the eye before they had attacked. Vericoos found that it wasn't that hard to imagine the flora, which was swaying slightly in some kind of hypnotic dance, reaching up and dragging him into the earth from which it grew. Or perhaps those delightful blue strands would come down and drag him upwards; wrapping him up like some unfortunate fly trapped in a spider's web.

'I like it.' replied Vericoos and she smiled at him, it was a sweet smile but also one he could imagine etched across her perfect face as she stood over his corpse.

'So,' she said. 'Clearly not much of a talker. You come to me for healing, is it that simple Vericoos? Is that all you would have?'

'Yes,' he replied instantaneously. 'I seek to destroy Veo and you know this to be for the benefit of the world. Won't you please recover me as swiftly as you can, for my quest is on the verge of failure?'

She laughed, and to his ears it was a terrible sound.

'You lie!' She cried and she sounded both exhilarated and amused. 'How powerful do you think you are Vericoos that you can lie to me?'

'I lie not.' he shouted and at the sound of the distress in his voice she seemed to grow more exhilarated still, her nipples standing hard on her breasts.

'Then why should I believe you then?'

'Would your defences have let someone through if all they came for was to satisfy their own selfish needs?'

This seemed to interest her and he felt her mind reach out to his, extraordinarily powerful, yet he resisted as best he could and though she gained much there was one thing which he managed to protect. The most important thing.

'Hmmmm, it seems that you really do seek recovery so you can open the 'god chamber'. Tell me this then Vericoos, do you really think you can succeed.'

'Yes,' he replied in a moment, and as he spoke her sexuality seemed to blossom out of her, engulfing him. For the first time he thought about something other than magic…

Concentrate, he told himself, appalled that he'd lost his focus even for the briefest of moments. You're so close now, just hold your mind together, stick to your story. Sheeba was one of the guardians and despite all the power she held, she was bound to the world which she was there to protect. If Vericoos had lost his talent, well what was that to her? He shouldn't have used his gift so excessively. In point of fact he shouldn't even have been using it at all. It was only because he'd destroyed something of her creation that he was using his skills in the first place.

But if Veo were to emerge, that was another matter.

Yet still she doubted him, he could feel it.

'At least it's a chance,' he cried in tones that Shabwan and the boys would have recognised, although usually they would have been saying something like, 'just one more batch, please!'

'If you heal me, he might still emerge it's true. But if you choose not to heal me then he will emerge for certain.'

Vericoos stopped, realising how desperate he now sounded. He looked up at her expecting to see mockery in her eyes.

He saw none.

'You realise that a healing comes at a price?' she said and Vericoos' heart leapt.

'What do you require?' he asked, tasting the magic all around him, tasting what would soon be his again.

She laughed once more, and this time there was a mocking element in there with the sweetness.

'Me? You think I would require some kind of payment for my services? Gods Vericoos, I overestimated you. It is not me that requires payment but the source. I will be able to heal you but be warned, the source will not take this lightly. What you ask of me is a powerful ritual and I have no doubt that when it is completed the source will need to restore equilibrium.'

'Payment?'

Vericoos, was perplexed. He'd never heard of the source being spoken of like this before; like a conscious entity.

'You could look at it as payment certainly, but perhaps at least try to think of it as balance, for this is how the source will see it'

As she said this she was no longer completely herself, she seemed to have become another...someone who he recognised.

'Everything requires balance,' she was saying. 'And what you are about to receive is seen, in the grand scale of things, as an exceptionally good bit of fortune. Few men rupture their talent and are lucky enough to see the use of magic again but you will and for this I have no doubt that the source will see fit to put some extremely bad piece of fortune in your path. Will you accept my help still?'

Vericoos was looking down at the unimaginable flora that was swaying so mystifyingly around his feet.

Then he spoke.

18.

They were growing inpatient which, for Shabwan, was most certainly bad news.

They seemed to be of the opinion that, if Shabwan had understood this one word, then he must have gained a completely understanding of whatever the hell it was they were trying to communicate.

'Veeeeeeah koos.' They had said and Shabwan had reacted. They could only mean one thing after all.

Once they had realised that he understood, they had all started shouting the same word along with the other two they had been originally trying.

'Veeeeahhh koos'

'Nwoooooooah.'

'Stoooooooooo.'

The effect was maddening, but the urgency with which the little things now spoke told Shabwan that the level of danger he was under had gravely increased.

'I don't understand!' he yelled.

Suddenly the atmosphere changed. It was odd because Shabwan could see nothing of these little creatures that would display any kind of outward emotion. Their eyes were hidden behind the great flaps of hair that sprouted from above their noses. Their mouths too were hidden. You might as well try and work out how a duck was feeling. Yet, despite the fact that nothing about the physical appearance of the creatures could tell you what they were thinking, Shabwan knew exactly what it was all the same.

His time was up.

The efforts to communicate were over and now the little creatures, small enough that he could defeat ten maybe even twenty of them, but not thousands, had decided to kill him. He and Vericoos had come so damn close and yet still they were to fail. What was worse was that Shabwan wasn’t going to fall at the hands of some mighty adversary, wasn’t going to be slain at the hands of some terrible divine being. He was going to be killed by these god dammed human moles or whatever the hell they were. His thoughts went out to Kayleigh, he had failed her just like he’d failed everyone else, but he wanted hers to be the face in his minds eye as it winked out forever...

And then, right then when he was just about willing to give up everything, he heard something.

Something which filled him with hope.

'SHABWAN!'

Vericoos voice bounced around the huge catacomb and dust fell from the darkness above. Shabwan tried to rise but was instantly overwhelmed by the little things. They pinned him down and stuffed some thing in his mouth so that he couldn't shout back. Then he saw a glimpse of something that could only mean one thing; a sharp steel edge, brilliantly reflecting the light of the strange little church which he had once thought was the exit to this hell hole.

If only that were true.

He could not see the blade any more but he was sure he would be *feeling* it very soon. Vericoos roared his name again. He sounded closer this time but Shabwan didn’t think he was close enough. He felt an increase of pressure in his side and prepared himself for the worst.

Then there was a crack.

The little men were flung off him in all directions and a force which certainly wasn't physical hauled Shabwan to his feet. Standing in front of him was Vericoos his eyes blazing and steam billowing all around him. The little men who had not been killed in the original blast were trying to flee and Vericoos threw his arm out in a circle cutting them in half as they ran. The scale of the death was terrible to behold but Shabwan felt nothing but relief.

He was alive! They had not failed and Vericoos had his magic back.

He’d never imagined he’d be so happy to see the old git.

The sorcerer wordlessly grabbed his arm and they were flying. When they had flown away from the field outside San Hoist it had been a sketchy affair and on a couple of occasions Shabwan had feared that they might fall out of the sky. This time they flew true as an arrow, rocketing upwards into the darkness, which became lighter as they passed through it. The crackly lightning which surrounded them as they flew illuminated the now deserted streets that ran along the rock ledge. Shabwan saw a little sphere of light above them, true daylight not the mockery of it he had seen at the bottom of this terrible cavern. Then they were out.

19.

The brightness hurt Shabwan's eyes and they took a long time to adjust. By the time he could see again they had landed on a small rocky ledge, although to Shabwan it felt like a king sized bed complete with full feather mattress. He fell to the ground and lay there panting. It was a long time until he could speak.

'Thanks!' he said to Vericoos.

The old man smiled at him and as he did Shabwan felt the warm rush of magic sweep over him.

'I see you're better then.' he said as the healing force began to do its work.

Vericoos smiled at him again and replied:

'Never better.'

'What were they?' asked Shabwan, shuddering slightly as he recalled those eyeless, hairy faces, pinning him to the ground.

'They're Oo-ja's,' replied Vericoos, in a tone that suggested it wasn't really important. 'Soul eaters.'

'What?' Shabwan gasped, 'soul eaters!'

'Yes.' replied Vericoos.

Why did he seem not to want to speak about this?

'They seemed to be trying to talk to me,' said Shabwan, determined that after what he'd just gone through he was entitled to some sort of explanation.

'Well they would,' said Vericoos. 'That's their way.'

Shabwan was beginning to get extremely annoyed now. He needed to know what had just happened to him.

'Sorry if I'm inconveniencing you in some way,' he said. 'But would you mind telling me why I almost just got cut to pieces by those hairy little trolls down there.'

'They're not trolls, they're Oo-ja's,' said Vericoos with the same uninterested tone that made Shabwan feel like throttling him.

'They drag unwary travellers off into their lairs and, once they get them there, they eat their souls, but to do this they need to gain the trust of their victims. I imagine they were trying to converse with you in a way that would suggest they were trying to help you, and once you'd placed even the slightest bit of trust in them they would have been able to feed.'

Shabwan felt sick, remembering how he'd reacted once they'd started chanting the old sorcerer's name. How close had he been to giving them that little bit of trust which would have made him theirs?

'But it seemed like they were going to kill me?'

'Yes,' said Vericoos still not looking at Shabwan. 'And when was that?'

Shabwan thought back to the horrible floor of that deep chamber, dark except for the strange simulation of daylight which came from the little church.

'Once they heard your voice.' he replied. In his confusion Shabwan didn't realise that it had, in fact, been slightly before this. Shame really; this little difference, so quickly forgotten in the mind of our protagonist meant everything.

'Exactly,' said Vericoos. 'Once they realised they had no chance of a feast they decided to dispatch of you, luckily I was able to save you.'

For the first time since they had left the cave Shabwan followed Vericoos' line of sight and he understood, at once, why the old Sorcerer had not been looking at him or paying much attention to what he had been saying.

They had arrived.

Chapter 2.

The Chamber.

1.

Below them lay the city of Hardram; and what a sight it was. Shabwan had tried, while listening to Vericoos' story to picture the size of the place but he now found that he had failed miserably.

It was huge.

It stretched right up to the foot of the mountains, far below the ledge where they now sat and sprawled for miles in the opposite direction. As Shabwan looked now, towards the far end of the city, he saw a thin black line, not unlike a trail of ants weaving its way out of the city towards the horizon.

People were leaving Hardram and he didn't blame them, for above the city, floating like some ludicrous cork popped from a bottle, was the God chamber (that was what Vericoos called it, wasn't it? Shabwan remembered disliking the term, thinking it sounded like a place of respect rather than a prison). And the God chamber was clearly about to break.

'Do you see how it is cracking?' asked Vericoos, his eyes never leaving the floating tube. 'Do you see why we must go? If it breaks he will be one again.'

Shabwan could only nod, the red light which was stabbing out of the brick walls was a clear enough indication that whatever force was holding Veo back would be unable to contain him for much longer.

So they flew again, it was the last time they ever flew together. The young man who would soon be three and the old sorcerer who would hold his sanity together as he split.

As they flew they pondered different things. Young Shabwan pondered what the third division would be, for recent events had removed any chance they'd had of working it out together and still he had no idea. One look at the God chamber however, and any fool could see that there was no time to ponder. They would just have to go for it.

Vericoos thought not of the third division, for he had a strong idea what it would be, he had seen the three doors when they had first been created, and it was not a division he would share with young Shabwan. Much better that he didn't know.

No, that was not what Vericoos thought of, instead he thought instead of the words the guardian had spoken before she healed his talent.

A piece of bad fortune would be thrown into his path.

It was, of course, an unsettling idea, but it mattered not. For the part of the quest that was 'his path' would very soon be at an end. Perhaps this 'all knowing' source that Sheeba had spoken of had missed the boat. Perhaps he, Vericoos, had been faster even than the great power.

Still, as pleasant as these arrogant musings were, he mustn't get ahead of himself...But things were looking rather optimistic all of a sudden. As long as he could get young Shabwan into the three rooms then his part was done and, if all went well, a force would emerge from those three rooms which could match anything that the source could hope to produce.

Yes, thought Vericoos, a warm feeling flooding all through him, unless something were to strike them out of the air as they flew then what else could threaten his goals now?

He could not have known, even with all his power and wisdom that the source had already struck. For as they flew they carried something with them that neither Vericoos or Shabwan knew existed, something which rested in a small leather moleskin bag, that one of the people, who Vericoos referred to as 'soul eaters', had bravely slipped into the pocket of Shabwan's trousers just before the sorcerer had struck him down.

In his arrogance Vericoos assumed that, when the source attempted to restore balance, it would be an event of epic proportions, something he might not be able to overcome and conquer, but something he would most definitely be able to see. What minds obsessed with their own brilliance sometimes forget is that the littlest actions sometimes have the greatest consequences.

2.

As they neared the little hatch in the bottom of the God Chamber it swung open as if to greet them. Inside it was exactly as Shabwan had imagined. The only thing his minds eye had left out was the dagger, a dagger which, had he seen it in any other place, would have probably not even caught the young man's eye, save that it was a bit shinier than most. It was mounted on the wall.

You could feel, just from the air in here, how fragile the chamber was, the doors still looked like they were shut fast but that wouldn't matter if the whole room were to crumble and fall apart. There really was no time at all.

Shabwan knew what he must do and he took the knife from its bracket. It felt strangely comforting in his hand. He looked at the three doors, reading the inscriptions which Vericoos had told him would be there. He had absolutely no idea what to expect once he stabbed himself, let alone once he opened the doors, but he trusted Vericoos. No, it was more than trust, it was friendship. He knew the old man would help him as much as he could. And they had identified two of the divisions, hadn't they? Surely that would be of some help.

Shabwan thought of Kayleigh and tried with all his might to send his thoughts out to her. He wanted her to know that he wished she was here, that the only thing that had given him the strength to come this far was the thought that he was protecting her.

He turned to look at Vericoos, he knew the old man didn't know the answer to the question any more than he did but he wanted to ask anyway.

'Do you really think I can beat him?'

Vericoos nodded, it was another lie, and like all the other lies it bothered him not. The boy had eaten up everything he had told him, about himself, about the Lubwan and about Veo. He had even swallowed the stuff about the Oo-Ja's. Like all the other lies Vericoos had told it was perfectly delivered. Shabwan should not be blamed for the complete trust he had in the old sorcerer.

'I cannot tell you what is beyond those doors, only that you must destroy him.'

Shabwan nodded once making his last eye contact with the old man. He turned and held the dagger out in front of him. The three doors beckoned. He thought one last time of Kayleigh and then stabbed himself.

Vericoos lowered his head as if to concentrate.

'My Lord,' he muttered under his breath. 'I have delivered your key.'

Lightning Source UK Ltd.
Milton Keynes UK
UKOW051955100712

195775UK00002B/1/P